After taking a Modern Languages degree at Oxford, Elizabeth James taught at various comprehensive schools and also worked with maladjusted children. She then ran a bookshop with her husband in Essex but since 1987 has been writing full-time.

By the same author

Life Class
Life Lines
Lovers and Friends

ELIZABETH JAMES

Crossing the River

Grafton

An Imprint of HarperCollins*Publishers*

Grafton
An Imprint of HarperCollins*Publishers*
77–85 Fulham Palace Road,
Hammersmith, London W6 8JB

A Grafton Original 1992
9 8 7 6 5 4 3 2 1

A catalogue record for this book
is available from the British Library

ISBN 0 586 20986 7

Set in Times

Printed in Great Britain by
HarperCollinsManufacturing Glasgow

In memory of
Beatrice and Eleanor Southwell

1

Annie Tyrell sat idle at her sewing-machine, waiting for Leonard Floyd, the factory manager. The set of her body gave nothing away, but inside a jabbing tension mounted. Her head ached and rings of sweat showed below the arms of her striped flannel blouse. It was the end of April, an average spring day, but already, in the long workroom of Ballard's Garment Factory, the atmosphere was thick, hot and noisy. And there'd be worse to come: the stifling summer months. Floyd wouldn't have more than just one window open – it was against the regulations, but who was going to complain? He claimed the dust settled everywhere, so the garments went out dirty. The rattle of forty-five sewing-machines combined into a loud, oppressive thrumming that vibrated dully inside her head.

'Arseholes.' Edie Black, to her right, cursed softly. The cheap flannel she was working on frayed easily. Edie ought to watch herself. Cursing carried a threepenny fine if Floyd, or his bum-licker Doll Durrant, heard. Annie caught Edie's eye. The two of them exchanged glances. Just a narrowing of the eyes. You daren't risk more. The look signalled frustration, resignation, solidarity. They understood each other.

Where on earth had that bastard Floyd got to? She'd been idle more than half an hour. He'd have been on her like a ton of bricks if she'd downed tools to take a breather. Edie was on her third pair of boys' knickers. Time was money. For Floyd, too. *He* got the bonus if they reached their target. The rest of them got fined if they didn't. Then again, he was quick off the mark with fines for pretty near anything. Tuppence if you laughed or looked out of the window, threepence for going behind the screen for a piss outside break-time, a shilling an hour for being late. Plus you paid for your own thread. It was a wonder some of the younger ones took anything home at all at the end of the week. Floyd loved it, loved being a slave-driver, the only man among near enough sixty women, apart from the bloke who maintained the machines. He didn't get much change out of Annie, though. She was a fast worker, and old enough to know the ropes, and she was as tough as he was.

Finally, the manager approached across the factory floor, a crooked leer pasted across his long, rawboned skull. His slimy look, the women called it.

'They said you wanted me, Annie, my girl. Is there something I can do for you?' He laid an oily stress on the words lending them a lumbering sexual innuendo. Behind her a young girl sniggered obligingly. As he drew alongside, Floyd's sweaty hand rested briefly below the ringleted topknot in the nape of Annie's neck.

With an effort Annie mustered one of her broad, knowing smiles. It was taken for granted that there was no love lost between the two of them. All the same, he *was* the boss. 'This machine's playing up, Mr Floyd. Thread keeps snapping off.'

He bent down and peered at the mechanism. An odd smell of nervous perspiration hung about him always, strong and fusty like long-stewed meat. 'What you been doing to it?' A jovial, patronizing tone as if he were talking to a backward child.

'I've done nothing,' she replied sharply, just managing to stay on the right side of civility.

He fiddled, adjusting knobs, checking the bobbin, turning the manual wheel. Annie sat by, waiting for him to finish. She'd done all that, but there was no point saying so.

'Must be the tension.'

'I've checked that, Mr Floyd.'

He frowned. 'What've you been doing?' he repeated, lapsing into his more natural, hectoring style.

It was impossible to hide her irritation. 'If I had a guinea for every mile of stitching I've done on this machine I'd be a rich woman.' A metal clamp seemed to be tightening round her throbbing head. 'I know this machine inside out. It's playing up. Wear and tear. Got to happen some time.'

Lips compressed, Floyd tinkered on. An ex-soldier and an ace disciplinarian, he was no mechanic. His good humour had evaporated. Annie's tart reply had rubbed him up the wrong way. He tutted. 'This'll cost you, Annie.'

'What d'you mean?'

'You're slapdash, Annie. I've seen you. You've done it this time. You'll have to pay.' He spoke with an insulting certainty.

She was struck dumb by the magnitude of the lie, the injustice. Nine years she'd spent in this shit-hole and never laid off, not even at the slackest of times. She was too valuable, too experienced a hand.

Floyd gave the wheel a final impatient turn. Annie found her voice. 'You can't do that!' A flat, harsh, overloud statement. She sensed some of the women faltering and pricking up their ears. But they kept their heads down. It was safer to act deaf and dumb. A shrill giggle rose from somewhere, instantly suppressed. Floyd flushed. Any hint of ridicule maddened him.

'You know I'm a good worker.' Annie was sickened by the pleading tone in her own voice.

The manager gave a short, dismissive laugh. 'Too good to be fined, Annie, are you? No one's too good for that if it's merited.' He had an irrational, vindictive hatred of women he considered uppity and Annie was a prime example of the breed.

His temper was rising. She looked into his eyes. They had the hot, dangerous glint all of them knew, the look that kept them cowed, as if he'd kill anyone who tried to get the better of him. His mouth twisted malignly. 'Let's see. A bob a week for four weeks. Can't be less. Firm's not going to foot the bill for your clumsiness.'

She shook her head and lifted one hand absently to her forehead, finding that the curls of her fringe were plastered to her skin with sweat. Her eyes felt hot and dry in their sockets. She was aware of the furtive, fascinated glances of her co-workers. Something snapped inside her head. 'You can stuff your fine, you bugger,' she spat. 'I hate your bloody guts.'

For a second or two the factory foreman's pock-marked face was a picture. Rebellion didn't enter into his scheme of things. Day in, day out, his word was law. Floyd's eye-popping look of outraged disbelief filled Annie's soul with a fierce, unholy joy.

At the same time she had the presence of mind to use his dumbstruck floundering to her own advantage, defending herself loudly for the benefit of her mesmerized co-workers. 'We're not slaving all hours in this sweatshop for the love of it, I can tell you. Can't make ends meet on the pittance we get paid as it is . . .' She gave a quick, head-tossing sideways look, inviting the others to step in and support her. Not that she had much hope of that. They were a weak-kneed lot at the best of times. 'And now you've pulled a new trick out of the hat. *We* pay when the machines go arse-about. If you get away with that one, mate, we may as well forget the idea of wages altogether!'

Her voice held the hectoring, brassy edge that made weaker souls back down. She'd slipped into the tone out of habit, but her bravado was faked. Already she was having second thoughts. She couldn't afford to lose this job. For once in her forty-three years she was genuinely abashed at the enormity of what she'd done. Sworn at Leonard Floyd. Christ! She was fleetingly aware of Dot, the factory's skivvy, on her way to empty the cat's dirt-box, stopping to gawp with her big, pale eyes and loose mouth.

A crimson-purple flush now mottled the manager's moustachioed features. Sweat glistened visibly at the roots of his thinning hair. But already, with his native self-discipline, Floyd was regaining control. Big and bony, he towered head and shoulders over Annie. Taking advantage of his superior height, he smiled down at her and shook his head, with a look that was both pitying and amused. 'My God, Annie, you've really done it this time. Gone a bit too far, wouldn't you say?' Stressing the words, slow and sarcastic, like a schoolteacher boosting his own popularity by tormenting one of the slower pupils. 'I don't think we need you here any longer, love. Far as I'm concerned you may as well sling your hook right now.' Floyd paused and gazed at her with a steady, impersonal interest as if examining some new species of bug. 'You've got too bloody big for your boots, Annie.' He made as if to turn away. The machines, which had fallen silent, began, one by one, to hum again.

'You . . .' Her first impulse was to insult him again, but she was overtaken almost at once by a monstrous sense of futility. What was the use? What on earth had she hoped to gain? Leonard Floyd had all the power. It was as simple as that. She was out of a job and everyone was too damn scared to say a single word in her defence.

'Excuse me, Mr Floyd, but that's not right. It's unjust.' A third voice chimed in, seemingly from nowhere. Startled, Annie looked about her, identifying in the confusion of the moment a blur of white face, a black dress. Daisy Harkness, standing over by the wall to her left, holding a couple of filmy silk garments over one arm. The whir of the machines died away again as the workers watched stealthily for further developments.

11

Floyd stopped in his tracks. 'Who said that?' He scanned the women, searching for the owner of the voice. A hard tension glittered in his eyes. Above everything he feared losing face. Among the watching women there was no longer even a pretence of activity. The silence was breathless.

Daisy Harkness stepped forward. 'I did.' Her tone was even. She rarely raised her voice. There was no defiance in her manner, but in the stillness her slight figure, the plain, dark dress had something heroic about them. 'What you said wasn't fair, Mr Floyd. Machines do break down. It's wear and tear like Annie said. We can't be made responsible.' Her words dropped into the hush with cool logic. The South London accent was overlaid with an odd, unique lilt.

Daisy worked upstairs where the finer clothes were manufactured. Still in her mid-twenties, she was a widow – a foreigner, Polish or something – who lived in the next street to Annie. They didn't have much to do with one another. Daisy kept herself to herself, never joining Annie and her group to gossip and laugh outside the factory gates before they went home at night. Publicly Annie dismissed her as stuck-up, but she had a secret, unwilling curiosity as regards her exotic fellow-worker.

Floyd was seriously taken aback. Daisy was one of his favourites. He admired her un-English good looks, her competence. 'You stay out of this, Mrs Harkness. It doesn't concern you . . .' But her quiet certainty had undermined his command of the situation.

Daisy's intervention could face him with a quandary, Annie recognized. She herself was a good, fast worker, handy and reliable. But she only did plain sewing and when it came down to it, she could be replaced. Daisy was special. She did embroidery and fancy-work. There weren't too many around with her skill. Ballard wouldn't thank Floyd for dismissing her. Annie glimpsed a tiny ray of hope.

Daisy showed no signs of backing down. 'It does, it concerns all of us. If you're talking about fining people when the machines break down, then we'd all better mind our step.'

The women watched, still and avid as waiting vultures. Wonderingly they saw that Daisy's attack had put Floyd on the defensive. The mottled flush blotched his skin again, and hot anger filled his eyes, veiled but visible, like a furnace glowing behind mica doors.

Challenged, he fell back on the accusation he'd made earlier. 'I'm not talking about all of you. It's Annie. She's careless. She's flogged that machine into the ground.' His voice sounded rusty. He cleared his throat. Visibly Floyd hoped that the singling out of a scapegoat would let him off the hook. It was obvious he hadn't foreseen these complications when he'd had the bright idea of introducing a new fine.

His dilemma gave Annie heart. She returned to the fray, making an all-out effort to rouse her mute co-workers. 'He's lying! You know he is . . . Edie!' She appealed directly to her neighbour. '*You* know I'm not slapdash. He's just made it up. You know, don't you?' She turned a basilisk gaze on her friend, fixing her with the full force of her baleful brown eyes.

A large and normally ebullient woman, Edie was daunted at becoming so abruptly the focus of all attention, and more particularly that of Leonard Floyd. But Annie, with her righteous wrath, was even more compelling. Edie hesitated and looked down at the grey flannel knickers she was working on. Then she raised her frizzy, reddish head. 'I've never seen you slapdash, Annie, not in nine years . . .' The words came with an air of reluctance, but with the unmistakable ring of truth.

'There you are!' Annie flourished the testimonial at

the factory manager, then whirled to her left, seeking confirmation from a second source. But she met the dull, blank stare of Dot, the dogsbody, and turned away. No use trying to rope her in.

At the same time she heard murmurs of support from other corners of the room, isolated at first, but rising to a groundswell. The buzz was indignant, sympathetic. It was hard to pick out particular words, but behind her one of the new girls muttered, 'About time someone stood up to him . . .' Annie was warmed. Across the room she caught Daisy Harkness' eye. They exchanged a wary, understanding glance.

Floyd stood, tall and glowering, exuding a watchful hostility, like that of an animal at bay. Abruptly, from a side-table, he picked up a wooden box that held reels of thread, and raising it high above his head, he dashed the container violently to the ground. The reels slid and skittered in all directions across the wooden floor, bringing a new and expectant hush.

'I've lost patience,' the manager snarled, with an ugly, forced rasp, designed to bring them to heel. He turned to Annie. 'You sling your hook, missis . . . And the rest of you . . .' He scanned the women slowly with the hard look that normally served to subdue them. 'Get back on the job. Sort yourselves out. Sooner the better!'

Smartly, as if the matter was settled, he turned on his heel and began to walk towards the door of his office at the far end of the long, low workroom. Cheeks burning, he looked neither to left nor right, but his ramrod figure was followed by a crescendo of jeers from the women. For the first time they'd seen weakness in him and they were drunk with the wonder of it.

Reaching the doorway, the manager stood with one hand on the brass knob, and roared above the rising hubbub, 'Get back to work, I say. Right now. Else tomorrow you'll find the door locked.' He paused a second or two, for form's sake, before retreating through the door, slamming it behind him with a viciousness that shook the building.

Annie turned to face her fellow-workers, raising her arms in the air and flinging back her head, her face a mask of heathen jubilation. She laughed, an infectious, throaty, derisive cackle.

'Lock us out!' she shouted. 'We'll walk out! Let's see how the bugger gets on without us!'

2

A long, white banner fluttered, restless as a kite, against the blue of the April sky. It was suspended, in a makeshift fashion, between two waxed beech clothes-props, planted in the rich, manured soil of the shrubbery, close to the main gate. Across it, stencilled in bold, black lettering, were the words: PIMLETT FAMILY GRAND ANNUAL TENNIS TOURNAMENT 1914 A.D.

Stretched out on a rug on the lawn and munching a warm Cornish pasty, Mercedes MacInnes idly calculated how long she'd been coming to this yearly jamboree. Let's see now. Eleven or twelve she must have been the first time, and in August she'd be twenty-four. Today, for no reason, the tradition, the cosy sameness of it, made her feel vaguely depressed.

This time there was a small difference, though. Normally the tournament took place in July. This year it was early – not long after Easter. The reason, so Walter Pimlett confided, was his brother's wife, Cassandra, who was pregnant with her first child.

'Ma was scared that if they held it any later poor Cassie'd probably go into labour, what with the sheer unbridled excitement of it all,' Walter had told her, with a little gleam of bravado. Friends of the opposite sex didn't usually talk about things like pregnancy, but she and Walter had no patience with such mealy-mouthed taboos.

So this was probably her twelfth tournament *chez* Pimlett, in their sprawling house and garden on the Herts-Essex border. Pimlett senior had been at medical school with Mercedes' father thirty years or so

16

ago. The two men had stayed in touch ever since, the friendship extending to their eventual wives and children.

Scanning her fellow-guests, Mercedes gave the impression of distancing herself from them a shade, observing them with a vaguely speculative eye. Her skin was smooth and rather pale, though warmed to a slight tan by the spring sunshine. Her features were regular – straight nose, symmetrical arched eyebrows and a fullish, shapely mouth. Her eyes were the most striking thing about her – hazel, with a gleam of scepticism, but also at times a disconcerting unselfconscious steadiness. Her hair was straight and left so, a dark blonde in the sunlight, with reddish glints, mousy when the sun vanished for a moment behind a cloud. For the tournament she wore it hanging loose, the forward locks caught off her face with a narrow white ribbon.

She wore a plain white skirt, a pin-tucked blouse and a narrow belt which emphasized a slight, flexible body. The kind of figure that was just beginning to be fashionable, complementing the dashing new uncorseted bohemian styles, making the hour-glass-shaped, frizzy-haired Edwardian beauties of a few years back look overblown and a little bit *passé*. Though men of a certain age huffed that you couldn't tell the boys from the girls any more.

'Another pasty anyone?' Winnie Pimlett, Walter's mother, gave her good-natured, horsy smile and indicated the piled willow-pattern platter. A large, linen cloth was spread on the ground and most of the company lounged round it on the grass – the Pimlett household never stood on ceremony – but there were wicker chairs available for the older and staider members.

'These pasties are just the ticket, Winnie.' Alfred, a friend from the village, a beaky barrister, stretched out a lanky arm to help himself.

'Delicious.' Murmurs of agreement rose from all quarters.

17

The lunch-time picnic never varied. It was always Winnie's Cornish pasties, followed by Winnie's sticky gingerbread, washed down with ale or Winnie's ginger beer. Good old Winnie, Mercedes thought with a flicker of cynicism, basking in the credit and the compliments just as though she, personally, had been slaving over the kitchen range for days. No mention of cook or her skivvies. Nowadays Mercedes noticed things like that, things she'd always taken for granted. And tonight, no doubt, there'd be a proper sit-down meal for twenty or more, four courses at least, with wine.

Walter took a hefty swig from his tankard of beer.

'You're quaffing.' Mercedes gave him an ironic sideways glance.

'What?'

'Quaffing.' She grinned. 'Ale. Knocking it back like some Shakespearian ham. Sir Toby or someone.'

Obligingly he demonstrated again, wiping his mouth on his sleeve with actorish vulgarity. 'This stuff goes straight to my backhand. I'll play all the better for it. I've got to beat the Ballard boy after lunch. Wouldn't do to be trounced by a sixteen-year-old.'

Since she'd last seen him Walter had grown a moustache. To Mercedes' eyes it looked like stage face-fungus pasted on to his open, boyish countenance. They sat together, just slightly apart from the rest, on the green baize lawn that sloped down to the River Stort. Ever since they'd been toddlers the two of them had gravitated towards one another. They'd always been able to talk easily and frankly, the families accepting their special relationship. But their friendship was casual – often they went months without meeting.

Mercedes closed her eyes, turning her face up to the harsh spring sun. She thought back to the morning's matches. 'I had to umpire Ballard *père*'s game earlier. He really likes to win, old Edward. There was one ball

I said was out and he said was in. We had quite a scene. Lost our tempers in a well-bred sort of way.'

The hot vehemence in Edward Ballard's eyes had startled her. He was known as a charmer, affable and easy-going.

'Did you sort it out?' Walter asked.

'I stuck to my guns.' Mercedes gave a dry smile at the memory. 'He didn't like it, though.'

But Ballard's show of anger had struck a chord in her. She'd been both repelled and attracted. 'He reminds me of myself,' she admitted. 'Thinking it was terribly important to win some tuppenny-ha'penny game of bat and ball.'

The incident had rekindled the more-than-passing interest Mercedes had always felt in the Ballard family. Generally speaking, her once-a-year, tennis-playing acquaintanceship with the Pimlett family's friends and relations made almost no impression on her. But, from years back, the Ballards had intrigued her. They seemed different. Their three boys were so handsome and self-possessed. One of them had longish hair and gold-rimmed spectacles and was supposed to be brilliant at the piano.

Edward's wife, Mildred, too, was unlike the other matrons. Dark-haired, white-skinned, voluptuous-looking and slightly strange. Not that Mercedes had ever had much to do with her. But last year, she recalled, they'd had quite a long chat about H.G. Wells. Mildred had hinted naughtily at his reputation as a ladykiller, but she'd read the books too, and had opinions on them.

'He looks as if he's got over his fit of the pique.' Walter glanced across to where Ballard was talking to the visibly pregnant Cassie Pimlett. She was laughing at something he'd said and there was a smile of secret amusement on his face. The wings of his fairish hair had been ruffled by the tennis game and he looked relaxed and younger than the forty-odd years he must be.

Mercedes shrugged. 'Well, he won the match anyway.'

'Did you hear about the walk-out at his factory?' A confidential expression crossed Walter's fresh features.

'No?' She looked at him sharply.

'Yesterday. Something like sixty women. *All* of them. There was some row and they just upped and left.'

'So it's a strike?'

Walter nodded. 'I suppose so.'

Mercedes' response was unequivocal. 'Serve him right.' She spoke without thinking and was surprised by the feeling in her own voice.

So was Walter. 'Goodness, what venom. He must really have put your back up.'

She shook her head. 'Heavens, no. I don't hold our little spat against him.'

Walter was called away to fetch something for his mother and discreetly Mercedes looked across at Ballard again. Walter's titbit of news had stirred a memory that had lain dormant at the back of her mind for years – a conversation that had taken place at the Pimletts' long dining-table when she'd been sixteen or seventeen.

Above the shining cutlery, the cut glass, the good, rib-sticking food, some of the men were bemoaning the alarming rise of Germany and America as rival industrial powers. At first Mercedes didn't take much notice. She was more interested in observing Mildred Ballard, alluring but strangely overdressed in low-cut maroon satin, and speculating what, if anything, lay behind her silent, enigmatic smile. But gradually her attention had shifted to Edward Ballard. In this gathering of professional men – doctors, lawyers, their wives and children – he was the only one with direct experience of manufacturing. Inevitably he began to dominate the conversation. He talked wittily, keeping his touch light. Mercedes remembered that, as he spoke, he'd picked up a small silver knife and deftly peeled a peach, the coils of its skin snaking gracefully on to his plate.

Thomas Pimlett, Walter's father, had struck a lugubrious note. 'It's tragic, though, don't you think, this decline of craftsmanship?'

Ballard turned to him, smiling indulgently at the country doctor's sweet, old-fashioned notions. 'Productivity's the word nowadays, Thomas, old boy. Sadly we've no time for proud, granite-faced craftsmen.'

Thomas Pimlett had pulled down the corners of his mouth regretfully.

'Take my Bermondsey factory,' Ballard went on. 'I've got a first-class man in charge. Pay him handsomely and he gets the productivity up year by year, without fail, regular as clockwork . . .' An engaging, self-deprecating smile. 'I don't enquire too closely into his methods . . .'

Mercedes was stunned by the casual confession. Instantly she saw Edward Ballard in a startling new light. There was talk everywhere at the time – in Parliament and in the newspapers – of sweated labour . . . Mercedes had even been to an exhibition which exposed the scandal of women who toiled all hours in dark, stuffy rooms, without rest or fresh air, making clothes, ruining their health, paid the barest minimum, living their lives in grinding poverty. Her mother's friends clucked sorrowfully, deploring the faceless villains who exploited the poor so cynically.

And there he was. Ballard. Sitting at the table with them. Revealed suddenly as the embodiment of one of these mythical slave-drivers. Mercedes gazed, rapt and repelled, though no one else seemed to be turning a hair. His heavy, handsome features wore an attractively quizzical grin. The peeled peach glistened on the plate in front of him, looking, to her fevered eyes, as if it had been flayed alive.

'Wotcher, Sadie.'

With a start Mercedes looked up. It was Walter, back from his errand, looming over her. 'You seem miles away,' he said.

She pulled herself together, sitting up and smoothing her hair. 'Walter, while you're on your feet, be an angel and get me a slice of your mother's sticky gingerbread. Just a small piece – I've got a game to play in an hour or so . . . Interesting that,' she added irrelevantly. 'About the strike, I mean.'

Mercedes MacInnes won the women's section of the tournament, as she had for six years running. In the final she beat Agnes Cook, the willowy blonde daughter of the local vicar. Agnes had a trim, athletic figure, but just one look at her wide grey eyes told Mercedes that she'd think it beneath her dignity to scramble after difficult balls or appear to mind if she lost. Mercedes despatched her efficiently for the loss of only one game.

'Well done, darling!' Florence MacInnes called with unselfconscious enthusiasm as her daughter left the court. Mercedes felt herself blush. Her mother's irrepressible public affection was one of the few things that still had the power to call up the ghost of her old, embarrassed, adolescent self.

Later, sitting sedately on a long bench between her parents, Mercedes watched the men's final. It was a beautiful evening. At five o'clock the sun was still mellow and warm. In the wake of the physical exercise her body tingled with well-being. Idly, pleasurably, her eyes took in the familiar surroundings – the large, harmonious, coral brick Georgian farmhouse casting its long shadow across the smooth lawns, the herbaceous border, tidied and top-dressed, just starting into life with yellow leopard's bane and a patch of blue hyacinths, the apple trees lavish with white blossom, the shards of broken sunlight dancing on the surface of the Stort.

On court Walter Pimlett did battle with Edward Ballard. Walter was lithe and agile but, like Agnes Cook, he would have considered it slightly vulgar to get too fiercely involved in the game. He played well enough, but his movements hinted at an amused laziness.

'Dear old Walter,' Florence MacInnes whispered loudly to her daughter. 'Doesn't he look nice with his moustache?'

In some part of her mind Mercedes envied his detachment. It must be rather nice not to care terribly whether you won or not. But the nonchalance of it was alien to her.

Now she understood Edward Ballard. His teeth were gritted, his handsome face red and sweating and his yellow hair bounced in time to his exertions. His muscular body, slightly thickening at the waist, almost vibrated with his determination to win.

There was a discreet burst of clapping as he served a savage ace. As far as Mercedes was concerned the result was a foregone conclusion.

Her mind drifted away from the game and back to the subject that had preoccupied her on and off all day, an unseen backdrop to polite, playful conversations, the bouts of physical activity. Back to the absorbing thoughts and fantasies that had been triggered by Walter's report of the walk-out at Edward Ballard's South London factory.

3

Mercedes was a socialist. An 'ardent' socialist her father always said when explaining her to his friends, as if the two words were inseparable.

With time he'd become almost proud of the fact, though when she first announced it to the family, at the age of twenty, they'd been distinctly dubious. Her two elder sisters had never been much bothered with politics. They were wed now, settled, with children. In her parents' eyes Mercedes was the daughter-at-home, ripe for marriage, on display at parties and gatherings with other girls of her age, like choice fruit on a market stall. Her new enthusiasm wasn't likely to enhance her desirability. Ardent socialism was almost as embarrassing in company as religious fanaticism.

In fact Mercedes would have been the first to admit that her grasp of political theory was shaky to say the least. As far as she was concerned, the word 'socialism' was simply a convenient way of labelling a feeling that had been growing inside her for ages – for all of her life – a guilty awareness of the blindingly obvious fact that society was wickedly unfair and long overdue for a radical shaking-up.

One cold day in early December she'd visited an old schoolfriend in Chelsea, to congratulate her on becoming engaged to be married. Phyllis Goodwin was pretty and fluffy, with a sharp, malicious sense of humour. At school, Mercedes remembered, she'd always been at the centre of any high jinks. She hadn't seen her friend for some time and was unprepared for Phyllis's blithe, blatant involvement in the material preparations for her wedding. She looked a lady of fashion now, in a

24

draped lavender cashmere tea-gown, her hair arranged in upswept, sausagy curls.

'We'll be living in Belgravia, Sadie, imagine that,' Phyllis had gushed with a coy glance at Mercedes, never doubting for a second that her guest would be just as impressed as she was with the splendour of the address.

She tried on a new fur coat for Mercedes' benefit and boasted that she and her fiancé had ordered all their furniture from Liberty's. 'It's all being individually made,' she emphasized importantly, 'to suit the dimensions of our rooms.'

She giggled over some silk underwear she'd bought the previous day at Debenhams, but almost immediately a look of sharp petulance crossed her pert features, as she ticked off the nervous young maid who was serving tea, with an irritability Mercedes found shocking.

When she left the house Mercedes was in low spirits, disliking Phyllis heartily for her self-absorbed chatter, yet feeling her own disapproval to be stiff and priggish. She'd walked for some time, briskly, while random thoughts swirled and then crystallized inside her head. She found herself in the shabby back-streets of Victoria. Their mildewed dilapidation contrasted bleakly with the chic little drawing-room she'd just left, depressing her still further.

At breakfast the next morning in their house in Devonshire Place, near her father's practice in Harley Street, Mercedes tried to explain her moment of truth, while the maid clattered about in the next room, sweeping and dusting, and her parents attempted to listen with a suitable air of gravity, while at the same time not letting their bacon and eggs go cold.

'I was walking past a bakery. It was freezing and windy, but I was quite enjoying it. I had my warm coat on and I was coming home to a lovely fire and crumpets and cocoa. It was getting dark. There was this bunch of little boys outside the shop. They were dressed in ragged trousers and just thin jerseys. One or two of them had jackets, but nothing substantial. One was barefoot . . .'

Mercedes was uncomfortably aware of sounding like Mrs Chambers, a friend of her mother's, who was always dwelling on the sufferings of the poor with an almost gloating melancholy. She wasn't conveying the reality of what she'd seen and felt. Her mother was crunching noisily on a piece of fried bread. Mercedes ploughed on . . .

'One little boy asked me to buy him a cake. He had a horrible rough, scaly rash on his neck and legs – scabies or something. There were six of them, so I went inside and bought six lovely, hot, flaky sausage rolls. They took them and they didn't smile. Their eyes were sort of blank and hard. I remembered Phyllis bragging about her fur coat and lacy underpinnings . . . and I hated her, and I hated myself for having enough money and yet . . .'

Solemnity was much debunked in the MacInnes family and Mercedes could see that her father was dying to lighten the atmosphere with a well-timed witticism. George MacInnes wasn't a callous man, but for him the problem of poverty was too large a subject to get to grips with. It was something best left to the experts, whoever they were. His expression, behind the mask of his greying beard and moustache, was sceptical and discouraging.

She gave up and changed her tactics. For a few weeks there'd been mayhem. Mercedes felt raw and edgy but determined to make them understand her point of view. She shouted and slammed doors, deliberately making life disagreeable for the whole household. Her parents were easy-going people who liked their peace and quiet. They'd never been strict and hated the unpleasantness of rows. But now they began to ask themselves anxiously whether they hadn't been too easy with the girls, too indulgent . . . Perhaps finally, the chickens were coming home to roost.

'This socialism's turning you into a little bit of a virago, darling . . .' her mother ventured timidly during one of the rare moments when Mercedes was approachable at all.

But the warfare couldn't last. As a family none of them were good at keeping up sulks or ill-temper. Over the months Mercedes' socialism lost its novelty value, and with it the power to shock, and was gradually absorbed into the everyday scheme of things. Florence and George defused it, thankfully, by turning it into a family joke. It was their way of dealing with anything unfamiliar or disruptive.

They nicknamed her The Bolshevist and exchanged amused, parental glances when Mercedes dashed off after dinner to meetings of all sorts – to Caxton Hall to suffragette gatherings, to Essex Hall to listen to the giants of the Fabian Society, to draughty meeting-rooms in remoter parts of London to attend lectures by Lansbury and Keir Hardie. Privately they agreed that this kind of rushing about was better than her getting a bee in her bonnet about going out to work, like Margery Cannon, the headstrong daughter of one of George's patients.

In fact Mercedes welcomed her parents' good-natured teasing. It was useful, providing a smoke-screen, a humorous fuzz round her activities, making them less likely to be scrutinized or interfered with.

The truth was that, in spite of the solemn announcement of her conversion to socialism, Mercedes felt like an inept swimmer, splashing and kicking out in all directions, but not getting very far. She covered her confusion with a great show of bustle and purposefulness. She was always off to meetings and lectures.

'You're such a rush-about, darling,' her mother said constantly, with an air of dazed admiration. 'You'll meet yourself coming back one of these days.'

With all her heart Mercedes longed for some kind of all-enveloping involvement, the feeling that she was getting somewhere, changing something. But she was bedevilled by the suspicion that her activities were full of sound and fury, signifying nothing very much.

Her first foray had been into the realm of women's suffrage. She was fired by the stirring words of the queenly Mrs Pankhurst at a suffragette fund-raising concert and joined the local branch of the WSPU, instantly acquiring a whole new group of friends. They held discussion evenings and passed resolutions whilst drinking a great deal of cocoa.

Mercedes sold the magazine, *The Suffragette*, round Waterloo, braving the smirks and muffled giggles of the passers-by, and the loud, insulting comments from overdressed women about what frights these militants looked. Each time she found herself reduced to bristling, trembling rage.

'Good luck, young lady. You'll win through.' Once in a while a well-wisher, male or female, would smile or shake her by the hand, and Mercedes would be taken aback by the almost abject gratitude she felt.

She took part in a massive parade through the streets of London. The women who'd been to prison walked at the front in white. They were watched all the way by crowds four or five deep. That had been the best day – wonderful, emotional, exhilarating.

A few weeks later Mercedes was arrested, with some of her fellows, for disrupting a political meeting. She was carried out bodily by a large, ginger-haired policeman. He was red in the face and had the exasperated, embarrassed air of a young father dealing publicly with a child in a tantrum. She was taken to the station and booked, but ignominiously released as small-fry. She went home and never even mentioned the happening to her parents. There seemed no point in worrying them for so little.

But, in spite of her solid belief in the cause, Mercedes had always felt a nagging dissatisfaction. She seemed to be mixing almost exclusively with the kind of women she might have been at school with, or their older sisters, or their aunts. There was a jibe going round that what the suffragettes really wanted was Votes for Ladies. Ladies, not women. The barb prickled often in the back of her mind. She thought of the hostile, hungry children she'd seen that cold December evening outside the bakery, and it didn't seem to her that she'd done much to help them.

In Mercedes' group there was a woman called Ann Garvie. She was about thirty and unmarried, solidly-built, fresh-faced and bossy, with thick hair of a dense, dull brown. She had some medical training and twice a week she worked at a voluntary mother-and-child clinic in Lambeth. Mercedes wouldn't have chosen her as a friend, but she couldn't help admiring the brisk way she kept their meetings on course. Some of the women got side-tracked by their own personal hobby-horses, and the business went round in circles, but Ann gave this kind of dithering short shrift. One evening, walking home from a meeting – they lived in roughly the same direction – Mercedes confided her doubts to Ann.

Her fellow-suffragette was typically decisive. 'Come and help us out down in Lambeth. At the moment we're short of someone to deal with the paperwork.'

Mercedes was cheered. A clinic. The word had a straightforward, practical sound. Perhaps, at last, in some small way, she could actually feel she was involved in making things better.

Consultations were held in a large, bare hall behind a tall warehouse. The interior was murky, except where shafts of light came slantwise through the high windows, illuminating dancing specks of dust. The medical staff sat at the far end, a white-coated, exclusive enclave. A long expanse of bare floor stretched between them and the waiting women and children, who sat in rows, looking to Mercedes like dull-eyed immigrants in steerage.

Her registration table was placed sideways on, near the entrance, at the patients' end of the room.

A name would be called and the woman in question would stand up and advance the length of the hall, a lone, self-conscious figure, her boots clacking loudly on the wooden floorboards, often with an intimidated child or two clinging to her skirts.

Frequently they had to wait two hours or more, with nothing to keep the children entertained. And woe betide any mother whose infant was noisy or showed any desire to run about on the vast acreage of empty floor. Ann Garvie was even crisper with them than she was with the over-chatty suffragettes. In this context her bossiness edged over into outright bullying.

'Between ourselves, Sadie, I'm really rather proud of you.' It was at this stage that George MacInnes began to be reconciled to Mercedes' socialism, equating it vaguely with a memory of his mother taking rice-puddings round to needy families when he was a boy. He started to mention her doings to his friends and acquaintances in a modest, offhand fashion.

But, to her vexation, Mercedes found that she couldn't be altogether wholehearted about the clinic's work. It was better than nothing, of course, but she couldn't help seeing how unrealistic it was to think that these shabby, ill-nourished women could afford to buy eggs, oranges or full-cream milk for their whey-faced children, as they were advised. And the medicines and bandages prescribed would have to be paid for out of incomes already stretched to vanishing-point.

Her own comparative wealth rankled horribly. She was made profoundly uneasy by the cowed eyes of some of the women when she asked them questions for their registration-cards, and by the glinting hostility of others. Mercedes grew to loathe the overloud, hectoring speech of the medical experts, and tried to interview the mothers in a

30

normal, conversational tone of voice. Some of the women were confused by this unexpected approach and it slowed things down.

Ann Garvie became impatient. 'There's no point in trying to treat these people as equals!' she hissed one afternoon in a fierce stage-whisper that resounded round the bleak hall. 'They simply don't understand!' Mercedes flushed with anger and shame.

'I'm not sure, dear, after all, that you're tough enough for this kind of work,' Ann commented tartly, when Mercedes complained after the session about her lack of tact.

'I'm plenty tough enough,' Mercedes retorted. 'But that's not the same as being a brow-beating bully!'

After that, by mutual consent, they parted company.

For a time Mercedes did nothing. Dully she acted the part of the daughter-in-residence, visiting friends and participating dutifully in her mother's at-homes.

'It's lovely to see a little more of you, darling,' Florence sighed almost daily.

In the wake of Mercedes' political involvement, Florence too had begun to take a warm, amateur interest in social questions. At fifty-five she was too matronly and comfortable, so she claimed, to be doing anything active, but she quoted George Lansbury and Sylvia Pankhurst daringly to her staider friends. Over dinner, especially after a glass or two of wine, she would discuss the Vote and minimum wages and health insurance with a bright-eyed, pink animation, often disagreeing with her husband, and Mercedes would glimpse suddenly, in her mother's thickened features, the ghost of someone younger and more unconventional.

Mercedes herself felt savage and frustrated, constantly wondering whether she wasn't just hopelessly and congenitally over-critical. Other people seemed to manage to throw themselves into things and really believe in what they were doing. Why couldn't she be like that?

She became prickly and difficult about accompanying her parents to social events. Although they didn't say as much – not wanting to provoke an outburst – she knew they were worried because she showed no interest in meeting young men, displaying herself, attracting a husband. Mercedes was perfectly aware of their muffled concern and it exasperated her still further.

But it was true that she found most of the young men in their social circle bland and predictable. They bored her. There was something indistinguishable about them. It seemed to her that they all had the same polite smile, talked with the same charming, well-bred diffidence and offered the same safe opinions. Perhaps it was simply that they were all products of the same few public schools.

'They're mass-produced. Like those spotted china dogs that go on mantelpieces,' she said dismissively to George and Florence, who valiantly tried to turn her pickiness into one of their family jokes.

She made an exception for Walter. He was her dear friend, cheerful and reliable and easy to talk to. But he was more like a brother.

In fact, though she'd never have admitted it, Mercedes wasn't altogether happy about her own aloofness. As a girl she hadn't been like this at all. Her sisters used to be scandalized by her frank interest in the sons of her parents' visiting friends.

'Sadie's always pestering the boys,' the family joke used to run in those days.

She could remember one unreal tea-time spent kissing young Peter Drury behind the acrid-smelling laurel bush in the garden, while the adults had temporarily forgotten them. Even now the scent of the gloomy shrub recalled to her that strangely dream-like afternoon, Peter's long, black lashes and dry, slightly scabbed lips, his starched, unyielding Eton collar.

He'd had a waywardness about him when they were both

eleven years old that corresponded to her own. Now he had the same careful smile as the rest and talked about banking. He'd courted her for a time when they were twenty. Perhaps he'd been encouraged by the memory of their childish flirtation in the shrubbery, because it took a long time before Mercedes' coolness finally put him off.

She was glumly resigned to the fact that in this, as in all other areas of her life, she was critical and difficult to please. In any case, the prospect of marriage didn't attract her at all. As far as she could see, it made women fat and dull. Secretly she thought the idea of 'free union', as described in that subversive journal *The Freewoman*, sounded far more inspiring, if only she could find a man who really interested her. But at home she kept such opinions to herself. George and Florence worried enough about her as it was.

4

Daisy Harkness turned slowly on the narrow settee. A pale light piercing the limp floral curtains told her it was around five o'clock. Alex and Janie were still asleep, head to tail, on a mattress on the floor alongside her, and her mother snored softly on the bed by the wall. No sound yet from next door where her brother, Andrew, slept.

Seventeen months since Frankie had died, and it still felt strange and cold each morning to be lying alone. That had been one of the best things – his warm flesh, their tangled limbs, the drowsy cuddling, the solidity of him pushing into her while she was still half-asleep, the feel of it, the slow, deep, melting sensation. She missed all that almost more than she missed Frankie himself.

He was lovely, a handsome boy with dark curls that Janie had inherited, and a smile that was like the sun coming out. And he was steady, a good husband, a good provider. He worked all hours, and brought his money home. At the most he'd have a couple of pints on his way back to supper. He'd be dog-tired when he got in, with nothing much to say to her, just a kiss and his sweet smile. They had the children to talk about, and how to eke out his money, and that was about all. As far as Daisy could tell he never felt the lack. Frankie always seemed a foreigner to her. A closed book. She told him that once and he laughed, surprised. He held his arms out sideways away from his body, with a crooked grin, as if to show he had nothing to hide, and said, 'What you see is what you get.'

But he did like *her* foreignness, she knew. Once he whispered to her after they made love, 'It's like you're made out of a different metal than the rest. Something

34

silvery, none of your old brass like the other girls . . .'
She'd always remembered that because he didn't often
say anything that showed he had thoughts about her.

Then, the winter before last, he fell from a botched
scaffolding five floors up. It was a frosty Monday – you
could see your breath all day. When they told her she hid
her eyes in a useless attempt to block out the picture of
his warm body smashed to a pulp on the frozen ground.
The funeral was a nightmare. Imagining his brightness and
his smile nailed inside that coffin, about to be buried in
the grey, dead earth. But in a way Daisy felt worse for
Frankie's mother. She looked like a walking corpse and
there was the thought that if you let go of her she'd jump
into the grave and try to join him.

After that Daisy got a job at Ballard's and she and
the children moved into two rooms in Aquitaine Street
with her mother and brother. It wasn't so bad. She could
manage. She had to. These few minutes in bed in the
morning were the worst, when she had a little time to
remember Frankie with his curls in his eyes pulling her
close, the live feeling of skin on skin. But a feather of
anxiety brushed across her sleepy imaginings and she
recalled that it wasn't going to be an ordinary day. Today
she wouldn't be going into the factory.

In spite of everything, a part of her welcomed the
prospect. It'd be like when Frankie was alive. He wouldn't
hear of her going out to work right from when he knew she
was expecting Alex. She used to have time then to plan
ahead, think about looking after the others – Frankie,
and her mother two streets away, and the children when
they came along. There was time, too, to sort out the
money situation, shop around for the cheapest food and
bargains on the old-clothes stalls. She would mend and
make things for the family or for neighbours who would
sometimes give her cloth and thread in return, knowing
how clever she was with a needle. She had leisure to

35

make things then, slowly and skilfully, like the quilt that was on Andrew's bed now. It had taken months, getting the materials gradually, cutting up the good parts of what people gave her. It was different and unusual, put together from her own imagination. Everyone admired it and there wasn't another one like it in the land.

'You could sell that for a lot of money,' people told her. But she wouldn't. Daisy was proud of it. It added something to their shabby old rooms, like the plants she grew in pots along the window-sill.

She was able to use her imagination a bit at Ballard's, though not as much as she'd like. She did fine hand-embroidery on the most expensive blouses and petticoats. But you had to do the kind of thing that was wanted, nothing too different. Her own ideas were much wilder. The hours were far too long and the close work strained her eyes, but it wasn't as grinding and dull as most of the jobs there. Leonard Floyd didn't treat her like dirt, because the skills she had were thin on the ground in Bermondsey, and she got better money than most, though they still had her damn cheap.

Daisy decided to get up early and make some potato pancakes for Andrew to take to work. Might as well use the time while she had it. Only there was a chill of fear. This dispute wouldn't last, would it? Best not to think of what could happen. She'd keep busy, take the time to sort out all the jobs around the house that Mamma didn't seem able to think about doing any more. And play with the children. She'd enjoy it.

Only . . . there was that memory from when they were children and Daddy was still alive. A hard time when work was scarce and they hadn't been able to pay the rent. They'd gone out and when they came back the landlord had put their bits of furniture outside on the pavement and locked the door. And all the neighbours were standing on their doorsteps, looking down their noses at the beggarly

For the moment she was invaluable, looking after the children all day when Daisy was at the factory. But she was getting vaguer and vaguer and Daisy could foresee a time, quite soon, when she'd be forced to pay someone to mind not just Alex and Janie, but Mamma herself. And how would the money stretch to that? As it was, Daisy was getting less and less happy about leaving the children with her. She was so forgetful, and often cross for no reason that anyone could see. The only good thing about the walk-out was that Daisy could stay home and keep the children company for a day or so. It couldn't be good for them to be alone with Mamma for twelve hours and more every day. But what else could she do?

Andrew teased her that she only had to marry again and all her troubles would be over. Daisy knew she could if she wanted. She couldn't help knowing – she'd seen it all her life – that men singled her out, wanted her, tried to please her. And no doubt, if she chose a new husband, some parts of her life would be easier. Daisy had been born here, but still she felt a misfit. The people she lived with and worked with seemed alien to her, their spirits stunted by their hard lives, their bodies malnourished. The women and the men. Frankie, with his wholeness and his sweetness, had been the exception.

Deftly she flipped the potato-cake over, feeling unsettled, more so than usual, because of the walk-out, the uncertainty. She was only twenty-five and sometimes all she could see stretching ahead of her were years of grind and fear.

'Nose stuck in a bloody book! I thought as much!'

Annie Tyrell seized the novelette from her ten-year-old daughter's hands and slapped her black-stockinged leg. Maggie had been too engrossed to notice her mother's entry into the bedroom.

'I'll give you read! Get on and make those beds before I give you more!'

39

'Mum!' her daughter protested, grabbing for the book. Annie held it higher above her head. Resignedly Maggie flicked back an ancient plaid blanket that covered the double bed.

She was dark and wiry and self-possessed. Her hair hung down to her waist in two plaits, which bobbed about as she straightened the bedclothes. Her movements were quick and capable. Annie watched her with secret satisfaction. God knows where she'd got this habit of reading from. Annie blamed Rose, a mooney fourteen-year-old from down the street, who bought trashy books from the rag-shop, a penny for a great big pile, and lent them to all the younger girls. But, reading apart, Maggie was a kid you could be proud of – sharp as knives. Ever since she'd been able to toddle her daughter had held her own with the other kids. You'd have to get up early to put anything over on her.

Maggie finished her parents' bed and started on her own.

Then she'd go into the living-room and do the boys'. It was her job to sort out all the beds before she went to school.

She looked up saucily at her mother. 'Anyway, Mum, why do I have to do this? You're going to be home all day like Lady Muck.'

Annie gave her a humorous, sideways, exasperated glance. Most mothers wouldn't let their kids get away with such cheek. But she'd seen children that were squashed and punished all the time. They grew up timid and couldn't stand up for themselves. That wasn't going to happen to any child of hers.

'Don't bank on my being home like this for long,' Annie declared forcibly. 'The bosses need us too much. They're nothing without us.' They'd all agreed on that, she and her husband, Will, and the two boys. Since Friday they'd talked it over time and again. But if the deadlock *did* last, they were right behind her. They all hated the bosses. Things had been bad often enough in the past, and they'd lived to tell the tale. And they would again.

'Don't think you're going to get lazy, my girl.' Annie gave her daughter an old-fashioned look. 'And hurry up with those other two beds or you'll be late for school.'

When Maggie was gone Annie heated up the remains of the tea she'd made for their breakfast and sat down. It felt strange. For years she'd been in a rush all of the time, desperate for a bit of peace, and here she was free to do nothing for as long as she liked. It didn't matter providing that she had a meal ready for the rest of them when they came home. Annie tried to make herself enjoy sitting there, but her mind kept wandering.

It was easy when other people were around to talk big, convincing herself and them that this walk-out wasn't a giant-sized mistake. Floyd deserved it, God knows. The bugger had been asking for something like this for years. She'd no regrets on that score.

Only, no matter how hard she tried, one thing kept preying on her mind. The Burial Club. The weekly shilling she'd managed to pay regular as clockwork for a good few years now. Supposing they couldn't afford that any more.

Annie had been lucky with her kids. She'd had four boys before Maggie, all of them bouncers. But her fifth child had been a girl. Betsy they called her. She was different – tiny and delicate. Even now thinking about her wasn't easy. A little fighter she was, but her fighting did her no good. One night Annie had sat up holding her while the others slept. She could still recall the stillness of the two of them alone together, the pain of loving the mangy little scrap and knowing she was almost gone. Betsy died at about four in the morning and Annie carried on cradling her. Will was out of work then and only Jeff, the oldest boy, bringing anything home – about three bob for all of them. They owed money right, left and centre and she had to lay Betsy out in a cardboard box. A big van called to take her little body away. She was buried on the parish in a mass grave. For months Annie kept bursting out crying just to think of it.

41

Two years later Maggie was born and it was back to normal. Right from the start she was tough as old boots. It seemed to Annie that the little black-haired tot, with big, dark, knowing eyes, had changed their luck. Soon after she arrived Will landed a long spell of steady work, and when Maggie was weaned Annie took the job at Ballard's and left the baby with a neighbour. It was slave-labour, but at least she brought *something* home each week.

Things got better. They'd had this place in Picardy Street for a while now. It was a shit-hole, and the bugs were starting to get lively with the warm weather. But she made it as nice as she could, and they'd been able to keep up with the rent, even if Will was only in work for about half the time. He was chesty and breathless and getting that bit too old for labouring. The two elder boys were off hand, and the next two had jobs more often than not.

Since she started at Ballard's Annie had managed to keep up the insurance payments, so none of the rest of them would ever have to be buried like poor Betsy. No one knew – not even Will – how much that meant to her.

A sharp rapping came at the street door and Annie got up eagerly, leaving her morbid thoughts behind. The Tyrells' two rooms were on the ground floor, so it was a matter of seconds to nip into the hallway and open up. Edie Black stood on the doorstep, out of breath, green eyes sparkling in her doughy face. She grinned, showing a mouthful of broken teeth. 'Come quick, Annie. Betty's just found out that Sal O'Shea's been carrying on with her old man. There's a barney going on . . .'

Annie brightened. 'Just a moment, duck. I'll get my shawl.'

It was a sunny, blustery morning and a small crowd had already collected outside the house where Sally O'Shea lived with her parents and her sisters. Sally was a machinist at Ballard's along with Bridie, one of her older sisters. The young girl was standing on the doorstep looking scared. She hadn't done her hair yet. It hung to the middle of her back, stiff and crimped as if she'd slept with it in plaits. Her smooth, pale face was screwed as though she were on the point of crying.

'Tears now,' Annie commented. 'I've seen her with Betty's Josh, bold as brass. Bit late for tears.' She had no pity for the cornered girl.

'Bloody tart!' Betty Partridge was shouting. She appealed to the onlookers. 'Look at that! Butter wouldn't melt in her mouth. But she's been shagging my Josh in shop doorways!' Betty worked at home, sewing sacks. She had a lanky, uncoordinated look to her – a long neck, long thin arms, and a raw, red complexion.

'You tell her, Bet!' Edie called.

'Who can blame 'im?' a man commented audibly, and little eddies of laughter rippled among the crowd.

The remark and the giggling appeared to incense Betty. She rushed at the young girl, grabbing her by the hair, slapping and kicking her. Sally O'Shea seemed too dazed to put up much resistance as her head was pulled this way and that. Then Betty's fist struck her full in the eye.

'She'll have a shiner by evening,' Annie said.

Retreating struggling through the doorway, Sally spoke for the first time. 'I'll get my cousin Michael on to you.' The door slammed and she was gone. Ragged cheers arose from the spectators.

'I'll get my cousin Michael on to you!' Betty mimicked shrilly, relishing her moment of acclaim. She sauntered off victoriously, surrounded by a little knot of well-wishers, wiping her hands on her apron, then re-winding her back hair and fixing it with a comb.

'Only just got here in time.' Annie grinned. Her good humour had returned. 'Think,' she said to Edie. 'If we'd been down Ballard's we'd have missed this.'

Mention of Ballard's seemed to touch some undigested clot of anxiety in Edie. She grabbed her friend by the arm.

'What in God's name are we going to *do*, Annie?' she asked vehemently.

All her life people had looked to Annie to provide the solutions to questions they couldn't answer themselves. It was her own fault, Annie admitted ruefully to herself. She acted like a know-it-all, so it wasn't surprising that people were taken in.

She had as little idea of what the next step should be as Edie. But whatever it was, Annie knew she'd have to be the leader, so there was no point in confessing to her own doubts and uncertainties. If she did, the whole dispute would have collapsed by this evening and she'd be well and truly out of a job. She'd learned from experience that when nobody knows what they're doing, they'll follow the person who's best at pretending.

'We'll sort out a meeting for tomorrow,' Annie said decisively. An inspiration occurred to her. 'I bet Father Simpson would let us use his hall.' It sounded as if she'd worked it all out beforehand, she reflected with grim amusement. 'Let's say two o'clock. I'll take this road and Aquitaine Street. You let them know in Tooley Street. Tell everyone to pass it on.'

Edie was gawping at her, trusting and reassured. Silly cow. Annie was irritated by her look of blind faith. A sickly reek of boiling vinegar from the pickle factory had begun to invade the air above Picardy Street. She hated it and knew she'd have a headache before noon.

Annie had the confused suspicion that there were worlds of laws and rules and official procedures that she was totally ignorant of. If only there was someone she could ask. Still, Annie had found in the past that, if she bustled enough and was bossy enough, she'd convince herself in the end that she knew what she was doing.

5

In the spring of 1913 Mercedes had enrolled in a series of afternoon classes in typewriting and shorthand at a commercial college housed above a shop in Oxford Street. She embarked on the course with a sort of cold masochism. It seemed a sensible thing to do, though her heart was far from being in it. But Devonshire Place was closing in on her. She was thoroughly bored.

George and Florence approved cautiously. The course got her out of the house, while also keeping her out of mischief. As long as it didn't lead to any nonsense about setting up on her own and earning her own living.

Most of the class were women in their twenties like Mercedes, but one of them was considerably older. Hannah Spalding looked close to forty, though she was slim and smart, with silky chestnut hair which was always draped and twisted into a stylish, almost Grecian-looking chignon. She had a clean, clear profile, a very straight nose, and what Florence called 'good bones'. Her skin, stretched taut across them, had a matt, ivory look, only slightly dulled with age. She addressed the teacher, an over-blown blonde woman of about fifty, in a crisp, decisive fashion, with none of the ingratiating frills that passed for charm in most of the matrons of Mercedes' acquaintance. She had the impression that the teacher didn't much care for the brisk directness of Mrs Spalding's tone.

Mercedes was intrigued by her, but there was little opportunity for getting to know her better. The classes were formal and the pupils tended to rush off afterwards. But one day she had an evening lecture and instead of returning to Devonshire Place for dinner she bought herself a cup of tea and a bun in a nearby ABC café. It happened that Hannah Spalding was sitting alone at one of the tables and Mercedes asked if she could join her.

'Of course.' She nodded in her curt but pleasant manner. Mrs Spalding wore a high-necked blouse in an unusual shade of yellow-gold, and a straw hat that framed her face and the rich sweep of her chestnut hair. Close to, Mercedes saw that her eyes were underscored with the beginnings of small horizontal wrinkles. They seemed the only thing that gave away her age. She offered an impression of alertness and composure that interested Mercedes as well as intimidating her slightly.

Over Chelsea buns and tea in thick white china cups they talked about the classes and Miss Bentley, the teacher, and the uncanny difficulty of Pitman's shorthand method.

'Why are you taking this course?' Hannah Spalding asked suddenly.

It was Mercedes' turn to be disconcerted by the woman's directness. Any reasons she could give struck her as aimless and lacking in drive. She fell back on a teasing irony. 'Something to add to my female accomplishments, I suppose.' She added honestly, 'I can't say I'd relish earning my living by typewriting from morning to night, even if my parents gave me permission, which is highly unlikely . . . What about you? Why are you doing it?'

Mrs Spalding was typically unhesitating. 'I belong to an organization – a campaigning organization. We write a lot of letters and it occurred to us that they'd look more impressive if they were typed . . . As if we had secretaries and office-staff. And the shorthand'll be useful for taking the minutes of meetings.'

'What kind of organization?'

'It's called the Association for the Advancement of Women Workers. We campaign to improve pay and conditions for working women . . .' She smiled with an air of cool competence. 'We pester Members of Parliament and

46

employers of all sorts. We raise funds to help run strikes on occasion . . .'

Mercedes was surprised and immediately fascinated. 'And organize trade unions?'

Hannah Spalding shook her head. 'Not necessarily. We differ from other groups in that.' She swallowed the final cooling dregs of her tea with a small grimace. 'It doesn't always do to be too rigid, Miss MacInnes . . . We try to be, well, pragmatic.'

Though she wasn't too sure about the meaning of the word, Mercedes gave an intelligent, encouraging nod.

'In practice, you see, there are all sorts of reasons why poorly paid, uneducated women find it almost impossible to commit themselves to a union . . .' Now a rhythmic, lecturing cadence crept into her tone, as if this was something she'd said a hundred times before. 'For a start, they're terrified of the employers and getting the sack – and frequently terrified of their husbands, too. On top of that they've got too much to do at home to get out to meetings . . . And tuppence a week for the union dues can be a fortune to find – it's the price of a loaf when your children are hungry.' Her brown, almond-shaped eyes held Mercedes' with a stern fixity. 'But they still need help and encouragement, these women, in the struggle for a fair wage.'

Having said her piece, she sat quiet, unconcerned by the silence that followed. Mercedes was still dumbfounded by her discovery of this new aspect of the impressive Mrs Spalding. It was as though a flash of sheet-lightning had illuminated the unremarkable interior of the ABC café, with its dado and cream-coloured paintwork. Here, she fancied, was a fellow-spirit, and one who was firmly engaged on a worthwhile course of action.

She began to confide the story of her own unsatisfactory involvement in social affairs, shyly at first, but with rising intensity. Her companion listened with a cool, sympathetic attention.

Eventually, a tired-looking elderly waitress, drab in her shapeless maroon uniform, came to clear their table. Such people always made Mercedes feel awkward and privileged. She handed over her cup with a smiling, embarrassed helpfulness, but Hannah Spalding didn't so much as glance in the woman's direction.

She took an interest, though, in Mercedes over the following weeks. The two of them met often in the same ABC café after class for tea or tart, cloudy lemonade when the weather was hot. And gradually, as they talked, the germ of an idea grew, of itself, into a seedling and then a full-blown plant: once the course was ended Mercedes would go and help out with the secretarial work at the offices of the Association for the Advancement of Women Workers in Victoria.

'You must understand, Mercedes, that you may find it dull at first,' Hannah warned, fixing her steadily with oddly inscrutable brown eyes, while her interlaced fingers rested composedly on the red check tablecloth in front of her. 'Don't expect to find yourself plunging into a maelstrom of heady, inspirational activity. But there'll be a purpose to it all, and there's so much you can learn – about working conditions and labour relations and effective campaigning . . .'

There was the implication in her words that Mercedes might have been too impatient in the past, unwilling to serve out any kind of apprenticeship. If anyone else had suggested such a thing, she would have bristled with indignation. But Hannah Spalding had the knack of offering this kind of truth with a smile and a semi-apologetic lift of the eyebrow. Mercedes felt strangely honoured that her new friend deigned to take note even of her character failings.

The prospect of joining the Association gave a much-needed fillip to her interest in the classes. She worked hard, and in the final examination, at the end of October, she came third overall, behind the two Misses Springham – pale, earnest, frightened sisters, recently orphaned. They gave the impression of being two gently-bred waifs left at the mercy of a brutal world and they studied with a ferocious, panic-stricken singlemindedness. In all conscience Mercedes couldn't begrudge them their success.

Hannah didn't sit the exam. On the appointed day she rushed into class, elatedly pink and out-of-breath, to explain to Miss Bentley that she'd been unexpectedly called away to sit in on some dispute at a box-making factory in Peckham. Then she dashed off to a waiting taxi-cab, looking wonderfully elegant in a snuff-coloured coat and skirt and a ruched velvet hat with a veil.

Florence and George were reasonably sanguine about her work at the AAWW, as some of the members called it, though the initials were almost as cumbersome as the full title. At least she wasn't getting any money for it. They still had an ingrained horror of the idea of any daughter of theirs working for a living. Mercedes had been careful to present the job to them as charitable and respectably office-bound.

Always keen to avoid conflict, George decided that he could still justifiably regard it as the up-to-date equivalent of his mother's Lady Bountiful ministrations.

As for Florence, she was fascinated to hear every detail of her daughter's work. 'Those poor women.' She would shake her head and screw up her face in distress when Mercedes talked about the falling rates of pay among sack-sewers and paper-bag makers. As far as she was concerned, her daughter's activities provided a live, personal link with her own new-found curiosity about social reform. Here was an interest both of them could share and, apart from that, it could bridge the gap nicely until Mercedes finally met some suitable young man.

The office consisted of a large upstairs room near Victoria Station with a WC and hand-basin next door, and a cubbyhole with a gas-ring where drinks and soup could be heated up. In itself the room was unimposing, with grey walls and two sash-windows, whose chipped and peeling paint gave off the sharp smell of grimed-in dust. The windows were shaded by a pair of ancient, intractable Venetian blinds. The furniture was basic and had seen better days and, at one end of the room, a network of deep varnished shelving was crammed with an assortment of files, books and papers.

To Mercedes it all had a workmanlike glamour. She loved the place, specially during late afternoon in winter, when the gas burned with a low hiss and the gas-mantles glowed, while twin rectangles of sky showed, dark and leaden, at the far side of the room.

Above the mantelpiece a picture hung, the only object in the office that wasn't sternly functional. It had been painted by the brother of one of the Association's members, an aficionado of the Camden school, and showed a thin woman of about thirty leaning wearily over an ironing-board. Her skin was luminously pale, her eyes and cheekbones and the contours of her arms emphasized with deep blue and mauve shadows. Her hair had an exotic violet sheen and straggled in graceful coils over her forehead and in the nape of her neck. The woman's attitude suggested a hopeless, dogged endurance. Mercedes had gazed at the painting until she knew every curve and shadow. It seemed to her to depict exactly the kind of person they were trying to help.

The Association consisted of a loose nucleus of a dozen or so women. All of them were comfortably off and most of them were married, though a couple were single women of independent means. A few, like Hannah, were activists.

Others were sympathizers, supporting the cause with money and good will rather than energy. Some members Mercedes had never met. They always seemed to be away, holidaying in Nice or Baden-Baden. Their patron, a Lady Flowers, had been in America for months, lecturing and cultivating contacts and, so they hoped, acquiring funds.

The office, Mercedes thought, was like a railway junction, the centre through which the members passed, on their way to or from assignments in the field. And she, with her heavy black typewriter and her brown leatherette swivel-chair, her baize-topped auction-sale desk, was like the man in the signal-box. She had the overview. She was the only one who knew what everybody was doing, where everything was. Within weeks she'd made herself the humble but capable linchpin of the organization.

By dint of typing letters for the others, reading their reports, collating the material they'd collected, she became tremendously *au fait* with all aspects of female employment and labour relations. And the more she learnt about the pitiful rates paid to outworkers in, say, the glove-making industry – slaving from morning to night, virtual prisoners in one room for up to eighteen hours a day – the more she burned with indignation. Sometimes she fantasized, privately, debating the issue with some imaginary cocksure Member of Parliament, and confounding him with her righteous, well-informed anger.

Hannah had warned her that the work might be dull and, looked at from one angle, it was. She was, after all, a glorified dogsbody, office-bound while the others were out in the field. But Mercedes wasn't in the least bored. She believed passionately in the end product of her work. And she'd taken Hannah's hints about patience to heart, regarding her present position as training that was going to lead eventually to her taking her place as a fully-fledged field-worker.

'Mercedes, you're a wonder – you're indispensable,'

51

Hannah would say when she produced, from the morass of paperwork stored in the office, the desired file of facts. Her tone was always crisp and energetic, without a hint of toadying, and Mercedes would secretly glow.

She was invited to dine at the elegant yet cosy flat in Bloomsbury that Hannah shared with her tall and sardonically handsome journalist husband, James. To Mercedes they seemed the ideal couple – companionable, equal, purposeful. Now, if marriage could be more like that . . . But they were one in a million.

In spite of Miss Bentley's classes, Hannah never did touch the typewriter. She gave her letters and reports, written in an even black hand on quality vellum, to Mercedes to copy, declaring each time, 'I just don't know what we did before you came . . .'

Hannah herself was like a whirlwind, addressing gatherings of working women up and down the country, pleading with them to help themselves, advising them on their disputes with management – all the practical work that Mercedes was going to have for herself in the near future, when she'd served out her apprenticeship.

6

Examining the person who'd come out of the blue to help them put their complaints to management, Daisy Harkness was far from reassured. They'd laughed about it before she arrived and decided that she was going to be one of those bossy old cows with corrugated hair and a loose double chin, like the health-visitor, who talked to you as if you were feeble-minded. Nobody liked her, but you knew where you were with someone like that.

Miss MacInnes was just a girl, and nervous with it, though she was making quite a good job of covering it up. Daisy felt a bit sorry for her. There was something about her that recalled that young student teacher who'd spent a few weeks at Ryland Street School last winter, and used to walk to work looking like a Christian about to be fed to the lions. Miss MacInnes was polite and nicely-spoken. The sort of person Annie Tyrell liked to get to grips with. She had her knife out for anyone who looked as if they might have had an easy life.

Father Simpson, the Catholic priest, had loaned them his cold, scrubbed church hall, mainly because he loathed Leonard Floyd, with his black cigars and his fourteen-year-old mistress. Miss MacInnes sat at the head of the pair of paper-hanger's trestle tables that had been requisitioned for the occasion. There were twenty-one women crowded round the benches, which was better than expected. Sally O'Shea wasn't there, Daisy noticed. She'd heard about yesterday's rumpus.

'Mrs Tyrell, perhaps you could describe for me in detail the events that led up to the general walk-out four days ago.' Miss MacInnes had a block of paper in front of her and a pencil held loosely in one hand.

Annie gave her neighbour, Edie Black, a wolfish side-long smile before she replied and Daisy felt a rush of dislike for her. She was the one who'd got them into all this and she was already laughing at the person who'd come along to try to help. Daisy guessed that Annie liked to see herself as leader and wasn't too pleased about this newcomer who'd dropped from the sky, even though she worked for some organization that dealt in strikes and could tell them all sorts of things they needed to know.

'I think so. I think I could describe the events . . .' Annie said, repeating the girl's words with a subtle, mocking emphasis. Daisy wasn't sure whether Miss MacInnes noticed or not. Daisy watched her as Annie talked about her set-to with Leonard Floyd. The young woman listened attentively, occasionally asking a question or sorting out a matter of detail. At the same time she made strange, flowing squiggles on the paper in front of her. Shorthand, Daisy supposed, though she'd never seen anyone use it before. The newcomer had got in touch by standing outside Ballard's factory and questioning passers-by. In the end a neighbour of Edie's had chanced along and taken her back to Edie's place. She'd offered her services and Edie had told her the time and place of the meeting, then rushed off to tell Annie the good news.

Miss MacInnes was middling tall with a neat little figure, but it didn't look as if she tried to make herself look flirty or pretty. Under the straw boater her fairish hair was pulled tightly back off her face. She was a pale girl with nice, smooth, even-coloured skin – personally Daisy didn't much care for rosy cheeks. Her face was longish, but not too much so, her lips full with little colour to them. She had hazel eyes, rather delicately shaped, under tidy, arched eyebrows. There was a clever look to her and Daisy wasn't surprised to see that she wore a Votes for Women button on her tucked blue blouse.

Most people would have said she ought to do something to her hair – fluff it out or arrange it in swoops across her forehead, or in a curly fringe. Daisy didn't agree. She believed people tried too hard to look like everybody else. There was something about Miss MacInnes's combination of youth and severity that was rather appealing.

'Floyd told me to sling me 'ook,' Annie was relating. 'And nobody said nothing.' Meaningfully she looked round at her captive audience of co-workers, relishing the opportunity to remind them of their lack of spirit. 'Except for Daisy. She stuck up for me.'

Some people changed when they talked to women like Miss MacInnes, Daisy thought. They became stiff and embarrassed and used long words. Annie made sure she didn't.

Abruptly Daisy became aware that everyone was looking at her expectantly. She'd been watching and listening idly, as if none of this had anything to do with her. She must have looked surprised because some of the other women laughed, though in a friendly fashion.

Miss MacInnes smiled too. 'You're Mrs . . . ?'

'Harkness.'

'Can you tell us what you said to Mr Floyd?'

'Just that he wasn't being fair. Blaming Annie over her machine.' Although born in London, Daisy was conscious that something in her manner of speaking betrayed her Polish background. There were times when it worked to her advantage. Men, on the whole, were intrigued by her way of talking. But women tended to brand her as different. Stuck-up.

'There's fines for this and fines for that,' she added, 'without him inventing new ones. Hard enough to take home a living wage as it is.'

Ragged, heartfelt murmurs of agreement greeted this

statement, but Daisy experienced a stale reluctance at going over the old, familiar ground. What was the good? They knew how things stood, but all of them needed the work. When she'd spoken up for Annie it had been simply to set Floyd straight, so he wouldn't try the same trick on the rest of them. She hadn't bargained on it coming to a walk-out.

'I think,' Miss MacInnes declared, pitching her voice to be heard above the hubbub, 'that before we go any further we must agree on something. I think we have to decide what is the aim of this strike.' She paused and looked slowly round at the assembled women, her eyes wide and solemn. 'Is it simply to get Mrs Tyrell reinstated? Or do we also confront the management with pay and conditions . . . ?'

Her raised tone momentarily took on a schoolmistressy shrillness, a bossy, emphatic quality that reminded Daisy of the infamous health-visitor. The murmur of voices died away, so that the ringing echo of her words lingered on in the chill quiet of the hall.

There was no immediate reply. The women eyed one another, each willing someone else to do the talking. Their hesitation was mingled with a feeling of resistance to this stranger's sudden brisk involvement in their affairs. And no one had used the word 'strike' before. There was an alarming finality about it.

Daisy, like the rest of them, had given small thought to the nuts and bolts of the situation. In some way she'd had the vague, forlorn hope that something would happen to get life back again to normal. Cautiously they'd welcomed the offer of help from this Workers' Association, whatever it was they called themselves. All the same, when an outsider came along and tried to get you organized it was difficult not to clam up.

'Jump to it, girls. The lady wants to know why you're on strike.' Annie's sotto-voce comment rustled into the silence like a hostile snake. 'Pull your socks up now. Get yourselves sorted out.'

There were furtive grins and muffled explosions of stealthy laughter. Edie Black gave Annie a barely perceptible nudge. A woman Daisy knew as Belle hid her smile with a hand as wrinkled as a monkey's paw.

Miss MacInnes blushed brightly and Daisy saw a quick, hurt look in her eye. But she managed to maintain her poise, sitting very upright and facing the two lines of smirking women with a resolute air of calm. Though, Daisy noticed, she met no one's eye, and the tips of her long fingers were tightly clamped against the shaft of her pencil.

When she spoke there was a strained note in her voice, but she carried on regardless. 'Has anyone got an opinion on the question? Any constructive suggestions?'

Annie Tyrell wore an amused, mocking smile. No one volunteered a word. Most of the other women were wary of Annie, intimidated by her sharp tongue, and they took their tone from her.

What a crowd of sheep they were. Daisy was filled with hot contempt for them. She'd never understood the power Annie had over her fellow-workers. If you ignored her there was really nothing she could do. She was a bully and couldn't stand girls like Miss MacInnes, well-off and nicely brought-up. Given an opportunity to make her look silly she'd seize it. Never mind if it meant throwing away any help the girl could offer, cutting off her nose to spite her face.

Daisy was distinctly half-hearted about the notion of striking. She'd never wanted it and none of them could afford it. All the same she spoke up, largely to demonstrate her scorn for Annie and her bum-lickers.

Turning to the MacInnes woman, she said, 'Seems to me while we're fighting for Annie's rights, we might as well push for more money for the rest of us as well. It's a good chance. We may as well try and get what we can out of it.'

Miss MacInnes nodded with an expression of judicious interest, but Daisy didn't miss the flash of eager, embarrassed gratitude in her eyes.

'I hoped you'd feel like that,' she commented. 'But I . . . That is we – the Association – we try not to lead people. We prefer *them* to tell *us* what they want to do.'

She appealed again to the women. 'Do the rest of you agree with Mrs Harkness?' Daisy rather admired her dogged determination to drag some response out of them.

There was a tense, profound silence. Daisy had decided to wait now, to say nothing herself, and see what the others would do. She half-sensed that the atmosphere had changed. The grins had died away. But still no one spoke. Daisy could feel gooseflesh on her upper arms, beneath the cotton of her blouse. How strange it was that the hall could be so cold. It was the beginning of May and sunny outside.

She sat and waited. Miss MacInnes waited. They could hear the rhythmic swishing of a stiff broom in the anteroom beyond the dark, varnished door.

Annie shifted in her seat. The movement seemed to have some kind of significance, though Daisy wasn't sure what it was. Obscurely she was put in mind of a tiger she'd once seen in a circus, defying its trainer with bared teeth and unsheathed claws before deciding to co-operate and perform its dusty routine of tricks.

The other women held their breath. Annie leant forward, resting her elbows on the bare boards of the table. 'It ain't just the money. It's rules and fines. They got us all ways. What we got to do something about is that pig Floyd.'

Annie Tyrell was going to be the key, the leader, Mercedes told herself, and it was quite obvious that the

58

woman was a tough nut to crack. Secretly Mercedes could understand and even sympathize with Annie's sly hostility towards herself. No doubt she'd been on the receiving end of the offensive condescension of her so-called betters times without number. Incidents from her months at the mother-and-child clinic in Lambeth flashed into her mind. They still had the power to make her cringe.

As Annie talked she examined her, taking her measure, almost as if the woman were her enemy. She must be about forty, Mercedes guessed, though she was hazy about the ages of people she considered middle-aged or old. In this company of faded, poverty-stricken women she stood out a mile by virtue of her sheer vitality. Though she was thin, like the rest, and haggard, her body had a tough wiriness about it. Her skin was coarse but in the muted light of the hall it shone with a robust olive glow. Her hair was a dull darkish brown and dry in texture. Still there was plenty of it and it was arranged in a complicated romantic chignon, with a fringe and a top-knot of curls. Most likely Annie had never changed her hair-style since she'd been a young girl, and it contrasted curiously with the expression of aggressive energy on her middle-aged face.

Mercedes felt herself prim and inexperienced in comparison. All the same, the two of them had something in common. The other women in the hall were dubious about the prospect of a strike. Ambiguous and faint-hearted. She and Annie, on the other hand, were determined to make it happen. For quite separate reasons the two of them were passionately dedicated to the same course of action.

Annie's aim was simple – to get herself reinstated. For her it was strike or nothing. Mercedes' motives were less cut and dried but, in her own mind, just as compelling. Against the odds she'd been given a practical chance to prove herself to the Association. The thought of the strike being aborted, of returning sheepishly to the office with her tail between her legs was too galling to contemplate.

Mercedes knew that her ambitions at this moment were far from altruistic. Come what may, she just had to demonstrate her own worth to Hannah, to the others. The desire to do so was like a clenched fist in the pit of her stomach.

She would have to go carefully, though, with Annie. The woman was rash, quite capable of jeopardizing the whole project, ignoring her own interests, for the chance of showing her claws, baring her teeth in defiance at Mercedes for what she represented. But as the afternoon progressed Mercedes' confidence grew. Her quietly capable middle-class air was, she came to understand, far more of an asset than a liability. By refusing to be side-tracked, remaining calm and good-natured, suggesting simply and clearly the points to be put before management, Mercedes felt she gave the illusion of bringing order to vacillation and chaos. And discussing the pitiful rates of pay, the petty rules and restrictions of factory life fanned the women's indignation, so that, by the end of the session they were far more militant than they'd been at the beginning.

To clinch her advantage Mercedes even touched on the likelihood of financial help to see them through possible hard times, though she wasn't absolutely sure there'd be enough money to spare. I'll arrange something, she told herself recklessly.

Am I manipulating them, she wondered dubiously. But she was elated, like an acrobat taking her first faltering steps on the high wire, then finding her feet, gaining assurance, and performing hand-springs and curlicues of her own invention.

'Prim little cow,' Annie commented after Mercedes had left.

There was a silence. Her remark hung in the air, carelessly malicious, taking it for granted that all of them would feel the same.

Abruptly Annie stood up, smoothing the back of her skirt. 'Come on, girls, let's sort these tables out.' Briskly she picked up a couple of chairs, one in each hand, and began to carry them towards the far end of the hall ready for stacking, ignoring her co-workers, confident that the rest of them would follow her example.

The other women began to get to their feet. They seemed dazed, as if, after a period of sustained, concentrated effort, they'd become aware of the real world again. Belle picked up a couple of chairs and hastily put one of them down again. She was slight and hadn't Annie's whippet strength.

'Tight-arsed little virgin.' Bustling back for another couple of chairs, Annie returned to her verdict on Mercedes.

'School-marm type. Know-it-all,' Edie Black endorsed, tucking in stray locks of her frizzy red hair.

Daisy paused with her hands hooked under a trestle table, waiting for Edie to take hold of the other end, voicing the thought she'd had earlier, 'She's got a neat little figure.' Though she couldn't see what Miss MacInnes' looks or love-affairs or lack of them had to do with anything. She merely offered the comment to register her separateness from Annie and her pals.

But Daisy, too, felt bewildered. Everything had happened so fast, and suddenly it all seemed decided, settled, and she'd agreed to it all.

'She's not as daft as she looks.' A woman named Kate Reeves was encouraged to suggest a somewhat more charitable view of Mercedes. Tall, thirtyish, with faded blue eyes and the remnants of a blonde prettiness, she was one of four who'd volunteered, or been coerced, into a deputation to beard management tomorrow or the day after, if Mercedes could arrange a meeting. The others were Annie, Edie and Daisy.

'Lift up her skirts, you'll probably find she's wearing chain-mail drawers.' Annie was gratified by the explosion of ribald laughter that greeted her quip. But a new thought distracted her. "'Ere, have you seen Bet Partridge?' she asked the others. 'Someone's given her a shiner. Eye's all swollen up and closed. D'you reckon it was Sal O'Shea's cousin Michael done his stuff?'

From the post office closest to the Association's headquarters in Victoria, Mercedes sent off a telegram to Edward Ballard, the factory owner. In it she asked him to agree, as soon as possible, to a meeting with the strike committee. She smiled to herself, thinking that the wary group of reluctant women would have been surprised to hear themselves so described. Somehow, before she met them, Mercedes had expected them to be . . . angrier and more determined. Now the thought struck her as naïve. Already she felt as if she'd learned a lot.

Then she hurried back to the office to finish some typing she'd promised to do for Hannah. Mercedes hoped there'd be someone there – she was bursting to talk about the afternoon's events. But to her disappointment the room was deserted. She sat down at the typewriter and banged out the remaining pages at top speed, without making a single mistake. Her brain felt alert, focused, and it seemed a crime to waste the mood on this mechanical activity. When she'd finished, Mercedes left the papers on her desk in a large envelope with Hannah's name on it.

To begin with Hannah had been curtly unsympathetic to Mercedes' suggestion that she offer her services to the striking women of Ballard's factory. Her mouth had turned down sharply and she'd shaken her head. 'You're far too inexperienced,' she told Mercedes, and then, 'you look much too young. You won't inspire confidence.' Mercedes had protested, but Hannah had been absolutely adamant.

Then, when Mercedes returned to the office after a

lunch-time break for a pie and a cup of tea at a nearby café, Hannah had quite simply changed her mind.

'I think you *should* take this on, Mercedes,' she'd urged, with as much conviction as she'd shown previously in arguing against the idea. 'It'll be a smallish dispute. Probably all over in a matter of days. I think you're right. It'll be valuable experience for you . . .'

Mercedes glowed with delight and gratitude, though she was baffled as to what had brought about this abrupt change of heart. And something in Hannah's eyes and her slightly guarded smile warned her not to probe. She wasn't tempted to anyway, in case Hannah performed another about-turn.

Mercedes draped a piece of green baize over her typewriter and locked up the office. She caught a tram travelling in the direction of the West End. Already it was almost seven o'clock. She was going to be late for dinner and cursed inwardly. Mercedes made a point of obeying rules at home. It lulled her parents into a sense of security and made them less curious as to what she might be doing elsewhere.

It was a fine spring evening and her favourite seat was free. The one on top in the front. The sky was darkening slightly and a mild breeze blew. The streets were still full of people going home from work. A plain, thin young girl sat down next to Mercedes with a large paper parcel. Mercedes guessed that it held garments ready cut out for her to assemble at home. For a pittance, no doubt. The girl appeared shabby and tired and there was a long-suffering look about her. She reminded Mercedes of the women she'd met that afternoon in the church hall in South London. Normally such people, when she encountered them, seemed alien, arousing her guilty socialist conscience. This evening the girl awakened in her a new sense of familiarity.

The conductor was a well-built young man with a

bold moustache. 'Nice warm hands you've got,' he told Mercedes and winked as he handed over her change. The good-natured flirtation made her blush a little.

As the tram swayed along, she closed her eyes, reliving moments from that afternoon, looks and tones of voice, turns of phrase that had caught her imagination. The face that recurred most often was that of Daisy Harkness. A *sensuous* face, Mercedes thought, with intriguingly shadowed eyes, a full, curved mouth, and blonde hair that curled just the way it should, like a painting or a statue. Daisy looked different from the others. Set apart. She seemed foreign. She also seemed friendly and encouraging, as if she could be an ally in this unknown territory.

'Mercedes, I really don't think it's too much to ask for you to be punctual for family meals.' Her father seemed out of sorts. Between his beard and moustache she could see that his lips were compressed at the corners. 'It's really not fair on your mother or Mrs Carter.' Blank-faced, the cook-housekeeper stood by, watching and listening.

'I'm sorry.' Mercedes sat down, abruptly reduced to dependent, daughterly status after her leading role in the afternoon's drama. But she kept quiet about that. She had the feeling that even her mother wouldn't approve.

7

This place. It's the arse-end of nowhere, Edward Ballard thought to himself as his chauffeur manoeuvred the Lanchester through the narrow iron gates and into the depressing yard of his Bermondsey factory.

'Glorious weather!' he remarked with ironic enthusiasm to Leonard Floyd, who stood waiting for him by a side-entrance. Or *lurking* rather, Ballard thought. There was something cagey in Floyd's manner that brought the word to mind.

'Good day to you, Mr Ballard. Mmm . . . Glorious.' The word was far too expansive for Floyd's grudging vocabulary and emerged with a tight reluctance. His expression suggested that comments on the weather were a luxury that could be dispensed with under the circumstances.

He led the way down the familiar gloomy corridor, lined to chest-height with mottled brown tiles. An unkempt young girl with a broom froze as they passed.

'Cleaning woman's put in an appearance then,' Ballard said.

'Dot's a good girl,' Floyd replied darkly. 'She does what I tell her.'

Ballard felt oddly buoyant and detached as he followed on the manager's heels, though the situation hardly warranted it. He grinned inwardly as they entered the man's office. Always the room seemed to be in a state of absolute readiness for some unexpected military inspection. Even on the odd occasions when Ballard had arrived unannounced it had looked no different.

The bare wooden floor had been polished to a high gloss and the distempered yellow walls were totally free of any kind of ornament. A set of shelves held fifty or so matching black ledgers, their backs perfectly aligned. On the desk, which gleamed with a deeper richness than the floor, a blotter, a glass inkwell, a folder of paper and an open oblong box holding pens, were arranged with geometric precision. Positioned flush against the desk stood a heavy wooden revolving chair. Two upright, ladder-backed seats were placed equidistant from it, one on each side.

Ballard wrinkled his nose. The one personal touch the room possessed was its smell. An odour of polish and strong disinfectant combined with the pungent, fusty undertow of Floyd's perspiration and the sharply acrid scent of the black cigars he smoked.

Through the single high window Ballard could see fluffy, silvery-white clouds drifting dreamily across the blue of the sky. The tight young leaves of a plane tree fluttered intermittently, and Ballard was fleetingly reminded of the way the world used to look through his classroom windows when he was a boy.

'Take a seat, sir.' Floyd indicated his own massive revolving chair. 'I'll call Mrs Durrant.'

Fat bitch, Ballard thought. He lowered himself on to the chair which his manager had obligingly pulled into a convenient position. 'Yes, Floyd,' he said. 'Go and call Mrs Durrant.' There was a lazy mockery in his repetition of the man's words.

For reasons of propriety Mrs Durrant had been taken on as the manager's deputy. She was a huge, lumbering woman and the fleshy weight of her face had dragged the corners of her mouth and her eyes downward into an expression of sleepy malevolence. But her somnolent air was misleading. She was keenly alert for any irregularities she could report back to Floyd in her rasping, emotionless voice. And in his absence she was every bit as zealous as he.

Floyd walked towards the door, an upright and yet

oddly uncoordinated figure. Ballard watched him go. His attitude to his factory manager was one of distaste. The man was a necessary evil. A martinet who kept everything ship-shape and achieved miracles of production from his employees with the minimum of outlay and fuss.

Ballard paid him well. It was a way of keeping the fellow at arm's length. As long as everything ran smoothly and efficiently there was little call for him to interfere. He found Floyd repellent, with his long skull and hard, opaque eyes, the smell of nervous perspiration that clung to him. And today he was worse. An unacknowledged embarrassment smouldered beneath the man's normal graceless manner. A hot-eyed, shamefaced, dangerous anger at what he saw as his own failure. Ballard was quietly amused at Floyd's mortification.

All the same, he personally didn't attach a great deal of importance to this little show of mutiny by the women. It couldn't last. After all, they knew which side their bread was buttered.

Edward retained his feeling of detached good humour even after the meeting proper had begun. He was only too aware of what an absurdly incongruous group they formed – he and Floyd and Mrs Durrant – lined up to face the deputation of women like three wildly ill-assorted mandarins.

Himself first, with his cultured vowels and Savile Row suit, occupying the Daddy-bear seat. Then the gangling, baleful figure of Floyd, perched forward on one of the other chairs, resting long, damp fingers on his bony knees. And, lastly, Mrs Durrant, who'd chosen to remain standing behind them, arms crossed, chin burrowing into her massive chest, like some silent, monumental duenna.

Having no idea how a meeting of this sort was conducted, Edward opted to give free rein to his affable state of mind. 'Well, ladies,' he breezed. 'This is an unexpected pleasure. Now, what is it I can do for you?'

The deputation – there were four of them – stood silent and obviously ill-at-ease, uncertainty in their eyes. His amiability had wrong-footed them and each waited for the other to take the initiative.

He was encouraged by their seeming confusion and he sensed that urbanity might be his best method of approach. On visits to the factory he'd always courted popularity by joking and flirting with the women. Generally his charm rendered them pink and incoherent and foolishly biddable.

The women were standing two and two. He concentrated on the foremost pair. One was a large, lumpy woman, sporting a top-knot of frizzy red curls, the other a tall blonde with a dry, faded prettiness. Edward had scant interest in women of a certain age, but he was good at humouring them with a cordiality he didn't recognize as contemptuous.

'Mrs Black, Mrs Reeves.' Floyd had previously introduced them by name and Edward had a quick memory for such things. 'Our charming militants. I suggest, ladies, that we lay our cards on the table. What is it that you're wanting us to do?' He smiled inwardly at his own unctuous turns of phrase.

The Reeves woman swallowed nervously and licked her lips, obviously steeling herself to take the plunge. Her expression became vacant and her eyes seemed to focus inward, as if she were trying to recall some previously agreed rigmarole.

'First of all we want Annie . . . Tyrell . . . to be taken back.' Her voice was hoarse and she cleared her throat. Edward greeted the statement with silence and watched impassively as she thrashed about in her memory for further demands.

'. . . Then, we want our conditions of work to be written down, so's Mr Floyd can't make up the rules as he goes along . . . Fines and suchlike . . . and break-times.' She

68

paused again and Edward saw that she was clutching the material of her dark skirt as if for support.

'And we want a minimum wage. Fifteen shillings a week . . . and more if we go above our targets . . .' This final claim emerged with a total lack of conviction, a dogged, embarrassed air, as if the woman was perfectly aware that she might as well ask for the moon. She closed her mouth and stared at her three interlocutors with a sort of scared defiance.

Her words were followed by an explosion from Floyd of some violent, inarticulate emotion. A guttural, graceless, incredulous rasp. Edward glanced across at him and mentally recoiled. He was a disconcerting sight, flushed and glowering, his eyes burning with a vindictive, wholly personal anger. At the same time his soldier's sense of hierarchy prevailed and he offered no comment. It was Ballard's place to act as spokesman.

Edward leaned back in his chair, still feeling unruffled, inwardly dissociating himself from Floyd's excesses.

'So.' He smiled seraphically at Kate Reeves and summed up her demands. 'It's Annie to be taken back. Mr Floyd not to make up the rules as he goes along . . . And fifteen bob a week all round.' He wasn't displeased with the humorous contrast of Kate's blunt vocabulary and his own suave tones. He smiled again.

'It's all a joke to 'im!'

An incensed cry went up from one of the women behind Reeves and Black, so strident it verged on a screech. Annie Tyrell. The woman who'd caused all the trouble in the first place. Edward turned his attention to her. She was crimson, beside herself with outrage, eyes flashing with sparks of an almost hysterical hatred.

With an effort Edward retained his calm. 'Did you say something, Mrs Tyrell?' Injecting a reproving note of cool courtesy into his tone.

'I said it's just a joke to you, isn't it! All this. You've been grinning ever since the moment we walked in!'

Edward felt his face flushing. 'I don't think I've been . . .' He was annoyed to find himself momentarily on the defensive.

'Yes, you have!' Annie was quick to seize her advantage and harangue him further. 'Well, it's no joke for us, I can tell you. And nor would it be for you if you had to work in this rat-hole . . . The hours we do for the money. *And* with old Floyd here taking as much of it back as he can in fines . . .'

Leonard Floyd could stomach her tirade no longer. 'Hold your noise, you bloody hag,' he hissed with truly blood-chilling vehemence.

'I'll have my say.' Annie treated him to a slow, insolent grin. 'It's nothing but the truth, as you well know.' She was emboldened and protected by the official support of her fellow-strikers. It enclosed her like a rampart, enabling her to utter words that, under other circumstances, would have spelled her downfall.

Edward felt the reins of the interview slipping from his grasp. He was irritably aware of Mrs Durrant observing the scene with her pale, fishy eyes. Silent and impassive but all-seeing. Up till now everything had been running smoothly. He'd almost been enjoying himself. Inwardly he cursed Tyrell and Floyd for toppling the meeting so abruptly into an abyss of undignified farce.

He remonstrated. 'Mrs Tyrell, Mr Floyd, surely it's in all our interests to discuss this matter rationally. Anger and insults aren't going to advance us in any way whatsoever.' For the second time that morning shades of schooldays drifted through his mind. But this time his point of view was different. His were the exasperated, impotent tones of a master attempting to curb his pupils' genuine passion and indignation.

Floyd subsided into seething silence with barely a

struggle. Ballard was his paymaster and a generous one. He wasn't likely to forget that for long.

Ballard saw the fourth woman – Harkness – touch Annie's arm. Up till now he'd not paid her much attention, apart from registering, with an independent part of his brain, that she was younger and more physically pleasing than her colleagues. She appeared to be whispering something to Annie, calming her. Annie seemed mutinous, but allowed herself, ungraciously, to be shushed.

In order to re-instate himself in the driver's seat Edward decided to attack on a subject that had, in fact, riled him more than a little. He aimed his complaint at Reeves and Black, as the more manageable members of the deputation, and anyway they were in the front row.

'I really don't see,' he declared forcibly, 'why you found it necessary to enlist the help of outsiders. This Association . . . Women Workers business. This dispute is nothing to do with them. It's between ourselves, a purely internal matter.'

Mrs Black gazed at him. Her eyes were greenish and expressed nothing. The woman's bovine blankness repelled him.

'We . . .' Again Kate Reeves plunged in as spokeswoman. 'Thought . . . that . . .'

'It's obvious, isn't it? You can see why from what's been going on today. You can run rings round us if you want by using long words and smiling to yourself . . .' Mrs Reeves was drowned out by the more full-blooded tones of the Harkness woman.

She stepped forward, neat and composed, in a dark coat and skirt. Her voice and presence touched some elusive and nostalgic chord inside Edward Ballard.

'We're ignorant.' She made the statement in a sprightly, challenging style and looked at him, her head slightly to one side, an enigmatic half-smile on her lips. 'So we need all the help we can get.'

*   *   *

Travelling through the lunch-time streets of the City, on his way back from Bermondsey to his town house in Onslow Square, Edward was profoundly rattled. Normally he enjoyed lounging against the smooth, richly aromatic tan leather of the Lanchester's rear seat, watching the world go by and exchanging the odd amiable snippet of conversation with Waters, his chauffeur. Today he was barely aware of his surroundings, his thoughts centring obsessively on the meeting he'd just left.

Nothing whatsoever had come of it. No progress had been made. Edward was used to moving through life on a purposeful tide of business and pleasure, so this morning's stalemate ran frustratingly counter to his sense of order.

The inept and ridiculous little deputation of women had proved to be hugely more obstinate than he could ever have foreseen. In spite of the fact that three of them at least could barely string a couple of coherent sentences together, they'd flaunted a passive and infuriating stubbornness, encouraged no doubt by this bloody interfering Women Workers' set-up. Waves of hot and angry indignation swept across him repeatedly at the thought of the Association's mischievous busybodying. Organizations like that should be banned by law. Irresponsible do-gooders meddling in matters they knew nothing about, throwing an ignorant spanner into the smooth running of the nation's business.

His thoughts went back to his employees. It was mortifying having to pretend to take these self-important female nobodies seriously. Wryly Edward entertained, in his mind's eye, the image of a giant boot descending and crushing them like bugs underfoot. The picture encapsulated his longing to demonstrate to them, conclusively, their own insignificance.

It was their voices he hated, perhaps more than anything. Voices of the underdog. Either whining or nagging.

Wheedling or stridently haranguing. Whether begging or threatening, they held a note of powerlessness that had a jangling, almost physical effect on him.

'. . . A real thrashing, so he did, Mr Ballard. Skin of the brute's neck was hanging like curtains . . .'

Ballard became aware that Waters was talking to him. His chauffeur was a devotee of dog-fighting and Edward took a democratic interest in his passion. But today he knew he couldn't stomach one of the man's graphic accounts of torn ears and gaping flanks.

'What was the profit?' He side-stepped the description by proceeding directly to the financial aspect, which, traditionally, they discussed last.

'Five bob, sir.' The chauffeur was disappointed, recognizing that his employer wasn't in one of his expansive moods.

'Better than a kick up the arse.' Edward offered an affable, seigneurial smile to the back of Waters' stocky neck.

He felt free then to return to his musings, and a mental impression of the Harkness woman took possession of his mind. Daisy. He'd heard one of them call her that. She wasn't like the others. Neither intimidated and abashed, in the manner of Reeves and Black, nor ready to boil over with class-hatred like Annie Tyrell. It seemed to him that she had an unconscious sense of her own dignity and worth.

Daisy reminded him of someone or something, but he couldn't think who or what. He wondered if she were foreign, though her name was English enough. He pictured the graceful sweep of her blonde hair, her erotic half-smile, the smoothness of her skin.

She'd reiterated the women's demands and he had argued. Their dialogue had, in his fevered mind, taken on a quite separate significance – the give and take of some kind of courtship or mating ritual. He'd felt disarmed and had the wild suspicion that Durrant, with her pale, protuberant cod's eyes, could see into his head.

Finally, he'd manufactured a show of anger and stalked from the room, as if in exasperation. Nothing was agreed – their respective positions were hardened. As he left, confusedly, he heard Leonard Floyd snarling at the women like a vicious-tempered dog and thought how much he hated the man.

That evening the Ballards were invited to dine with their neighbours, Hugh and Bridie Berton. Mildred Ballard looked forward to the dinner as a means of taking Edward's mind off the morning's abortive meeting.

The company of old friends, good food, fine wines, damask and silver, the warm, rose-coloured wallpaper and the soothing candlelight combined to create a sense of reassurance and changelessness. Mildred sipped her Sancerre from a goblet of amber-tinted bohemian glass and watched as, further down the table, her husband regaled his immediate neighbours with the tale of his encounter with the deputation of factory women.

'Lawks, sir. 'Ave a 'eart. You're laughin' at us,' he was wailing in a grotesque parody of Annie Tyrell's cockney accent, sounding for all the world like some lumbering Punch cartoon come to life. But his impression was greeted with gales of rapturous laughter.

After pre-dinner sherry, and two glasses into the wine, Edward appeared flushed and animated. He wore the inward smile Mildred knew so well, the smile that, with his handsome crest of blond hair, she thought made him look like an amused and secretive lion.

In a sense she was relieved that he felt able, now, to present the story in a humorous light. Arriving home earlier in the day, direct from the meeting, he'd raged and cursed the jumped-up fishwives he was forced to have dealings with.

'Edward's being awfully gallant about the whole situation,' Neville Kirkpatrick, to her right, remarked to Mildred. He was a banker, greying and hawk-like, and they'd known him for years. 'Terrible business,' he added.

'Terrible,' she agreed.

But, disloyally, something inside her welcomed this challenge to Edward's power, to his charmed and charming progress through life. She felt the stirrings of an odd kind of fellow-feeling with the women who'd opted to defy him.

A male servant leaned unobtrusively between herself and Neville, replenishing their glasses, then moved on. Neville pushed away the remains of his lobster salad. 'Worker bees seem to have turned into drones,' he suggested drily.

'Neville!' Her tone was a reproach. She grinned in mock exasperation. 'I'll never live that down!'

One evening, ages ago, when slightly tipsy, Mildred had confided impulsively, to this very group of friends, that she sometimes saw herself as a queen bee, white and sluggish, kept in luxury by the buzzing underlings of Edward's factory. She'd never been allowed to forget the comparison. It had become a long-standing joke, revived every so often to tease her.

Mildred took the joshing in good part, but remained secretly puzzled. No joke had been intended. The analogy had simply been her way of presenting the truth.

'And were they awful frights, Teddy? Those women?' Bridie Berton, their hostess, was asking eagerly. From way back in their youth Bridie and Edward had conducted a mock flirtation. Bridie used to be a pretty pink and blonde creature. Now Edward remarked privately that she was beginning to look like the back end of an omnibus, but the habit remained.

He flashed her a winning smile and crinkled his blue eyes. 'Harridans, Bridie. At least three of them were,' he told her and the table at large. 'But one of them was young and . . .' He paused and twirled imaginary rakish moustaches, '. . . a deuced fine woman.'

'Oh, Teddy!' Bridie was delightedly reproving and dimpled at him in a way she'd never lost. 'Trust you . . .'

'Little foreign filly.' Edward warmed to his parody of a stage roué. 'Quite a pleasure to discuss working conditions with her . . .' The remark trailed off into a hubbub of appreciative laughter.

There had been a time when Mildred used to think this persona of Edward's as hilarious as Bridie obviously did. But recently she surprised herself by finding the joke – and Edward's self-congratulatory manner – offensive somehow, and subtly threatening.

She put the laughter from her mind and turned deliberately to Neville with a bright, automatic smile. 'S'pose you were Edward, Neville, and all your workers downed tools. What d'you think *your* next step would be?'

8

Mercedes picked her way along the cobbled surface of Picardy Street, just around the corner from Ballard's factory. Tall grey buildings rose up on either side and a strip of blue sky showed between the twin receding lines of their roofs. Harsh spring sunshine illuminated the windows and awnings of the ground-floor shops, pointing up a shabbiness that was camouflaged when the weather was dull. From an open doorway she caught a whiff of shellfish, combined with the sharp tang of boiling vinegar.

In her boater and neat, striped blouse, Mercedes felt conspicuous among the hatless women, men in waistcoats and shirtsleeves, the strident, ragged children. She'd given up wondering why it was they weren't at school, accepting now that, at any given time, a sizeable proportion of the school-age population would be wandering the streets for one reason or another.

After the impasse of the meeting with Ballard four days ago, Mercedes had – with the enthusiastic encouragement of Annie and Edie – telephoned a couple of local newspapers. They'd been intrigued and sent journalists to interview the deputation of four almost immediately. The papers came out today and Mercedes had arranged to meet Annie and the others in the Picardy Café so that they could read over the reports together. Hannah was always preaching the virtues of publicity and Mercedes was curious to see how much space had been allotted to them.

Crossing eagerly to the other side of the street, she almost collided with a frail old man in a dusty bowler, plodding along the middle of the road.

'Watch out!' he said, testy and toothless. Powerless in spite of his truculence.

'I'm sorry.' Mercedes placed her hands on his shoulders, steering herself round his tiny frame. He looked up at her in dumb surprise and for an instant she wondered how it would feel to inhabit that desiccated little body.

But she forgot him almost at once, returning to her musings on the progress of the strike. When she heard Daisy's description of Ballard's ill-tempered exit from the meeting earlier in the week, and Floyd's surreptitious, growling threats, Mercedes had feared that the women might become disheartened and discouraged.

Nothing could have been further from the truth. They were elated by Ballard's retreat from his position of supercilious calm.

'Lost his rag good and proper,' was the phrase that spread like wildfire among the rest of Ballard's employees. The factory owner's show of temper had the effect of strengthening their belief in the strike. His anger was like a mirror, making their defiance seem real to them. If Ballard was riled, he must have good reason. And they rejoiced in Annie's gleeful account of Floyd, forced to swallow his own simmering rage, because of the presence of the boss.

Mercedes drew level with the brown-painted frontage of the Picardy Café, noticing that Annie and Edie were already installed at the table close to the window. A newspaper lay open on the table between them, and they were peering at it, laughing. She knocked on the glass. Annie looked up, saw her, grinned and flourished the paper, beckoning her to hurry in. In the spontaneity of the moment Annie's expression was open and welcoming, with none of the sardonic distance she usually placed between herself and Mercedes. She looked like a gypsy, Mercedes thought, with her bold, animated features and the olive tint to her skin. A red shawl was draped carelessly over her shabby blouse and skirt, adding to the effect.

'Come here, girl. Look at this!' Annie called, the moment Mercedes set foot inside.

A copy of the *South London Advertiser* lay open at its centre page. Annie's finger jabbed excitedly at a headline.

Mercedes leant over the table and read the legend DEADLOCK AT GARMENT FACTORY, which ran across three columns. Below, side by side, two grey faces stared out of two dark rectangles. Mercedes examined them more closely. The faces belonged to Annie and Daisy.

She looked up delightedly. 'I say . . .'

'Read it,' Annie commanded.

Beneath the picture of Annie, wearing a pugnacious smile, the words HOLY TERROR were printed in heavy black type.

'I called her that,' Edie explained, 'and they've taken it up.'

WIDOW AND MOTHER was the by-line attached to a sweet and soulful portrait of Daisy.

The paper's account of the strike was sympathetic, though Mercedes thought privately that there was something condescending in its approach to the story. Annie's cockney speech had been laboriously rendered, complete with missing h's, but for some reason quotes from the other three women were set down in perfectly orthodox spelling.

Edie Black and Kate Reeves were mentioned, but it was obvious that the reporter had picked out Annie and Daisy as providing maximum titillation.

Enormous stress was laid on Annie's aggression and fighting spirit. As well as Holy Terror, she was labelled Battling Annie and the Militant Machinist. "E ain't goin' to get the better of us, mate,' she was quoted as proclaiming. 'Mr Ballard's goin' to find 'e's got a battle on 'is 'ands.'

In contrast, Daisy was presented as a modest, respectable widow and devoted mother, worried sick about providing for her two young children and an ailing, dependent mother. It was obvious she had attempted to pin-point the cause of the strike for the journalist's benefit, but this was glossed over. On the other hand, Daisy's flawless skin and gentle eyes were commented on, as well as the refinement of her appearance and dress.

'Not bad, eh?' Annie was like a cat with the cream.

'Useful,' Mercedes agreed, making no mention of her reservations about the roguish-cum-sentimental tone of the report.

'Hark at her,' Annie said. 'Show a bit of feeling, can't you, girl?'

The other account, in the *Southwark Enquirer*, was succinct and factual. In a sense far more to Mercedes' taste. But she admitted to herself that it was unlikely to cause a stir and Annie was right to be jubilant about the spread in the *Advertiser*.

Daisy arrived and read both stories. Watching her, Mercedes guessed that the young widow felt much the same as she did herself about the newspaper coverage.

'Kate can't come,' Annie announced. 'Her old man's on the warpath this morning.' Edie and Daisy nodded, with unemotional acceptance of the information.

'Tea and bread pudding?' Mercedes offered.

The Picardy Café was housed in the converted front room of its owner's home. The floor was unevenly flagged, and the furniture seemed to have been bought, in dribs and drabs, from the second-hand shops that abounded locally. No table and only the odd chair matched any of its fellows. All the tables, though, were covered in matching black-and-white checkered oil-cloth, which the proprietor's wife, May, swabbed from time to time, doing the rounds with a dazed look, hunched and sickly, clutching a cloth that smelt of Jeyes fluid.

Charlie was the owner's name. He had a doughy white face that appeared to sit awkwardly on his shoulders, and a similarly pudgy body. His smile seemed rather vacant to Mercedes, but she'd heard Annie and Edie laughing that he couldn't keep his hands to himself. He treated her with oily courtesy and she found it impossible to detect in his stolid face any spark of lechery.

The bread pudding his wife made lay on the counter in a large, corroded metal baking tray. Mercedes had tried a piece when she came here before and, in spite of its repugnant appearance, it was one of the most delicious things she'd ever tasted.

Charlie brought the teas and huge slabs of the bread pudding to their table, bowed and clicked his heels. 'At your service, ladies.'

Mercedes paid. 'Courtesy of the Association,' she explained.

In fact the money was from her own allowance, but she was sure she could claim it back later. She had a compulsion to treat the women, of which she was half-ashamed, for it smacked of charity. But stronger was the feeling that it was partly her own ambition, her encouragement, that had brought them to this strike that none of them could afford. Filling their bellies, when she could, was her instinctive way of stifling her own guilty sense of privilege.

Annie showed Charlie the piece in the paper. He examined the photograph of her, his white slab of a face blank and immobile.

'Look as if you could go twenty rounds with Crusher Compton,' he told her, mentioning a local prize-fighter so celebrated that even Mercedes had heard of him.

Annie aimed a hearty kick at him with the heavy men's boots she wore beneath her skirt.

81

'Lovely of *you*, Mrs Harkness,' he said smarmily to Daisy.

Over tea they discussed what they should do next, their four heads converging in a conspiratorial huddle. Since Ballard had been so uncooperative, it was Mercedes' opinion that they should bide their time and not look for another confrontation. Let Ballard and Floyd stew. Let them understand that, without their workers, they were powerless and nothing got done. Let *them* request the next meeting. Clasping her hands round the warmth of the tea-cup, elbows on the checkered oil-cloth, Mercedes argued her view in a low, urgent tone.

She could see that the others took her point. Annie agreed wholeheartedly. Edie and Daisy were more guarded, their faces expressing reservation.

'It's all right for a week or so, while they're still blowing hot over old Ballard's tantrums. Two weeks maybe . . . Three at a pinch. Then the landlord'll come knocking . . . An' there'll be no more tick at the grocer's . . . That's when the going gets hard, an' they start to crawl back . . .' Edie's green eyes protruded with the effort of sustaining such a lengthy flow of words, but the truth of what she said was irrefutable.

Annie countered with an explosive raspberry. 'If *I* catch 'em at it there'll be hell to pay!'

Mercedes endorsed her sentiments, cloaking them in language more appropriate to a representative of the Association. 'It *is* important that we're all seen to pull together.'

Something in this statement put Annie's back up. Probably it was Mercedes' implied inclusion of herself in their struggle through her careless use of 'we'.

'It ain't *you* that's doing the holding out.' Sharply Annie put her in her place, isolating her from the rest, pointing up her position as a privileged outsider.

Mercedes shrugged with feigned indifference, but she

82

was hurt and had no answer to Annie's accusation. As she swallowed the dregs of her tea a stray tea-leaf stuck to her bottom lip. She removed it with a grimace.

The gesture seemed to anger Annie further. 'Too rough for you, is it, this caff?'

'It's only a tea-leaf, Annie,' Daisy said wearily. She looked tired today and the intriguing shadows beneath her eyes were more pronounced than usual. In the course of her short acquaintanceship with Ballard's workers, Mercedes had gleaned the impression that Daisy had little time for her colleague, Annie Tyrell.

But Annie had abruptly lost interest in the conversation. She rapped excitedly on the window, calling to someone outside. 'Joey! Joey!'

A slight, callow-looking youth of eighteen or so was passing by. He stopped short and peered in at the window, his face breaking into a broad smile that revealed broken, discoloured teeth.

He entered the Picardy and approached their table. 'Hallo, Mum,' he said to Annie.

'Take a look at this.' She thrust the newspaper at him and he read it, moving his lips. His threadbare jacket was a strange greenish-black colour and his boots were covered in a layer of chalky grey dust.

'Gawd help us.' He handed the paper back to his mother. His grin spread and his eyes revealed a kind of exasperated affection.

'What you doing about the streets at this time of day?' Annie asked him accusingly.

'Errand for old Harris.' It seemed to Mercedes that layers of mutual family understanding, experience, knowledge lay implicit behind the simple statement.

'I'll give 'im errand,' Annie said darkly. Then she dismissed the subject and nodded towards Mercedes. 'This is that Mercedes I was telling you about.' A pause. 'She's bossy, but she'll do.'

'Good morning,' Mercedes smiled at the young man. She was absurdly pleased by Annie's casual introduction and use of her first name, though some part of her mind deplored her own susceptibility.

'Mmm.' Joey nodded and looked her over, a half-smile on his lips. She found his direct, unselfconscious stare a touch unnerving. The lad was far from good-looking, yet she felt herself disturbed, and feared that Annie, with her quick, caustic eye, would notice.

But attention turned to Daisy, who got to her feet, pinning back a lock of her blonde hair that had flopped from its anchoring pin. 'I must get back,' she murmured.

Edie asked, 'How's the old lady?' Again Mercedes felt excluded from areas of knowledge that the others, through the interwoven fabric of their lives, had in common.

Daisy shook her head. 'Getting worse,' she said. 'I don't much like leaving them.'

Annie and Edie pulled sympathetic faces. Daisy picked up her untouched slab of bread pudding and wrapped it in one end of her shawl. She must be taking it home for her children, Mercedes guessed.

9

There was one good thing about the club, Edward Ballard thought. They left you alone here if you indicated in some small way that that was what you wanted. It was enough to shift your chair slightly. He sat with his back turned diagonally to the rest of the room, facing the rooftops of St James's Street, the gas-lamps, lit but not yet really necessary, and above them the darkening pink spring sky. With an after-dinner brandy at his elbow, he gazed out in abstracted contemplation of the gathering dusk.

Behind him smooth, worn leather armchairs were drawn into loose semi-circles under pools of electric light. Conversations droned and buzzed. He was distantly aware of newspapers being rustled, aproned servants passing with glasses on trays. He luxuriated tonight in feeling himself separate from the muted, familiar activity, temporarily suspended in time, with leisure to let his mind wander.

As his brain idled, the memory surfaced of a picture his sister, Blanche, used to have, cut from some magazine. It showed a twilight landscape with a lone figure, and above it in the sky a woman's face floated, a Pre-Raphaelite type with rippling hair and ripe red lips. He'd been six or so, three years younger than Blanche, and the image had fascinated him.

'Why's she in the sky?' he asked her once, after staring obsessively at the picture, absorbing every detail.

'She's only imagination,' his sister answered impatiently, as if the question had no importance. And yet she'd kept the cutting pressed under the glass of her dressing-table for years.

Now, as he gazed out into the crimson-grey sky, a face

lingered at the back of his mind, a female face, the features hazy, a composite impression, blonde, pale, breathing an aura that was sensuous and self-contained.

Over the last few days he'd been ambushed by memory, hedged about, in a way that had no parallel in his congenial and well-ordered life. He'd been washed by waves of nostalgia and vague, unspecified desire. It wasn't like him. The woman, Daisy Harkness, had aroused in him thoughts he'd not had for years, that he'd believed buried and suppressed.

When he'd seen her, four days since, he had known she reminded him of someone from long ago, but he couldn't think who. Later, as he lay sleepless, the answer came to him with easy inevitability. There was a quality to her that recalled Christiane Jochen. Christiane. The name delved back into his childhood and revived a particular, personal blend of happiness and shame.

She had been a young German woman, hired by his parents as Nanny to himself and Blanche, and to speak German with them. She was blonde and gentle, fun and pretty. She also had, at times, an odd, quiet air of dignity. Christiane wore clean-smelling cotton dresses and her fine hair draped, with natural grace, into the nape of her neck. The nursery consisted of four rooms, self-contained, in a wing that lay at right-angles to the rest of the house. After Christiane arrived it seemed, to his nine-year-old self, like an island of light and pleasure.

Edward sipped his brandy. Details of those days flickered into his mind, slow and hesitant from years of neglect. He recalled her guitar. It had red ribbons on it. She used to teach them German songs. He remembered *Röslein auf der Heiden*. He used to hide from her sometimes and when she found him she laughed and ruffled his hair, calling him 'vicked boy' in her irresistible German accent. In those days he often had bad dreams and she would come into his bedroom in a white cotton nightgown, half asleep, with

86

her hair hanging on her shoulders, and cuddle him until he felt brave again.

He loved her. In fact, Edward realized now, he'd been *in* love with her. He never wished she was his mother. Mothers were different. His was tall and busy, someone on the fringes of his life, with a sharp humour that sometimes made him feel small.

He and Blanche kept chickens in an elegant little blue-painted wooden house one of the gardeners had made. One morning they found a fox had got to them. A carnage of blood, offal and feathers lay strewn over a large area. Edward had cried from shock and childish fear, and Christiane held him against her warm body, soothing him and shielding his eyes.

Through his distress he heard his father remark to his mother in tones of cold distaste, 'I don't like the lovey-dovey stuff.'

Edward felt violently ashamed and pulled away from Christiane. He didn't think she'd heard or understood.

But the moment passed and he and Blanche returned to their charmed life in the nursery. One day Christiane kept humming a folk-tune. She couldn't get it out of her head, she told them, and to tease her they sang along, keeping it on her mind. There was a dance that went with it, Christiane said, and she showed them a few steps. They imitated her, and gradually the dance got rowdier and more hilarious. Edward became quite over-excited and red in the face, linking elbows with Blanche and Christiane, swinging them round wildly and clicking his heels.

As luck would have it, his father came across to the nursery that evening, a thing he almost never did. He stood in the doorway watching their capers for some moments before they noticed him. Abruptly the cavorting stopped and they stood facing him, foolish, sweating and embarrassed.

Ignoring the women, his father addressed himself to

his son. 'Take a hold on yourself, sir,' he hissed. 'You look like a bloody tart in a tantrum.' Edward had never forgotten the cutting, devastating edge to his voice. With humiliation his bowels lurched and he almost lost control of them.

Within a fortnight Edward was removed from the cosy classes he shared in the village with the sons of other rich families, and packed off to boarding-school a year earlier than planned. Nothing was said but he knew it was to get him away from Christiane's influence. She must be bad for him. Within a term he'd learned to cringe with burning shame at the memory of that exuberant, giggling dance. Christiane returned to Germany shortly afterwards and an English governess was hired for Blanche.

Term by term Edward learned to overlay his natural behaviour with a dry and half-amused stance that removed the rest of the world to arm's length. The more he succeeded in this, the more his father and mother seemed pleased.

'Fine boy,' a family friend remarked off-handedly to his father one day.

'Quite a man nowadays,' his father replied, with more affection and approval in his voice than Edward had ever heard and he glowed with pride. Christiane was never mentioned and Edward pushed her memory resolutely to the back of his mind like a shameful deed. Though the sound of the German language, spoken low and murmuringly, still stirred in him a diffuse, nostalgic and partially erotic ache.

The sky above the rooftops had darkened to a velvety mauvish-grey. Gas-lamps shone, silver-white and hazy. His glass was empty and most of the occupants of the lounge had drifted off to their evening's amusements. Edward didn't feel like going home just yet. Fleetingly he thought of a house he'd been to once or twice kept by a woman who called herself Lisette. But the prospect of the women's rouged faces and forced vivacity, their heavy sexual innuendo, was exhausting. He had a brief, disconcertingly pleasurable mental image of himself, at ease in some unknown, candle-lit room, absorbed in idle, undemanding conversation with the Harkness woman.

After her two elder sisters had married, the nursery, on the second floor of the MacInnes home, had been turned into a suite of rooms for Mercedes. She had a bedroom and a sort of library – with a desk and her books, from *Puss-in-Boots* to pamphlets by the Pankhursts, ranged on two sturdy sets of shelves built into alcoves on either side of the fireplace – and a sitting-room.

When dinner was over, she and Walter Pimlett went upstairs to chat. Her parents allowed them to be alone together, although Florence always reminded Mercedes privately to be sure to leave the door ajar. 'It's not that we don't trust you, darling. I'm thinking more of Winnie and Tom, what they might feel.' She underlined this reference to Walter's parents with a crooked, woman-to-woman smile.

Upstairs, in the former nursery, a maid brought them cocoa and fruit-cake. It had become a sort of tradition. By the window Percival, Mercedes' old grey-and-white rocking-horse, stretched his legs in a perpetual frozen gallop. A fire burned cosily in the grate. In early May the evenings were still chilly enough to warrant it.

Walter lounged back on the worn, plum-coloured sofa. It was still a shock to see the new moustache, a shade more ginger than his mid-brown hair and, to Mercedes' eyes, at odds with the fresh-faced, easy-going, adolescent look that she knew so well.

'It's good to be here,' he said, with boyish fervour. 'And so good to see you, Sadie. You know,' he cocked his head to one side, 'you're looking stunning. I love that dress. Is it new?'

'It's nice, isn't it?' Mercedes wasn't usually clothes-conscious, but she did like the rather stylish frock she and Florence had chosen a few days ago at Liberty's. Bottle-green silk and very Paul Poiret, so the assistant had claimed, with a high waist and narrow skirt.

'It isn't the dress, though. It's you. You seem so . . . full of bounce and sort of glowing. As if you had a secret.' The bluff openness of Walter's admiration was undermined by a wayward gleam of intensity revealed in his eyes. Not for the first time Mercedes wondered whether, on Walter's side, their long-standing friendship wasn't becoming tinged with something more serious. She hoped not. Walter was a dear, someone she didn't have to be careful with or measure her words.

They'd had champagne at dinner. Walter had just passed some law exam or other. The MacInnes family were typically vague about the details of his progress towards barrister status, but fondly eager to celebrate any success he reported.

With the unaccustomed wine, Mercedes still felt a little other-worldly, a little euphoric. She smiled with impish knowingness. 'If I look well,' she said, 'it's because of the work I'm doing.'

He looked surprised. 'Work, Sadie? Sounds mysterious . . . Something to do with Hannah Spalding and her ladies, is it?'

Mercedes was mildly put out to hear the Association so defined, but decided this wasn't the moment to make an issue of it. She nodded. 'Yes, it *is* related. But if I tell you about it, you must promise not to mention it to the parents, yours or mine. It's just . . . I'm not sure they'd understand.'

Walter pulled a face that expressed eye-popping curiosity. 'Sounds better and better. Okay, Sadie, I promise.'

She laughed. '"Okay", Walter? I thought that word was black-balled in your family.' As a girl she'd heard

Thomas Pimlett reprimand his sons for using it times without number.

He laughed with mock anxiety. 'Cripes, Sadie, don't tell the pater.' They exchanged nostalgic grins; the shared trivia of their childhood was precious to them.

Briefly Mercedes outlined for him her activities over the last few days. Walter listened closely. She thought he seemed impressed, but a trifle dubious. Edward Ballard was, after all, an old and valued friend of the Pimlett family.

'You're a close one, Sadie,' he commented, when she'd brought him up to date. 'This is awfully, well . . . enterprising of you. But what's going to happen when people find out? That's really going to put the cat among the pigeons.'

She was a little miffed that he'd chosen to highlight this particular aspect of the affair above any other. 'It's really only an extension of my other work with the Association,' she told him with an edge of impatience. 'Hannah's done this sort of thing lots of times, and so have some of the others – it's all part of what we're there for.' Mercedes noticed that her cocoa was forming a layer of skin. Wrapped up in their conversation she'd forgotten it. 'As far as Ma and Pa are concerned,' she added, more practically, 'I just go off to work as usual . . . And that's all there is to it.' Mercedes was displeased with a defensive note that seemed to have crept into her account of herself.

Tactfully Walter dropped this particular line of discussion. 'How do you find it? I mean, dealing with all those working-class types. A bit daunting, isn't it?'

She didn't answer straight off, giving her attention to the cooling cocoa, while she thought about what to say. Then she looked across at Walter and shrugged. 'I just feel terribly alive,' she told him simply.

His eyes expressed incomprehension. 'What d'you mean,

alive? You're always . . . You're the most alive girl I know.'

Mercedes stared at the coals in the fireplace, black and radiant orange, burning with a restless, unobtrusive energy. She and her sisters used to toast crumpets in this room, on the end of a long, brass fork, kneeling by the fire on a squashy old red plush cushion. Cosy winter tea-times. All at once she was overwhelmingly aware of her secure, sheltered girlhood.

She shrugged her shoulders again. 'You're a boy,' she said, 'and whether you've noticed it or not, you've always had a lot more freedom than me. Now, for instance, you live on your own, you come and go as you please. You're free to go to the most awful dives if you want to.' She flashed him a mischievous smile. 'Maybe you even do . . .'

Walter gave a bark of self-conscious laughter.

'Girls are protected from everything. We're restricted and kept in maidenly ignorance of anything at all interesting or juicy.' Her feet, crossed in front of her, neat in silk stockings and high-heeled shoes with bows, seemed symbols of the hampered life-style she was talking about. 'Although, to give them their due, my parents are a lot more liberal than most . . .'

With a grimace she drained the rest of her luke-warm cocoa and leant forward to replace her cup on the tray by the hearth. 'Today,' she told Walter, 'I was sitting in a run-down café in Bermondsey with three working-women, drinking tea and eating bread pudding. Nothing hugely remarkable. And yet to me it felt like . . . an adventure.'

She met his eyes. He wore a look of sympathetic interest, but she sensed that he was also secretly bewildered and she wondered if he could really understand anything of what she was trying to say. Mercedes offered him a quizzical grin, undercutting her earnestness, and he smiled back with the vulnerable intensity that surfaced from time to time, giving her food for thought.

In her mind's eye she saw Annie waving the newspaper at her through the window of the Picardy Café this morning, wearing a wide and piratical grin. She'd had a wild feeling, then, of being accepted. Belonging. Because, in spite of their massively differing backgrounds, she and these women were working towards a common goal.

It seemed to Mercedes that she absorbed energy from their salty speech and fight for survival – an exhilaration that made her decisive and persuasive. Did that make her a leech, she wondered. Some kind of a bloodsucker gaining nourishment from the hand-to-mouth hardship of their lives.

She hastened to reassure herself, confiding to Walter, 'I *do* think I'm useful to them. What with my experience at the Association I can organize them, get them thinking in unison. And I know how to approach the newspapers so they'll take us seriously . . . The thing is, though,' she added, with rueful candour, 'here at home I'm just the unmarried daughter, at the beck and call . . . If Pa finds out about this, he could order me to stop. I'd look such a fool. I'd die . . . of sheer humiliation.'

10

A triple knock – urgent yet timid – sounded at Annie's front door. She cursed inwardly. It'd be Kate. On the scrounge again, most likely.

Sitting at her sewing-machine, hair still in curling-rags, Annie was busy negotiating the curved parallel lines of stitching on a scalloped collar. Without breaking rhythm, she carried on. It was too easy to make a pig's ear of a job like this.

The knock came again.

'Give us a chance!' she called sharply, not taking her eyes off the intricacies of the stitchery, her feet still moving steadily on the treadle. Finally, reaching a point where she could safely break off, Annie slowed down and stopped. Removing the material from under the metal foot of her machine and snipping off the thread, she then laid the garment with unhurried care over the back of her chair.

Sure enough, it was Kate Reeves standing on the doorstep in a light spring drizzle, her blonde hair a mess, looking like a dying duck in a thunderstorm, as usual.

'What is it, Kate?' Annie's tone was indulgent, resigned.

'Can you lend me sixpence, love?' The request came out in a wheedling rush. At the same time something uncharacteristically hard and meaningful in her neighbour's eyes reminded Annie that it was on her account that Kate was reduced to begging and borrowing.

Annie gave a thin smile. 'Course I can, Kate. You know I'm rolling in it.'

'I'm serious, love. Jack's only given me three bob this week.' Annie's living-room opened to the right off the

94

narrow hall. Kate drifted through the doorway, as if by accident.

Annie followed. She had no patience with this kind of talk. 'You should stand up to that husband of yours. I'd like to see my Will try and palm me off with three bob if he was in work.'

Kate drooped her head, saying nothing.

'He's still drinking himself silly, your Jack, when the fancy takes him.' Another thought occurred to her. 'Go through his breeches when he's asleep.'

Kate gave a faint, irritating smile, refusing to be drawn. She looked round the room with a wistful air that always got Annie's goat, as if Kate herself lived in a cardboard box or something. There was nothing to choose between their respective lodgings, just that Annie kept hers nicer.

The room was spartan, but clean, furnished with a table, five upright chairs and the sewing-machine. Two narrow iron beds stood at right-angles to one another alongside connecting walls, where Joey and Danny slept, the two of Annie's four sons who still lived at home. The wallpaper had a faded pattern of vapid pink flowers and was mottled with two large, ineradicable patches of damp. They'd lived here for a good few years now, in this room, and a poky kitchen and a bedroom, where she and Will and Maggie slept.

Kate's eye fell on the half-finished garment draped over the back of Annie's chair. 'What's that?'

Annie held up the partially-assembled dress in pinkish-grey worsted. 'Jessie Martin's getting wed.'

'It's lovely . . . Tricky, though.' She examined the tucked and scalloped overskirt, the decorative collar, the tight, fitted sleeves. 'How much are you getting for this?'

'Two and six.' The bald statement spoke volumes. 'They know I can't afford to turn it down.'

Kate ignored this instance of exploitation, remarking enviously, 'If *I* had my own machine it'd make things a lot easier.' She had the knack, from way back, of implying that other people had all the luck.

'I paid this off myself, bit by bit, as you well know. When we were *both* a bit more flush,' Annie retorted pointedly. Then she returned to the matter in hand. 'If I lend you this sixpence, when can you pay me?'

Kate brightened. 'Tomorrow – promise. I just need to get some bread and stuff for the children tonight. We got nothing in the house . . . I can pay you tomorrow,' she repeated. 'Bet's off to Waltham Cross to see her sister's new baby. She's given me her day cleaning the schoolhouse. I'll be getting one and six.'

'All right. Just a tick.' Annie vanished into the bedroom and fished under the mattress, pulling out a draw-string bag with some coins in it. Two and ninepence – she knew without looking. Will was having trouble finding work nowadays. The boys'd bring something home tonight, but there was the rent to pay . . . At least they were still up-to-date with that.

She took six coppers out of the bag, went back to the living-room and handed them to Kate.

'Thanks. You're a pal.'

To Annie's mind the heartfelt relief in Kate's eyes was pathetic. Her Jack was a bus-conductor, on regular wages. But he kept most of it for himself, relying on Kate's meagre earnings to keep the children fed and clothed. She ought to have it out with him instead of coming down on the neighbours. Money'd be tight, in any case, with their four kids, none earning. Jack was a bully and still saw himself as a ladies' man. And Kate let him get away with it.

'Bugger off now,' Annie said amiably. 'I've got this frock to finish.' She sat herself down at the machine again.

Kate began to wander off, but paused in the doorway, clutching the coins against her grimy blouse. 'I'm not sure how long I can keep this up, love, this striking lark.' A plaintive note in her voice implied that all of them were only doing it on Annie's account. Just as if they weren't looking to get anything out of it themselves, Annie thought with a rush of resentment.

Kate quavered on. 'It's been three weeks now since I brought any money into the house. I put the clock in hock last week and now Jack has to check next door to find out if it's time to go to work . . .'

'God's sake, woman, show some fight!' Annie's irritation got the better of her. 'What about *them*? Don't you think they're getting windy? They got a damn sight more at stake than we have. If we can just hold out we'll be quids in! Anyway,' she said, in a more encouraging tone, 'that Mercedes said she might be able to bring us something from the fund tomorrow.'

'Mmm.' Kate screwed her mouth doubtfully. 'Wouldn't bank on it. She'll try though. She's a trier, I'll say that for her.'

Annie experienced a flash of annoyance at hearing Mercedes praised, however faintly. She gave a short laugh and crossed her arms with a grin that was mocking and sceptical. '*I'd* say she was having the time of her life down here with us commoners. No money worries herself, and running round in circles feeling important. Still, if she delivers the cash, I won't be the one to turn it down.'

Mildred Ballard didn't take much at breakfast-time. Now past forty, she found it increasingly difficult to maintain herself on the right side of the thin, crucial line that separated voluptuous from stout. She drank tea – several cups – accompanied by half a slice of soft white bread. Always she spread the bread thickly with fresh butter and made sure there were plenty of whole strawberries in her large spoonful of jam. Her meal was over in a couple of mouthfuls, but at least those mouthfuls were worth having.

There seemed an oppressive silence this morning over

the dining-table. She was intensely aware of the gulping sounds in her throat as she swallowed the tea, and even more painfully conscious of the muffled, thunderous rumbling of her own stomach. Holding her cup between two hands, more or less at eye-level, she watched Edward as he munched his way absent-mindedly through a stack of buttered toast. He'd made short work of a pair of kippers – the plate, with two skeletons and some repulsive folds of shiny black skin, was pushed to one side – and he was engrossed in a letter. How heavy and red his face looked this morning, she thought. Coarse even. He was ageing, as she was.

'Who's the letter from?' she asked.

'Neville Kirkpatrick,' he replied, without looking up.

Mildred didn't question him further. Often, in the mornings, he was slighting and cold, and she had no wish to provoke his hostility.

The slit envelope was too large for a simple letter. It appeared to contain something else. Edward inserted two fingers and drew out a folded sheet of newsprint. She watched as he opened it and found the place he wanted. As he read she saw, with resignation, that his temper was rising. After twenty-one years of marriage she was all too familiar with the signs. A kind of glowering luminescence beneath the skin that darkened and intensified into a choleric shade of crimson, lending him a slit-eyed, brutal look.

To Mildred, the silence of the room seemed to deepen and reverberate. Oblivious to atmosphere, Papageno the parrot, perched in his golden cage by the window, uttered a brief burst of garbled chatter.

'Christ!' Edward's anger exploded in an abrasive monosyllable. With an abrupt movement he pushed the sheet across to her. 'Read that! Neville's housekeeper came across it in a dentist's waiting-room.' This fact seemed to enrage him as much as the paper's actual contents.

The pages, from the *South London Advertiser*, were dated a fortnight ago, and the story was headed by the photographs of two women. One was about Mildred's age and wore an aggressive smile. The other was younger, pensive and rather beautiful, the sort of person who would arouse the readers' sympathy, their chivalrous instincts.

In the text below, Edward Ballard was described as a charming and wealthy businessman, who owned a mansion in Onslow Square as well as a 'country seat' on the Herts-Essex border. His evident affluence was contrasted with the average weekly take-home wage of one of his employees. Twelve shillings.

'Actually 'e's not much seen at the factory,' the one they called the Holy Terror was quoted as saying. 'We'd know if 'e was – *we're* there seven till seven every day of the week.' Mildred couldn't deny a flash of amusement at the woman's dry aside.

'Oh dear,' she said to Edward, offering the rueful ghost of a smile.

Her calm infuriated him further. 'Oh dear!' he mimicked, with a grotesque, overwrought shrillness. 'Good Christ, Mildred, is that all you can say?'

His angry flailings intensified her sense of calm. 'What d'you want me to do?' she asked. 'Tear my hair and ululate?'

He stood up from the table. The force of the movement was blatantly hostile. Mildred stared at him. Above the white shirt, and with a backdrop of dark, striped wallpaper, his face resembled a boiling ham. It was the way he looked when things weren't going his way. When he was losing something. A game of tennis or a dispute. He hated to lose.

Edward strode towards the door. 'I'll be at the factory all day,' he said. 'I've been patient too long. Stupidly patient. Time I set about actually doing something to sort out this whole bloody mess.'

'Will you be in to dinner?' She put the wifely question hastily, before he could fling out of the room and be gone.

'No!'

When Edward wasn't home to dinner she was left high and dry. However grumpy he was at breakfast-time, she needed his return to punctuate the emptiness of the day, to give it a focus. Did he realize that, she wondered, and concluded that probably he didn't. His daily decision was so random, depending on mood and whim as much as anything. And he rarely bothered to give a reason. Just yes or no. And then he could leave and do whatever he wanted, wherever he wanted, until whatever time he liked. She marvelled at such power and insouciance.

In theory, of course, she was perfectly at liberty to live her own life and look out her own entertainments. In practice her freedom amounted to little more than the right to visit other women of her own social class, drink tea and talk about what their servants, children and husbands were up to. It was like being in a Greek chorus, Mildred thought, commenting while everybody else was doing.

'I'll clear the table, shall I, ma'am?' It was Iris, the new housemaid. Mildred liked her, approving her wholesome, uncomplicated prettiness.

She nodded and smiled, deciding to adjourn to her own sitting-room on the first floor. There was a book of Algernon Blackwood ghost-stories she wanted to finish. Mildred stood up, smoothing her skirt. 'Mr Ballard won't be in to dinner. Could you please tell cook, Iris?'

She climbed the stairs, leaving behind the busy chink of crockery as Iris stacked plates, cups and cutlery. Above her, on the second floor, one of the other maids was turning out the bedroom. Mildred could hear her attacking a carpet vigorously with a stiff brush. She sauntered into her sunny sitting-room. It had already been dusted and straightened, a fire laid in the grate to be lit if she needed it. Around her the house was a hive of purposeful activity. This room was a retreat, an island of peace.

Idly she crossed to the window and looked out on to Onslow Square. Already a brisk nursemaid, in a navy coat and skirt, was giving her employers' baby an airing in his perambulator. The day ahead of her would be mapped out, a series of fussy nursery chores. Mildred watched and wondered. All *she* needed to do was lower herself into her favourite armchair and take up her book. She was a parasite. That was the word the radical journalists were bandying about nowadays. People like the fiery Rebecca West who'd lived on her wits from the age of sixteen or seventeen. God knows, Mildred admired her spunk, but she seemed like a creature from another world.

She turned away from the window and surveyed her own comfortable room, with its clean, bright, cheering colours. Her piano stood in one corner. There were shelves of books, and a half-finished watercolour was propped on an easel. At this time of the morning her day bristled with possibilities. It was only later, when the sun moved round to the other side of the house, that the emptiness began to make itself felt.

Edward used to laugh at her habit of spending the day painting or playing the piano, or curled up in a chair with a good book.

'It's like having a mistress to come home to,' he used to tease her. Around six o'clock he'd pour them both a glass of the light, dry sherry they both liked. They'd talk and laugh. Sometimes he used to sit on the floor by her chair and she'd stroke his yellow hair. It amused him that she wasn't like his friends' wives, playing a domestic role, clucking over the slapdash ways of the servants.

Mildred left the running of the household to McKellen, the butler. He was dour and vigilant and made sure everyone came up to the mark. He treated Mildred like a wayward daughter and the relationship suited both of them very well.

'He loves patrolling the place with his rod of iron,' she used to tell friends with a cat-like smile. 'So who am I to spoil his fun?' And Edward used to touch her hand, signalling his approval.

And now she felt betrayed because, as she grew older, he seemed to imply that she'd do well to become more like Bridie Berton and Winnie Pimlett, dull, settled matrons, catering to the needs of everyone but themselves, hand-in-glove with their domestic staff, without a spark of glamour or romance in their lives.

Over the years Edward had gradually withdrawn from the amusing kept-woman fantasy they'd shared and she was left without a role to play. Once in a while Mildred gritted her teeth and made an effort to attend to the nuts and bolts of household management, plan menus, consult with McKellen and cook. But the attempts were farcical. They didn't want or need her. The house ran perfectly smoothly without her interference.

And there were the children, the three boys. Adorable little creatures they used to be, with sturdy-soft limbs and smooth, fresh cheeks. They'd always had a nanny, of course, who dressed them and fed them and put them to bed. But when they were little she, Mildred, used to have fun with them making up games, getting them wild and over-excited. They were playmates. But then they went away to school and became priggish, too old for her silly, loving nicknames. They treated her politely now, and without interest, like any female relative of a certain age.

In company she missed the undertow of sexual admiration that used to tug towards her from Edward's male friends, looks that lingered on her shapely white shoulders and breasts, an awareness of possibilities. The half-mechanical jollying, reserved for people like Winnie and

102

Bridie, was a poor substitute. The other night, after undressing, Mildred had stared at her naked self in a mirror. The criss-crossed red weals from her corsets cutting across her over-ripe flesh had put her in mind, bizarrely, of a religious painting – some poor, tortured female martyr. But she could no longer see any allure in her body.

Edward was getting a paunch and wrinkles and wore spectacles now to read with. She noticed the details of his physical decline with a chilly exactitude. But in the eyes of the world he was a man in the prime of life, charming, wearing his casual authority like a coat. Young women blushed and twinkled when he spoke to them. Watching, with cold, all-seeing eyes, she hated him for the difference between his status and hers, for the fact that she was nothing without him, that he had power and she needed him.

With a flash of grim pleasure, Mildred turned her thoughts to the women who were challenging him, challenging his authority and his will. So far he'd been unable to charm or bend or overpower them. In her mind's eye she saw her husband's workers as a rabble of hags – *tricoteuses* – with greasy locks and missing teeth. She relished the idea of their rowdy, graceless defiance, and unconsciously Mildred's lips curled in a wolfish smile.

From a low table she picked up the red-bound volume of ghost-stories. Her place was marked with a fringed strip of leather. Her morning was spoken for. It was good to lose yourself in a book.

11

Kate Reeves sat waiting for her husband to come home. The children had settled at last, all four of them sleeping head-to-tail in the big bed in the other room. The door was propped a little way open with a stool, so that Sally, who was scared of the dark, could see the flicker of Kate's candle. The bed smelt something awful. Paul, the youngest, still wet himself sometimes, and it soaked into the mattress. But what could she do? If they ever got any money together – Kate gave a cynical smile at the unlikeliness of that – a new mattress was the first thing she'd buy.

She wasn't sure what time it was. Somewhere between eleven and twelve, she guessed. Every time she went down Flanders Road she passed their big kitchen clock sitting in the pawnshop window. It wasn't even theirs in fact, but fixtures and fittings with the two rooms they rented.

No sign of Jack, but that wasn't surprising on a Friday night. She just hoped he'd be happy-drunk and not spiteful-drunk when he did get home, whenever that might be. Rose Gretton said she'd seen him with the Cannon girl a couple of times.

'A word to the wise,' she'd whispered hoarsely, with a sly, warning grin that suggested Kate had better be on her mettle.

She *was* pretty, the Cannon girl, with her coppery, dyed hair, bold smile and plump little body. Kate couldn't see her sticking to Jack for long. But what did it matter? If it wasn't her it'd be someone else.

Curled in the one sound, comfortable chair in the place, Kate didn't feel too bad. Her flannelette nightgown was soft against her skin and her stomach full. With the sixpence borrowed from Annie this morning she'd bought bread, a pennyworth of loose tea and a little bit of butter. Sophie upstairs had lent her the end of a pot of jam. Kate hadn't bought the food till supper-time, so the children couldn't eat it too early and get hungry again. And tomorrow she'd clean the schoolhouse from top to bottom and get one and six. She might get a bit of bacon for all of them. Paul loved bacon.

Kate thought of Jack, swilling beer to his heart's content. On top of a bellyful of pie or something, more than likely. She ought to feel angry with him, but all she felt was dead. It seemed as if she couldn't work herself up to anger any more – just sit here, not doing anything, burning a candle to save gas. They still had a few of those in the table drawer.

Tonight she'd got to thinking about her sister, Allie. Kate knew that things wouldn't seem so bad if Allie still lived close by. But she'd married years ago now and gone to live in Hove, of all places. It might as well be the moon. Kate couldn't imagine ever having money enough to spare for the fare down there. Allie used to be so sweet and funny, it cheered you up just to see her. Kate remembered a night when she and Jack were still courting and they'd gone to a fair with Allie and her Tom. A lovely, warm, blue summer night. Jack had been flush and bought them all drinks. She could hardly credit that now. He kept telling her how nice she looked and kissing her right in front of Allie and Tom. Kate shook her head. Had they really once been so young and careless and kind?

She heard the slam of the street door and her heart sank. Thinking about that night at the fair she'd forgotten about the present for a moment. When Jack got home she held her breath, waiting and watching, tense, as his footsteps came up the stairs.

He always opened the door with force, as if wanting to

catch her at something shifty. As he stood framed in the doorway, his black hair was tousled, his cheeks flushed and his eyes bright from the beer and the company. She felt drab next to him in her nightgown, hair lank and colourless on her shoulders. Seeing Jack so handsome, some foolish part of her still swelled with disbelief and pride that he'd chosen her to marry.

But almost at once his look changed, and he screwed up his face in ugly disgust. 'Fucking room stinks of piss.' He said it every other day.

'It's the mattress. What can I do?' Kate heard the whine in her own voice.

'Stinking bloody hole.'

Jack sat down on the bed, on the moth-eaten red counterpane, and leant to untie his boots, fingers fumbling with the laces, getting nowhere. His eyes were glazed and his lower lip drooped with a mixture of drunkenness and ill humour.

'Leave it. I'll do your boots.' Kate knelt by the bed at his feet. She was nervous and over-eager and couldn't see properly in the dim candlelight. He'd got the laces all knotted and it took her a long time to sort them out. Jack sat like Lord Muck, watching her, and there was something in the air between them, a dull excitement at her servility, and she guessed he'd want to do her when they got to bed. The Cannon girl must have let him down. After Kate had pulled off his boots and socks he patted her head, ruffling her hair carelessly like a pet dog.

'What's to eat?'

She felt a lurch of terror. She hadn't thought of this. On drinking nights he'd normally eaten before he came home and then went straight to bed. When Kate was working she always made sure there was something – bread at least and some tea – in case Jack felt the need. But tonight they'd polished off the lot. The children had been starving hungry.

'There's nothing.' Her voice was toneless.

'Nothing!' His disbelief had an abrasive, unholy, gloating edge to it.

Kate closed her eyes for a moment, betraying her fear. 'You know I got no money. I borrowed sixpence to buy stuff. We ate it all. The kids were ravening.'

'You ate the fucking lot!' It was almost comical, the wealth of outrage in his tone, like a child's, but a sudden massive clump to the side of her head made Kate see stars, sent her sprawling on the bare wood floor.

'No!' She curled into a ball, protecting her head with her arms, trying to twist away from him.

'Greedy bloody bitch!'

He began to kick her in the back and sides, his bare feet landing bluntly, viciously on her flesh and bones. 'I've had about enough!' he shouted as he attacked her. 'You get back to work, start bringing something home!'

Jack knelt astride her, pulling her arms away from her face, trapping them between his knees. Then he slapped her face again and again, the blows landing wildly, catching her nose, eyes, splitting her lip. From somewhere Kate heard a howl like an animal's and realized that it was her. With a dream-like remoteness she saw Sal's white, frozen face in the slit of the door.

'Sal! Close the door! Get to bed!' The commands jerked out in hiccups between his blows.

Jack turned, his attention distracted. He snarled at the child, 'Get back in there!' Then, with a menacing agility, he stood up and crossed the room. Leaning in at the door, he thrust his daughter into the darkness of the bedroom and slammed the connecting door. Kate heard the collective siren wail of the children's frightened crying.

She lay on the floor. Nothing. Dirt. No fight, no feeling left in her. The way Jack liked her.

He came and knelt beside her. 'Katie. I'm sorry, love.' She felt his forehead laid against her own and smelt the

107

beer on his breath. 'Lost me temper. I'm a bastard.' As if
it were happening to someone else, she was aware of him
lifting her nightgown and fumbling with his own trousers.
His fingers probed between her legs.

'Katie.' The word was hoarse, a growl.

He began to thrust into her. The floor beneath her skin
was cold and splintery. She lay still, then after a bit, out
of habit, she began to move with him a little.

12

Daisy's brother, Andrew Sitek, sat at the table in her first-floor living-room, mending her boots. It was Saturday afternoon. He ignored Mercedes and his sister as they stood talking about the best way to share out a grant of money Mercedes had managed to wangle from the Association. Holding the worn boot, sole uppermost, he tapped in small nails with a deft delicacy and skill that constantly distracted her from the conversation.

He was extraordinarily handsome; his face long, and thinner than his sister's, the fair skin moulded to the bones beneath. He had the same wavy fair hair as Daisy, which flopped over his forehead as he leaned forward, concentrating. His cheekbones were prominent and there was the shadow of a cleft in his chin. He had grey eyes, with a smudge of darker skin below each one, like Daisy. His nose was straight, his lips full and clearly defined. There was something Slavic in his looks, Mercedes thought, though perhaps the word sprang to mind because she knew he was Polish.

'I think we'll have to meet together with Annie and the others,' she told Daisy. 'And we can all decide together how to divide the money. Although, personally, I think a simple equal division might be the best way, without trying to reckon out who *needs* it most . . .'

Daisy nodded judiciously. 'You can tie yourself in knots trying to be fair.'

With startling and inexplicable clarity, Mercedes noticed Andrew's hands, long and elegant, but capable and strong-looking, his wrists stippled with fine hairs, protruding from the sleeves of his grey jacket. He wore a striped shirt and a thin, loosely-knotted scarf. His clothes looked worn, but clean.

Daisy broke off from their conversation to ask him, 'Can you keep them in one piece for a bit longer, my boots?'

'Is there a choice?' He looked up with a crooked grin. Mercedes was charmed with the quick, natural grace of it, and with the husky note to his voice. He seemed shy, addressing Daisy, averting his face slightly from Mercedes.

'Not now there isn't,' Daisy laughed back at him. In a sudden flash, Mercedes saw them as a pair of natural aristocrats, like in a fairy-tale, living among wood-cutters and peasants. Daisy was as lovely as Andrew was handsome, in a way that was unmistakable. She wasn't an acquired taste. And yet something about her – a reserve in her expression, a definition to her features, the way her skin took light and shadow – removed her a million miles from insipid, conventional beauty.

'Will you have some tea?' Daisy asked, rather doubtfully.

'I'd love to.' Mercedes gave a warm, reassuring smile, and thought that she looked and sounded like her mother attempting to put some social inferior at her ease.

'Sit yourself down.' Daisy positioned an upright chair near the table, opposite Andrew, and left to put on the kettle.

As Andrew carried on with his rescue-operation on his sister's boots, Mercedes looked around the room. Its clean, bare simplicity was exotic to her. She approved the white walls, the pots of plants lined up on the window-sill, back-lit by the afternoon sun. There was a pink geranium, a cactus, and some other things she didn't recognize. The light filtered through a thin blue curtain that was partly drawn. On the wall above Andrew hung the framed sepia photograph of an old and upright Victorian. Mercedes thought she saw a resemblance. Perhaps it was their father.

The table and upright chairs were almost the only furniture. But a plaited rag-rug lay on the floor by the empty fireplace, and there was a bed in one corner, covered by a patchwork quilt of unusual design. Perhaps Daisy had sewn it. Above the bed were pinned four or five pictures of actresses, cut from some journal or other. Most smirked demurely from clouds of luxuriant hair, but one looked modern and saucy, a ragtime type, wearing an osprey feather in her turban head-dress.

Andrew must have noticed her staring at them. 'My harem, Daisy calls them.' Again there was the huskiness in his voice, an edge of diffidence.

'Oh.' Mercedes was unaccountably embarrassed and could think of no sensible reply. 'That's *your* bed, is it?' she blurted and, stupidly, became even more flustered. Yet in her own circles she was known for the frankness of her conversation, her impatience with the old-fashioned prudery of her elders.

He nodded. 'That's right. Bit of privacy.' A wry grin. 'Being the man of the house . . . Daisy and the kids and Ma sleep through there.' Pointing vaguely towards the door behind him.

Andrew set the boot he was mending down on the table and tested it, bending it carefully back and forth. Mercedes observed his concentration and air of knowing what he was about. Finally he was satisfied. 'That'll have to do.' He put it down on the floor next to its twin.

He smiled across at her with a hint of flirtation. 'Boot repairers to the gentry. Anything I can do for you while I'm at it.'

Mercedes glanced down at her feet. 'I don't think so.' She could think of nothing wittier to say, and felt dull and wrong-footed. She found herself powerfully affected by him. By the singular mixture of his startling good looks, and practicality, the unassuming manner that bordered on

111

shyness, yet underlying it the suggestion that he was not unaware of his own attraction.

Daisy returned with the tea and poured three cups. They went back to the subject of the money. With a corner of her mind Mercedes hoped that Andrew would take note of their discussion and appreciate her active role in the dispute.

The money was sorely needed. Three weeks without pay had produced serious hardship in some quarters, and Daisy warned that some of the women were wavering on the point of giving up.

The fact was that, up to now, Mercedes had been unable to lay her hands on any of the Association's funds. Hannah Spalding had been away, staying with friends who owned a villa in the South of France. She'd returned two days ago and authorized Mercedes to withdraw a little over twenty pounds from the communal bank account. She seemed surprised and impressed – and mildly put out – that the strike was still a going concern.

For the first time Mercedes' hero-worship of Hannah had been nibbled a little by doubt. She couldn't suppress the unworthy suspicion that Hannah's sudden change of heart – her decision to entrust her, Mercedes, with responsibility for the Ballard strike – had simply been a result of the tempting, unexpected invitation abroad. Mercedes felt proprietary about the strike now. It was *her* brain-child. And she hoped desperately that, back in London, Hannah wouldn't want to take over her role.

Andrew finished his tea and stood up. 'I'll be off,' he said to Daisy. 'Don't reckon to wait supper for me.'

She raised an eyebrow. 'What supper?' she teased.

Once again, confronted with glimpses of the hardship overtaking Ballard's employees, Mercedes experienced a chill of responsibility, and for the umpteenth time she prayed fervently that it would all turn out to be worth it in the end.

Andrew faced Mercedes. He seemed awkward now, as if he felt that some kind of social gesture was required and wasn't sure what. 'Expect we'll be seeing more of you,' he offered with a slightly sheepish smile. Was it her imagination or had he coloured a little, as if the curiosity that lay between them wasn't all one-sided.

'My little brother,' Daisy said, wryly, fondly, after he'd gone. 'It's hard on him,' she confided. 'All this. He's only twenty-two. He ought to be able to keep a few bob back at his age, to enjoy himself. The way things are he's got me and the kids, as well as Mamma, like a dead weight round his neck.'

Mercedes nodded sympathetically, hoping that her eyes weren't betraying a too-eager interest.

'If only I had a sewing-machine,' Daisy continued. 'I could make a reasonable bit, even now. But all I can do at home is embroidery. I've been doing handkerchiefs to sell to the big shops. But they pay next to nothing. Then they go and sell 'em at two bob a time . . .' Daisy's tone was merely factual, with no edge of bitterness.

'Can I see?' Mercedes was curious.

'If you like.'

Daisy disappeared for a moment and came back with some samples folded in a cardboard box. The handkerchiefs were highly decorated with delicate flowers, sinuous, stylish and elongated, in the William Morris vein, purples, ochres, and shades of green predominating. Each one was different.

Mercedes examined them enthusiastically. 'They're wonderful! Where did you get the patterns from?'

'I made them up.' Daisy shrugged, a touch embarrassed by Mercedes' raptures. 'I enjoy it. Only it doesn't bring in much.'

'Can I buy a couple?' Mercedes asked impulsively. 'They're so unusual. I'll pay what they charge in the shops.'

113

'Oh no!' Daisy was adamant, and Mercedes understood that her offer had a ring of charity, and however much she needed the money, Daisy wasn't having that.

She was mortified for a second by her own tactlessness, but realized that Daisy had taken her suggestion in good part. With some of the other women, notably Annie, Mercedes sometimes had the impression that she was walking between land-mines, skirting half-buried resentments and hostilities which would blow up in her face if she didn't watch her step. But she'd noticed before that Daisy seemed to accept her with a matter-of-fact good will, making allowances for the middle-class clumsiness that she was unaware of until it was too late. It made her easy to get along with and, without further ado, they agreed on a compromise price for the handkerchiefs.

Light, pattering steps could suddenly be heard on the stairs. 'That'll be the children and my mother,' Daisy said. 'I sent them for a walk to get them out of the way for a while.'

A child pushed open the door and burst into the room. A boy. He looked about four, though Mercedes wasn't good at telling children's ages. He was as beautiful as a Renaissance angel, with almond-shaped grey eyes, coral lips and soft hair the colour of champagne. His blue sailor shirt and knickers were neatly patched and his face shone with eagerness.

'We saw the wolf-dog, Mam,' he told Daisy breathlessly.

She bent to his level. 'Did you, Alex?'

'Janie was frightened.'

'I wasn't. I talked to him.' From the doorway Janie aimed a slap at her brother, a token aggression, not meant to connect. She was sturdy and earthbound, younger than Alex, maybe three. With her mass of curly dark hair she seemed a changeling in this family of blonde heads. Perhaps she took after her father, Daisy's dead husband.

She was followed by an elderly woman dressed all in black, with a black shawl of some thin cottony material covering her grey hair, which was drawn straight back from her forehead. Mercedes was struck by her eyes, which had a distant, haunted vacancy. But she was physically imposing, with the remains of a grave, seemingly unconscious beauty.

'My mother,' Daisy said. 'Mamma, this is Miss MacInnes.'

Mercedes moved forward to greet her, but the woman made no acknowledgement of her presence, almost gazed through her, and the friendly words froze on her lips. She was left wearing a foolish, automatic smile, her impulsive right hand semi-extended, looking for a moment like a monument to the empty insincerity of social manners. Daisy's mother turned silently and left the room.

Daisy shrugged and explained. 'I'm sorry. We can never tell . . . She's not always strange like that, but as she gets older . . .' The sentence trailed away.

'Time I went, anyway . . .' Still taken aback, Mercedes registered that the sentence didn't sound quite right, as if there were some connection between Daisy's mother and her own departure . . . But she trusted the other woman to grasp her meaning.

Before Daisy could reply, though, a new set of footsteps sounded on the staircase outside, and then a knock came at the door.

It was Annie Tyrell, looking hot and hurried, hatless, her hair bedraggled and losing its curl. She wore a blouse and a skirt that was almost hidden by a brown sacking apron.

'No bloody peace for the wicked,' she proclaimed forcibly. 'Listen to this, Daisy . . .' Annie caught sight of Mercedes. 'Oh, you're here. Good. Listen, Kate's gone back to work.' She curled her lip, with a look of disgust. 'That's bloody Jack's doing. He's made mincemeat out of 'er face . . . Bastard!' she spat, then returned to her informative tone. 'And Ballard's been down at the factory all day yesterday and today. He's hiring scabs!'

13

Edward felt far happier now that he was taking an active role in the course of the strike. The weeks of doing nothing, just simply waiting for the women to give in, had run so counter to his nature as to put him in a permanently filthy mood. The mere fact of hiring this makeshift workforce – however poor a substitute they might be for the real thing – gave him the impression that he was once more in the driving-seat.

In this situation Leonard Floyd was a tower of strength. He had years of local knowledge and used it to track down likely recruits who might not have seen the large notice on display outside the factory inviting them to apply within. The winkling out of candidates had become a point of honour for him, even, Edward thought, a personal crusade. He was indefatigable. His long, rawboned features wore a permanent look of brooding determination, and his eyes smouldered with something akin to suppressed rage. At times he made Edward think of an old-style religious fanatic – a John Knox or a Savonarola – and he could imagine that, given an inch of leeway, Floyd would happily have burned the striking women at the stake as heretics. His restless, pig-headed zeal was useful under the circumstances, and effective, but it struck Edward as unbalanced, and he experienced renewed misgivings about his unholy alliance with the man.

The appalling Mrs Durrant imported a pair of nieces from the Berkshire countryside to fill two of the vacancies. They, at least, were experienced dressmakers – many of the new women they'd engaged had only the most basic skills. She introduced her youthful relatives to Edward with a complacent look of ownership on her sleepy, malevolent features. The young women were surprisingly presentable – country girls with nice manners and fresh faces. Edward decided to charm them, and did so, teasing them in a flirtatious but fatherly fashion. Soft-soaping the peasants, as Mildred termed it scathingly. They responded with blushing smiles and Edward warmed to them. Some young women were surly and complicated nowadays.

Throughout the strike the factory had been kept swept and cleaned by a child of fourteen or so.

'Dot's a good girl,' Floyd assured him with monotonous regularity, though Edward suspected that she was half-witted. To him she was a shadowy wraith, haunting the corridors, always with a broom in her hand, slack-lipped and vacant-faced.

One day he'd seen her out in the yard sitting on a bench, taking a breather. Edward noticed with surprise that she was smoking one of the thin, black, malodorous cigars that Floyd was addicted to. As she drew in the acrid smoke, there was an expression almost of ecstasy on her bloated features. He was fascinated. The girl seemed barely human. She made him think of some kind of organism feverishly absorbing the substance it needs to sustain life.

Within four days they'd managed to hire a total of thirty-one women. It meant that the factory would still be operating far below its full capacity, but perhaps the threat would be enough to ruffle the feathers of his obstinate employees.

Edward felt energetic and pleased with himself. It occurred to him that ever since initiating this new plan to foil the strikers he'd ceased his unhealthy brooding about Daisy Harkness. He wondered whether this might not be a good time to approach her – while his mood was still bullish.

In fact an unofficial meeting might turn out to be just

the thing, offering him an opportunity to present himself in a more sympathetic light. He could emphasize to her his reluctance to use scab-labour and sound her out as to whether the women were weakening. And if some kind of personal relationship should emerge from their talks . . .

Floyd had stressed several times that Daisy was the most reasonable and intelligent of the original deputation, so he had every reason to try to make contact.

There was no chance of a clandestine visit. Aquitaine Street was lined with nosey, barge-arsed old bags, with nothing better to do than stand on their doorsteps gawping at all-comers and whispering to their hatchet-faced neighbours. They got Edward's goat. He glared contemptuously at a couple of them, hoping to shame them out of their brazen curiosity, but they simply snickered and left him feeling a bloody fool. After that he pretended to ignore them.

Floyd had told him where Daisy lived and that she had rooms on the first floor. There was a brother, he gathered, who worked at Annakin's the furniture-makers. But at two o'clock on a Tuesday afternoon Edward assumed that he'd be out.

The street door stood open in the mild weather, so Edward walked straight up the stairs and knocked.

It was Daisy who answered the door. She looked bewildered at first, as though she couldn't place him, then her eyes widened in recognition.

Seeing her again required a readjustment on Edward's part. His mental image hadn't done her justice, confused as it was with his memories of Christiane and his sister's picture of the woman's face in the sky. Now he had her before him in the flesh, with her loosely-waved fair hair, smooth-sensual mouth, fine skin and shadowed eyes. His eyesight seemed keener suddenly and his brain mimed a sharp, reverential intake of breath. Daisy's expression was watchful, without a trace of the coquettishness that might have trivialized her beauty. She

118

looked at him with severe, questioning grey eyes, saying nothing.

'I wonder if I could have a word with you, Mrs Harkness?' The directness of her gaze made him feel insincere and somehow shifty.

She made no move to motion him inside, speak or smile.

Uncomfortably Edward asked, 'May I come in?'

'Yes.' Daisy's reply was simply factual, her tone unwelcoming. But she moved aside to let him pass.

He entered a domestic world, its unpretentious plainness dictated by poverty, and he was thrown off-balance by a powerful feeling of nostalgia. It was inexplicable. He'd never lived like this. There'd always been servants around him, and space. Was it the memory of his close, short-lived nursery life with Christiane that made him feel as if he'd been here before? The sun shone into the room through a screen of plants and he recalled Christiane trimming dead leaves and flower-heads from her geraniums, getting Blanche and himself to grow acorns and apple-pips in pots.

Edward felt that his presence ruffled a calm that had existed before he came. Two children had been playing on the floor. Now they were round-eyed with his sudden appearance. One was a blond, beautiful boy, the other a sturdy little girl who didn't look like Daisy at all.

'Go and sit with Grandma for a little while in the other room,' Daisy told them. The children gathered up the rag-dolls and stuffed animals they'd been playing with, colourful, characterful creatures, he noticed – Daisy's creations perhaps. They left the room and he heard their voices next door, telling someone about his arrival.

The last time Edward had seen Daisy she'd worn a hat and a dark coat and skirt. Her hair had been formally arranged. Today she was in a faded cotton frock – the kind he thought of as a servant's dress – and over it there

119

was a large apron. Her sleeves were rolled, exposing most of her arms, and her hair hung down her back, caught simply with a piece of wool in the nape of her neck. He was intrigued and aroused by the intimacy of this private face. It looked as if she'd been doing some hand-sewing. Now she cleared away cloth and thread into an open cardboard box.

Edward explained to Daisy, with a flattering air of confidentiality, that he was frankly unhappy about using scab-labour. The sooner some alternative could be worked out the better he'd like it. In a sense he was sincere in what he was saying. On another level he saw himself as manipulating Daisy. He still believed – in spite of Mildred's growing crustiness and sarcasm – that women were gullible creatures, easily amused and easily led. He expected Daisy to nod respectfully at his words. He assumed that she'd like him better for his scruples.

So he was a little thrown when her grey eyes remained sceptical as she faced him across the table. She was too courteous to be openly cynical. But her too-innocent smile seemed to mock him subtly and signal that she thought him a bit of a humbug.

He renewed his efforts, still confident of convincing her. He liked Daisy. He liked this room. He felt expansive. The more he spoke, the more he believed in what he said. But, with mounting surprise, he noticed that Daisy's scepticism was becoming more overt.

'I don't see,' she declared suddenly, during a lull in his monologue, 'why you're doing this if you hate it so much.' She sounded like the boy in the *Emperor's New Clothes*, voicing his honest bewilderment.

Edward was stopped in his tracks. He fell back on a cliché that most people found unanswerable. 'Business is business,' he said.

'Oh.' The ghost of an inward smile.

She sat quiet. Her slim, mutinous figure was achingly desirable. Her serenity exposed him as a charlatan. Edward found himself at a loss and felt ridiculous. Passively Daisy had taken charge of the situation. He'd exposed himself with his lame excuses and explanations, with his sentimental pleasure in this woman's domesticity. He was mortified. By rights Daisy should have been gratified and overwhelmed by his favour. Edward had a clear idea of how women should behave in relation to himself, and it ruffled him if they tried to play the game differently. And to be slighted by one of his own workers was doubly galling.

He could feel defensive anger rising and knew his cheeks were burning. With an effort he controlled himself. If he lost his temper he'd look even more foolish. Deliberately he transformed his anger into cold disdain and shrugged with an insulting air of indifference.

'It doesn't matter anyway, in the long run, what I do or what you think. You'll lose this dispute . . . The only question is when . . .' The chilly antagonism made him feel more in command, but it distanced him from Daisy. He'd wanted to get closer.

'Mrs Reeves has thrown in the sponge, I see,' he added with a small, hateful smile.

'Only because she's been beaten black and blue.' Now her tone was one of frank dislike. 'What's that supposed to prove?'

Edward held up a pacifying hand. 'You're right. In itself it proves nothing. Only . . .' He turned on her the full force of a stern and meaningful look. He'd recovered himself quite remarkably. '. . . To be frank, I think you've been led astray by this . . . Women Workers' League.' Edward spoke the words disparagingly, as if it were beneath him to recall the Association's proper title. He paused, then continued in judicious, measured tones. 'People like that have their own motives. They're agitators. It's not *your*

121

interests that they've got at heart. To them it's a matter of supreme indifference if their manoeuvring drives you into Queer Street . . .'

'You're wrong!' She was indignant. 'Miss MacInnes helps us with money. She worries about leading us into . . . Anyway, we walked out before she ever appeared on the scene . . .' Brusquely Daisy got to her feet. 'Excuse me, Mr Ballard, but I don't know why you came here and I don't think there's any point in us talking any more . . .' With an automatic gesture she reached into the open box of sewing, as if she'd wasted enough time and now planned to carry on with her work.

What she took out was a largish handkerchief. He caught sight of a bold and arresting design of elongated lilies, worked in shades of scarlet, mauve and black, with dark green leaves and tendrils undulating round them, sinuous as jungle vines.

Edward was distracted by their strangeness. Without thinking, he held out his hand. 'May I see?'

He spread out the handkerchief on the table in front of him. The design seemed to him immensely strong and original. He was oddly disturbed by it. He would have expected bluebells and daisies. Simple shapes and light, bright colours. He was startled to think that this woman's imagination held these exotic, almost erotic blooms.

'They're wonderful.' He smiled at her with spontaneous surprise and pleasure.

At the same time it dawned on him that everything about her – looks, style and, within the limits of her poverty, the way she arranged her lodgings – all pointed to a strong and confident artistic sense. She's got taste, I'll give her that, Floyd had confided perfunctorily. But this went further.

His interest in her was primarily sexual, but also nostalgic, harking back to some almost forgotten golden age of his boyhood, before he'd adopted the stiff, protective carapace society imposed on its men. Now his obsession took on a sudden, fresh dimension.

'I sold some to Mercedes – to Miss MacInnes – the other day. From the Association.' Some part of Edward's mind reacted to the name, but he was still absorbed in contemplation of Daisy's handiwork. He examined other specimens. They seemed to him just as remarkable.

'You sell these to the West End shops, do you?'

'Yes.' She pulled a face. 'And a fine profit *they* make.'

On an impulse Edward claimed, 'I think I could get you a fair price for them. I've got contacts . . .' An inspiration had occurred to him. He turned on the charm. 'Look, we've been a little short with one another. I regret it – it wasn't necessary.' Edward had no idea of what he could do with the handkerchiefs, but he'd sort something out. If Daisy were willing, it would be the perfect excuse for seeing her again.

He pressed on. 'Do you think you could meet me on Thursday? Three o'clock? Not here – it's too out of the way. Let's say Oxford Circus?' Edward prayed that his decisiveness would carry her along, leaving her no time for doubt. He lifted his hands in a gesture that swept away any suspicions her mind might be forming. His smile appealed to her, person to person. 'I know this is a bit sudden, not to say unorthodox. But, after all, this factory dispute's nothing personal. I think I know someone who might be interested. I'd simply want to put you in touch . . . Please say yes!'

She was dubious, but didn't resist the tide of his persuasion. 'I suppose so.'

14

It was six forty-five in the morning. For late May it was chill. Above Ballard's factory the sky spread, whitish-grey and empty. But there was a fair crowd outside the gates, Mercedes thought. Forty at the very least. The women stood and talked among themselves, subdued and seeming absorbed in their chat. But an almost tangible sense of expectancy hovered in the air, poised like a waiting bird of prey.

To the left of the gates someone had lit a brazier. The vitality of its flaring orange flames emphasized the cheerless look of the street, the drabness of the picketing women. In a crowd, like this, their poverty was pronounced. When you met them separately it never seemed quite as bad.

There were their boots, always clumsy and dilapidated, salvaged from second-hand stalls and generally shared with some other member of the family, their clothes threadbare and much-worn. Some of the younger women had a freshness about them, an optimism, a shine in their eyes, aspirations to fashion within the narrow limits of their resources. But from the mid-twenties on, the signs of age and ill-health came thick and fast – poor teeth, a parchment pallor, a stooped, hollow-chested set to the body, hair as dry and dull as rope. Along with these symptoms came an air of tough disillusionment. Either that or a look of hopelessness. Mercedes pictured her own mother, shapely and well-dressed, still with the smile of a girl, a child's delighted sense of fun, though she was older than any of the women here.

At this hour even Annie's bravado had a bedraggled

quality, like that of a peacock in a zoo. Her face looked slack and lardy, but she greeted Mercedes with a ruffianly grin. 'Bet *you* don't see this time of day very often, do you, girl?' The dig was followed by a burst of strident laughter from her companions.

Mercedes shrugged indifferently. 'I'm a pretty early riser.' She was learning to show no emotion at Annie's jibes, but she was hurt. Yesterday ten or twelve of them had spent the afternoon closeted in the church hall, thrashing out the details of today's demonstration. Mercedes had felt accepted, useful, part of a team. But today, once again, Annie was treating her as an outsider, some idle, privileged sightseer.

Then, over Annie's shoulder she caught sight of something that took her mind off these contradictions. She nodded covertly. 'Look what we've got here.'

Two policemen had appeared on the scene. Even to Mercedes they looked young, hardly more than boys. And they obviously thought the protesting women a huge joke. Their taut, youthful faces were split into mocking grins.

Annie turned to see. 'Oh Gawd,' she said satirically, 'it's the boys in blue.'

As a child Mercedes had been brought up to look upon the police as her friends, and most of the families in the MacInnes's social circle still held staunchly to the faith. Mercedes had been a suffragette, so her belief in the dogma had taken a hefty knock. All the same, she'd been unprepared for the sustained and cynical hostility displayed by all the Bermondsey women she'd encountered towards the guardians of law and order.

'. . . I bleedin' nearly fainted when 'e pulled his truncheon out . . .' A woman called Queenie began to sing some bawdy music-hall song. She was about thirty, with a gypsy look about her, black hair tightly braided and a hard, sultry expression. The two policemen showed signs of embarrassment, but Annie shushed her.

'Shut your face, Queenie,' she ordered amiably. 'No point in getting their backs up.'

Queenie broke off at once. It seemed that Annie always got her way.

They were ready. Mercedes stole a moment to savour her glow of pride in the scene, a leap of exhilaration at her own part in it. It was socialism in action, the kind of involvement she'd dreamed of. There was a feeling almost of disbelief that she was here organizing and participating in a demonstration of working women. The sense of unreality was heightened by the fact that this had to be a secret side of her life. She'd justified her early departure to her parents by claiming that she was accompanying Hannah to some prosaic court case in Brighton as her secretary, sitting in and taking notes.

Recently there'd been times when she was afraid that the whole strike was on the point of collapsing. Rents were going unpaid and children were frankly starving. The handout from the Association hadn't gone very far and Mercedes was making desperate efforts to raise more funds. But they'd gone this far and it would be just awful simply to give in. Ballard's decision to hire blackleg workers had outraged the women and re-galvanized them. Kate Reeves' defection had also been a powerful spur. Her hangdog look and discoloured, shameful, battered features acted as a grisly deterrent, like the head of a traitor displayed above the city gates. She was seen as a victim and pitied, but also, however unfairly, despised.

Mercedes surveyed the scene in front of her through bedazzled eyes. Privately she saw in it a bleak, heroic beauty like some romantic, revolutionary painting, with the fierce red and orange glow of the brazier and the uncompromising but somehow picturesque poverty of the women, the banner hoisted above the factory gates. TURN BACK, it proclaimed. YOU ARE BETRAYING YOUR FELLOW-WORKERS. The wording was Mercedes' own.

The figures of two men rounded the corner.

'It's Floyd.' Pale and slight in a dark frock, Daisy was the first to spot him. Perversely, her sleep-drugged eyes and dawn pallor had the effect of underlining her beauty. She nudged Edie Black who stood next to her.

'Here he comes, the bugger.' Edie broadcast the news in a searing stage-whisper.

'Don't say nothing,' Annie urged the women. 'Just stare at him.' It was the strategy they'd agreed on yesterday in the church hall. Some of them had boasted about the insults they'd hurl when the manager walked past. Mercedes had argued that for now their demonstrations must be kept dignified. It would be foolish to put themselves in the wrong. Rather to her surprise Annie had seconded this opinion. Though they'd agreed to try to talk to some of the blackleg women – but calmly.

All eyes were on Floyd as he approached them down the road.

'Who's the bloke with him?' Queenie asked the company at large.

Annie shrugged. 'Never seen him before.'

After that no one said anything. All attention was focused on Floyd and his companion as they came closer and closer. As always, Floyd's walk was stiff and upright, but Mercedes thought she saw something constrained and self-conscious about it. It was the only sign he gave that acknowledged the women's presence. She remembered Daisy had told her that he was an old soldier. He'd served in the Boer War and his ideas on discipline had barely changed since that time.

The man with him was younger. He made her think of a bulldog with his blunt, pugnacious features and squat, powerful body. His hair was light, frizzy and close-cut, his colour high. He wore a collarless shirt and a waistcoat and, unlike Floyd, he appeared to relish the attention he was attracting.

The hush that greeted the two men had a life of its own, deep, coiled and watchful. Floyd drew nearer. He passed close to Mercedes between the ranks of silent women, walking towards the factory gates. His gaze, focused straight ahead, took in the provocative banner.

Mercedes saw his eyes and a shock passed through her. They smouldered. A baleful, personal fury was visible in them, though deliberately damped for now, as if a layer of soot had been laid across glowing, naked coals. She experienced a frisson of fear. He wasn't someone to anger lightly. Mercedes saw him as a circus lion, outwardly docile, but awaiting his chance to kill.

They watched as he unlocked the factory gates with one of a large bunch of keys that hung from his belt. In the cool morning air, Floyd's face was crimson and sweating. The younger man opened each of the pair of iron gates, propping them ajar, then the two of them passed through and disappeared inside the building.

All attention had been riveted on the two men so that the ponderous approach of the massive forewoman, Mrs Durrant, and her two nieces had gone unnoticed. The two young country-women appeared terrified by the crowd of pickets. Mercedes thought what a difference there was between them and the watching factory-hands. They seemed to have a freshness and a gentleness that their town-bred counterparts lacked. One of them clung to her aunt's arm as she passed between the ranks of Ballard's employees.

'Silly cow, she's scared shitless,' Queenie murmured. Her hard gypsy looks contrasted strikingly with the soft prettiness of the country-girls.

'Look at her.' Annie turned her attention to Doll Durrant. 'Like a bloody battleship on wheels.' But, mindful of keeping the peace, she made the remark sotto-voce. The forewoman lumbered past, sleepy-eyed and seemingly oblivious, chin tucked well in, so that the roll of flesh that framed her lower face swelled, resembling a pale, bloated sausage.

Without stopping to think, Mercedes called to them: 'Can't you see what you're doing? You're helping the management to exploit working-women. Women just like you. You're making it easy for them.' In the dull morning her voice sounded thin, bleating. But she knew beyond doubt that her words were wholly urgent and vital. 'Think about it. Think! *You* might be in this position some day. What would *you* feel about people who tried to cut away the ground from under your feet?'

Silence followed her outburst. Mercedes felt conspicuous and somehow stupid. Her heart beat furiously against her rib-cage. But the young country-girl hanging on her aunt's arm turned and gave her a stricken look, her eyes docile and vulnerable.

'That's made her think, Mercedes,' Annie muttered, warming Mercedes with her approval.

Mrs Durrant's measured stride never faltered. She stared straight ahead, drawing her niece firmly through the factory gates. The other young woman was left a few paces behind. She looked about her like a startled animal and took a few hasty, skittering steps to catch up, not wanting to be left to the rough mercies of the pickets. The girl's panic was comical and spontaneous laughter bubbled up from among the crowd of women.

Other scab-workers were beginning to appear. Generally they arrived in groups, as if anticipating the possibility of trouble from the strikers. They approached warily down the road. This time little difference was discernible between the substitute workers and those they were replacing. But on second thoughts, Mercedes reflected, that wasn't quite true. If anything she had an idea that the blacklegs looked dowdier, more down-trodden, less intelligent, though perhaps that was a trick of her imagination.

She noticed the two young policemen again, standing by, with their hands behind their backs and expectant smirks on their faces. The road to the factory was lined with tenement buildings. Many of the occupants had come to stand on their front doorsteps, lured by the prospect of some kind of scene. Mercedes saw a man of thirty or so, an outdoor worker – he was tanned and sturdy for a slum-dweller – watching with his arms crossed, wearing the same kind of smile as the policemen. His wife stood just behind him, hair loose and uncombed, mouth half-open, with a look of passive enjoyment, as if she were watching a play or a cinematograph show.

'Feel good, do you?' A woman called Rose Gretton quizzed a small knot of scabs as they passed.

'How would *you* like it?' Edie demanded. But she kept her tone moderate and conversational, as they'd agreed.

One of the scabs, a gaunt young woman with a bony face and a severe hair-style turned and shrugged. 'It's just life, isn't it?'

Her careless, joyless fatalism sent an abrupt wave of indignation through Mercedes. She flushed and stepped forward. 'It doesn't *have* to be like that. There's such a thing as . . . helping . . . helping one another . . . comradeship . . .'

Their eyes met and locked. At close quarters Mercedes noted scaly patches on the girl's face, the remnant of some kind of skin disease, and a septic-looking blister at one corner of her mouth. The young woman's stare took in the solid quality of Mercedes' blouse and skirt, the newness of her straw boater, the smoothness of her complexion. Her look was eloquent. She smiled with a cool derision that clearly demanded, what's all this got to do with you, what would you know about it? Mercedes held her gaze, determined not to back down. She wasn't one of them, but that didn't mean her opinion was worthless. The thin young woman tossed her head and walked on, with an abrupt, yelping laugh.

Rose Gretton hissed, 'Here comes Kate.'

'Oh Lord,' Daisy said, awed. 'Look at her.'

Kate was on her own. She walked in a dazed, lingering fashion that reminded Mercedes of a man she'd once seen as a child, meandering down the main street of the Pimletts' small village, the first person she'd known to be a drunkard. Kate wasn't drunk – her gait expressed a hideous, shamed awareness of being on show, the focus of everyone's rapt attention. Her eyes were downcast, her head bare. She'd allowed the forward locks of her hair to hang down across her face in a useless attempt to camouflage the signs of her husband's violence.

Both eyes were massively swollen and so was her mouth. The lower lip was split in two places, now marked by prominent, scaly, purple scabs. Dried blood caked her nostrils as though the bleeding from her nose had still not altogether stopped. Kate's face was one vast, puffy bruise, a ghastly grey-purple, turning now to dull, sulphurous yellow. There was silence as she passed. No one called out to her. The woman's sense of agonized humiliation seemed to throb and quiver in the air about her.

At the sight of her Mercedes' skin crawled with horrified empathy and her insides lurched with a convulsive shudder, forcing her to catch her breath sharply.

Annie turned to her with eyes that held a corrective cynicism. 'She's never stood up to that husband of hers. Not for one minute. And now look what she's got.' For a second Mercedes looked at the older woman wonderingly, and it dawned on her that life had taught Annie that weakness was something to be condemned and routed out – never pitied.

Edie, too, gazed at her battered co-worker, seemingly unmoved, as if she'd seen such sights many times before.

'Don't suppose you get much of that sort of thing up

your way.' Queenie addressed Mercedes with a provoking grin, cocking her head casually in Kate's direction.

'Decent people don't get much of it down *our* way,' Daisy retorted tartly.

Mercedes thought that Queenie seemed to take a perverse pride in this repellent aspect of neighbourhood life. As if it demonstrated the Bermondsey women's superior guts and powers of endurance. She was positioned near the gate and Kate passed close by her. Their eyes met momentarily. Mercedes proffered a tentative smile, but Kate flinched and turned away, slinking towards the doors of the building.

A largish group of scabs – there were ten or twelve of them – had arrived in Kate's wake. Their numbers lent them courage and they milled around the factory entrance, ignoring the pickets, defiantly good-humoured. The strikers began to talk to them, trying to persuade them to return home. The majority of the scabs were well-known to the picketing women, some were even neighbours, so their exchanges were direct and personal. But Mercedes was gratified to see that Ballard's employees succeeded in sticking to the moderate tone they'd agreed.

At this point a portly photographer in a·black bowler arrived from the offices of the *South London Advertiser*. Mercedes made herself known to him as the person who'd telephoned the paper to give notice of the demonstration.

He set up his equipment deftly to the right of the gates. The man's presence lent an official stamp to the proceedings, and people began to play their roles with increased conviction. Mercedes was glad he'd come. The whiff of publicity was likely to give a fillip to their determination and make them all feel that they counted in the outside world.

Playing up to the photographer, a large, loud-mouthed woman, one of the scabs, took up a battling posture. Grey-haired and full-bosomed in a greasy-looking black dress and shawl, she stood head and shoulders above her companions. She challenged the pickets in a hoarse, pugnacious voice, enjoying herself.

'Who's going to stop me, eh?' she cackled throatily, brandishing fists like a prize-fighter's. 'Come on, I'll take on any five of you!' Her fellow-scabs laughed in a rowdy, admiring fashion.

'Fancy yourself, don't you, Beth?' Annie shouted back with amiable scorn, exhilarated by the woman's provocation. 'Queensberry rules, don't you know.' Pronouncing the words like a music-hall toff. It was the pickets' turn to laugh.

Sotto-voce, Annie added, 'That bleedin' Beth Coster. I'd strangle the bumptious old bitch for two pins.' Catching sight of Mercedes' look of consternation, she grinned. 'But I won't, mate, don't worry.'

The mutual heckling was noisy, but easy-going and good-natured. Then suddenly a commotion broke out among the blacklegs. They filled the gateway, so it was impossible to see what had caused it.

'Get inside!' The order came, abrupt and flat, in Leonard Floyd's voice.

In a trice the scabs had scattered, streaming towards the factory door and the pickets found themselves face to face with Floyd and his young henchman, each of them holding one of the large, heavy-duty hoses kept for sluicing down the yard and in case of fire.

'All right! Go ahead!'

Floyd yelled over his shoulder to someone out of sight and in an instant Mercedes found herself deluged, at point-blank range, by a forceful jet of freezing water. Almost immediately her face, hair and clothes were saturated and her hat lay sodden on the ground. She'd not even had time to protect herself with her arms. Then the jet moved on to someone else. In the dream-like confusion she encountered Floyd's flushed features twisted in a gloating leer, his

133

eyes shining with heated, intimate excitement. In contrast the younger man's face appeared blank and emotionless.

Too late the pickets understood what was happening. All those in the front rank were drenched, gasping, spluttering, too dazed to take evasive action. Queenie and a woman called Belle had been knocked to the ground by the thrust of the water. Another striker, forced into them by the press of retreating bodies, lost her footing and sprawled on top of them. The brazier was doused. It hissed and sizzled. Still the water came, directed higher now, to reach the women behind.

The photographer hadn't escaped. In the mêlée he'd lost his hat and Mercedes caught a glimpse of him smoothing dripping locks back off his forehead, tubby and outraged. Miraculously his camera was still upright and he set about recording the scene with angry vigour.

Annie snarled like an animal at bay. Her skirt was sodden, her top-knot askew, and black, slick rats' tails of hair clung, dripping, to her forehead and cheeks. She yelled at Floyd, 'You fucking bastard!' Her voice held an awesome concentration of loathing and contempt.

'You watch your mouth, Annie,' the manager sneered. Then, deliberately and still with the evil, dancing exultation in his eyes, he redirected the hose full at her.

'This is monstrous! It's criminal!' Mercedes heard herself scream before the jet was once again transferred to her. The cold water splattered hard against her face, painful, choking, humiliating, before she had time to turn away. She was helpless in the teeth of the relentless torrent. But as soon as it moved on she began to harangue Leonard Floyd again with the full force of her lungs.

'This was a peaceful demonstration! We weren't trespassing, we didn't obstruct anyone and we kept our tempers! This attack is completely unwarranted! It's vile, unspeakable, bullying!' Her own voice resounded in her ears, no longer thin, but full-blooded and furious. It seemed to her hugely important to point out the facts of the situation. She was barely conscious of what was going on around her, or of the figure she cut, her drenched clothes clinging to her, head thrown back, arms raised, hair half-down and plastered across one shoulder of her blouse, her whole body shaking with rage.

Shortly afterwards she was aware of Floyd shouting, 'That's enough!' and the water was shut off. He and his stocky, unknown sidekick closed the gates silently, their faces rigid, responding to the jeers and insults of the outraged women.

The two men retreated across the yard and disappeared inside the factory. Gradually the hubbub died away and the women were left outside the gates like drowned rats, cold and shivering, invaded by a dull sense of anti-climax. A further show of anger seemed pointless.

They shook out their sodden skirts, smoothed back their hair, emptied their boots and contemplated the ignominious walk back home through the early-morning streets bustling with workers.

Rose Gretton picked up the man's cap she always wore, wrung the water out of it and jammed it back on her head. Daisy wrapped her arms around her body, looking white and frozen. 'He won't get away with it,' she said flatly. No one contradicted her. The bald, emotionless words seemed a statement of intent, reflecting the resolve of them all.

As the women began to drift away, Mercedes caught sight of the two policemen. They'd retreated to a discreet distance and now formed part of a band of onlookers, wearing the same expression of idle curiosity as the rest. Faced with the brazen indifference of the two young men, their casual dereliction of duty, a wave of almost murderous anger rekindled inside her.

'Proud of yourselves, are you?' She bore down on them. 'Doing a superb job, aren't you, of protecting the public!'

They gazed at her, insolently unruffled, their eyes taking in her bedraggled figure with amused contempt.

An older man, with greying side-whiskers, who seemed to be a friend of theirs, stepped forward with a slow, offensive grin. 'Here, Bob,' he said to the taller of the policemen, 'I reckon she's one of them suffragettes.'

Mercedes ignored him, addressing the two guardians of law and order with a well-bred smile, consciously relishing the middle-class precision of her speech. 'You'll find out who I am soon enough. You'll be hearing more from me, I promise you.'

The threat was merest bluff, but she hoped it would give the two young policemen a sleepless night or two.

15

In the *South London Advertiser* the following day a smudgy but dramatic photograph of Annie Tyrell – the so-called Holy Terror – appeared. Her head was thrown back, her mouth a gaping, agonized black O, her arms raised in a gesture of supplication or aggression – it was difficult to tell which. Meanwhile a high-powered jet of water had splattered her full in the face.

The headline ran COWARDLY ATTACK ON DEFENCELESS WOMEN and underneath was an eye-witness account of the incident, related by the *Advertiser*'s staff photographer, a Mr Nathaniel Hardy. If the strike committee had composed the story themselves, they couldn't have told it better than the tubby photographer. Repeatedly he stressed the peaceful nature of the demonstration, the moderate and lady-like behaviour of the pickets, the total absence of a warning in advance of the hose-pipe onslaught.

Mr Hardy described Leonard Floyd as 'resembling a demon from hell' as he played his hose on the stunned and gasping pickets. 'He directed the powerful water-jet vindictively and selectively' the photographer claimed, and mentioned Mrs Annie Tyrell and Miss Mercedes MacInnes as particular victims of Mr Floyd's brutality. At the same time the manager's attack was frenzied and random, extending to innocent passers-by who had no part in the picketing activities. 'I myself was unceremoniously saturated and had a new and expensive bowler ruined. I shall be seeking reparation.'

The photographer identified the manager's sidekick as Ernest Powell, an up-and-coming young prize-fighter from

Bow. 'One cannot but question Mr Floyd's motives,' he mused, 'in enlisting the services of such a man.'

The whole episode was dubbed a scandal and Mr Hardy mentioned the presence of two young officers of the law, who made no attempt whatsoever to protect the shamefully beleaguered working-women.

The account in the *Advertiser*'s rival newspaper, the *Southwark Enquirer*, was in truly staggering contrast. It could have been relating some quite separate happening.

Under the heading UGLY INCIDENT HEADED OFF, the picketing 'females' were described as unruly, rowdy, aggressive and threatening. Accordingly, the loyal employees of Mr Edward Ballard were 'forced' to resort to protective tactics in order to prevent an already ugly situation from deteriorating still further. The quick thinking of Mr Leonard Floyd had saved the factory premises from damage and destruction at the hands of a mob of female strikers running out of control.

'Old Floyd must've hot-footed it down to their offices the moment he dried his hands,' Annie laughed ruefully, as she and Mercedes, Daisy and Queenie, scanned the papers over tea and bread pudding in the Picardy Café which had become the unofficial headquarters of the strike committee.

'Not to worry, though.' Annie grinned with an expression of conspiratorial cunning. 'I've thought of another way we can scupper the bugger.'

That afternoon Daisy had reason to be glad she was something of a loner. It meant she could leave the district without having to lie to anyone. None of the neighbours presumed to question her, Andrew was at work, and Mamma was used to minding the children and never troubled to ask where she was going. Daisy offered a probable time for her return, but she wasn't sure Mamma took it in or cared one way or another. Daisy had the impression that her mother simply waited without curiosity until she reappeared. But she showed Alex and Janie where the hands would be on the brass clock.

Daisy had serious doubts about meeting Edward Ballard. If anyone found out it would look suspicious and strange. The thought bothered her a great deal. Still, when it came down to it, she told herself forcibly, her seeing Edward Ballard could have nothing in the world to do with the outcome of the strike. But it might help her family, and she owed them that.

A whispering voice inside her head kept asking whether Mr Ballard had some ungentlemanly motive for wanting to meet her. What earthly reason had he, after all, for trying to help her? But she pushed these fears to the back of her mind as well. She was a grown woman. If he tried to take liberties she could look after herself. If she was honest, there was a kind of fascination in meeting people who had more on their minds than where the next meal was coming from. Like Mercedes. Daisy had to admit she enjoyed a chat with her more than with any of the women down Aquitaine Street, even though she'd been cushioned all her life from the kind of worries Daisy had.

She set off early and walked to Oxford Circus. It meant she saved the fare, though it was hard on shoe-leather. Daisy had promised herself that, if this meeting yielded any cash in hand, she would ride at least a part of the way home.

Mr Ballard was already waiting when she arrived at Oxford Circus, feeling tired and sweaty. He was tall and she saw him from a distance, marvelling at how distinguished he looked, with his well-cut, new-looking clothes, polished shoes and air of total confidence.

She felt intimidated, but knew better than to show it. All her life she'd been good at seeming calm and composed even when her heart was beating wildly and her knees knocking together. Though it wasn't quite as easy with this wealthy-looking man, her employer. To help herself Daisy called up her feelings of dislike and contempt. However well-bred he appeared, this person paid his workers a pittance, and yesterday his man had turned a hose-pipe on women who were asking only for a living wage.

Daisy held her head high as she approached him. She cleared her throat and touched his arm. 'Mr Ballard?'

He turned, recognized her, and raised his Homburg. 'Mrs Harkness, how charming to see you,' he said, just as if they'd run into one another by accident.

Against her will Daisy was affected by his courtesy and style. Edward Ballard's face glowed with health. He wore a smile that was humorous and vaguely foxy. His yellow crest of hair ruffled a little in the wind. He smelled of bay rum and something spicy like snuff. And of port, as though he'd come here direct from a good lunch. Altogether a rich smell.

She could think of nothing conversational to say. It seemed unnatural to ask after his health as if the two of them were friends. She plunged straight in with the question that had filled her mind ever since the day before yesterday. 'Did you manage to see your friend about the handkerchiefs?'

He drew his head a little backward with a quizzical look as though he were startled by her bluntness. 'Straight to the point, eh?' But he grinned to show he wasn't offended. 'Quite right, too.'

A pause. Daisy was on tenterhooks.

'My friend has a high-class . . . draper's I suppose you'd call it. In South Kensington. I told him about your work. He was very interested . . . You've brought some samples?'

She nodded and patted a paper packet she was carrying under her arm. 'I've brought ten.'

'Splendid.' He nodded approvingly. 'On the strength of my enthusiasm he'll buy those outright for sevenpence

apiece – I'll give you the money before you go home . . .
If he likes them he'll want more at the same price – as
many as you can supply. Will that be agreeable?'

Daisy nodded, dazed and exultant. Her brain totted up
the cash she was to receive. Five shillings and tenpence.
A fortune the way things were at the moment. She'd been
getting threepence apiece for the handkerchiefs up to now.
Best keep quiet about that.

The stream of passers-by skirted them as they stood face
to face on the corner of Oxford and Regent Street. 'Look
here, Mrs Harkness,' Edward said. 'We've conducted our
business in record time and you've come a very long way
. . . May I offer you a cup of tea before you start home?
Then we can sort out the money at our leisure.'

Ten minutes later Daisy found herself sitting opposite
him in Schroeder's, a small but comfortable tea-room in
a back-street off Piccadilly Circus. It had rich, cyclamen-
coloured carpets, lamps made of a patchwork of coloured
glass, and a frieze of rather stiff nymphs in complicated
drapery. Like Mr Ballard, the other customers looked sure
of themselves and well turned-out. Daisy felt out of place,
but after her long walk it was a relief to take the weight
off her feet. And a drink wouldn't come amiss. She was
glad she'd put on the respectable coat and skirt she'd cut
down from a man's suit bought off an old-clothes stall in
Picardy Street.

Edward ordered tea and cakes from a red-haired young
waitress. Daisy thought the girl gave her a snooty look, but
it could have been her imagination.

When she'd gone Ballard leant across the table, steepling
his fingertips and smiling. 'You know, you're a very artistic
person.' The tone was warm and confidential.

'Thank you.' Her reply was cool. Flattery made her
suspicious and uncomfortable. She wanted him to know
he couldn't flannel her. Though his remark did no more
than put into words a feeling she sometimes had about

141

herself. That she saw things differently from most of the people she knew, and liked different things.

'We're lucky to have you at the factory.'

She let this comment pass. The hypocrisy of it was breathtaking, given the pitiful wages the man paid, the state of the strike. Ballard must have sensed her scepticism, because he changed the subject at once.

'Mr Floyd tells me your family's Polish,' he proffered.

Daisy nodded. 'That's right.'

'How long have you lived over here? You sound English . . . Though there's something in the way you say your words . . .' He looked at her curiously, head to one side.

She couldn't deny a feeling of . . . interest, that this powerful man had observed her to this extent.

'I was born here. But Mamma and Daddy always had an accent and it must have rubbed off on me.'

'Why did they leave Poland?'

She smiled and shrugged her shoulders. 'We never really knew. Daddy would never tell . . . He just used to hold up his hands and say "politics, politics" – make a joke of it. In the end we stopped asking.' Daisy considered for a moment. 'All I ever saw him do was work, work, work, to keep all of us. He never had time for politics here.'

Edward's eyelids drooped, with a flash of cynicism. 'Best kept separate . . . Work and politics, I mean.'

His words puzzled Daisy and she didn't reply at once, but by the time she'd decided to take him up on the remark, the tea-things arrived, distracting her from her purpose.

Everything was elegant and luxurious. The tea came in a silver-plated pot. The cups were made of fine white china, with a pattern of long, narrow trees and oddly-shaped leaves that fascinated her. A matching cake-stand held pastries, squares of moist fruit-cake and delicate almond macaroons. She experienced the wild temptation to sweep them all into her handkerchief and take them home for the children. You could do that in the Picardy Café, Daisy thought wryly, but it wouldn't go down so well here.

'Were you a big family?' Edward asked after the waitress had poured their tea and gone away.

She shook her head. 'Four children. I had two brothers older than me – they're in Manchester now – and one younger. We live with him and my mother, the children and I.'

'You're a widow.' It was a statement, not a question. 'I imagine you must find life quite a struggle.'

Daisy sipped her tea – she could think of no useful comment to make. It didn't seem to occur to Mr Ballard that there was a direct link between the struggle that was her life and his own tight-fistedness as an employer. He spoke as though some higher power had arranged their respective destinies and he had no say in the matter. Several sharp remarks sprang to mind, but she bit them back. No point in queering her pitch – the friend who'd bought her handkerchiefs – whoever he might be – was a lot more open-handed and could be useful in the future.

Edward pushed the cake-stand towards her as if his action might temporarily relieve her poverty. 'Do take some of these.' He gave a quirkish smile that made him seem likeable in spite of his blind complacency. 'They're paid for.'

She took a square of fruit-cake, a solid chunk of nourishment that would carry her back to Bermondsey and beyond. She had a sudden dizzying sense of the unreality of her presence here in this smart teashop with this worldly, wealthy man. Edward Ballard filled her field of vision. He was facing the window and the sunlight illuminated the wrinkles and sagging flesh below his eyes with harsh clarity, making her see him in a flash as older and more vulnerable.

They talked some more about her family. Ballard drew her out. His interest seemed genuine and he had a nice,

143

irreverent sense of humour. Daisy relaxed her guard a little. She confided her fears about Mamma. Ballard was sympathetic. His manner was kindly, pleasant and respectful, but Daisy didn't miss the gleam in his eye, the nakedness, showing that his thoughts were earthier than his conversation. It excited her a little. She wasn't offended. Since she'd been fourteen or fifteen most of the men she talked to had had that same look in their eyes.

After a time they exhausted the topic of family and a silence fell. Daisy took an almond macaroon and bit into it. The cakes really were delicious.

Edward began to speak again. 'Floyd showed me the *Southwark Enquirer* this morning,' he said. He looked at her across the damask tablecloth, half stern, half ruefully amused, as if he'd taken the decision to broach a slightly touchy subject. 'With the account of your co-workers' demonstration.'

Daisy had a mouthful of cake. She swallowed it hastily and with an effort. 'Lies!' she declared forcibly. Impossible to keep her mouth shut about this one, even if it did mean kissing goodbye to her unknown generous patron, Ballard's friend.

'I beg your pardon.'

'That report was a pack of lies from start to finish. It doesn't say a word about the small matter of Floyd drenching us with hoses. It says we were out to damage property. It's all the most . . . sickening . . . lies!'

'Drenching you?' Edward's bewilderment was unmistakably genuine.

'Didn't you know?' Her emphatic tones attracted the attention of their fellow tea-drinkers. Daisy noticed a fat middle-aged woman in a burgundy velvet coal-scuttle hat pause in the act of lifting a cream-cake to her mouth. She lowered her voice. 'Floyd and some prize-fighting bully he hired turned hoses on us. Cold water, great jets of it . . . no warning or nothing. And we weren't trespassing or causing a nuisance . . .' She leaned forward, narrowing her eyes. 'I don't suppose Floyd showed you the report in the *Advertiser*, did he? He soaked their photographer by mistake, so the things they said weren't quite so cosy.'

Ballard was frowning, perplexed and dismayed. Daisy could tell, without a shadow of a doubt, that he had no previous knowledge of the facts of yesterday's kerfuffle.

He was silent for a moment, looked at her with troubled sincerity. She experienced a ripple of exhilaration. Her words had hit home and no mistake. Finally he spoke. 'I can only apologize and assure you, Mrs Harkness, that I had no knowledge of this whatsoever. I'll be looking into it, I promise.'

Daisy said nothing, though she nodded to acknowledge his apology. It occurred to her that perhaps some good would come out of this secret, half-guilty meeting, not just for herself, but for the others, too. The thought comforted her, justified her.

She glanced at the handsome black-and-white inlaid clock on the wall. 'I ought to be going,' she told Ballard.

'Not without your earnings, remember,' Edward said. His reminder was quite unnecessary. The prospect of the cash had flickered at the back of her mind like a warming fire throughout their shared tea and conversation.

Edward felt in his pocket, counting out the coins by touch, transferring the cash to her hand with swift discretion. She was impressed by his deftness and dexterity.

He suggested that they meet again the following Monday. By then he'd have his friend's verdict on her samples. Daisy agreed.

'I'm certain he'll be impressed,' Edward added. 'So do keep working at your sewing in the meantime.'

There was an awkward pause. Daisy wondered whether she should get to her feet. But he hadn't paid for their tea. Ballard's eyes held a fixed, rather embarrassed expression.

'Look,' he said suddenly. 'Could we take tea again? I've so much enjoyed it. You know, you remind me enormously of someone I used to know. A German woman . . . she was charming . . . It was a long time ago . . .' Daisy was taken aback by his momentary loss of poise. Could it be her imagination or had he gone quite pink?

In spite of herself she was flattered by his surprising but increasingly obvious interest. She had to admit she'd enjoyed it, too. Sitting in this comfortable tea-room, talking about herself to someone who seemed to admire her, she had the feeling of being a million miles from the headaches of her ordinary life.

'Yes,' Daisy said. 'I'd like that.'

With a lordly gesture Edward summoned the red-haired waitress and paid. 'Would you happen to have a box to spare,' he asked her, 'that I could put the rest of the cakes in?' His confidence and flirtatious smile made the request sound endearing and perfectly natural. The waitress blushed and seemed intrigued by the novelty of his suggestion.

'I'm sure we can find something,' she said and whisked away, full of purpose, slim-waisted in her black skirt and lace apron.

Edward grinned conspiratorially at Daisy and she couldn't help grinning back. He'd quite recovered his composure.

The waitress returned carrying a stiff white carton with a paper frill round the outside. Deftly she transferred the cakes from the stand into the box, smiling at the amusing outrageousness of the idea.

'Thank you, my dear,' Edward said urbanely. 'You've been most sporting.' He stood up and bowed briefly over the young woman's hand. She laughed breathlessly, quite won over.

Halfway up Regent Street he offered the box to Daisy. 'I wish you'd accept these as a gift from me to your children.'

Daisy hesitated. She was tempted, but hated to be beholden. On the other hand she could picture the children's faces in her mind's eye. In the last weeks they'd eaten precious little but bread and marge. Tonight she planned to make a big stew for all of them with neck of lamb, carrots and potatoes. And the cakes would make the whole meal seem so . . . special.

She made the decision and looked up at Ballard. 'Thank you,' she said.

16

For the last month or so, since the strike began, Mercedes had had the impression that she was living in two separate worlds and she found it hard to decide which felt the most unreal.

This morning, a Friday, she'd visited Annie in her two cramped rooms in Picardy Street to talk about the new plan for undermining Leonard Floyd's team of scab-workers. The living-room – which doubled as bedroom for two of Annie's sons – was poky and dark with large patches of damp on the wallpaper. It still smelled rankly of sleeping bodies, though the beds had been straightened and the boys gone to their jobs. Annie's husband, Will, who had no work that day, was slumped at the table, unshaven, in his braces and shirtsleeves, drinking a cup of watery tea. Maggie, her daughter, had been kept off school to unpick some sugar-sacks Annie had got hold of. She planned to dye the material and make it up into children's shirts and breeches then try to sell them for a few pence on the market.

Annie greeted Mercedes with her piratical grin and a juicy bit of gossip. 'They say Sal O'Shea's in the pudding club.'

Mercedes knew Sally O'Shea to be one of Ballard's workers, though she'd taken no positive part in the strike, a young girl who'd been running around with another woman's man. Then Annie exhorted her husband to get up off his arse and make himself useful – call in at a baker's on the other side of London Bridge who sometimes had stale bread to give away.

The whole scene had appeared fascinating and exotic

to Mercedes. She found Annie's salty speech exhilarating, liberating, and she recognized, with a flash of guilt, that Annie's harsh reality was, to her, a picturesque dream. The Bermondsey women's poverty-stricken lives excited her like an addiction.

She remembered the bulging, self-important eyes of a schoolfriend who'd whispered to her one playtime about a book she'd found in her father's study that described respectable men who had the dark compulsion to visit low bordellos in shady parts of town. And, in her inner-most soul, Mercedes wondered whether she didn't share something of the same urge.

After spending a morning at Annie's it seemed equally unreal, come evening-time, to be sipping sherry in Hannah Spalding's elegant Bloomsbury flat, with Walter Pimlett and Hannah's urbane husband, James.

Hannah's drawing-room was a womb of comfort and good taste, suffused with the luminous amber glow of three exquisite Tiffany lamps. On the long settee Mercedes relaxed against yielding tapestry cushions with a design of medieval flowers in mellow, autumnal shades. Oriental rugs were strewn across the gleaming parquet, and gold velvet curtains shut off the outside world of poverty and squalor.

Hannah presided in a high-waisted dress of russet silk that echoed similar shades in her shining hair. The soft, golden light was immensely flattering to her, as she lounged decoratively in a curved ebony armchair, cradling the stem of her slim glass with stylish negli-gence.

Hannah's husband, James, was tall and dark. He had a thin, sharp-featured face that seemed set in a permanent expression of fastidious amusement. He was a journalist on *The Times* and diffused an air of being enormously well-informed – more so than he could discreetly reveal in casual conversation.

149

Walter had met the Spaldings before and was tremendously impressed and rather intimidated by them. But he kept up his end of the conversation gamely, while at the same time deferring suitably to James's superior knowledge.

This evening James was in a doom-laden mood, talking about war with Germany as a racing certainty within the next two years.

'But, darling, you've been saying that for at least the last *five*,' Hannah protested with a wide-eyed, ingenuous smile. Mercedes shared her scepticism. Ever since she could remember, her father and his friends had been making the same prediction, to the accompaniment of much judicious head-shaking, and it still hadn't happened.

But James was not to be side-tracked, and he continued to hold forth to Walter who, as a fellow-male, couldn't allow himself the luxury of Hannah's flippant, debunking tone.

Mercedes and Hannah drifted into a private conversation. Hannah showed her a copy of the *Woman's Dreadnought*, the newspaper of the East End working women's group led by Sylvia Pankhurst. The avowedly socialist group had separated off, earlier in the year, from the much larger WSPU movement run by her mother and sister, Emmeline and Christabel. Eagerly Mercedes flicked through the pages of the broadsheet. It was written by the women themselves, with indignation and passion, from their own personal experience. Mercedes was enchanted.

'I think it's a wonderful thing Miss Pankhurst's doing,' she enthused. Sylvia Pankhurst was a heroine of hers. Her opinion that the suffragette movement was too narrow in its aims and undervalued the contribution of its working-class members harked back to Mercedes' own feelings about the organization.

Hannah disagreed. She deeply regretted the split,

declaring that it pointed to a lack of discipline on Sylvia's part. 'She should be ready to submerge her personal notions for the greater good of the cause,' Hannah claimed. 'The only effect of this kind of individualism is to divide and weaken.' She pronounced the judgement in measured, modulated tones, head to one side. Her manner and slight smile seemed to take it for granted that Mercedes would now see the error of her ways.

Before Mercedes could decide whether to embark on a full-scale challenge, dinner was announced. As she got to her feet Mercedes reflected yet again, with surprise, that her former hero-worship of Hannah Spalding was spiralling into a set of emotions that were altogether more complex.

George and Florence MacInnes had gone to spend ten days with friends in Scotland. Until recently it had always been assumed that Mercedes would go with them on their jaunts away. But two years ago she'd protested that she hated being dragged along on their staid trips like some awkward, bulky appendage.

Her parents had been dismayed, but Mercedes refused to back down. And in the end, after deedy consultations with Mrs Carter, the MacInnes's motherly cook-housekeeper, they'd given in.

The periods she spent alone in the house were times of luxurious freedom for Mercedes. It wasn't that she kicked over the traces in any spectacular fashion. But the mere fact of not having to explain herself all the time, report where she was going, calculate when she'd be home, gave her a wonderful feeling of lightness and independence.

Quite quickly she and Mrs Carter had come to an unspoken agreement. Both had things they wanted to do and no desire to be tied down as to time. Mrs Carter had relatives all over London. One evening, by chance, they'd returned home at the same time and met in the

151

hallway. The housekeeper's breath had smelt of beer and Mercedes saw that Mrs Carter was relishing her freedom just as much as she was herself.

George and Florence gradually came to terms with the realization that their absence wasn't necessarily going to unleash a plague of fire, flood and pestilence. Mercedes suspected that they secretly enjoyed the peace of being alone together, the freedom to be sedate, middle-aged and dull without the reproachful presence and bored, restless eyes of their youngest daughter.

The Spaldings' dining-room was small and cosy, the table was spread with a damask cloth in the colour Mercedes' mother called old rose. The chinaware had an intriguing peacock design and the tulip-shaped goblets were made of a glass that was attractively mottled in a misty shade of green. In here the light was filtered through a mauve-pink shade that lent the room an atmosphere of warmth and intimacy.

Mercedes had to admit that the picturesque luxury was heartening to the soul. She was wearing her favourite modish green silk dress and the sherry seemed to glow in her veins, making her feel happy and expansive, blunting the prick of guilt she suffered at the thought that Annie and her family were probably, at this very moment, dining off stale bread and whatever meagre spread they'd found that was cheap enough to do five of them.

A pale, quiet young woman served lobster salad and poured a tart, chilled French wine. Mercedes was no gastronome but the combination was delicious.

The salad was followed by a saddle of mutton, caper sauce, and all the trimmings. Hannah encouraged Mercedes to talk about the strike. Her questions were shrewd and detailed. Though Hannah didn't say as much, Mercedes again had the impression that she was impressed by the factory-women's persistence, and by Mercedes' role.

Though, heaven knows, Mercedes herself was constantly tortured by a sense of her own clumsiness and inadequacy. But she supposed it was results that counted, and so far the dispute still held.

At the back of her mind the familiar nerve of anxiety throbbed, that one day – soon – Hannah might exercise her superior right, step forward, and take the running of the strike into her own slim and capable hands. If that happened Mercedes knew she wouldn't be able to bear it.

'What are you doing about raising funds?' Hannah asked.

As it happened, that very afternoon, Mercedes had visited an acquaintance of hers, a Priscilla Gordon, whom she'd known since her days in the WSPU. Priscilla was wealthy in her own right, and married to a modern, thrusting, affluent young businessman. She was an active suffragette who had been imprisoned and endured force-feeding. Mercedes respected her unemotional stubbornness and courage.

Priscilla had received her at her house on New Cavendish Street, in her smart, pared-down, beige and apple-green drawing-room. Her wide pale eyes had been thoughtful and steady as Mercedes stated her case and appealed for financial support for the striking women. She knew Priscilla gave money to a wide variety of unselfish causes.

But her friend had shaken her head with cool finality. She had hair like corn-silk, smooth and centrally-parted. 'I'm afraid I'm out of sympathy with socialism, my dear. In my opinion it's a recipe for dangerous chaos. I believe the working-classes deserve a better standard of living. But if this kind of disruptive action is rewarded . . .' She let the sentence drift, but showed her misgivings with an expressive tightening of the lips.

'Mind you, I can see her point,' Walter ventured eagerly and unwisely, but was shouted down by the other three.

'Lady Flowers is back from the Americas.' Casually Hannah referred to the Association's roving patron. 'I think we should go and see her. I'm sure she can be relied on for some backing.'

'Oh Amy'll cough up all right,' James agreed with a languid smile.

Privately Mercedes' reactions were confused at the thought of Hannah succeeding where she, so far, had failed. Another injection of money would be a godsend for the strikers of course. More than that – it was absolutely vital. But still the sneaking possessiveness re-asserted itself, however hard Mercedes tried to stifle it as immature and selfish. The truth was that something inside her protested at the vision of Hannah appearing on the scene like Lady Bountiful and putting Mercedes' own nose out of joint.

The self-effacing young maid reappeared and served portions of feather-light soufflé floating in a creamy sea of lemon sauce. Resolutely Mercedes pushed her unworthy thoughts to the back of her mind.

She hadn't yet given Hannah an account of Wednesday's demonstration. Impulsively Mercedes launched into a description of the picketing activities she and the other women had staged earlier in the week, conjuring up the comical panic of the young country girls, Mrs Durrant's nieces, the racy exchanges between strikers and scabs, the posturing of the unknown prize-fighter, the hoses, Leonard Floyd's demonic glee and the puffing indignation of the photographer. By now all four of them had consumed a fairly reckless amount of wine and, as Mercedes proceeded with the story, she became increasingly aware of its farcical qualities.

'Damnedest thing I ever heard,' James murmured incredulously.

Her tale was greeted with amazement, a rush of questions, and a sort of admiring dismay. Willy-nilly Mercedes experienced an unexpected few minutes of total success as a raconteuse. The hilarity of her three listeners had a black, almost hysterical quality, like gallows humour. Even James, who – so she'd confided to Walter – seemed to ration his laughter as if it came through a meter and had to be paid for, reacted to her story with rusty, but irrepressible guffaws.

There was a shamefaced honesty in their dark, shared mirth, interrupted by the arrival of the maid with a ripe Stilton. Almost reluctantly they allowed sanity to seep back as they sliced the cheese and passed the biscuits.

Hannah recovered herself first. She began to eat her Stilton with etiquette-book skill, at the same time advising Mercedes what her next steps should be in the Ballard dispute. Mercedes listened glumly. It was more like a lecture from expert to novice, she thought, and Hannah was becoming far too proprietorial for her taste, talking about 'we' and 'us' at every turn. She also took the opportunity to remind Mercedes that there was an awful lot of typing needed doing at the office in Victoria.

Walter seemed quiet, Mercedes noticed. She thought how terribly man-about-town he looked with his moustache and his well-fitting dress-suit. Seeing him like this, it was easy to lose sight of the boy he'd been, her childhood friend.

Actually he was more than just quiet, she reflected, as Hannah droned on. He seemed to exude something – a kind of misgiving that bordered on disapproval. It was as if he couldn't bring himself to condone Mercedes' part in the challenge to Edward Ballard, the Pimletts' family friend. It saddened her. She glimpsed the ghostly beginnings of a cooling. She and Walter had always been so open with each other, and now, in Mercedes' eyes, he was showing distressing signs of the priggish conventionality she saw in most of the young men of her own class.

Then again, maybe the wine was making her feel

morbid. *Vin triste*, Leon, her sister Sybil's husband, used to quote from somewhere. And she wasn't used to drinking.

'. . . So I think we must have a meeting. All of us. Say, at the end of next week,' Hannah was declaring energetically.

Mercedes nodded meekly. But she and Annie had a plan. Fiercely possessive, Mercedes hugged it to herself.

17

After lunch on Saturday they always drank coffee in Mildred's pleasant sitting-room on the first floor of the house. The bacon roll and onion sauce – a homely favourite from his schooldays – sat heavily and satisfyingly in Edward's stomach as he stretched out in one of Mildred's comfortable armchairs with his long legs crossed in front of him.

Before she came down to lunch Mildred had been painting, and immediately afterwards she put on her vermilion smock again and started to dab at the canvas, titivating and adjusting, with her coffee beside her on the piano. She was using oil-paints. Edward had always liked the smell of all the paraphernalia and he inhaled it with nostalgic pleasure.

He wasn't too keen on the picture. Some lemons and some greenish drapery, an old earthenware jug. He'd never been able to see the point of still-lives, or still-lifes should that be? A set of random, unremarkable articles, artificially grouped together, while Mildred fiddled and dabbed, obsessed with texture and highlights.

'Are you pleased with it?' he asked, for something to say.

She cast a mock-despairing look over one shoulder. 'I never am. You should know that by now.' Her words and expression suggested depths of artistic temperament.

'Silly girl,' Edward said comfortably. 'You're far too self-critical.'

He watched as she daubed. Under the smock she was wearing a soft, dark charcoal dress that he liked. Only a few years ago, a very few, with her hair puffed and piled up like that, Mildred would have been stunning. What was the difference? An inch round the waist? The merest sagging of flesh below the chin? And now she simply looked like . . . his suitably middle-aged wife. His spouse.

Her artistic efforts irritated him rather nowadays. They seemed pretentious and vaguely futile. And yet similar traits in Daisy interested and intrigued him. Again, what was the difference? Merely the fact of Daisy's unfamiliarity, her youth, he supposed. Her looks, still fresh, yet overlaid with enough experience to make them meaningful.

He thought, with rueful amusement, of the collection of her embroidered handkerchiefs in his desk-drawer, stuffed under some personal correspondence. In the end, rather than fart about finding prospective customers, it had seemed simpler to buy them himself at a generous – but not improbably generous – price. The ploys a man would descend to for the sake of a desirable woman. Dignity and *gravitas* went out of the window. He could be a panting twenty-year-old again. Though he was better now at covering up with a bland, public face.

He tried to picture Daisy as she'd looked the day before yesterday. She'd been wearing a coat and skirt that had obviously been fashioned from some masculine garment. Though she'd done it skilfully, it was shiny and worn in places, and too heavy for the time of year. All the other women in the tea-room had worn colourful clothes, new-looking and rich in texture. And yet Daisy had shone like a star, pale and lovely, making the others look ordinary and overdressed.

Edward took a sip of coffee and screwed his mouth. He didn't know what to think of his chances with her. He had the impression she'd rather welcomed his obvious interest and concern. For a time she seemed to thaw out and talk to him quite easily, laying aside her mistrust – before the question of Floyd and his antics came up. It seemed to him that she'd liked the elegance of the surroundings. Probably seemed like luxury to her and there'd be precious little of that in her life. That could be a point in his favour. He could supply that kind of interlude *ad nauseam*. And there was the money of course, the supposed client . . .

But he couldn't take anything for granted. Daisy had a prickly sense of pride; if he said the wrong thing she might even throw up the chance of earning the cash. She was bright and wary, didn't let things pass. He was literally frightened to flatter her in case she saw him as some middle-aged, middle-class lecher with dishonourable designs. Which of course he was.

What he'd really like would be to set her up in a pleasant apartment. With the children of course – no way round that. Some comfortable place, not too central, that he could treat like a second home. Go there to sleep a couple of nights a week. Eat and relax. A kind of secret alternative life. The vision seemed enchanting. A domestic idyll spiced with sex. It *ought* to be easy. There must be millions of women living hard lives who'd leap at the chance. But he very much doubted that Daisy was one of them.

'Buggeration and crapulence!' Mildred reached for a rag and began scrubbing vigorously at her canvas.

Edward winced inwardly. Such expletives formed part of his wife's repertoire of small bohemianisms. He used to find them bold and amusing, but now they sounded merely stale with repetition.

'What's the matter?'

'Hamfisted blunder.' She didn't turn her head.

'Turn it to your advantage,' he laughed.

Mildred didn't reply. There was an edge of strain between them. Over lunch she'd pontificated shamelessly on Leonard Floyd's exploits with the hose-pipe.

'The man's a fool,' she declared with calm conviction. 'If ever anything was calculated to consolidate the opposition.' She'd shaken her head with weary contempt. 'The only sane policy is to let things peter out slowly and miserably. An attack like that . . . It's absolutely designed to get them all stirred up and excited again!'

Edward had argued, but in his heart he couldn't deny the logic of her words.

He didn't like the oblique personal interest Mildred took in the affair. She seemed obsessed by the women themselves, putting herself in their place, analysing their motives, setting herself up as some kind of an expert. Why couldn't she just shake her head and bemoan the breakdown of order and respect, like the Bertons and the Pimletts did?

Personally – in spite of the hangdog demeanour he'd put on for Daisy's benefit – Edward had felt a secret rush of glee on hearing of the hose-pipe onslaught. At last, no more pussyfooting or long-faced pretence of concern. Just a loud and vulgar raspberry towards the arrogant ambitions of these muddle-headed female nobodies. He'd had to caution Floyd, of course – that kind of thing wouldn't do, not too often – but he'd done it in such a way as to let the man know that privately he'd a degree of sympathy . . .

Experiencing a subversive excitement, Edward allowed his mind to linger on the image of Daisy soaked and humiliated, her clothes clinging to her breasts and legs, her cool composure routed. God, he'd have loved to have seen her like that . . . But he dismissed the thought with an effort of will. This wasn't the time or the place . . .

'Those scabs are turning out pretty hopeless, aren't they?' That had been another of Mildred's forthright and oddly complacent statements over lunch.

'Hell's bells, Mildred,' he'd expostulated. 'Give them time!'

Unfortunately she spoke the truth. Production was at rock-bottom and Floyd was hamstrung. He had to go easy, there wasn't an endless supply of substitute workers. He couldn't use his normal tyrannical methods for licking them into shape. All the same, Edward was adamant. In the foreseeable future they were going to stay, as a stick to beat the malcontents with, if nothing else.

He didn't *depend* on the factory, though it was a jammy source of income, quite a little gold-mine in fact. But he'd got investments he could live off handsomely for quite some time. He wasn't going to have to pull the boys out of Eton or pawn the family silver. Just as well, because he was buggered if he was going to let a crowd of jumped-up hags and harpies make a fool of him in front of all the world.

At least he'd had one small stroke of luck. Reading that interview in the *Advertiser* with the little puffing billy of a photographer, he'd come across the name Mercedes MacInnes, and a light had come on in his head. Mercedes MacInnes. So she was the interfering busybody who was egging his workers on to defy him. It came back to him then that Daisy had mentioned the name once, but he hadn't really taken it in.

He'd been amazed once he placed her. The youngest MacInnes girl. That whey-faced, bossy kid who came to the Pimletts' tennis tournament year after year and won it more often than not. If he noticed her at all, he'd always rather liked her pluck. No beauty, but she'd got a neat little body. She'd argued with him this year, he recalled, over a bad ball. Her small, peaky face had blazed with righteousness. He'd got quite hot under the collar at the time, but later on he'd smiled with Thomas Pimlett over her stubbornness in not backing down.

Seeing her name in the newspaper, Edward had experienced an almost laughable sense of relief – that *she* was the fly in the ointment and not some old suffragette harridan bristling with savvy about the finer points of industrial law. There should be no problem in getting the MacInnes child dealt with. It would be simply a question of telephoning her father and getting him to spank his daughter's bottom. MacInnes was on holiday, he'd tried him yesterday at his surgery. But as soon as he came back . . .

Edward set down his coffee cup on a small, carved table next to him. He stretched and yawned, feeling restless, and decided to get Waters to drive him out to the club. It was a fairish day. He could take a stroll in the park and then drop by for a drink and a smidgen of company.

He hauled himself out of his chair. 'I'm going out for a bit, Millie.'

She nodded, still engrossed in her painting.

He peered over her shoulder at the work in progress. 'That lemon rather brings to mind one of Mr Wells's space-machines.'

Mildred turned and treated him to one of her we-are-not-amused looks, but there was a redeeming glint of laughter in her eyes.

He turned to go. 'See you anon, old thing.'

'Edward,' she called as he opened the door. 'Don't forget we're dining *chez* Kirkpatrick tonight. Do please try and be home on time.'

18

Mercedes watched as Daisy washed her children's clothes in a galvanized iron bucket hoisted on to a chair. She had brought water upstairs from the stand-pipe in the backyard and boiled some of it in a kettle. A wash-board was laid across the top of the bucket and she scrubbed the garments with a stiff brush and the last of a bar of unpleasant-smelling soap.

'Not much left of this,' she commented with a quick grimace. Then she grinned. 'We'll just have to go dirty.'

Over her skirt Daisy wore a sacking apron and her blonde hair hung down her back, caught back loosely with a piece of thread. She'd taken off her blouse – to save it – and stood working in a threadbare white chemise top, the square neck neatly mended, Mercedes noticed. After she'd scrubbed each small garment Daisy wrung out the water with practised dexterity, revealing the wiry muscles in her slim, bare arms. Then she draped them over the back of a neighbouring chair.

Mercedes felt privileged to witness this homely rite. It seemed to her that Daisy had admitted her a little further into her life, that there must be at least a grain of friendship in the young widow's attitude towards her. In fact, this Saturday afternoon, she'd been invited to stay for supper. 'I've come into a bit of cash, what with my embroideries,' Daisy explained diffidently – and Mercedes felt as though she'd been offered a delightful and unexpected present.

Down here in Bermondsey she was referred to as 'That Mercedes', the prefix serving to keep her at arm's length, point up her separateness. But she'd overheard Daisy once talking about her to the others, and she called her simply 'Mercedes'.

It was in Daisy's two rooms in Aquitaine Street that Mercedes had taken refuge last Wednesday morning, to take off her soaking clothes and dry out. Eventually the two of them had seen the funny side of the embarrassing public walk home through the busy streets, the gawping faces, and they'd laughed about it shyly together. But Daisy had taken matters briskly in hand, wringing out Mercedes' skirt, blouse and petticoats and stringing them above the gas-rings, using up three prodigal pennies' worth of gas. Mercedes left some money so she wouldn't be out of pocket, but Daisy refused to accept a single farthing more than she'd spent.

A few weeks ago Mercedes had been to a private viewing of an exhibition of paintings by an artist called Hugh LeGrys. He was the brother of one of the Association's founder-members. In fact one of his canvases dominated the Association's office in Victoria. His paintings featured working-class women engaged in domestic tasks, their faces tragic and beautiful, their flesh blue-tinged and luminously pale.

'Sentimental twaddle.' Hannah was crisply dismissive of the man's work – even the painting in the office – but privately Mercedes was rather taken with his pictures.

As Daisy toiled over the wash-board she was illuminated by the sunlight that filtered past her pot-plants and through the thin blue curtains. The soft filaments of her hair were haloed and the bluish light caught her face and arms. To Mercedes her figure and movements had a timeless, classical 'rightness' and she seemed for a moment the embodiment of one of LeGrys' oppressed beauties.

'Andrew'll be home soon,' Daisy said, as she wrung out the final small garment. 'I'll get him to bring up a couple of buckets of rinsing water.'

Mercedes felt the sweat break out under her arms. Her

skin prickled with anticipation and nervous excitement. In spite of the rush and tumble of the week since their meeting last Saturday, she'd found quiet times to picture the strongly-boned face of Daisy's brother, his practical hands and grey, steady eyes, even to think his name, Andrew Sitek, over and over like a charm, knowing it was stupid, but unable to resist the private pleasure.

'Talk of the devil . . .' The sound of male footsteps on the stairs.

Andrew entered the room and silently Mercedes caught her breath. In the flesh there was an immediacy to his looks and presence that no mental image could match. He seemed to bring into the room a hint of the early-summer air outside, a touch of the sun. He stood in the doorway for a moment with his working-man's scarf loosened and his jacket open. There was a bloom on his pale skin and his fair hair was ruffled. The sunlight from the window made his grey eyes appear startlingly clear, their pupils hard and diminished.

Glancing round the room, he caught sight of Mercedes, and she saw that his eyes widened a little, out of wariness or surprise. He nodded. 'Hallo, Miss MacInnes.' She recalled the slight distinctive huskiness to his voice.

Mercedes made a deliberate attempt to breathe calmly and regularly, to adjust her expression to one of pleasant neutrality. 'How do you do, Mr Sitek.'

'Mercedes is staying for supper,' Daisy announced. 'As we're high on the hog for once.'

Andrew nodded, but made no comment. He was carrying a sugar-bag like those she'd seen at Annie's, partially filled with something. He held it out towards Daisy. 'Been down to old Tanner's piece of ground on the way home. He's let me have a bag of soil for your plants. Don't want no payment – just a cutting of something or other.' Andrew grinned. 'And he says you got to bring it down yourself.'

'The dirty old man.' But she laughed at his cheek. 'Thanks, love. You're a good boy.'

She took the sack to stow it in the corridor. 'Don't sit down, Andy,' Daisy said mischievously as she went. 'There's a couple of buckets of water want fetching. And you can get rid of that one over there. Then my broom-handle's come away from the head. If you could do something about that, love . . .'

Andrew hoisted the bucket from the chair, pulling a face. Then he grinned at Mercedes. 'It's a dog's life.'

She glowed at being included in the wry joke. 'No rest for the wicked,' she agreed sympathetically. It was a phrase she'd heard Mrs Carter use often and one which seemed meaningless to her. But she thought it had the right ring of humorous resignation.

Andrew's smile widened. Mercedes thought he looked pleased that she'd answered him back in kind.

After he'd lugged the two bucketsful of water up the stairs, and Daisy had rinsed the clothes, Andrew had taken the water down again, then settled on the floor to mend the broom. He appeared to whittle the shaft and prod at the cavity in the broom-head, then slice two tiny wedge-shaped pieces of wood from the top end of the handle. Mercedes watched the process intently, but found her attention lingering on Andrew's strong hands, the frowning concentration of his expression. He seemed to her a new and intriguing species of male. She admired his manual skill, and was touched by his willing practicality in the house.

'Mamma'll be back soon with the children,' Daisy confided. 'I always try and send her out for some fresh air on a Saturday. If I didn't make her, I don't think she'd ever go out at all now. She's supposed to be buying some faggots down the market. Alex'll jog her if she forgets . . .' A pause. 'Don't worry, Mercedes, if she seems quiet and strange. It's the way she is these days. Nothing personal.'

*   *   *

Daisy fed the children first because there were only four seats, not counting Grandma's dilapidated wicker easy-chair kept in the neighbouring room. Afterwards Alex and Janie crossed hand-in-hand to say goodnight to Miss MacInnes. Mercedes' experience with children was pretty well confined to her own young nephews and nieces, but she was charmed by the earnest solemnity of the angelic-looking blond boy and by the little girl's huge brown eyes and dark curls.

'Dream of lots of nice things,' she told them and their faces lit up with shy, pleased smiles. Janie wriggled one shoulder and snuggled her cheek against it with winsome bashfulness.

Around nine o'clock the adults gathered at the table. It was beginning to get dark and Andrew lit a stump of candle to save gas. Its flickering light emphasized the outer darkness and made the room seem cosy and intimate.

As Daisy had predicted, her mother sat on her side of the table, silent and withdrawn. Physically her eyes were like Andrew's and Daisy's – grey, but seeming darker because of their black lashes, the smudge of shadow beneath them. But, where her children's eyes were responsive and bright, Anna Sitek's held a far-off vacancy.

Mercedes addressed conventional pleasantries to her, but she took no notice until the remarks were passed on via Andrew or Daisy. Then she would nod, or even venture a monosyllabic, emotionless reply, always to her son or daughter, ignoring the stranger.

As she had been last Saturday, Mercedes was struck by the immobile beauty of her lined face. She couldn't be all that old. Between fifty-five and sixty perhaps. At times she seemed simple-minded, but occasionally she would make some remark of her own – either in accented English or Polish – that revealed an intelligence still intact somewhere within her apathetic person.

Daisy ladled faggot stew, with barley and dried peas, into four dishes from a large battered and misshapen saucepan.

'This pan's older than me,' she told Mercedes. 'Mamma brought it with her from Poland.' She glanced at her mother with a crooked smile, but Anna Sitek gave no reaction.

Yet somehow the older woman's presence was restful. The stew was thick and filling, made savoury by the floating chunks of faggot. The candlelight had a gentle, vibrant quality. The homeliness of the scene was magical to Mercedes.

'Haven't eaten like this since God knows when . . .' Andrew attacked his portion with relish. Mercedes saw his sister eye him and form her lips into a silent ssh. She supposed Daisy thought it tactless to dwell on their straitened circumstances in front of a guest.

All the same, Mercedes had the feeling that, in this household, she was more than tolerated – she was accepted, liked even. It was the first time she'd had such an impression since she first came to Bermondsey, and the warmth of the stew inside her body mingled with a private glow of pleasure.

'You'll walk Mercedes to London Bridge, won't you, to catch a train?' Daisy suggested to Andrew later.

He nodded and got willingly to his feet, then seemed to sense that he'd been over-hasty.

'I *had* better be off,' Mercedes said, sparing him the awkwardness of feeling that he'd hustled her departure.

Down in the street he offered her his arm. 'No place for a lady, these streets. Specially on a Saturday night.'

It was a new side to Bermondsey, with the dark sky and the stars, and the streets given over to enjoyment rather than workaday bustle. Mercedes had always thought what a lot of pubs there were here. Every block of tenements seemed to boast one and all of them were doing a roaring trade. As you passed, the hum of conversation was punctuated with shouts of laughter, male and female, that sounded reckless to Mercedes, slightly threatening, but exciting too. There were lights everywhere, gaudily welcoming beneath the velvety sky.

They approached a pub called the Tiger's Eye. It was a fine night and three or four tables had been set out on the pavement, where people sat around drinking in the open air.

'Don't look now,' Andrew told her. 'But your pal Leonard Floyd's sitting out front.'

Mercedes walked on, her head facing resolutely forward, but her eyes slid sideways. Sure enough, Floyd was drinking with the frizzy-haired plug-ugly from Wednesday, his face red and shiny. His free arm was round a woman, a young girl . . . very young. With an inward twitch of surprise Mercedes realized that she couldn't be more than fourteen. The child looked drunk, her mouth hanging in a slack, foolish grin. Her dull brown hair was coming loose from its moorings and, like Floyd, she held a slim black cigar between her fingers.

'Disgusting old cradle-snatcher, eh?' Andrew looked down to see how she'd reacted to the sight. 'That's Dot Faraday. Cleans up down at Ballard's. 'E started with her when she was twelve.' There was a note of condemnation in his words, but also of acceptance.

'Oh.' Mercedes was embarrassed and shocked. But she was physically disturbed too, by Andrew's pale good looks in the lights from the pub, the appealing huskiness of his voice, his confidential smile and the sexual content of his words. She couldn't deny an insidious flame of excitement that flickered in the pit of her stomach.

He went on, 'She's kept out of the strike. He's made sure of that.' Andrew lowered his tone. 'Funny kid. Not too bright . . . Her mother, well, she's her sister, too, if you see what I mean.'

'Oh.' She was even more taken aback. He must be hinting at some kind of incestuous . . . She worked it out in her mind. 'Good heavens!' She felt the exclamation made her sound like a prudish maiden aunt.

He grinned as if amused by her disarray. 'This way.' Steering her courteously across the road.

They reached London Bridge and stopped outside the station. 'Beautiful night.' He raised his arms to indicate the stars, the general balminess of the air. 'Would you fancy walking a bit longer, Miss MacInnes? As far as the next stop?'

She was surprised and gratified by the suggestion, but succeeded in keeping her reply light and neutral. 'Yes. Why not?'

Halfway across the bridge they stopped to stare at the black, oily-looking water, the boats and the moving, shimmering pools of light reflected in the surface of the river. Outside Bermondsey, the usual few streets, they seemed isolated together. Mercedes had regained her calm and a free, unhurried sense of well-being.

'Looks different at night, the river. You can't see the dirt and the junk.' Andrew leaned forward against the parapet and gazed down into the water, then turned his head to face her. 'Daisy likes you, you know.' He sounded as if he'd needed to pluck up courage in order to voice the thought.

He amplified the statement, slowly, as if the words came with difficulty. 'I like to see her . . . Daisy cuts herself off a bit. Some people think she's stuck-up. She ain't had much of a life since Frankie died – her husband. Just work. And worry.' He shrugged his shoulders. 'She's gone sort of . . . dead inside. I was well pleased when she invited you . . .'

The pleasurable feelings that had been gathering inside her all evening flooded through her body like a state of grace. 'I'm glad you think she likes me. I like Daisy . . . I feel as if she's on my side . . .' Mercedes wasn't sure

170

whether Andrew would understand this last comment. He couldn't know her self-doubts as regards Ballard's workers.

She said impetuously, 'If only this strike could be over. Won . . . Over. It bothers me, all the hardship . . . I feel somehow responsible.'

'But you're helping them,' he said with total conviction.

Mercedes let the remark stand. Her motives were so mixed. She didn't feel like admitting, even to herself, the part self-gratification played in her actions. Perhaps it didn't matter, anyway. This wasn't the time to be analysing her reasons . . . It was strange. With this young working-man she discovered that she felt the way women in books are supposed to feel, women in love-stories. Sort of disarmed . . . Softened. The way she never felt at all with the men she knew.

On the far side of the bridge they came to yet another pub, The Ship Arms. It was small and looked cosy inside but not too crowded.

Andrew asked hesitantly, 'Would you feel like having a drink with me?'

In a pub! Mercedes was bowled over by the thought. She'd never set foot . . . But who would know? She nodded. 'I'd like to.'

'No saloon here.' He looked at her indecisively for a moment, as though half expecting her to change her mind. 'It *is* quiet, though.'

Inside, the smell of sawdust strewn on the floor mingled with the yeasty tang of fresh beer. The low-ceilinged room was furnished with old-fashioned, high-backed, dark wood benches, their polished gloss reflecting the brightly burning gas-lights. The place looked comfortable and homely and, to Mercedes' avid eyes, disappointingly respectable.

Andrew escorted her to a secluded table in one corner.

'What can I fetch you?'

Mercedes racked her brains. She was dubious about his spending money on her, but guessed he'd be mortified if she passed any comment.

'A shandy, please.' It was a drink her father sometimes had on hot days, swigging it down with the air of being a man of the people, wiping his mouth ostentatiously with the back of his hand.

'You sure?' Andrew seemed doubtful about her choice.

She nodded emphatically, as though her mind were quite made up.

He crossed and bought the drinks from a fat barmaid, who looked to Mercedes as if she rouged her cheeks and lips and dyed her hair. The woman smiled flirtatiously at Andrew and they exchanged snippets of well-worn banter. It occurred to Mercedes, with rueful suddenness, that if she found Andrew attractive and intriguing, it was only logical that others would, too. Probably he had a host of women-friends. And if he had, it was no concern of hers. All the same, the thought was displeasing.

'You look . . . as if you're not used to places like this,' he said as he carried the drinks back to their table.

'I'm not. But there's a first time for everything.'

Andrew bent and placed the glass of shandy in front of her, looming a little above her and grinning, with a gleam of mischief in his eyes. 'Hope I'm not leading you into bad ways.' He must have taken a sip of his beer before he crossed from the bar. She could smell it faintly on his breath. He seemed very close for a moment and tantalizingly attractive.

But when he sat down Andrew seemed shyer, less in control, as if it was his job now to entertain her and he wasn't sure how.

Mercedes, too, was ill-at-ease. He was such a stranger to her. With a kind of awkward rush, she returned to a subject he'd mentioned earlier. 'What was he like, Daisy's husband?'

'Frankie? Lovely bloke.' Andrew took a ruminative sip of his beer. 'Good-looking, too – Janie's the image . . . Always good-natured. Hardworking, *and* brought his money home. Daisy struck it lucky . . . Only . . .' He hesitated.

'Only what?' she encouraged.

'Sometimes I think Daisy wanted more. Once she told me they'd never talked much. I don't know.' He shrugged with a kind of bewilderment. 'They talked as much as anyone . . . Daisy's a deep one. Strikes you as so sure of herself but . . . she's complicated. I mean, to me, Frankie looked like the perfect husband . . .' He smiled across at her, wry-flirtatious. It seemed he'd regained his self-assurance. 'There's no telling – with love.'

Mercedes reached for her glass and took a swallow to mask the renewed onslaught of some feeling that felt like . . . lust. In her fevered state the drink seemed strange – watery, gingery, brackish.

Andrew went on, 'A mate of mine had a lovely girl, a florist. Classy, too. And he threw her over for some runty little shrew, not five foot tall.' He paused for thought, then added, 'Mind you, there's something about her . . .'

Mercedes said feelingly, 'It's like my sisters. They both married men that . . . Well, I think they're so dull. But they must love them.'

'Stuffed shirts?' He looked at her quizzically over the top of his glass.

She nodded eagerly. 'Stuffed shirts. That's it exactly!'

They laughed together, the ice suddenly broken. Mercedes relaxed, leaning against the polished back of the bench. It occurred to her that, until this moment, she'd been sitting bolt upright.

Andrew drained his glass and placed it on the table. He asked her, 'Would you care to come for a walk with me tomorrow evening?'

19

Daisy Harkness leant back on the park bench and turned her face up to the sun. Her elbows were hooked over the slatted back. The position raised her breasts, made them jut. Edward resisted the dizzying desire to slip his hand inside the ugly dark jacket she was wearing and close it over the soft solidity of her flesh. He could see himself doing it so easily it was frightening and he thought what a slim and tenuous thread it was that held one to the path of acceptable behaviour.

Less feveredly he imagined taking her, now, to a fashionable shop, dumping her heavy, hideous coat and skirt in a bin, and buying her a dress – a light one in a bright colour – that would set off her supple body and erect, beautiful head with its swept-up pile of softly curling blonde hair.

After they'd met and exchanged her second consignment of handkerchiefs for the agreed money, he'd suggested they take tea again. But Daisy had opted for a walk in Hyde Park.

'It's not often I get the chance to feel the grass under my feet, and it's such a beautiful day.'

Edward wasn't sure whether to feel encouraged or not by her proposal. It could be that, in choosing the open spaces of the park, Daisy was trying to avoid the intimacy of a tête-à-tête. On the other hand her suggestion did seem to take for granted the fact that the two of them would be keeping company, questioning only their possible options. And Daisy had been lively and talkative as if, in the intervening days, she'd reconciled herself to the idea of him as a friendly presence. Also, he sensed obscurely, she'd become more used to the fact of his sexual interest, and appeared not to be unduly disturbed by the thought. At any rate she seemed more free and easy than she had last Thursday. Even sitting like this, with her eyes closed, indicated a certain trust, the feeling that she didn't mind his watching her unawares.

The mellow early June sun warmed the pallor of her skin. A slight breeze had ruffled her hair a little into separate fronds, and she looked more alive and approachable than he'd seen her before.

Edward gazed at her upturned profile. It amazed him now, the thought that he'd jogged along in recent years with merely a general, periodically urgent, interest in women and sex, which he satisfied easily with Mildred or, more often, with some pretty whore. Now suddenly, from the blue, this focused passion that at times made him feel as raw and hot as a boy. Avidly his eyes took in the curve of her neck, the fullness of her lower lip, the dark eyelashes on her cheeks, the peculiar sensuousness of the shadowed area beneath her eyes.

'You're such a beautiful woman . . .'

He heard his own voice make the fervent, involuntary statement and for a moment was dismayed. But almost at once a feeling of recklessness gripped him. Why the hell not say what he thought? He could skirt round it for weeks and get no nearer to what he wanted. Win or lose, he'd taken a step.

Daisy's eyelids fluttered open and she turned her head towards him. At first her eyes looked glazed, as though dazzled by the sun. Then her gaze became neutral and steady and he realized that she wasn't going to put on a show of outrage or flounce off. The expression on her face showed bemusement and a faint, subversive gleam of humour.

It was up to him to follow through. Edward smiled disarmingly. 'There, I've said it.' A frank grin that he'd learned to summon up at will, and which put him in control of most situations.

Daisy smiled too, reluctantly, wryly, quizzically. She moved her shoulders in a small shrug. 'I don't know what to say.'

'Don't say anything. Just carry on looking beautiful.' This time his gallantry had an awkward ring and there was a silence between them.

Two well-dressed children, with shiny shoes and tautly pulled-up socks, passed by with a rosy young nanny. 'Possess your soul in patience, Master Simon,' she was saying. 'You can't always have what you want just when you want it.'

Edward looked at Daisy, laughing. 'Teach 'em resignation early on in life.' Turning the young woman's words to his advantage and filling the embarrassed hush.

Then he added, switching smoothly to a tone of engaging diffidence, 'I hope I haven't offended you, Mrs Harkness. It's just . . . I'm flesh and blood, you see, susceptible as the next man to a desirable woman. But I promise I won't be making any dishonourable advances . . .' Keeping his manner light and ironic, as he'd learned to do ever since his first miserable days at boarding school. Though mentally he smirked at the patent insincerity of his final statement.

Still Daisy said nothing, her face expressing confusion, indecision.

He concluded, 'I hope our little business arrangement will still stand. And I'd like to keep . . . I enjoy just walking and talking with you.'

A flush had spread beneath the clear skin of her face. To Edward she looked lovelier than ever, with his compliments ruffling her poise. He saw that she wasn't indifferent to his interest, though he didn't go as far as to flatter himself that it was returned.

'Have I offended you, Daisy?' For the first time he used her Christian name.

'It's difficult, isn't it?' She looked him squarely in the eye. 'You being the boss. Us being on strike. Doesn't look too good.'

'We're just two private people,' he urged, 'who enjoy one another's company. That fact's quite separate from any official relationship. It's got nothing to do with anyone. Look, Daisy, I'm not asking you for anything, but I can't pretend I'm indifferent.' Edward finished on a note of pained honesty, but privately he registered the contrast between Daisy's bluntness and his own seductive wiles.

He observed her keenly. He thought she appeared torn, and he wondered whether, even laying aside the lure of his money, she might not be reluctant to give up the diversion of meeting with him. The idea encouraged him hugely.

He wouldn't press her now, but if she *did* agree to see him again, then to a certain extent she'd be condoning his courtship of her. He could bring up – cautiously – the prospect of his installing her in some kind of flat. Perhaps the whole affair would turn out to be easier than he'd dreamed.

The bedclothes, twisted and trailing on the floor, felt like clinging fronds of water-weed, tangling round her limbs and pulling her under to drown. Sweating and heavy-eyed, Mercedes lay on her back, one arm across her eyes, one outflung leg clear of the sheet. Her nightdress lay next to the bed, a pool of white muslin cloth. Her damp flesh was tinted by the light from outside glowing through the red linen curtains, and the morning sun pierced the gaps between them, casting bright spears of light across the floor and bed. Mercedes' left hand rested on her stomach. The skin seemed preternaturally sensitive. She felt tense, feverish, exhausted. She'd not slept a wink – just turned over and over in her mind a jumbled kaleidoscope of visual impressions, conversations, tones of voice, smiles, expressions from her last two meetings with Andrew Sitek.

They seemed to swirl round her as she lay in the dark, then the watery dawn, and finally the raw, strong light of a summer morning.

When she'd arrived home last night from her Sunday evening walk with Andrew in Hyde Park – where they were unlikely to meet anyone they knew – Mercedes had the elusive impression, as she crossed the hall and climbed the stairs, that she was underwater, that her movements had a floating unreality, that she'd entered a new realm of strange, drugged wonder.

In her bedroom she lit a candle. At that moment she'd been unable to face the harshness of electricity. Placing it on her dressing-table, she'd unpinned her hair and gazed at herself intently in the mirror.

The face that stared back had shocked and impressed her. It had her features, her dark blonde hair falling straight to the shoulders, and yet she was undeniably altered. It was as though the emotions she was discovering had entered her body, effecting a strange and subtle chemical change. Her small, pale face had a bloom on it, a humid, delicate flush, like that of some hot-house orchid, one of those rare, strange flowers that seemed to Mercedes almost human. Her eyes were deep and black, appearing to glow with some new kind of knowledge. And for the first time in her life – seriously – Mercedes wondered whether she was desirable.

She'd tried to read the answer in Andrew Sitek's eyes as they walked arm in arm on the grass, under the black trees and the stars. He'd not paid her any compliments. She suspected he was too shy of her.

'What colour are your eyes? That what's called hazel?' he'd asked her, with the awkward, vulnerable grin she found so touching and attractive. At any rate that had been a personal remark. Her mind repeated it, hearing again his exact inflection.

She thought it was his very lack of the seamless veneer

178

she was used to in the men of her acquaintance that aroused the strength of her response to him. She felt almost out of control and it frightened her, as if she might do anything. And yet, in another way, she welcomed the feeling like a mythical being she'd heard tell of all her life and never yet encountered. Did other people feel like this? She thought of her sisters before they were married, with their young men, and could recall no sign of the wildness that seemed to have invaded her.

As she lay in bed now, the morning after, a knock came at the door. 'Miss Mercedes, it's half past six!' It was Mrs Carter, giving her the early morning call she'd requested the previous day.

'Thank you, Mrs Carter!'

Last night in the park, Mercedes had noticed a striking couple out for a walk, like herself and Andrew. The woman wore a red blouse and spangly earrings. She was pretty and sharp-faced, the kind of female Mercedes had been conditioned since earliest childhood to think of as common. The man was tall and swarthy, hook-nosed. Gypsy-type, her father would have said, with an odd tone in his voice – half damning, half almost envious. As the couple passed, the man's hand rested lightly in the nape of the woman's neck, in a gesture rich with possession.

'Look – his chattel,' Ann Garvie, from her suffragette-group, used to hiss scathingly when she saw such things, and Mercedes would agree.

But, as she watched the couple disappear through the park-entrance towards the haloed lights of the street outside, Mercedes had longed, with all her heart, to be held with such casual intimacy.

Andrew had walked her home to Devonshire Place. It was midnight when they arrived. He looked up at her tall, prosperous house with a wary glint in his eye, then he bent and kissed her simply and softly.

'Like sweethearts,' he said huskily. Then that smile again, flirtatious but unsure.

Stretched out under the twisted sheet in the early-morning sunshine, its rays warmed by the insulation of curtains and glass, Mercedes imagined Andrew's body lying next to her on the bed. Moving her fingers lingeringly across her breasts and stomach. Imagining they were his.

20

The dream had come again last night. She hadn't had it in years, though a long time ago it used to come back every four or five days. Annie jammed her fist against her mouth as she remembered.

She was digging, with her bare hands, in some stony, hard-packed soil, finding bodies – half-rotted flesh and bones, coming across vile, tangled knots of worms. But she kept on digging, searching for someone. For Betsy, her baby. She'd let them take her away to this god-forsaken dump. Her whole soul cried out to the helpless, ill-used little scrap.

'I'm coming, love. I'll find you!' Annie called as she scrabbled with her black, broken fingernails, dark blood trickling from underneath them.

But she never did get to Betsy, just jerked back into consciousness, sat up in bed, crying, waking Will and Maggie. After that she couldn't go back to sleep. Always the next day the dream hung about her like a damp, grey, felted blanket, her head ached, and she snapped at anyone who so much as addressed a word to her.

This week, for the first time, Annie hadn't been able to find the shilling for the Burial Club – the reason why she'd had the old dream again – and whenever she remembered, a feeling of panic gripped her. People said she was fearless, but this secret terror gnawed at her like a rat.

As far as Annie was concerned it didn't matter half as much that they hadn't got the rent-money. The fishy-eyed bastard of a landlord could bluster all he liked. When it came down to it he was scared of her. If he came to the door she'd tell him anything, promise him the moon. He'd back down for a couple of weeks at least.

At the moment the worst thing was the lack of breakfast. Annie had managed to hang on to some ends of bread for the children, but she and Will had gone without, though both of them needed their strength today. He'd got a job this morning, painting window-frames for a neighbour. Poor old boy, he'd be dropping by ten o'clock.

And she, Annie, was waiting on Mercedes. The two of them were going to tackle old Rawdon, the shop-steward down the furniture factory, about Ballard's scabs. He was a bloody-minded sod and it wasn't going to be easy. A bit of something in her stomach'd do wonders for her fighting spirit – specially after that dream last night. Perhaps Mercedes would suggest a bit of bread pudding and a cuppa in the Picardy before they went. She was gasping for one. But she wasn't going to ask any favours from that little goody two-shoes.

Annie opened the windows to air the room. It smelt something awful what with the boys sleeping in here. She took a deep breath of the soft summer air. But you could only leave them open for an hour or so, before the choking vinegar stink from the pickle factory began to spread out and take over.

As it happened, Kate Reeves was walking past on her way down to Ballard's, but she turned her head away as she passed Annie's house. Hard-eyed, Annie watched her go. She'd seen her recently buying bacon off the market, making eyes at runty Dick, the stall-holder. Her face was healing, though it was still puffy. None of her friends would talk to her now, but at least she didn't have a bloody great empty hole where her belly ought to be.

Kate seemed to have palled up with Bet Partridge, whose husband had been knocking about with the O'Shea girl and put her up the spout. Annie had seen Sal yesterday. Face as long as a wet week. Some boys had called out after her and she'd run home like a scared rabbit with tears in her eyes.

The hooter sounded from Ballard's. Seven o'clock. Mercedes had said she'd try to get here by eight.

Annie went into the bedroom to pin up her hair. She felt old this morning, and discouraged. Must be the dream that had made her feel like that. It struck her that, if she'd been one of the others, with nothing much to gain but a bit of extra cash, she might have given up by now. But she couldn't afford to. It wasn't just money for her, it was the job itself that was at stake . . . and her pride.

Sometimes, on her own, Annie felt fed-up and tired, but she had to keep egging the others on. Even this morning, down in the dumps and famished as she was, Annie knew that if Edie or Queenie or anyone walked through the door, she'd be laying down the law in no time, cocky as you please.

Still, today Annie would be glad to see Mercedes, even with her well-fed looks, her know-all ways. She had guts and she wanted to win this strike as much as Annie herself. God knows why. To make herself look good, Annie supposed, make her feel important. A lot of the time Mercedes gave her the arse-ache. All the same, this morning it'd be good to see the bossy little cow.

Mercedes hadn't had time for breakfast so she insisted on taking Annie to the Picardy Café for tea and bread pudding before they bearded Mr Rawdon down at Annakin's furniture factory where Andrew worked.

The inspiration had been Annie's. She'd cottoned on to the fact that a large proportion of the scabs had husbands, brothers, fathers at Annakin's. Since they were the largest employer hereabouts, this was hardly surprising. The same was true of the strikers themselves. Rawdon was well-known in the district, an ardent trade-unionist. If the two of them could talk the bugger into coming out against the blacklegs, they'd be home and dry, so Annie claimed sagely.

'What's he like?' Mercedes asked, spooning two scoops of sugar into her tea, by way of boosting her energy. The café was deliciously scented with the lardy, spicy aroma of freshly-baked bread pudding.

Annie pulled a face and swallowed her last mouthful. She'd wolfed it down in record time, Mercedes noticed. The older woman took a swig of tea before replying tersely, 'He's a pig – and cussed with it. That's all you need to know, love.'

'Daisy's brother works at Annakin's, doesn't he?' Mercedes said, not because she didn't know, but for the sheer pleasure of mentioning Andrew.

'That's right. You've met him, have you?' Briefly Annie screwed her features into a sort of music-hall parody of lust. 'An eyeful, isn't he? I tell you, Mercedes, he could put his boots under my bed any day of the week.'

Mercedes was massively taken aback. She took a big bite of pudding to disguise her disarray, and suspected she was blushing. What an awful thing to say. Such sentiments were just plain embarrassing in a woman of Annie's age.

But Annie had transferred her attention. 'Can't you wait till we're finished, May?' she snapped at the proprietor's wife, who'd taken it into her head to swab their table with an unsavoury-looking dish-rag that reeked of disinfectant. The woman turned mild, cow-like eyes on Annie, but she continued with her mopping.

'Daft,' Annie remarked audibly as May proceeded to wipe the tables on the other side of the room, and Charlie, her dough-faced husband, laughed appreciatively from his place behind the counter.

Annie used to be at school with Hal Rawdon. He'd been an overweight bully then, and as far as she could see, he was an overweight bully now. He'd put a cockroach down her back once and, after she stopped screaming, she'd taken off her boot and landed him one on the side of the head.

His surprised yelp of pain and the laughter of the others had made up for the fright she'd had. Edie had walked out with him for a time when she was twenty or so, but gave him up because Hal had a fight with her younger brother and broke his nose.

She led the way to Sefton's Wharf on the river, where the factory and warehouse towered, a pile of gloomy blackish red brick, above the water. Annakin's was a firm that allowed trade-unionism. Annie thought they got on better putting up with union activity than fighting it. They were fair employers, everyone knew, so they had their pick of the best men. Will worked there for a time, best job he ever had. But then one winter he got ill with his chest and had to quit. He'd never had a regular job like that since.

It always amazed Annie how Hal, the little tyke, the bane of Ryland Street School, had grown up to become a big man in the district. People respected him, bought him drinks. But she couldn't forget him pulling up the girls' dresses to see their drawers. He used to wear a grey flannel shirt, all stains and patches. It was always hanging out of his breeches, and sometimes his trousers used to work their way down till you could see the top of his bum. Then the girls used to nudge each other and snigger.

And now he was storeman, with an office of his own on site, even if it was only a wooden shed with a stone floor and a piece of threadbare carpet stuck in the middle. She and Mercedes stood waiting for him to arrive. There were papers and folders on the shelves, just like a real office. Annie could hardly keep a straight face.

'Look at all this.' She gestured towards the signs of officialdom. 'He and his brother used to go round the streets with a little cart, selling horse-dung when they were kids.'

A skinny young lad of fourteen or so had gone off in search of the storeman. Now he put his pinched little face round the door and announced, 'Mr Rawdon's on his way.'

Soon afterwards Hal Rawdon appeared in person. Annie hadn't had much to do with him for years, though she saw him round and about sometimes. He was balder than she remembered, and there was a grin on his face that showed he was tickled to be receiving an old classmate on his own turf. She must want some kind of a favour or she wouldn't be here.

'Annie, love, good to see you.' She recalled the pale blue eyes that bulged a little, the girlish pink skin. 'Handsomest girl in Ryland Street, and still a looker after all these years.'

'Hallo, Hal,' Annie said dryly. She distrusted compliments. They meant people were taking you for a fool.

His eyes flicked curiously towards Mercedes. Annie smiled inwardly at his obvious bewilderment. She and Mercedes made a fine pair. Herself in her hand-me-downs and Mercedes with her snooty air, clean striped dress, dainty shoes and tilted boater.

'This is Miss MacInnes,' Annie told him. 'She's from the League . . .'

Mercedes butted in. 'Association for the Advancement of Women Workers.' Her voice was cool and strong. She offered him her hand to shake. He took it with a look of bemusement.

'Pleased to meet you.' He hesitated. 'How can I help you, ladies?'

The flesh of Rawdon's chin and jowls, overhanging his shirt collar, was soft and dimpled. But his belly, stuck out in front of him, was tight as a tick. 'Can we sit down, Hal?' Annie asked.

'Course you can, Annie. Don't stand on ceremony.' He waved an arm towards a couple of dusty upright chairs. Annie noticed that he took out a crumpled handkerchief and quickly dusted off the seat of the one nearest Mercedes.

Then he lowered his own rear on to an identical chair

186

behind the desk. A folder of some sort was open in front of him with columns and writing in red and blue ink.

'Annie tells me you're a trade-union activist, Mr Rawdon,' Mercedes proffered. Normally her toffee-nosed way of putting things got Annie hot under the collar, but it made her smile to see Hal Rawdon on the receiving end.

He nodded. 'Man and boy.' Hal didn't know quite what to make of her. The interest of a smart young lady was flattering, but Annie could see he was suspicious. So would she have been in his place.

'I suppose you've heard about the strike at Ballard's Garment Factory.' She looked him straight in the eye, her tone bell-like and precise. Mercedes wasn't bad looking, Annie admitted grudgingly to herself. She'd always thought of her as a whey-faced little thing, and prim with it, but she was wrong. There was something about her . . .

'I've heard.' He wasn't giving anything away.

'What do you think of it?' Her directness challenged him.

He became even cagier. 'Don't know enough to judge.'

'Perhaps Annie would tell you the whole story.' God, she was a bossy piece. Annie had half a mind to . . . But she pulled herself together. This wasn't the time to pick a fight.

'Yes, tell us about it, Annie.' There was a note of mockery in his voice, as if, like her, he found Mercedes hard to take.

Annie launched on the story of her run-in with Leonard Floyd, the walk-out, interview with Ballard, scabs, picketing, the hoses. It was the sort of thing Hal loved. Boss and management as villains. Workers banding together against them. But as he listened there was a silly smile on his face.

When she'd finished he was frankly grinning and his piggy light-blue eyes danced. 'Sorry, love, but I don't understand. What d'you want me to do?'

187

Mercedes cut in suddenly. 'I think Mr Rawdon's amused, Annie. He seems to find your story funny.' Her voice was clear as cut glass and sharp as a whip. She turned her eyes on him. They were bright and steady. 'And I can't help thinking that the only reason he finds it funny is because *this* particular dispute is being fought by women.'

Mercedes' voice shook, but her passion was contained, making it all the more startling. The silence that followed was shocking, seemed to quiver with her anger, the blatant truth of her words blazing in the hush. Annie was stirred and impressed by her venom. Quick as the tide covering shingle, Hal Rawdon flushed beetroot red.

'Not laughing.' He was on the defensive. 'But . . .'

'But what?'

Hal was on surer ground, trotting out arguments he must have aired hundreds of times. 'You can't compare a man's and a woman's struggle. Girls go to work just as long as it takes them to find a man to look after them . . . After that they're working for pin money.'

'I've been the wage-earner in *my* family for years . . .' Annie began.

But she was drowned out by Mercedes, her voice low but intense and full of indignation. 'I don't know the circumstances of all the women who are involved in this dispute. But looking round the strike-committee, I see Annie whose husband's not been able to get regular work for years. And Daisy Harkness, a widow with two children to keep . . . Kate Reeves who was forced to go back because her husband expects *her* to shoulder all the household expenses. And you sit there and tell us they're working for pin money!'

'Steady on, miss.' Hal sounded aggrieved now. 'I didn't ask you to come here. And I still don't see what all this has got to do with me . . .'

Annie was warmed by Mercedes' righteous anger. But she wasn't sure it was the best way to tackle Hal. From way back he liked flirty, stupid little women who flattered and teased him – like his Lily used to be. Only she'd sharpened up a bit since marrying him.

'We come to you, Hal,' she said, 'because you're the big man in this district on things like this . . .'

His pale eyes were hostile still. He knew she wouldn't be buttering him up if she wasn't trying to get something out of him. But she could think of no better way. 'People respect you,' she went on doggedly. 'And if you was to give the say-so . . .

'Just tell me what you come here for,' he interrupted. 'Sorry, Annie, but I'm a busy man.'

'Course you are, Hal,' she soothed, hating herself for crawling to the self-important jackass, thinking back with relish to the time when she'd landed him one with her boot.

But she took a breath and embarked on her explanation. 'It's like this, see. A lot of the scabs filling in at Ballard's've got husbands and fathers and brothers working here.' She dropped a few previously selected names of women whose men were no great friends of his. 'There's Beth Coster and the Terry girls . . . Molly Planer.' Annie watched closely for his reaction, but he gave no flicker. 'Now if you was to say to Lol Coster or Ted Planer that you didn't think much of their wives blacklegging . . .' She left the sentence hanging. The conclusion was obvious.

Hal leant back in his chair, hands clasped beneath his proudly jutting belly. He let out an explosive, derisive exhalation of breath. 'You're living in the past, Annie. Once upon a time women'd let themselves be told, or if they wouldn't you'd clump 'em one. Nowadays they've got their own ideas.'

'So, as a union man you're happy to sit back and watch this blacklegging, and do absolutely nothing.' Mercedes had regained control of her feelings. Her words were barbed, but her tone sweetly reasonable. 'Suppose the

189

same thing happened, say, at Roper's lumberyard. I imagine you'd have something to say then.'

'Course I would.' He was quick to defend his union-man's pride.

'Can you tell me what the difference is between that and what's happening down at Ballard's?'

Stolid and self-righteous, Hal Rawdon compressed his lips and shook his head with slow deliberation. 'What I will tell you is this – I'm not getting involved in any women's disputes.'

There was a timid knock on the door. 'Delivery from Roper's,' the pinch-faced lad announced.

'Tell Ted Mercer to sort it out,' Rawdon replied grandly. 'I'm a bit tied up here.'

Mercedes had the impression that the order was designed more to demonstrate his importance to herself and Annie, rather than to offer them any hope of a possible change of heart.

Between the two of them, she thought ruefully, they'd managed to rub him up completely the wrong way. She, Mercedes, had taken exception to the belittling smile he'd worn during Annie's blow-by-blow account of the Ballard's dispute – and let him know as much in no uncertain terms. Then Annie had tried flattery. But it had been delivered with a hard-eyed reluctance, not calculated to bring out the best in a man like Hal Rawdon.

But Mercedes was used to getting her own way in most things – simply by hanging on, like a fox-terrier with a bone. Rawdon had blanked them – unequivocally. Yet, illogically, Mercedes clung to the certainty that she and Annie could still win him over.

A pig – and cussed with it. Annie's description had a jaundiced accuracy, although Mercedes suspected it wasn't the whole truth. She could picture Hal Rawdon in some sawdust-strewn public bar, swigging with relish from a succession of pint tankards, and arguing his own brand of politics with all-comers . . . The image gave her fresh inspiration.

Now if *she* could get him involved in a discussion, get his pale, bulbous eyes to gleam with fire and interest, make him lose himself, forget his male self-importance . . . The more she thought about it, the more she felt that this might be an answer.

She began to talk, in a general way, about the problems faced by women workers, keeping her eyes fixed on his face, as though Rawdon were the expert and she was anxious to hear his opinions. After her months of secretarial work for Hannah and the others, she had pools of knowledge to draw on and facts coming out of her ears.

Trade-unionism had been Rawdon's passion from the age of about sixteen. All his adult life he'd been to meetings and conferences. He began to match Mercedes point for point, sometimes agreeing, sometimes differing, adding riders of his own and offering comparisons from his personal experience.

As they talked he changed physically, his eyes filling up with life and interest, his large, stolid face becoming mobile and animated, far more likeable. He abandoned his defensive, backward-leaning posture and sat forward, elbows on the desk, playing unconsciously with a pencil as he listened and spoke. At times his expression betrayed a grudging acknowledgement of the breadth of Mercedes' knowledge.

She sensed that Annie had tuned in to her strategy and was going along with it. As she followed the discussion her brown eyes had a canny look. From time to time she butted in with a leading question or some anecdote about her own working-life. A momentary gleam of remembrance surfaced in Mercedes' head. The way she and her classmates used to combine to distract a teacher of theirs who'd been to the Holy Land and carried in her handbag a small phial of Jordan water and was only too happy to waste whole lessons in reminiscing . . .

Several times Mercedes made the point that Ballard's workers posed no threat to any male worker – the trade they plied was an exclusively female one.

'You know the trouble with women?' Rawdon asked rhetorically, leaning even further forward and nudging aside the open ledger on his desk. 'They work cheap and undercut the men. They're a menace.'

Mercedes guessed that his thinking didn't often extend to the industrial rights of women. He'd left himself open. She pounced. 'That sounds to me like a reason for supporting our efforts to get higher rates. If women earned as much as men, they wouldn't present the same threat . . .'

Another thought occurred to her along the same lines. 'At any of your conferences have you ever come across Lancashire textile workers?'

Rawdon nodded, with a flash of intuition. It was obvious that he knew what Mercedes was going to say before she said it.

'They have the same union for men and women. They get the same piecework rates. So there's no reason to hire a woman in preference to a man or vice-versa . . .' She was suddenly aware of the hectoring intensity in her voice and shrugged, smiling. 'I get carried away on things like that. It's a bit of a hobby-horse of mine.'

Rawdon grinned with more simple friendliness than he'd yet shown. 'I know how it is. You should hear me down the pub sometimes, sounding off. I get given a wide berth, I can tell you . . .'

He shook his head. 'It'll never happen like that, though. Not in the real world. Women'll never be equal. Got to keep popping off to drop kids 'n' look after 'em.'

Mercedes let that pass. She wanted his help. No point in antagonizing him.

Abruptly Rawdon glanced up at the wall-clock and

grimaced in sudden alarm. Then he resumed the guarded air he'd worn earlier in the interview, a sort of fobbing-off look. He rose from his chair. 'You'll have to excuse me – Annie, Miss MacInnes. Time I was about me business.'

Mercedes and Annie got to their feet. Hal Rawdon shook each of them by the hand.

To Mercedes he said, 'We'll have to have another talk some time, you and I. You got plenty of ideas, but some of them's a bit . . .' He looked down at her with benevolent condescension, retracting his chin into the dimpled flesh of his neck.

'Good day, Mr Rawdon.' Her heart was in her mouth. She prayed for him to say he'd do something to help, but knew it would be fatal to ask him outright.

'Good to see you, Annie.' Hal Rawdon stood for a moment, clasping her hand in front of his football-shaped belly. His smile was warm and patronizing. He nodded his head, a wise old owl. 'Don't worry, love. For old times' sake . . . I'll put in a word for you.'

The sun dazzled as they left the gates of Annakin's factory behind them and strolled, by some mutual instinct, along the quayside bordering the Thames. The air was unusually clear and the surface of the water sparkled with reflected light. Even the low background stench of sewage couldn't spoil the beauty of the morning. Far ahead a ship was moored. It looked blue and hazy like something in a dream. Tiny men were unloading cargo in a scurry of distant, ant-like activity.

Annie gave a sideways look, a crooked smile. 'You're not as daft as you look, Mercedes.'

Mercedes shrugged, saying nothing. She couldn't see they'd gained anything you could count on. Hal Rawdon hadn't said that much.

On the quay in front of them, next to an iron bollard with a trailing length of chain, a bench with blue, peeling

193

paint looked out over the river. They drifted towards it and Mercedes sat down, idly watching the scintillating ripple of the water.

Annie stayed standing, staring out over the Thames. Suddenly she arched her body and threw back her head, raising her arms towards the sun, standing like that in a kind of ecstasy.

From where Mercedes was sitting, her figure was darkly silhouetted by the haloing glare. She was strangely impressed. Annie no longer seemed a shabby working-woman. She was statuesque, her body filled with vitality, a physical joy, like some pagan sun-worshipper.

She turned her head towards Mercedes. 'Best bloody day since the strike began.'

Mercedes longed to share Annie's conviction, her exhil-aration, but she didn't dare. 'He's not promised anything, Annie. Nothing solid.'

Annie sank down on the bench beside her. With a spon-taneous movement she flung one arm round Mercedes' shoulder, pulling her momentarily close. 'Don't be a killjoy, girl. I know that Hal Rawdon. If he says he'll put in a word, it's as good as done . . . And it's *your* doing, Mercedes. If you hadn't got him going, sounding off the way he loves to . . .'

Mercedes turned her face towards Annie, open, trusting the older woman for once, in her desire to believe. 'You honestly think he'll have that much influence?'

Annie nodded, her expression shrewd and knowing. 'Hal loves to throw his weight about, and there's plenty of it. And he's good at it – ever since school.'

Mercedes stared at the sun through half-closed lids. At that moment Annie's cause was her cause. Nor did it occur to her to brace herself against a rebuff. 'Be good to get the scabs on the run,' she said dreamily.

And for once Annie included her without reserve in their struggle. 'We *got* them on the run. From now on.'

21

'He's killing her!' Alex's soldier-puppet prodded unmercifully at Janie's doll with a wooden sword Andrew had made, till she lay spilled on the floor, a tangle of raised petticoats and pink rag-doll flesh. Janie left her there for about ten seconds.

'She's alive again!' The doll was roughly jerked upright. Janie's eyes gleamed with malicious triumph as she shook back her dark, tangled curls.

Both puppets had been fashioned by Daisy out of the odd rags she'd managed to collect together over the years.

'No!' Alex's angelic face blazed with conviction. 'Dead stays dead!' He was adamant. A year older than his sister, he scorned games that weren't true-to-life.

'All right.' Janie was unexpectedly docile. Once again the doll lay splayed on the bare, wooden floor. 'But next time she kills you!'

Alex nodded. He was reluctant, but knew you got nothing for nothing.

Daisy was quietly relieved. They'd sorted out the difference between themselves and she didn't have to stop working to see to them. Time was money. She couldn't suppress an unjust flash of irritation at the sight of Mamma, sitting like a cabbage in her wicker chair, blank and incurious, hands folded in the lap of her black dress. Only a year back she'd have been ready to step in if needed. The thought of that now was almost unbelievable. Almost all the time Mamma was happy just to sit. It was hard to remember that – since forever – her mother had been bustling and capable, never without work to do. A wise, reassuring presence. So sad how you forgot, robbing Mamma of the truth of her useful, active past. And always there was that edge of fear. If . . . when . . . the strike was over, how fit was Mamma to look after the children from morning till night?

Daisy sat sewing by the window in the warmth of the sun. She'd started at half past five that morning and now it was nearly midday. Good thing it was summer and got light early, it gave her that much more time. She couldn't cut corners with this kind of work, didn't want to. She was proud of it. The designs were all different, strong and unusual, almost like paintings. It pleased her to think of them on display in a shop, being admired, their specialness appreciated.

All the same, even with the goodish rate she was getting, it was sweated labour. Daisy screwed up her eyes. They were beginning to itch. But it was nice working here in the sunshine, with the children under her eye, and working on something of her own, something that interested her. Not like the pale, spindly designs they liked down at Ballard's. At least this job kept them in bread, with a little something extra a couple of times a week. And there was still enough to give Andrew a couple of bob towards the rent. God knows what they would have done without Edward Ballard.

But the kids were looking peaky – like real slum children. She'd have to stop for an hour later on, take them out, give them some air. She couldn't keep on like this, not for much longer. Annie was all smiles over what Hal Rawdon had said, but Daisy wasn't sure it amounted to much. Two more of the girls had given in and gone back. Sal O'Shea was one of them. Not that she'd ever been that keen on the strike. She was going to have a rough time of it. Everyone knew she was in the family way and who the father was . . .

Secretly, as Daisy sewed, an impression hovered in her

mind of Edward Ballard. His thick yellow hair and heavy, handsome face, the suppressed heat in his eyes. Half despising herself for it, she allowed the image to linger and excite her.

It wasn't really that she was attracted to him. Compared to Frankie he was old, with slackening skin and a softened belly. But she was fascinated by what she read in his eyes – an interest that he joked about in a man-of-the-world way, but which was keener and hotter than he was prepared to admit.

'Look, Mam, she's taken off her drawers!'

Daisy jerked back into reality. Janie was waving her doll, its petticoats hitched up to show the join of its pink legs and frog-like body.

Daisy shook her head with smiling disapproval. 'Put them back on, love. She'll get cold.'

'Janie's rude! Janie's rude!' Alex chanted.

Janie flourished the doll at him with saucy bravado.

Daisy had a ploy when their boisterousness threatened to slow down her work. 'Alex, Janie, go and get some water for the plants. Alex take the brown bottle, Janie find a cup. Go downstairs right now and fill them for me.' It was a measure of the restricted life they led that expeditions like this were a distraction, an adventure almost.

'Don't spill any!' she shouted after them as they clattered down the stairs.

In the sudden quiet she noticed her mother's head droop to one side and she began to snore quietly. Nowadays Daisy found it a relief when she slept. Somehow it justified her passivity.

She snipped off a length of blue-mauve silk and threaded her needle. She would get this one finished before stopping to spread the remains of yesterday's bread with a bit of tasteless dripping the butcher had given her. He saved her things like that sometimes, always handing them over with some suggestive joke, knowing she'd take it because she had to. Edie Black always sent her fifteen-year-old daughter along to beg bones or a bit of suet, and she got the same treatment.

Half-reluctant, half-obsessive, Daisy returned to thoughts of Edward Ballard. After yesterday afternoon she couldn't fool herself that his offers of help were fatherly or neighbourly. She was clear about the fact that he wanted her and that was why he was busying himself on her behalf, finding customers for her work. That being the case, if she met him again, she was encouraging him. It was as simple as that.

Even laying aside the question of money, she hung back from ending her relationship with Ballard. Her hands moved with quick, economical movements, totally independent of the doubts in her mind. Daisy couldn't deny that it was lovely – so lovely – to escape for a while from the grind of her life, the worry, the lack of pleasure. Eating cakes in a chic tea-room, or strolling in the sunshine in Hyde Park made her feel like someone else. They made her remember that she was nice-looking and only twenty-five, and that there were other things in life besides work and money-worries. She couldn't help enjoying talking to someone who had a bit of a way with words, and seemed to have time on his hands, and gave off a feeling of pleasure and leisure. Just being with someone who was smart and clean, and smelt of cologne and cigars did her good. She didn't want to banish it from her life. Not yet.

Anna Sitek woke up with a start as the children came back with the water, and Daisy turned away from the distressing vacancy of her open eyes.

'The old man from upstairs said we was pests and Janie stuck out her tongue,' Alex reported, his small hands tightly clenched round the brown bottle full of water.

'Only a little bit,' Janie protested. 'Mam, I'm hungry. I smelled bacon downstairs. Can *we* have some?'

Daisy felt a dull lurch in her insides, as she always did when the children asked her questions like that. But she was careful not to show it. Experience had taught her that trying to explain only made things worse. If you ignored their demands for meat or milk or anything they couldn't have, they forgot in time. Deliberately she turned her attention to the old misery from upstairs.

'You mustn't put your tongue out, Janie. Not even a little bit. You have to be polite to old people.'

Balanced on a chair, Janie tipped up her cup over one of the geraniums, spilling generous amounts of water on to the window-sill and floor.

'But he smells,' she said self-righteously.

22

She had let herself out without waking anybody. Her sister, Kathleen, in the same bed, was snoring like a pig in muck. Lying beside her, Sal O'Shea felt as if the room was spinning round and around. It made no difference if her eyes were open or shut. She lay there watchful as a cat, feeling her eyes were glowing in the dark and certain, all at once, that in the swirling darkness the ceiling would suddenly shatter and split open, with a ripping of wood and plaster, a life of its own. She hadn't slept, not for nights and nights, and even in the daytime the world would start turning as soon as she heard anyone snigger, or when the boys shouted names after her, or the women down at Ballard's laughed together, then looked across at her over their shoulders, shutting her out.

Down on the empty wharf she felt like a slinking, shadowy rat, but the silence and darkness soothed her soul. Sal sat at the top of the stone stairway that led down to the black water. She felt safer sitting, closer to the ground, so if the world started spinning she could cling on until it stopped. Her hands gripped the step each side of her. The sky was huge and dizzying, gunmetal grey, stars glittering millions of miles above, the cranes towering giddily like black, burnt-out skeletons; below, the water moving all the time, sucking and slapping against the steps and the hulking shapes of the barges.

She couldn't go back to the factory again tomorrow. To Leonard Floyd with his sweating forehead and burning eyes, his grin. And those women she hardly knew, though they seemed to know her and all about her, and talk about it endlessly through break-times.

'Little love-child, is it?' the big woman – Beth – had called out as she passed by on her way to the privy, then the others gave a great roar of hard laughter and she felt sick, only just managing to hold on long enough to throw up into one of the stinking buckets behind the screen. Everybody must have heard. It seemed like the whole world knew she'd fallen for a baby before she'd even known it herself.

In a flash of hopelessness Sal felt as if she'd been sitting alone like this for half her life. She could remember at school, in the yard, often as not she'd had no one to play with. Just sat on her own on the ground by the wall. Even at home, with the seven of them kids together, it seemed like they paired off, all except her. She was the quiet one, the one they forgot. Only her cousin Michael seemed to like her much. He used to carry her around on his back when they were children, strong as anything. But they said he was half daft.

And since she was expecting Ma wouldn't even speak to her, only got Father Simpson round to give her the rough side of his tongue. He hated fornication, he was known for it. But it was a bit late talking to her now. The strike had been a blessing in a way. It meant she didn't have to face people all the time. But in the end Ma said she wouldn't feed her any more unless she got up off her backside and brought some money home.

When Josh Partridge came along last winter, everything had seemed different. A grown man of nearly thirty and he was after her. She felt important and pretty. They used to go walking nearly every night, all the way down to Tanner's allotments. Josh hid a piece of sacking in one of the sheds and they used to lie on it and cuddle where there were a few bushes. He used to unpin her hair and say it was lovely, when her brothers had always told her it was like frayed rope. She knew she shouldn't let him stick her, but he was stronger than she was, and anyway it was worth it. At the time.

Because now he wouldn't even look at her. When he was with his mates they'd all laugh together and she knew it was over her. And when she saw Betty Partridge in the street, Betty would smile right at her, a gloating little grin. Josh used to tell her he couldn't stand Betty any more – ugly and bad-tempered with a neck like a turkey's. And now the two of them were going round like love-birds as if to show her. She'd seen them last week. She couldn't bear it. Her head went muzzy, there was a roaring in her ears, and she felt as if she'd burst.

Sal looked up at the sky. So wide, and the stars seemed to be quivering. She felt as if she were going to be alone like this forever, with no one liking her, no one on her side. All by herself by the black water, in the cold, under the big dark sky. And not one happy thing in her life. But the worst was the thought of going to the factory tomorrow, with all of them jeering, and she couldn't get away. She'd do anything to get out of that.

For the last few days Mercedes had been filled with a buoyant energy, a euphoria, invading every corner of her life – irrational, intense and almost painful. The cause was Andrew and their growing, urgent, tentative friendship, their long evening walks, miles removed from the problems of Bermondsey and the strike, untroubled by worries of parents waiting up for her at home. In her dazed state of mind, Mercedes saw her days and nights suffused with a dreamy, opalescent glow, like that of a melted pearl.

He was so different from any man she'd known before. Apart from anything else, she'd never met anyone whose physical presence affected her so powerfully. When they were together she was rapt, her eyes fixed on his pale, strongly marked features, discovering fleeting expressions in his grey eyes and new aspects in the curve of his lips, appraising time and again the unconscious elegance of his body. She was entranced by the casual skill of his hands and the flat huskiness of his voice, intrigued by the singular combination of his diffidence with a rooted self-confidence.

With her Andrew was conscious of his lack of education and middle-class graciousness. He remarked on the difference between them often, sometimes with a smile that verged on the sheepish which made her long to cradle his head against her breasts like a child's, his clumsiness transformed into yet another charm.

On the other hand he possessed certainties that frightened her because – at least where she was concerned – they were so fully justified. For instance, he seemed to place an absolute trust in the conviction that anything he confided to Mercedes about himself, his life or his past would be of breathless interest to her. And it was. She couldn't pretend otherwise.

All her life Mercedes had lacked faith in her own beauty. She was too pale, her hair too straight and mousy, her figure far too slight. But Andrew, without vanity, took his physical attraction negligently for granted. And Mercedes couldn't begrudge him the assumption, since she was enslaved. Her desire for him was running out of control. Every nerve in her body seemed alive. At night her brain flashed like a cinematograph show, with fevered images of sexual lore gleaned from friends with wide, secretive eyes. She imagined Andrew lying naked alongside her and felt she'd give anything for the irresistible, half-terrifying experience.

All the energy she had made her take the long way round, beside the river, on her way to Daisy's. She walked for the sheer joy of being out in the sunshine, feeling the vigour in her limbs. The river sparkled this morning, and the bustle of St Saviour's Wharf was heartening, with its barges and cranes, the men laughing together as they worked. On grey days it seemed merely bleak and sordid.

Mercedes had news to pass on. The previous afternoon she'd had a meeting with Hannah and Lady Flowers, the Association's president. She'd pleaded the Ballard workers' cause, given them an account of the meeting with Hal Rawdon, presenting it in the light of a triumph – far more so than, in her heart of hearts, she actually believed to be the case.

'If they can just hang on another two or three weeks,' she'd urged. 'The strike's as good as won.'

No point in undercutting her argument by revealing her doubts.

'But they need money desperately – two more women have given up and gone back this week . . . And others'll be forced to unless we can help them financially.'

Lady Flowers had hummed and ha'd and asked a lot of probing questions. She was a fresh-faced woman of sixty or so, her white hair cut daringly like a medieval pageboy's. Hannah had been to stay with her once, on her country estate, and been expected to get up at some ungodly hour to go ferreting. Under her scrutiny Mercedes had felt less like a leader of women than an inky-fingered fourth-former. But she'd finally agreed to release an initial sum of ten shillings for each of the women still on strike.

Ahead of her, Mercedes noticed, quite a crowd had gathered. She could see a semi-circle of backs – men and women in working-clothes, with a couple of policemen off to one side, looking more than usually earnest and self-important. Her curiosity was aroused, but she couldn't make out the cause of the gathering.

Drawing level, she approached the knot of bystanders and asked a hatchet-faced man with riotous black side-burns what the matter was.

He nodded towards the area in front of him. Mercedes wasn't tall enough to see.

'Body,' he said tersely. 'Just been fished out. Looks

like suicide. Young girl. They're waiting for the police-ambulance now.'

'No!' Mercedes' reaction was instant, horrified.

The man looked at her with amused cynicism. 'Happens all the time. Couple of stiff 'uns a month, give or take . . .'

He moved aside to let her pass and she saw a dirty tarpaulin spread on the ground, covering what was obviously a human figure. The sunny, cheerful bustle of the wharf emphasized the bleak finality of the sight. Mercedes stared, morbidly fascinated by the still form beneath its soiled covering. A young girl, the man had said. Mercedes' present world seemed so full, so spacious, she found it inconceivable that some youthful creature should see such despair in life that death, in the filthy water, appeared preferable.

'Mercedes!' Someone called her name.

She looked up. Annie Tyrell and Edie Black stood opposite, savouring the commotion. Mercedes walked across to join them.

'It's Sal O'Shea,' Edie whispered eagerly, revealing her row of broken teeth. 'I identified her.'

Mercedes caught her breath, covering her mouth with one hand. So it was one of Ballard's workers. She didn't know the girl – she'd taken no prominent part in the strike – but throughout the five or so weeks of its duration so far, her doings had provided the main subject of gossip, a constant riveting backdrop to the progress of the dispute. Mercedes had lived with her legend. A nondescript girl, only eighteen, who'd carried on shamelessly with another woman's husband, been insulted by his wronged wife in the street, and got her slow-witted cousin to give the woman a black eye. Then the reckoning – a pregnancy, and the man had deserted her. It seemed the very stuff of Victorian melodrama. Yet suddenly the story was made real by the presence of this inert body under a dirty cloth.

'Poor thing,' Mercedes breathed with horrified pity.

Annie and Edie gazed at her, impassive, curious.

'S'pose it was your man she'd been running around with,' Edie said stolidly.

'I wouldn't wish her dead!'

'Little cow never had no guts.' Annie shrugged with majestic certainty. 'If you're going to pinch another woman's man, you got to have the front to take what comes to you.'

There was no trace of pity in her tone. To Mercedes her words had the effect of sheet lightning, revealing with quick, blinding clarity a dark landscape. And she was reminded graphically, yet again, of the difference between Annie's life and her own. In Annie's world the weak went under and no bones about it. Mercedes marvelled at her ruthless realism. It seemed beside the point to condemn.

'Anyway, she was a blackleg.' Dourly Edie compressed her lips.

''Ere!' Annie exclaimed, changing the subject with breathtaking rapidity. 'Molly Planer's pulled out from down Ballard's. So that's one scab less.'

'One!' Edie mocked.

But Annie remained supremely unruffled. 'First of many. Mark my words.'

23

Each evening Mercedes had the impression that London belonged to herself and Andrew. Between them a wild alliance had sprung up. They were two roaming alley-cats, anonymous and answerable to no one. She had never known anything like it before, this heady freedom, heightened by her own obsession with the hungry good looks of Daisy's brother. And he seemed as susceptible as she was to the singular enchantment of their night-time rambles.

Above her head hung the dark weight of retribution ready to fall, but Mercedes ignored it, along with every cautious precept of her secure upbringing. She was doing wrong and knew it, wandering at night alone with a young working-man. But beneath the threatening shadow of society's condemnation she roved recklessly, revelling in their shared escape.

In four days her parents would be home. Her wings would be clipped. Mercedes pushed the thought away, famished for the liberty she was tasting. There might never be another chance.

Always they skirted Bermondsey. No one there knew about their friendship. Tonight they drifted towards South-wark, up-river. Andrew wanted to show her some fields he used to sneak off to as a boy with his mates. He seemed nostalgic about his childhood as a time without care or responsibility, and he took pleasure in displaying his haunts to Mercedes' avid eyes.

'We had a den down there in some trees. We took boxes down to sit on, and we used to swipe pasties off Dick's stall in the market and take them to eat.' He gave a wary sideways glance to see how she took this information. Mercedes found herself wide-eyed and uncritical. The glimpses he gave her of his young life seemed rich and bizarre to her, vastly more exotic than her own.

As they walked she talked to him about the shock she'd had that morning, happening on the drowned, canvas-covered corpse of Sal O'Shea. 'I didn't know her,' she explained. 'But I almost feel as if I did. Ever since I've been here there's been so much talk.'

Andrew knew about the suicide already via the word-of-mouth network that spread all news through Bermondsey like forest fire.

'She was one of them people who's always been there, but you never gave her two thoughts. Sal never had much to say for herself . . . That great ape of a Josh Partridge, he's been strutting round the place for months like a dog with two tails . . . Like he's some kind of big ladies' man . . .' The tone of his voice reflected Andrew's contempt. They walked a few steps in silence, then he said, 'Poor little cow.'

She liked his compassion, so different from the tight-faced dismissiveness of Annie and Edie. Perhaps a deprived life didn't have to harden you. Though Andrew was still young – younger than she was by eighteen months or so.

'Annie and Edie seemed so . . . unforgiving.'

'Married women close ranks,' he commented sagaciously, and she was touched by his air of sober world-liness.

Impulsively she said, 'I'm glad you're not so hard.' She had an image of him as chivalrous, decent . . . He turned to her with a smile she'd come to know – shy, yet mocking and, at the same time, warmed by her approval.

Bridge Fields was a tract of wasteland, set back a bit from the river, behind some dilapidated warehouses. Rough grass and bushes covered hard, pebbly ground, starred with ragwort, rose-bay and yarrow.

'People do their courting here,' he said.

'Do they?' The slightest mention of love or sex from Andrew affected her in the most acutely personal fashion. Talking to Walter she could discuss such things with airy indifference. With Andrew she broke out in a foolish sweat.

'Seems smaller than it used to be.' He looked around. 'We thought it was a forest or a jungle. About twenty of us used to fight wars here.'

'I envy you,' she said, without thinking. To her his words spoke of an instinctive, unconscious freedom. As a child, she'd always been accompanied everywhere, always had to account for her doings.

'Envy me?' He looked at her as though she were mad. 'I've seen the house you live in.'

'It's not everything.' She thought of her safe, comfortable life.

'Easy to say that when you've got it.' She glimpsed a hint of the hostility that sparked frequently from Annie and the others.

Mercedes changed the subject. 'Show me your old hiding-place.'

It was around nine-thirty in the evening. A group of children who'd been playing war in two noisy gangs drifted away, leaving the field to silence. The east side was bounded by a picturesquely broken wall, punctuated by bushes, a few trees, and a couple of ruined outbuildings. Andrew led her in that direction, towards the far corner, until their way was barred by a screen of thorn bushes grown to the height of eight or nine feet. They seemed to present an impenetrable barrier.

He looked doubtfully at her white blouse and skirt. 'We used to squeeze through here.'

Mercedes had no thought of being hindered by prudence. She spied a place where the branches seemed slightly thinner and began to push her way through, ignoring the thorns pulling at the threads in her clothes and tugging at her hair, prising it free from the tortoise-shell combs that anchored it.

Behind the screen of bushes was a clearing some ten feet square, carpeted with grass that seemed softer and lusher than the rest, as though this part might once have been under cultivation. Here the boundary wall had a decorative, arched section of brickwork and was criss-crossed with the gnarled, branching stems of an ancient rambling rose. High up at the top of the wall, where the sun would reach, festoons of lax, pink blooms trailed, mingling with the wild, self-sewn vegetation. To one side of the clearing the roots of a tree snaked sinuously at ground level, dividing the clearing-floor into oddly-shaped sections. A fallen tree lay across the grass, with clusters of ferns growing from its dead bark. Between two bushes a torn net curtain hung, as if subsequent generations of children had made a camp here. There was an earthy, damp, green smell to the place. Mercedes looked about her. From the façade of tough, dull thorn bushes she could never have guessed what lay behind.

'It's like a monastery garden or something,' she said. 'So quiet and secret.'

Andrew sat down on the trunk of the fallen tree. He seemed pleased that she'd recognized the specialness of his old hiding-place. He held out his hand to her. 'Come and sit down.'

She sat beside him on the log, looking about, noticing other things. An elder in bloom, with its acrid scent. A tiny mauve creeping plant growing out of the broken places in the wall.

Andrew watched as she gazed about her. 'You're so nice,' he told her suddenly. 'I'd never have thought . . .'

She looked at him in surprise, meeting his grey eyes, so like Daisy's.

He said, 'I've never seen you with your hair hanging

loose,' then leant across and kissed her – one of the slow, cool kisses he'd been giving her the last few nights when they said goodbye at midnight or later.

Something quick and impatient in her protested at the respectfulness of his approach. In an unthinking movement she reached for one of his hands and laid it on her right breast. A split second later Mercedes realized what she'd done. She was shocked and unbelieving but, at the same time, exhilarated by her own boldness.

'Mercedes . . .' His voice was low and wondering. His hand moved on the mound of her breast and he pulled her closer. Dazedly she wondered what she'd meant by her action, and what he thought she meant.

'Mercedes . . .' He became urgent. His free hand tangled in her hair, held her still, while his lips ground into hers, forcing them open, and his tongue entered her mouth.

His new passion disconcerted her, but her confusion combined with a small thrill of triumph and a cooler edge of curiosity. His mouth, crushing hers, made it difficult to breathe. His hand fumbled with the buttons of her blouse and found an entry, encountering the material of her chemise and also the curved area of flesh above it. The intimacy of his hot hand on her bare skin was so intoxicating that she took fright and confusedly pushed him away.

'I'm sorry . . .' His face was changed, his eyes hot and heavy. Reluctantly he let her go. She was scared and excited by the way he looked, this transformation from the shy, correct companion he'd been just minutes ago. It was what she'd wanted and yet now . . . she was unsure. At the same time a part of her cried out at the thought that he might stop kissing her, might go back to his former controlled frame of mind.

The realization occurred then that in a few days her parents would be home and this freedom would be lost.

She would no longer have the choice. And she knew with a fierce certainty that, if she pushed Andrew away, clung to the proprieties, every nerve in her body would ache with regret. By leading him on she would be entering deep, dangerous waters. So be it. She might be terrified of the unknown, but the grey anti-climax of pulling back had suddenly become unthinkable.

She shook her head. 'I was scared. But I like you kissing me.' Abruptly she unfastened the remaining buttons of her blouse, pulling it open to reveal the white cotton of her chemise, the bareness of her neck and the upper half of her breasts. The action seemed quite natural to her, and at the same time unbelievably brazen.

He kissed her again, caressing the naked skin above her chemise.

'I love you . . . love you . . .' With some lucid, watchful section of her mind, she thought the words meant nothing. They were a chant, an incantation, expressing his arousal. Hesitantly, deliberately, Andrew pushed his hand down inside her chemise, so that it rested on her bare breast. His thumb played with her nipple. Mercedes heard her own sharp intake of breath. Her arms pulled his thin, hard body close. She was weak with her own excitement.

In a convulsive movement Andrew laid one of her hands over the fastening of his breeches. Beneath the cloth she felt a hard, unfamiliar lump. A flash of recall. Phyllis Goodwin at school telling a group of them about this, sitting by the ornamental pond in the spring sun. They'd been sceptical at the time, but the memory had remained, surfacing now like a fish. Mercedes thought she should pull her hand away, but she left it where it was, unmoving and yet acquiescent. There was a sound from Andrew like a groan. A strange, animal sound. And still she didn't draw back.

'Let's lie down.' He looked at her with feverish eyes.

Mercedes nodded, thinking she must look like him. As if she were drowning.

Slowly he disentangled himself. Standing up, Andrew took off his jacket and then his shirt. She stared at him, mesmerized, like some small targeted animal fascinated by a snake, her gaze riveted to the sight of his lean, tightly-muscled torso. He laid the two garments end to end. Then he sat on the ground, taking her by the hand so that she too was pulled down on to the spread jacket.

'What d'you want, Mercedes?' he asked. His eyes held hers, level and searching.

She was silent, looking at him. He was asking her to make a decision and all she wanted was to be carried forward, swept along, not have to think. Her brain teemed with incoherent, contradictory images. How could she decide anything?

And yet some parallel urge overrode her confusion, summoning up a low, clear voice. 'I want to know what it's like . . .' She moved her shoulders in a small shrug of emphasis. 'I just want to . . .'

'You know what you're saying?' Andrew pressed her, incredulous.

She nodded. 'Yes.'

It was unreal, this rational, sotto-voce conversation. Her mind flashed the comparison of a general giving the order to attack.

Andrew touched her cheek with an intake of breath expressing some emotion she couldn't guess at. Then he pulled her down gently alongside him and began to kiss her softly, caressing her in a slow, insistent fashion, as if to calm her, and himself. Touching her breasts through the material of her chemise, her hips and thighs through the cloth of her skirt and petticoat, which had crept half way up her legs. She was lulled. In the twilight his face was close, pale and beautiful, mirroring her night-time imaginings. Her fantasies. She trusted him like a child.

He paused for a moment. 'You got to take your drawers off,' he whispered huskily. The very baldness of the order aroused her beyond belief. As if hypnotized, she obeyed.

Mercedes lay down beside him again. He held her and kissed her. Then, after a while, his hand probed between her legs. The enormity of the intimacy made her gasp. He began to caress her in the way she'd touched herself at night in bed. She closed her eyes, blotting out reality, shame, concentrating on sensation.

Far away she was conscious of him fiddling with his own clothing. He rolled on top of her and a hard, blunt shaft of flesh pushed against her, forcing an entrance.

'I love you. God, I love you . . .' As he thrust into her she heard the rhythmic, mechanical incantation, as if from another world.

24

At ten minutes to seven Leonard Floyd sat on the bench outside Ballard's factory, smoking his early-morning cigar, long legs stretched out in front of him, eyes narrowed against the curling smoke and raw sunlight, his mind empty, ready for whatever pictures drifted in. Best moment of the day, he always told himself, before the sluts filled the place with their cackling.

But a tiny cloud of disquiet hovered on the far edge of his horizon. There was something that didn't quite add up. The way the Planer woman, then the scraggy Richardson bitch, had given notice, upped and left, when they were in clover here, getting decent money for shoddy work, as Doll Durrant pointed out all day, every day, like some fat bloody parrot.

There was something funny about the way they told him, too, as if they were hiding something. It bothered him. Though, God knows, with three of the regular workers back in line – not counting Sal O'Shea – he'd no cause to worry. They were worth five of any of the scabs. Barring Doll's nieces – he'd give *them* a job any time. Good, clean workers and no side to them.

Sal O'Shea's face shimmered for a moment in his mind. She was another one, the kind of girl he liked, even though he'd always thought she looked like a skinned rabbit. She was quiet and eager to please, a fair worker, and no trouble. She used to tremble when he looked at her work, in case he found anything wrong. He liked that. She was just the kind of girl to fall for a baby if anyone took two pennyworth of notice of her. He could tell the type from miles off. If it hadn't been for Dot, he might have been tempted himself. Hard to believe the kid had drowned herself, though. That took guts and he never thought she had any. And it left him one good worker the poorer.

His lips curved briefly in sardonic amusement. Good reason for sticking with Dot. She wouldn't get knocked up, not yet awhile. Too young for that. A flash of tenderness crossed his mind. She wasn't a bad girl, always did what he told her and never got above herself. He felt like her father sometimes, telling her what was what. With a flicker of arousal he remembered her touching him under the table last night at the Tiger's Eye. Nice at the time, but he wasn't sure he was keen on her getting ideas of her own like that.

They were a funny family for sure. He recalled Dot's old man, with the strands of oily black hair pasted across his head, sparse as violin-strings. Everyone knew he shagged his own daughter, Lil, Dot's mother. But people still drank with him, accepted him. Seems you could get away with anything.

The sun, red through his half-closed lids, and the waft of tobacco, made him think of Africa suddenly, his soldiering days. Thinking back, they seemed good times, though he wouldn't have said so then. He could see the white-hot sun over the wide, dusty hills. Freer than here. Wilder. You could do things no one could get away with in this country. With a half-pleasurable disgust, he remembered the Boer women in the camps, starved, like skeletons in sun-bonnets, with big, sunken eyes and hair like rope. Now they knew what it was to be rock-bottom. No fight left in them. Not like the sluts he had to deal with here. Floyd pictured Annie's face, twisted in a snarl, defying him. Be good to see *her* like that, crawling in the dust, begging for a drop of water . . .

His musings were broken by a peal of strident laughter. He recognized the braying tone. Beth Coster, the slack-chinned old bag. She was another one like Annie. Time to sort them out. Floyd hauled himself to his feet with a dull gleam of foreboding. Unreasonably, something told him that this morning another of the scab women would've thrown in the sponge.

Hannah had presence, Mercedes admitted to herself, with a twinge of mildly ill-natured envy, which she immediately tried to repress. The meeting – in Father Simpson's cold, clean, dispiriting church hall – had come to revolve round her elegant person.

First she had presided over the distribution of funds authorized by Lady Flowers. Father Simpson had fulfilled the role of impartial witness, and Mercedes was reduced to right-hand woman, ticking off names on a list with clerkly anonymity. She longed to advertise the fact that it was her persuasion, and not Hannah's, that had secured the release of the money, but of course it would have been way beneath her dignity to do so.

Hannah was discreetly resplendent in a slim dress of palest pink gaberdine, with tucks and a sash. It was superbly cut but absolutely unostentatious. Her straw hat echoed the pink of the frock, combining it with a soft dove-grey.

At present she stood at the head of the table addressing the women, who were ranged untidily on chairs alongside the decorator's trestles borrowed for the occasion. The prospect of money had ensured that the gathering was a large one.

Hannah's voice was pitched low and urgent, as unobtrusively right as her clothes. 'You see, you women can withstand so much. *Together*. I'd like you all to picture a collection of sticks of firewood . . . Now, singly each stick can be snapped and broken.' Illustrating the words with a graceful gesture. 'But put those sticks together – in a bundle.' She lowered her voice dramatically. The women strained to hear. 'Pack them together.

Then try to break them . . . You can't,' she concluded triumphantly.

The comparison wasn't a new one. Mercedes had read it in an article by the trade-unionist, Mary MacArthur, and in many pamphlets since. It was a commonplace to her, so she'd never thought of trying it out on the Ballard's workers. Perhaps, on reflection, she'd taken their commitment too much for granted. Maybe they'd have appreciated a rousing speech or two of this nature.

'*Talk* to your work-mates,' Hannah continued. 'Some of them will be wavering, showing signs of quitting the strike. Talk! Persuade! You can do it. Band together and you can make yourself as unbreakable as that bundle of firewood . . .'

The women sat in silence, watching and listening. Mercedes envied Hannah her supreme lack of self-doubt. Her lack of a sense of the absurd, too. Never, in her wildest dreams, could she, Mercedes, have harangued an audience in that low, thrilling, *throbbing* tone.

Hannah continued in this vein for some time longer. Her voice rose and fell with hypnotic intensity, and her words were greeted with a breathless hush. She looked imposing and beautiful with her chestnut hair piled beneath her hat into a chignon of sculptured perfection. It must be gratifying, Mercedes thought, to have this goddess on your side, encouraging you, adamant that you could win. She felt redundant and graceless on the sidelines, like some substitute player in an important football match.

Hannah's speech reached its emotive climax as she looked forward to a new dawn for working people of all nationalities, just so long as they held fast to the golden rule – a passionate faith in their own solidarity. Proclaiming these words, her voice flicked like a whip-lash. The silence that greeted her pronouncement was bottomless.

Then, mundanely, she consulted her watch and adjusted her veil, addressing Mercedes in her brisk, everyday tones.

'I'll have to go now, Mercedes, dear. James is picking me up in the motor. Can we offer you a lift back into town?'

'No, thank you, Hannah. I'll stay on. There are one or two things the committee ought to discuss.' It was the truth and Mercedes was glad of it. She didn't relish the thought of being swept from the hall in Hannah's regal wake.

'Very well, my dear.'

It occurred to Mercedes that Hannah seemed more than usually the *grande dame*, though she played her role with faultless conviction.

When she and the majority of the women were gone, Mercedes was left alone with Annie and Edie, Daisy and Queenie. Soberly they began to talk about the best way of getting the strike money to those women who hadn't been able to come to the meeting. Then there were a couple of gravely sick children whose hospital bills had to be met somehow. Today Mercedes was painfully aware of her own matter-of-factness compared to the charged atmosphere that Hannah's presence had generated. All the same, she reflected, these details had to be sorted out.

'Friend of yours, is she?' Queenie asked abruptly, with a jerk of the head towards the door through which Hannah had exited. Her hard little face below the tightly-braided hair was inscrutable, and her eyes were like two black glass beads.

Once upon a time, without a moment's hesitation, Mercedes would proudly have answered yes. Now she was acutely conscious of the ambiguities that clouded her feelings for Hannah Spalding.

'Hannah's a colleague,' she replied. 'It was she who introduced me to the Association.'

'Thinks she's *it*, don't she.' Queenie's comment rang harsh and abrasive in the chill quiet of the hall.

'She does a lot of good work up and down the country, strikes like this, labour relations, that sort of thing.'

Scrupulously fair, Mercedes was aware that her defence lacked warmth.

'Does she talk to *everyone* like they were kids? Or idiots?' Queenie's forthright question seemed to slice through the layers of respectful pretence that had surrounded Hannah's visit.

'Good job we got you,' Edie said. 'With that other one, I'd've been spitting in her eye after five minutes.'

25

'You look tired, Daisy,' Edward said, his face twisted into a worried look, as if he were a family friend.

A needlepoint of exasperation pierced Daisy's well-being. 'So would you if you did nothing from five in the morning till ten at night but sit and sew.'

He bowed his head. 'I'm sorry. I was thoughtless.'

She could have said a lot more, but why spoil things? She sipped from her shining glass of chilled white wine. Each time she did so a childhood memory flooded her veins. Twice, or three times at the most, Daddy had felt rich enough the night before Christmas to buy a couple of green bottles of German wine and they'd all had to have a taste, even the children. She used to pull a face and say it was sour, but she half liked it even then. And tonight, with the memories it brought her, the cold pale-gold liquid seemed the most delicious thing she'd ever tasted.

The restaurant was homely and comfortable, on the river at Richmond. They'd come by cab. Here, she guessed, he was unlikely to run into anyone he knew. Leaving home, she'd told Mamma not to worry if she was late. There was work to deliver and sorting out the next batch might take time. She'd told Alex the same. He took in such things better than Mamma nowadays. And she'd left a note for Andrew, though he seemed to keep later hours than ever recently, and the chances were that she'd be home before he was.

Daisy looked about her. She didn't feel out of place here. There was nothing snobbish about it. The waiters were middle-aged and friendly, all wore aprons. The walls were panelled in dark, shiny wood and a wine-red carpet covered the floor. The tables were partitioned off one from another and you sat on high-backed leather benches. Daisy had slipped off her jacket and wore the old-fashioned coffee-coloured lacy blouse that Mamma wore at all family festivities when she was young. Daisy used to love her in it and she knew it suited her as well.

'Tiredness becomes you,' Edward said. 'One of the first things I noticed about you were the shadows under your eyes. They're so alluring. They make you look as if you had some kind of tragic secret.'

It was a funny thing to say, Daisy thought. He was probably a little bit drunk. He seemed to think it was in order now to make personal remarks and pay her compliments. Perhaps he was right. Just being here, with him, meant she'd accepted something. Though what exactly still wasn't clear. All the same, she didn't feel like being frosty, standing on her dignity. Although she was drinking the wine as slowly as possible Daisy thought it was affecting her, making her feel less careful than she normally did.

Their waiter, a nice moon-faced cockney with a walrus moustache, brought them plates of dressed crab. It smelt good and Daisy was determined to enjoy the meal, come what may. Her stomach felt like an empty cave. She would have to remind herself to try and toy with the food a little, and not wolf it as if she'd barely eaten for a week. Although she hadn't.

'I suppose you've not heard whether my handkerchiefs are selling?' Daisy asked hesitantly. It was wonderful to be able to place them at all. At the same time, she couldn't help being curious about how they were going. It seemed to her that, through having the time to concentrate on them, they were getting better. More unusual, more striking.

She thought Edward looked a bit sheepish as he replied, 'My friend seems pleased with them. Keeps asking for more. So they must be selling. Otherwise he wouldn't bother.'

'I suppose so.' Foolishly she'd longed for a bit of praise. But that wasn't the way business was done. You took the money and were grateful.

They ate in silence for a while. Outside the window it was a carefree summer evening on the Thames, with punts and rowing-boats, men in blazers and women in light dresses. Their voices seemed to float across the water. In her mind Daisy felt part of it as she sipped wine and ate controlled mouthfuls of the delicious sharp-salty crab. No matter that later she'd be back in her cramped rooms, with the children restless, Mamma snoring, and herself getting up at the crack of dawn for another sixteen hours of work.

'I was talking to Leonard Floyd this morning. He says the substitute workers are learning the ropes quite nicely.' There was a hint of black mischief in Edward's eyes.

'Oh Leonard Floyd!' Daisy was startled at the contemptuous venom of her tone. Must be the wine. Normally, with Edward Ballard – with everyone – she took care not to venture outside her protective shell of control.

'Her eyes flashed coals of detestation.' He looked amused. She supposed he was quoting from some book. 'Why do you hate him so, Daisy? I know he's the boss, but he's only a man doing his job.'

'He's vermin.'

'Why?'

'He treats us like dirt. Not me so much – he needs me. I'm skilled. It's the younger ones specially. The scared ones. He loves to treat them like they're nothing. Step on them. He gets a thrill from it, I reckon, a dirty thrill.' Her tongue ran away with her. She was half-amazed by what she was saying, but beginning to enjoy this new recklessness. Deliberately she took another swallow of her wine.

'He hasn't pinched your bottom? That's not why you're so down on him?' Edward entered into her mood of frankness, his eyes bright and over-eager.

Daisy was scornful. 'He wouldn't dare! It's the weak ones he goes for.' A pause, then she added, 'And anyway I'm too old for him. He likes them young. Kids who've never had the rags on.'

With satisfaction she saw him recoil in genuine shock. 'What do you mean?'

'You've seen Dot. She's fourteen and none too bright. He's been with her for two years already.'

'Is that true?'

She could see that this had made more impression on him than all her talk of Floyd's tyrannical ways.

Daisy shrugged. 'Why would I lie?'

Edward didn't reply at once, giving his attention to the final morsels of his crab, not meeting her eye. Then he looked up. 'Well, that's none of my business. The man's a good manager. He gets results.'

She gave him a bemused smile. 'He's got you a five-week strike. Nearly six. And it's not over yet.'

They noticed the waiter who was hovering silently. His expression betrayed a keen interest in their conversation.

Edward flushed as the man took their plates. 'That was delicious,' he commented stiffly.

'Thank you, sir.'

When he'd gone, Daisy continued warmly, 'Haven't you ever thought that your factory is one of the biggest employers round our way? We *need* you. D'you think we'd have walked out if we'd been treated halfway decent? Annie was just the excuse. It was all there before, bubbling under . . .'

Edward cut in. 'Let's agree to disagree.'

She shrugged. 'If that's what you want.'

He was still ruffled, abruptly refilling his glass and

downing the wine in a few longish swallows. The waiter reappeared with a trolley of roasted meats, which he carved to their order. Faced with a platter of beef slices, ham, and tongue in Madeira sauce, Daisy experienced a moment of nausea. She'd never seen such plenty and it struck her as almost . . . disgusting. A few potatoes nestled to one side of the plate, and she cut into one. It seemed a more palatable, familiar object. Perhaps, in time, she'd be able to work up to the meat.

Edward ordered another bottle of wine. He seemed to know all the names. It was red this time she saw when it arrived. Daisy still had an almost full glass of white and she thought it would last her for a bit.

When the waiter was well clear of them again, Edward paused in his eating and looked at her across the table. He seemed serious, and there was something swimmy about his eyes. 'Daisy, I don't want to quarrel with you.'

She was surprised. 'We were just talking. Nothing personal. Better to be frank, though.'

'My feeling exactly.' A hint of relief in his voice.

Daisy found that she could eat the meat a little at a time. Her nausea began to fade. She ate manfully, as if gathering strength for the weeks to come.

'There's something I'd like to say to you.' He sounded a bit sharp. His statement cut into her careful concentration on the food. She looked up enquiringly.

Suddenly he was vehement. 'You're *so* composed. Why is it? Why do I feel so . . . clumsy?'

It wasn't a comment she could find an answer to. He was rich and had power. She didn't understand his sudden agitation. Daisy simply asked, 'What was it you wanted to say?'

She waited. He looked hot and bothered. One of the wings of his hair fell across his face, which was florid and puffy.

'I want to look after you, Daisy,' he blurted. His lips were wet and there was a slackness about them.

She was silent.

'Do you understand what I'm saying?'

She shook her head. 'Not really.' Though some half-luminous cloud of premonition had begun to form inside her mind.

Edward paused and seemed to recover himself. 'To be baldly honest, I'd like to find you a flat. I'd pay the rent. I'd like to be your lover.' There was a kind of defiance in the statement, as if the self-revelation cost him an effort. His eyes were hard and looked deep into hers.

It seemed to Daisy that somewhere at the back of her mind she'd expected him to say this, ever since they'd first been alone together, and it was a relief to have it out in the open. All the same, she'd never really allowed herself to think what her reaction would be.

'Don't dismiss the idea outright, Daisy.' He'd regained self-control and his eyes held hers insistently. 'You seem different tonight. I feel as if we can be honest with each other. I'd like to know what you *really* think, without morals getting in the way.'

Daisy felt cornered, but before she could begin to work out her own attitude, practical obstacles crowded in, pressing their claim. 'I've got two children, young ones, and a mother depending on me.'

Edward made a sweeping gesture that pooh-poohed these objections. 'Daisy, I respect your family obligations. They'd be no problem. We can easily find a place that's big enough for all of you. And I'd be discreet when I came to visit . . .' He seemed encouraged that the obstacles she'd raised were concrete and not moral. His hand reached across the table, covering hers. It was warm, reassuring and somehow authoritative. 'What I really want you to think about is how *you* feel, truthfully, without being . . . coy.'

Thankfully Daisy gave up her unequal struggle with the daunting plate of meat. She took a swallow of wine, as if it might help her to picture the reality of what he was proposing. Pleasing images flickered in her brain of a large, sunny flat, far from Bermondsey, in some green suburb, perhaps with a garden where Mamma could sit and the children could play. Andrew couldn't be there. He'd never approve of her being kept. All the same, he might be pleased to shed the burden of Mamma and set up on his own. For a second or two she let herself be lulled by the tempting prospect. But all the time she knew that the dream was impossible.

Slowly she shook her head. 'I couldn't.'

Displeasure showed in his eyes, and behind that something more vulnerable, which he tried to hide with impatience. 'Why on earth not? Your life is drudgery, day in, day out. I could change that tomorrow.'

'I'm my own boss.'

He was contemptuous. 'Economic necessity is your boss.'

Stubbornly she shook her head. 'That's not what I mean. I'm free. Nobody owns me. If I let you keep me you could tell me what to do.'

'In a manner of speaking I can already. Under normal circumstances I'm your employer, don't forget.'

'That's different. I'm just one of a crowd.'

'May I take your plates, sir, madam?' If the waiter had overheard their exchange, this time he gave no sign, gathering up the detritus of the meal, comfortably unhurried. Without consulting Daisy, Edward ordered two ices.

When they were alone again he leant forward across the table, a kind of pain on his handsome, prosperous features. When he spoke it was with a hushed urgency. She had to strain to hear.

'Daisy, if only I could convince you . . . Everything I've said so far has made it sound as if I'm trying to set up some monetary transaction.' His warm, masterful hand closed round her wrist. 'You're so beautiful and young. You're artistic. You shouldn't have to slave day after day . . . I find it so hard to talk about these things. I've never been able – never really tried – to make you see how desperately I want you. I don't think I've ever wanted anyone so much. I'm like a boy. Helpless. The last thing I want to do is exercise power . . . control you . . .'

There was pleading in his eyes and tone. She was impressed, surprised, but barely moved. Edward belonged to a class that held all the cards. It was difficult for her to see him as human.

She shook her head again. 'You'd call the tune whether you realized it or not. And you soon would realize it. I couldn't take that.'

With the ices, cheese, coffee, Edward consumed a lot of alcohol. They didn't speak a great deal, not from embarrassment – the wine had taken them past that stage – but more because they'd reached a kind of impasse.

As she sat opposite him, with her food and drink, Daisy tried to visualize herself in bed with Edward Ballard. She found it hard to imagine him naked, without the disguise of his well-cut clothes, clean shirt and hand-made shoes. Just a man with slackening muscles and a slight belly. And when she tried to picture them making love she kept seeing Frankie instead. She tried to imagine Ballard's face, feverish and inward, concentrating on his body's sensations, the way Frankie used to look. The thought was repellent, though exciting, too.

She noticed Edward give a brief wave to someone behind him.

'A friend?' she asked.

'Just someone I know. Surprising to see him here.' But he didn't look unduly put out.

At one point, after the waiter had removed the goblets

that had held their ices, Edward said, 'If you ever change your mind, Daisy, tell me. The offer's still open.'

She gave a brief smile. It was more of a grimace. 'Thank you, but I don't expect I will.'

After that he seemed to become morose and more hostile, as if her rejection of him were beginning to rankle in earnest.

Over coffee she asked quietly, 'What about your friend? Will his offer over my handkerchiefs still stand?'

'I don't think so.' His face twisted in a bleakly cynical smile. She thought there was something brutal about it. 'You see, there *is* no friend. I've been buying the things up myself. I've got stacks of them at home. It was just to get you into bed with me.'

Daisy gazed at him dumbfounded and dismayed. Then a brief, vivid picture flashed into her mind. A pile of ornately embroidered handkerchiefs stuffed hastily into the back of some bureau drawer. The image had a kind of absurdity and she gave an abrupt, anarchic yelp of laughter.

26

A tender blue dusk was falling as Mercedes walked home from the Association's office in Victoria to her home in Devonshire Place. She was well used to walking now, and it seemed quite as natural for her to embark on a four-mile ramble through the paved streets as a walk in the country. Her parents would be there when she arrived home. It was the first night in ten that she hadn't seen Andrew.

Still, his aura was with her in the warm air that brushed across her skin, in every lift and twist of her body. Her walking felt like a dance. Her nerve-endings seemed close to the surface and she found the soft summeriness of the night almost suffocatingly beautiful.

She passed a pair of young lovers, recklessly entwined, like actors populating her stage. The woman's smile was quick and radiant and Mercedes could feel the dazzlement that lay behind it. She could imagine the warm weight of the man's hand at her waist, visualize soft flesh beneath the material of the woman's dress, light in the dusk. It was as if she could superimpose the ghosts of herself and Andrew on to their passing figures.

She felt drugged, suffused with the memory of him. He was a presence, with her all the time, a series of fragmented sensations. Constantly Mercedes recalled the feel of his skin against hers, the insistence of his hands, the texture of his mouth, hair, every part of him. She seemed to scent his body each time she moved. She felt annihilated, a slave to this fusion of their bodies. They'd resolved to keep on meeting whenever they could, though it would no longer be easy. Mercedes felt ready to take chances, defy convention, in order to hold on to this passion, this new addiction, which seemed to her worth more than everything else.

Yesterday they'd spent the evening in a room in Southwark that belonged to a work-mate of Andrew's who'd lent him the key. It was half below ground. A basement like a womb, cool, at the back of the house. There was a fire laid and Andrew had lit it. He'd heated water in a saucepan and a bucket, turn and turn about. There was a tin bath in the room and he'd soaped Mercedes, smoothing the lather slowly into her naked body.

'You got flesh like a baby, Sadie,' he told her.

The orange firelight had been bewitching. Mercedes was passive in his hands, luxuriating demurely in an intimacy she would hardly have dared imagine for herself. Since the evening in Bridge Fields, Andrew had set the pace. His lack of education and social graces were irrelevant in the world they'd begun to explore. He seemed practised and confident now – smoothing her awkwardness – imaginative, no longer shy. He washed himself as well and dried them both. Then they'd climbed between the coarse, unbleached sheets that felt sensuously rough against her skin, and made love naked for the first time.

Mercedes said she loved him, but it seemed beside the point. There were no phrases that weren't weakened by centuries of use, and it felt as if she wanted to say something quite new. But she could find no words that served her purpose.

Mercedes caught her breath when she saw him cross the room naked. Adonis, she thought, though she couldn't remember who it was the name referred to. She just knew it was the word for such unconscious grace.

'You got skin like silk,' he told her. 'Christ, to feel your body under my hands, so tight and so alive . . .' She'd never thought of herself as attractive, but began to wonder now whether perhaps . . .

231

As she walked down Oxford Street, Mercedes reflected idly on the future, though it had no reality for her yet, blinded as she was by the immediate past. Almost reluctantly she tried to conjure up a wedding-scene – like all the weddings she'd ever been to – with herself as bride and Andrew as groom, and smiling relatives doing their social duty. But the mental picture was grotesque. It applied to her sisters and the dull young men who'd chosen them, and couldn't by any stretch of the imagination encompass the secret, singular alliance between herself and Andrew.

In the last days the phrases 'free love', 'free union' had been hovering in her thoughts, an idea she'd read about in avant-garde magazines, a daring and intriguing novelty. She imagined the two of them living together unmarried in a small workman's cottage – something slightly more salubrious than most of the tenement lodgings she'd seen. He going off to work, herself looking after the house, cooking and cleaning. It was a diverting fantasy, though her own role remained a little hazy round the edges, since she couldn't even boil an egg and was frankly bored by the prospect of learning.

There was something in the air when she got home. Always, when she hadn't seen them for some days, Mercedes experienced a wave of love for her parents, for their familiarity and good humour, their obvious pleasure at seeing her again.

But today was different. On the surface they were as she would have expected – healthy-looking after their holiday and bursting with anecdotes. Florence had bought a new tartan blouse that suited her colouring. George had had his hair trimmed into a style which made him look younger and more dashing. She exclaimed at it, miming admiration. But her mother's broad, girlish smile seemed tinged with some private anxiety and her father was distinctly cool as she questioned them eagerly about their trip.

At first, obsessed as she was with the relationship between herself and Andrew, Mercedes thought she must be to blame. Perhaps their sexual experimentation had marked her in some way, perhaps it was blindingly obvious to George and Florence what their daughter had been up to while they were away.

'Your father would like a word with you, darling,' Florence whispered, with a warning look, when George had gone briefly into the next room to pour himself a dram of the special souvenir whisky he'd brought back with him. 'He popped into the office to see if there were any messages and there was a note from that Ballard man, the friend of the Pimletts.'

'Oh.'

The reason for George's coldness was abruptly clear to her. She experienced a sinking of the heart, a dead, resigned apprehension. Conflict was inevitable, conciliation out of the question. They had no common ground. Her father would be adamant that his daughter's interference in Ballard's affairs was nothing short of scandalous and she was absolutely determined to see the strike through. The confrontation she'd hoped to avoid now loomed, dark and threatening as a summer thunderstorm.

Florence withdrew discreetly, claiming she had to go and speak to Mrs Carter. George remained, enthroned in his old leather wing-chair, clutching a tumbler of pale, rare malt whisky. Behind him the curtains formed a graceful, draped backdrop of green and gold chenille. Her father had on his worn, claret-coloured velvet smoking-jacket. On his feet were slippers of soft Moroccan kid. Seated on the other side of the fireplace, on a low chair upholstered in dark brown plush, Mercedes viewed him with a mixture of affection and irritation.

She liked his clinging to old things, worn things of good, solid quality, finding a kind of reassurance in it. At the same time, she couldn't help thinking of Annie, Edie and the rest of them, a community where such prime creature-comforts were absolutely unknown.

'You realize, Sadie,' George began, 'that you've put me in a very difficult position . . .' His use of her pet-name, even in this moment of displeasure, touched her.

'I'm sorry you feel that,' she replied gently. 'I honestly had no intention of affecting you at all.'

George shifted his ground a touch, as though it occurred to him that his protest had a self-centred ring. 'But the people I'm really concerned about are the Pimletts. You must see that this is terribly embarrassing for them.'

'I'm sorry about that, too. I'm very fond of them.' She paused. 'But it's only a matter of sensibilities being bruised. What *I'm* involved with is genuine poverty and deprivation.'

She sensed that her father was ill-at-ease with this high moral tone. He tried to cut her down to size. 'But can't you see you're just meddling. Like a child. Ballard really must be presumed to know what's best for his own business . . .'

She cut across his words with full-blooded impatience. 'Father, he's indifferent! Those women work like slaves for . . . paltry, pathetic money. They're badgered with petty regulations and arbitrary fines. The manager's unspeakable – a browbeating petty tyrant . . .'

George's anger – and his colour – were rising. 'But it's none of your business!'

'If everyone said that, there'd be complete *laissez-faire*. I can't believe you'd approve of that. You're a kind man. I can't believe you want people to work in appalling conditions!'

'I think reforms are best left to the experts. Not sentimental, meddling little girls. Mercedes, I *forbid* you to take any further part in this dispute!'

There was a silence. Once upon a time, if an argument had come this far, Mercedes would have backed down. But the last few weeks had changed her. Until that moment she hadn't realized how much.

She and her father looked one another in the eye. In a sense, Mercedes thought, they'd never shared a moment of such honesty. Their family life was oiled by laughter and private jokes, lubricating the wheels of harmony. Most of the time their relationship was glancing, superficial, pleasant. Now they glared at one another like the generals of two opposing armies.

She shook her head. 'I'm sorry, Father, but I don't accept your authority in this. I'm nearly twenty-four. I'm a separate person.'

'You're financially dependent, my dear.' An icy note in his voice, all the more chilling for being rarely heard. '*That* gives me authority, if nothing else.'

'You've also got more to lose than I have.' It was threat for threat. Never before had they talked like this. 'At the moment my work in Bermondsey is almost a secret. Hardly anyone knows about it.' Mercedes paused to let the implications of her words sink in. 'If you insist on my stopping, I can create an awful scene. I can tell all sorts of people about it, and about this row. I can make the whole thing a lot more public . . .'

'Sadie!' The exclamation held shock, sorrow and outraged affection.

'Or you can leave me to carry on as I am. Discreetly. I'll offend Ballard and the Pimletts but, as far as most people are concerned, all I'm doing is the good works you've boasted to them about. Father, I'm sorry, but you might be better off leaving me to my own devices.'

27

Annie watched as Rose Gretton sat and shook. Under the man's cap she always wore, her mouth was pulled down at the corners like a clown's painted mask. Every so often ugly sounds of pain jerked from her. They made Annie think of a dog she'd seen once, caught in a trap, suffering and silent, then coming out with a howl that froze your blood.

Two of Rose's children stood by, barefoot, their eyes round and scared. The basement room was dirty and almost empty. She must have sold everything to help pay for the hospital.

'I'm hungry, Mum,' the boy whined. He was like a cross between a little old man and a baby, Annie thought. A little bullet-head. No flesh on his face at all. A patient look about him, as if he'd seen all the troubles in the world.

'I'll find you something in a minute,' Annie lied briskly. 'Leave your ma alone now. Go out and play in the yard for a bit.' Though they looked beyond playing, poor little mites. She looked around for their shoes. Maybe they didn't have any. Well, it wouldn't hurt in this fine weather. The children were frightened of her and they vanished.

'Bawling won't bring him back, Rose,' Annie said, when they were alone together. No point in being soft. It'd only make her worse. Annie felt as if her own belly was sticking to her backbone. It made her feel shaky. She could have bawled herself. She'd looked after Rose's Bobby enough times. All of them loved him. Maggie used to make faces at him and he'd crow with laughter. He had the deepest laugh she'd ever heard on a baby. A dirty laugh, the boys used to say. Even at ten months, a year, he'd been a real little character. It choked her up to think of his scrap of a body all stiff in the hospital morgue. She closed her mind to the picture. The funeral was the thing now. Rose was in no shape to sort it out.

'What about the insurance, Rose?' she asked.

Rose shook her head and tried, without success, to stifle a sob that seemed to shudder from deep down in her chest. She couldn't speak.

'Lapsed?'

A nod.

Annie's lips tightened. She thought as much. Tony Gretton was in work, but with Bobby in the hospital, five other kids to feed and Rose on strike, they'd never have kept up the payments. Mercedes' money was a drop in the ocean. And once it lapsed you lost benefit.

'Two pounds is about what you need for a decent kid's burial.' What with the death-certificate, tipping the grave-diggers, a few flowers. The sum was branded on her memory. It was what she'd needed for Betsy, but she might as well have howled for the moon. She'd been like Rose, shaking, half-mad, in no shape to go round trying to beg or borrow.

Something inside her cried out at the thought of Bobby being taken away, like Betsy, in a van no better than a dustcart. Times were hard, but maybe she could raise the cash. She could have a damn good try. If she sat at home doing nothing she'd get to brooding about Betsy.

She had two sixpences. Nobody knew about them, not even Will. They were her disaster money. They could miss meals before she'd break into it. They *had* done, a fair few times.

'I got a shilling, Rose. That's a start.' Annie said it out loud, before she could change her mind.

After she'd tramped up and down twenty or thirty stair-cases, Annie's legs felt limp as bits of string. She'd had nothing to eat that day and there'd be no cash till Danny got paid tomorrow. Still, collecting the money took her mind off the gnawing of her stomach. And the thought of little Bobby being buried right gave her a secret satisfaction.

No one seemed to know – not even the hospital – what had been wrong with him. He just started wasting, the way some children did. She wondered, if Rose had been able to afford milk and eggs and that sort of thing, whether the little dot might have pulled through. But there was no point in supposing.

Funny how different people were. Some looked at her cross-wise, as if she was begging money for herself. Others she knew couldn't afford it stumped up with a few coppers, even if it meant going without. Not that she'd got anywhere near enough yet.

She knocked at Queenie's house in Aquitaine Street and Queenie came to the door. Seeing her suddenly like that in the harsh sunlight, Annie noticed how queer she looked, how thin and grey. Her cheekbones stuck out like shoulder-blades.

Queenie shook her head. 'I'd give if I could, Annie. Honest. But I've nothing. And the kids are playing up awful. I'll have to get hold of something for tonight.' She gave a crooked grin. Annie thought she looked like a skull. 'D'you think if I offer the butcher a bunk-up he'll give me a few soup-bones?'

'I reckon the way things are he's spoiled for choice.' Annie was about to trot out her piece about Hal Rawdon doing his stuff, scaring off the scabs, how it couldn't be long now, but she couldn't work up the energy. It seemed like they'd been dragging out this strike forever. Annie felt as if she'd forgotten why they ever started.

The next day was Saturday. In the afternoon Annie resumed her collecting. She felt better. Danny had bought some bread and marge and some tea at midday on the way home with his wages. The food gave her heart. She felt optimistic. Saturday was the time to collect, when there was a bit of money about.

In Picardy Street market she ran into Kate Reeves, out doing her shopping. Annie hadn't spoken to her in weeks, not since she'd gone back to work at Ballard's. This was a chance to make it up, and Kate ought to be good for a bob, or sixpence at least. Kate always looked like a wet weekend, but compared to Queenie, yesterday, she was in the pink. She seemed pleased that Annie would talk. She smiled and a touch of colour came to her cheeks.

'You heard about Rose's Bobby?' Annie asked, after they'd chatted about nothing for a while.

Kate nodded and put on a sad, respectful face. 'Terrible, isn't it.'

'I'm trying to collect enough for a decent funeral for the poor little sod. Rose is broke, what with everything . . . I was wondering, love, if you could spare a bit of silver.'

Kate's eagerness was doused, like someone throwing a cup of water over a flame. She gazed at Annie worriedly, as if she was trying to think what to say, then she shook her head with an embarrassed look. 'Sorry, Annie. I would if I could. But Jack'd kill me. He counts up all my money nowadays . . .'

Annie felt the old impatience boiling up inside her at Kate's cowardice, but hotter and deeper. She and Jack could afford to give a bit. Others who were worse off had coughed up. 'Just tell the bugger what it's for! Surely he wouldn't begrudge a kid a decent send-off!'

Kate looked past her, avoiding her eye, in the way Annie remembered. 'I'm sorry, love.'

Annie felt the anger washing over her like a wave. 'I won't forget this. You'll regret it, you skinny cow, I promise you, when this strike's over and done with!' Her voice sounded loud to her, harsh and strung-up. Recently her moods came stronger and more sudden. It must be the lack of regular food. Turning away from Kate, she found herself shaking.

As the afternoon went on she calmed down, and her bag of ha'pennies, pennies and sixpences became heavier. She got ninepence from Daisy Harkness. Annie warmed to her. True, Daisy kept herself to herself, but she gave a hand when it was needed. All the same, as the day passed, Annie knew she'd collected nowhere near enough. And there was no point in going round a second time. You couldn't get blood from a stone.

Back home she counted out the money, arranging the coins in piles. It came to nineteen shillings and fourpence, less than half of what was needed. Dully Annie eyed the towers of coppers and sixpences. She felt nothing, not even disappointment. Something inside refused to credit the fact that all her efforts had been in vain.

As she sat at the table, chin in hand, her mind a blank, a knock came at the door. It was Mercedes. Each time she saw her nowadays, it struck Annie that the girl had changed. Even today, when her mind was on other things, it hit her in the eye. The difference was difficult to pin down, but it was there. Annie used to think of her as a goody two-shoes. In some way now she was harder, wilder.

She told Mercedes about Bobby and nodded towards the piles of money. 'I been collecting for a decent funeral, but what I got don't come near it.'

At once Mercedes asked, 'How much do you need?'

'One pound and eightpence.' Annie had the sum off pat.

'I think I can help.' From the small bag she carried Mercedes produced a leather purse. She counted out the amount in florins, half-crowns, larger coins than anything Annie had collected so far. She made it up to the sum

Annie had mentioned, then added another florin in case it was needed. She smiled. 'You can always give it back to me if it's not used.'

'Rose'll be pleased,' Annie said flatly. She felt empty. Thanks to Mercedes they had the money for the burial. But she'd rather have raised it without her help. It was too easy.

Annie registered that she felt hungry again. But they were going to eat all right tonight, and for the next two or three days. After that she didn't know. And yet almost without thinking Mercedes had counted out more money than Annie had flogged herself collecting in two days. Some people just lived in a different world. And even if they won the strike, nothing would have changed.

They all stood round the fresh, dark pit that had been dug for Bobby Gretton. Rose wore a shawl over her head, instead of her usual cloth cap. Her hair showed at the front, a blackish brown, streaked with grey. She was dry-eyed now, her skin the colour of paper. She clutched a bunch of delicate red and white roses, trailing some kind of soft, feathery leaves. Tony, standing next to her and holding her arm, looked years younger, too young to be the father of six children. He had a gingery moustache and had borrowed a black suit that was shiny and too tight on him. After the funeral he would go straight home, take it off, and get back to work.

The tiny coffin was made of white wood with shiny handles. Annie had heard that they took the handles off again when everyone was gone. She didn't know the vicar. He was new, a tall young man, his thick fair hair parted in the middle. He looked solemn, as if the funeral meant something to him.

Two other little coffins were going in the same hole, but you could see them as company for Bobby, Annie thought. Not like the great tangle of old and young bodies surrounding Betsy. Rose and Tony would be able to think of their child's burial without shame. Annie experienced the solid satisfaction of a job well done.

This morning the sky was blue with a ragged line of small, silver-rimmed white clouds. The sun shone dazzlingly on the vicar's white robe. It seemed wrong to Annie, all this light, bright sunshine over a child's coffin, as if the world didn't care.

There was a good turn-out. Apart from relatives, it was mainly women from Ballard's. Only a couple of men had taken the morning off. In a crowd Annie noticed how thin and grey the women looked, the way she'd noticed it about Queenie the other day. Their clothes looked dusty. In the harsh, revealing sunshine black cloth took on a greenish tinge.

There was a feeling in the air – though no one put it into words – that Bobby had died because of the strike, because Rose had been too poor to buy him decent food. He was a victim. A sacrifice. The feeling was like a communal secret that everyone knew and accepted. But no one seemed angry at the thought. There was a sense, too, that this was the way of the world, and anger would simply be energy wasted. Annie looked round at the rows of blank faces and she knew that the strike wouldn't hold much longer.

28

Mildred Ballard sat drinking tea with two friends in the small garden behind her town house. At ease in the dappled shadow of the cherry tree, she found it possible to forget for a time the many imperfections of her life. She wore a muslin blouse, beautifully embroidered, white on white. Her dark hair had been teased into a becoming loose onion-shape, from which a few locks escaped with simulated carelessness. She knew that the sun lent a bloom of animation to her creamy skin. It was an extraordinarily pleasant afternoon. Temporarily Mildred felt as if nothing had changed, and she was still the ironic, quick-witted, languorous beauty she'd always known herself to be.

She and Bridie Berton and Victoria Borden sat at a wicker table, on ornate, white wicker chairs. A duck-egg blue lacquered tray lay in front of them with fine white china cups and a dish of small lemon-cakes. Their gossip was idle and undemanding. The image of three pairs of chattering clockwork false teeth kept popping disrespectfully into Mildred's head.

From another, more shadowed area of her brain, she observed her friends with cool curiosity. Sometimes she felt like an old, dry, unblinking lizard, the way she examined people. She did it with everyone, with Edward, with her sons, the servants, summing up their small strengths and weaknesses. With her own contemporaries she noted down the small, continuous signs of their ageing.

Summer had never really agreed with Bridie, Mildred thought. She'd once been a pretty, fine-skinned blonde but always, even in her youth, the heat swelled her, thickened her features. Today she looked positively florid. The pistachio green dress she was wearing didn't help matters either. And with her hair – her best feature, still glossy and fair – she was a positive clash of ice-cream colours.

Mildred's attitude to Victoria was warier and less patronizing. She was often outspoken and sometimes a sharp wit glinted through the conventionality of her conversation. Mildred rather admired her. At times she even thought that they were two of a kind, genuine friends. At other moments Bridie's good-natured fluffiness seemed preferable, safer, less . . . sly. Mildred watched Victoria as she described a dinner-party she'd been to the night before, laughing about some awkward, embarrassing incident. Her dress was dark, patterned with flowers, a material that looked French. Victoria had always been thin and wiry. There were times when Mildred had the illusion she was listening to some cynical, knowing monkey.

Inevitably they started talking about the strike. Automatically Bridie's puffed, pink face assumed an appropriate expression of soulful concern.

'Is there any sign of a solution, Millie?' Her tone hushed as if she were enquiring about some family sorrow.

Mildred thought, then gave a doubtful nod. 'There *are* signs.'

Bridie was beatific. 'Oh, darling, I'm so pleased. This wretched business has gone on for much longer than anyone expected.'

'For the last week or so the substitute workers have been drifting away. Giving up, in twos and threes.' Mildred found a perverse pleasure in cheating Bridie's glad expectations. 'Edward thinks there's some kind of external pressure on them. But he can't find out from where . . .'

'Millie, that's dreadful. So sinister!' Bridie was genuinely shocked. 'This awful creeping socialism . . . Everywhere.' Repeating parrot-wise a phrase she heard bandied often over dinner-tables.

'It's dreadful from our point of view,' Mildred said dryly.

'But rather nice for the workers.' She enjoyed teasing Bridie with her wilful fairness.

'Mildred, how can you! Sometimes I think you're on *their* side.'

Mildred gave a sphinx-like smile, deliberately opposing her own serenity to Bridie's shrill dismay. All the same, her friend's observation was a shrewd one. As the weeks passed Mildred became more and more aware that – although she had little personal sympathy for the striking women – she *did* want Edward to be defeated. She wanted him to know what it felt like.

Ever since they'd met he had breezed through the world, taking it for granted that everything would be arranged for his satisfaction, confident that this was how it would always be. For once in his life Mildred wanted him to know what it was to be humbled, to be beaten.

Bland and unruffled, she offered the dish of cakes to her two companions. Bridie refused, patting her waistline.

Victoria accepted, with a look of bright enquiry. 'How *is* Edward?'

'Much as ever. Bearing up really quite well.'

'Did he say? Jonathan saw him the other night when he took his parents out to dine.'

'Oh really. Where?' Mildred's interest was faint. She regarded Victoria's husband – a banking colleague of Neville Kirkpatrick's – as a dull little pipsqueak, with a high voice, pale eyes and hair like an anaemic poodle's.

'Bentley's restaurant down in Richmond.'

'Oh?' Mildred attempted to conceal her surprise. What on earth had Edward been doing eating down there? He hadn't mentioned . . . Though, now she thought, he *had* been late home one night last week and the next day they'd not had a moment to talk.

'Jonathan was *so* curious,' Victoria continued. 'Mildred, you must tell! Who was the ravishing young woman he was dining with? A relation? Niece or something?'

Mildred felt slow and cloddish. Victoria's words were meaningless to her. She stared, perplexed, still holding out the dish of cakes.

'Blonde, Jonathan said. Soft, curly hair. Lovely hair, he said, and a pale complexion.' Victoria seemed strident, insistent. 'She was wearing a lace blouse. Oh, Mildred, you *must* know!'

Her friend's lively monkey-face grimaced vivaciously in front of Mildred's eyes. She knew she must look foolishly vacant. Mildred tried to arrange her features into a smooth mask. All her life she'd been able to do that. But it took a huge amount of effort. And she still had no idea how to reply to Victoria's questioning. Her wits seemed to have totally deserted her.

'Oh dear!' said Victoria, her small monkey's paw of a hand pressed to her mouth. Her eyes were stretched wide with a sudden fearful suspicion. Mildred couldn't tell whether her horror was real or faked. 'I hope I haven't said anything.'

Desperately Mildred hid behind the white mask that was her face. Her mind was a blank. The figures of her two friends appeared unnaturally sharp and threatening, though plump Bridie seemed as perplexed as she was. Victoria's quizzical eyes showed a little gleam of malice. Or was it her imagination?

Edward found he couldn't remember why he'd come here. Alongside him in the large, soft bed lay a child about the age of his eldest son. Her face was painted into a doll-like oriental mask and locks of her black, crimped hair undulated across the pillow. A musky perfume hung in the air, its heaviness somehow familiar. Nirvana. The word came to him from nowhere. Yes. There was a decorative dark bottle on the table by Mildred's bed that bore the name in long, twining letters.

Her duty done, the child lay beside him on her back, one arm dreamily extended in front of her. Lost in her own world, she contemplated its elegant lines from shoulder to fingertips. Dazed by her own beauty, oblivious to him, now their transaction was completed.

Their coupling had been satisfactory. She was a pretty creature with a lithe young body. He'd worked himself into enough of a frenzy to perform what was expected of him. There were times recently when he feared he wouldn't be able. Now his body was at peace, but he couldn't remember why it had seemed desirable to do this, why he'd passed the requisite money into the long, dry fingers of Lisette, who kept the place. Looking back, Edward marvelled that he'd summoned up the enthusiasm.

'I'm getting too old for these larks,' he told himself, gazing up at a cluster of plaster cupids on the ceiling. The room was decorated in sensuous colours, warm rose, claret, autumnal browns. There were gilt mirrors, printed velvet cushions and draperies, designed to bring out the sultan in you, the hedonist. Edward ached to be gone.

Abruptly he sat up, swinging his legs over the side of the bed. He got to his feet and crossed the room to where his clothes lay, feeling paunchy and graceless, deploring the indignity of pulling on socks and underdrawers beneath the indifferent gaze of the young stranger. He'd bought her, but she had the arrogance of youth and physical perfection.

Five minutes later, having completed the tying and buttoning, tugging and tweaking involved in the process of getting dressed, Edward walked towards the door.

'Don't say goodbye, will you,' the girl pouted. Under the disguise of her elongated eyes and painted mouth, she seemed a hurt child. Edward felt suddenly rude and boorish.

He went back and kissed her forehead. Something about her nakedness, the perverse contrast of his own formal clothing, excited him, reminding him of why he'd wanted her in the first place. One hand closed almost brutally over her small, hard breast. His lips moved to hers, his tongue entering her mouth. When he paused for breath, she giggled. 'Naughty old man.'

Edward fled.

'Edward, I've got to talk to you.'

Mildred was a dramatic apparition in the entrance hall at home. White-faced and heavy-eyed. For some reason she was holding a candle. He caught a hint of that perfume the young whore had been wearing. Nirvana.

Edward was dog-tired. Presumably Mildred had packed the servants off to bed. He'd been expecting a confrontation ever since he'd seen that little pissquick Jonathan Borden across the restaurant the other night. He was prepared for the scene and knew exactly what he was going to say. In a sense his exhaustion might make it easier.

'What is it, Millie? I'm terribly tired.'

'Can we sit down somewhere?'

'I'd rather not.' He smiled apologetically. 'I don't think I'd be able to get up again.'

'This is serious, Edward,' she hissed with muted vehemence.

'If it needs my full attention, then perhaps it had better wait till morning.' He made as if to mount the stairs.

Mildred grabbed roughly at his jacket. 'Edward!' Her voice was sharp with outrage.

Her manhandling of him, her insistence raised his temper gratifyingly. Impatience was necessary for the reaction he'd planned. 'For God's sake, Millie, say what you've got to say! Say it now!'

She stood at the bottom of the stairs, looking up at him for a second or two in hurt, dignified silence. But she could see he was immovable and that if she wanted to state her case it would have to be here, in the makeshift setting of the entrance hall.

'Jonathan Borden saw you dining with . . . a ravishing

248

young woman.' She pronounced the phrase satirically, as if in quotation-marks. Her brittle tone grated, increasing his resistance to her.

He replied with bitter energy, claiming for himself the role of injured party, neatly pre-empting Mildred. 'Pity the little squirt hasn't got something better to do than make a song and dance about things that don't concern him!'

'Well . . . who was she?'

Wearily he told her. 'One of the women from the factory. She's been acting as a sort of go-between. We were discussing the strike.'

'Oh, Edward!' A note of pitying contempt. 'Surely you can do better than that.'

He acted the part of a man whose patience has been tried too far and finally snapped. 'Quite frankly, Mildred, it's a matter of perfect indifference to me whether you believe me or not. If you think I'm deceiving you, then you're at liberty to leave! My conscience is clear.'

Edward turned on his heel, walking swiftly up the two flights of stairs that led to his bedroom on the second floor of the house, satisfied that he'd wrong-footed his wife, something he was practised at doing. She was far too emotional.

Her voice pursued him, angry but somehow impotent. 'That's the best you can do? You swine! It's pathetic!'

He locked the door to his room. It was a refuge, cool, simple, ordered as he liked it. The dark green curtains had been drawn and billowed a little in the breeze from the open windows. The walls were green too, a soothing shade, the colour of sage leaves. The top sheet on his bed had been turned down ready for him to step in. The place smelt of polish and fresh night air. Edward sank down in the large leather armchair near the window, savouring his peace.

He heard Mildred try the door, find it locked and begin

hammering like a crazy woman. 'Let me in! I want to talk to you. I've got the right!'

A towering fury swept through him at this invasion of his retreat. He launched himself across the room and fumbled madly with the key, desperate to confront her.

She was distraught, her eyes swollen with tears, cheeks streaked, mouth contorted with rage and pain. Always before, even in their worst moments, he'd retained at the very least a half-contemptuous affection for her. Now she seemed merely a ranting, tiresome hysteric.

'God's sake, woman, get to bed! Pull yourself together. Think of the servants!' Injecting all the bullish anger he could muster into his commands, trying to get through to her.

'We've got to talk! You can't just act as if nothing's happened.' Her voice was a high, insane wail that drove him crazy.

'Christ, let me sleep!' He grasped her shoulder, pushing her away from him with all his might. She staggered, grotesquely clumsy, against the wall of the corridor. The sight of it gave him an evil pleasure. 'Now get to bed. Fucking lunatic!'

Back inside his locked room, Edward heard no more from Mildred. But his nerves were jagged and jangling. He took off his jacket and shoes and stretched out on the bed in the dim light of a small lamp, trying to make his mind a blank.

He couldn't relax, though. The blubbering, hysterical presence of his wife was still with him. Resentment boiled in his gut, as though the lie he'd told her was truth. She'd doubted his word. He ached to punish her effrontery, teach her her place.

But after a while his thoughts of Mildred gave way to another image. The perverse, alluring, cosmetic mask of the girl he'd bought that night. The memory bothered and depressed him. He felt sickly humiliated by her view of him as an ageing lecher. He cringed to recall his own foolish, belated show of lust, exposing him to the child's shallow ridicule.

Gradually Edward's nerves began to calm and a new mood stole over him like creeping mist, an unfamiliar feeling he couldn't place. It spread and took shape, part regret, part longing. At first he didn't think to wonder where it came from, but in time, with a kind of inevitability, he found himself picturing the luminous face and cool grey eyes of Daisy Harkness.

There had been occasions, thinking about her, when his body had burned helplessly like an adolescent's. But tonight she seemed to him the embodiment of peace, the soul of calm, a blessed contrast to Mildred's hysterical claims and the sly contempt of the young prostitute.

Daisy was sanity, a woman whose needs he could fulfil simply by offering her a decent life and money for her mother and her children. In return she'd provide the sensuality he still craved – without indignity or extravagant emotionalism. Lying in the dim bedroom, Edward felt old. His longing for Daisy overwhelmed him like a sickness. But she refused to be bought.

He hovered for hours in some state between sleeping and waking. And without conscious effort, Edward took a decision. He would end the strike. Too many things in his life now were messy and diffuse. He would impose order where he could.

In any case, the new workers were drifting away in ever-increasing numbers. Edward *knew* there was a reason for it. Once upon a time – not so long ago – he would have rooted around, he wouldn't have rested, until he'd found out the source of the sabotage. At present he lacked the effort of will. Best to simply cut his losses.

And another thing. He was going to sack Leonard Floyd and find a new manager. He'd always hated the fellow. True, he'd been a loyal employee, worked his guts out down at the factory. That couldn't be helped. Edward longed to be rid of the man's stench, his hot fanatic's eyes. Apart from anything else, he hadn't liked the story Daisy told about that half-witted child, the factory skivvy. It would be as good an excuse as any for getting rid of him. It seemed to Edward, in his fevered state of mind, that sacking Floyd would be a kind of message from himself to Daisy. A parting gift to her.

Drowsily he became conscious of the sound of wild weeping. Mildred again. If he could hear her from this range she must really be going at it, no thought about the servants' dumb insolence tomorrow. Reckless as that, she might do herself an injury. But he was too exhausted to deal with the thought.

29

Today was Sunday. Mercedes told her parents she was going to Bermondsey to see about some new development in the Ballard's dispute. The information was received in hostile silence. In fact her explanation was just an excuse. There were deeper levels of outrage, hidden, like the juicy inside layers of an onion. Her supposed 'meddling in affairs that didn't concern her' was a front for something even more unforgivable. She was picnicking alone in the country with Andrew Sitek. Carpenter. Factory worker. Lover.

Mercedes had entered a new state of calm lawlessness. She did as she pleased. Her parents watched her, tense, appalled, unbelieving. The atmosphere in the house seemed white-hot. Airless.

In a sense she was blackmailing George and Florence with her reckless willingness to embarrass them, create a scandal, kick up a public fuss. They shrank at the thought.

Rashly George had brought up the question of money, but he dared not push it further. With her commercial qualifications Mercedes was perfectly well-equipped to earn her own living. And her parents dreaded that idea almost more than anything else.

All they could brandish at her were moral claims, their love for her, their hurt and disappointment. Their reproaches were more powerful than any threat. But Mercedes steeled herself against them. She couldn't afford to weaken. She felt as if she'd turned a corner and must keep going. Otherwise nursery ties and habits of loving would jerk her back, like a child on a walking-rein. They'd rule her life and she'd never be free.

All the same, she kept quiet about Andrew's existence. If George and Florence knew about him, it could tip the balance, send them as mad as she was, so they'd throw aside their social prudence and match her scene for scene, threat for hysterical threat. That wouldn't do. In the foreseeable future Andrew must remain a secret.

The two of them had taken the train out into the Kent countryside as far as a diminutive village in the vicinity of St Mary Cray. Mercedes smuggled a small basket out of the house. In it were pies and a few cakes she'd bought the day before. Andrew carried a stone flagon of beer cradled in his arms. Mercedes had assured him she'd be happy to drink it. In her eyes, the ale added to the exotic, alfresco nature of the escapade. She was entranced with the simplicity of it all. In her experience picnics had always involved servants, table-linen and cumbersome wicker hampers. This way you could pack up and go at a moment's notice. It was quite unbelievably easy.

She was elated, like a child playing truant, and Andrew seemed to feel the same. The train was crowded with people – mainly family groups – off to spend a day in the country. She and Andrew saw themselves as outsiders, quite different from these pillars of society. They were skittish. The families seemed plodding and faintly ludicrous to them. They noticed a fair sprinkling of stuffed shirts. The phrase had become a joke between them, ever since the evening when Andrew had first walked her home and she'd tried to explain how she felt about her sisters' husbands. On the train were a number of sedate young men and earthbound paterfamilias types. Covertly the two of them counted stuffed shirts. Andrew marked off the tally silently on Mercedes' fingers. It seemed a hilarious secret.

The tiny station where they alighted was part of a small hamlet, the houses dotted like irregular teeth round a central green, reminding Mercedes of the village where the Pimletts lived. She and Andrew struck off down a lane bordered with white cow-parsley, then skirted a couple of fields until they found a likely spot with a brook and a willow-tree.

The picnic felt to Mercedes like playing house when she was a child, only being with Andrew made the smallest activity seem vivid with excitement. He poured the beer, warmish from the journey, into two glasses that Mercedes had hidden at the bottom of her basket.

'I'll get you tipsy,' he told her. 'Then I'll have my wicked way with you.' The laughing words, the sound of his voice and the half-joking, half-suggestive look in his eyes left her helpless with lust.

Lust was a word she'd always thought sort of biblical and melodramatic. But now, in her mind, she used it all the time. And she wondered if that was what she meant when she told Andrew she loved him. Just that the way he talked and looked, the texture and shape of his body, the gestures he used, all combined to make her want to touch him and hold him, press up against him, hard, hard. Melt into him. Were love and lust one and the same thing? She'd never felt anything so powerful, but it wasn't the idea of love she'd got from the books she'd read.

The stream sparkled in the sun. 'I'm going to paddle.' Mercedes took off her shoes and stockings, sure her parents would faint on the spot if they could see her. She sat on the grass, dabbling her feet in the water, her skirts pulled up knee-high, swigging from the glass of beer, feeling bold and carefree. A fallen woman.

Andrew lay beside her, watching, leaning on one elbow, the opposite hand curved loosely round his glass. 'Wish I had a camera. Then I'd have a picture of you, the way you are now, for the rest of my life.'

She turned, smiling at him, but his eyes were serious, startling and disconcerting her.

Not trusting herself to reply, Mercedes burrowed in her basket, bringing out two cold chicken pies. She handed one to Andrew, wondering again why her elders fussed with plates and starched napkins, when life could be made so much more practical and simple.

Halfway through his pie, Andrew remarked, 'Best thing I've eaten in weeks.' He said it factually, without a trace of self-pity, but the statement hit home. For Mercedes the pies were humble fare, merely convenient. But to him, specially with the household's straitened circumstances, they were a feast.

She'd brought some bread pudding from the Picardy Café, and they shared that next. The taste and texture of it conjured up echoes of meetings held there with the strike committee.

'Annie Tyrell loves this stuff,' Mercedes reflected idly as she ate. Then she remembered something and said with a grin, 'Annie told me once that *you* could put your boots under her bed any time.'

She thought it a joke, but to her surprise, Andrew coloured a little. 'She's not a bad-looking woman, that Annie.'

'But she's old!' Her exclamation rang in her ears, quick and artless as a child's.

He laughed, sensing an edge of jealousy in her objection. 'Not *too* old. There's plenty to be said for experience.'

Mercedes was silent, intrigued by Andrew's view of Annie, so different from her own, as if it revealed a new way of seeing. She found it rather baffling that, at the same time as saying he loved her, he could assess the sexual potential of another woman. She felt, herself, as if she had no eyes, no energy, for anyone else. Andrew poured her some more ale and she sipped it, forgetting the passing ripple of doubt.

After they'd finished eating, the two of them decided to explore. The area was mainly open meadowland, with grazing cattle and long grass, pinkish and drying at the tips, shot through with blurred drifts of magenta and yellow flowers. Above them the sky shone, a clear, mild blue, seeming spacious after the restricted skylines of London. They didn't say so but both of them knew they were looking for somewhere to make love.

They found a place. Beneath a tall beech some low, scrubby bushes of goat-willow clustered. Between them and the trunk of the tree was a small, secluded space, carpeted with moss. Studded, too, with the prickly husks of beech nuts, but you couldn't expect perfection.

Andrew spread his jacket. 'Let's sit down.'

She sank down beside him. In the greenish shade his eyes looked very clear to Mercedes, his skin very white. She felt, herself, as if all colour and expression had drained from her face, as if she were stripped of all emotion but a blind pull towards him.

Without preamble he kissed her, pulling her down into a lying position. She'd never felt so ready, damp and swollen with lust. But they proceeded slowly, holding back, to make it last. She had the brief, bizarre illusion that they were making love underwater, with balletic, dream-like movements.

She looked for it now, that expression on his face, the half-closed eyes, a sort of anguish. It excited her beyond measure. They had their clothes on, but where their skin was exposed and touched, it felt hot, tender and terribly intimate. Something – the beer? – had altered her body, making her responses slower, deeper. Each sensation was separate, perfectly vivid, but they were gathering deep inside her, gathering in every nerve-end. Slowly gathering. To be resolved in a final, wild, twisting, prolonged release. From a long way off she heard Andrew groaning with agonized pleasure. Then they lay still, his body covering hers. She had no idea for how long.

*   *   *

'What's going to happen to us?' Andrew asked, some time later, when they'd moved and stretched, adjusted their clothes, and lay side by side looking up into the spreading branches of the beech tree. Outside the wood, the sun was high and hot. It slanted through the boughs of the tree, dappling their cool green shade.

'I don't know.' It was a question she'd asked herself often, but in the lazy afterglow of sex it seemed unimportant. Mercedes kissed him, running her tongue round the soft lining of his mouth, something he'd taught her.

'Think about it, Sadie.' He resisted being side-tracked by the distraction. Tangling his fingers in her hair, he touched his lips softly to hers, as if in reproach for the teasing sexuality of her kiss. 'I love you that much I'd ask you to marry me . . .' She took in the declaration with a fleeting, flattered incredulity . . . 'Only . . .' His tone became rueful, subtly mocking. 'What've I got to offer a well-set-up girl like yourself . . . ?'

His words hardly seemed real to her. Mercedes was still exhilarated and half-abashed by the unlooked-for abandon of their lovemaking. She could see nothing domesticated in their passion. She grinned at him, evading the issue. 'Can you see us living together till we're old and fat?'

He smiled too, but reluctantly. 'What if you turned out to have a bun in the oven?'

There was a touch of animosity in the question, as if to punish her flippancy, bring her back to earth. His grin changed subtly, acquiring an edge of amiable malice that she found perversely erotic.

It was a thought she'd always pushed to the back of her mind. She shivered, thinking of Sal O'Shea. 'Don't say that. Don't even think it.' And yet a part of her was strangely attracted to the extremity of such a scenario. It would stir everyone up. Everyone and everything . . .

'These things happen.' He pressed home a kind of

advantage. Obscurely Mercedes saw in it a flash of Annie's class-antagonism, and alongside that, the complacency of the male, whose pleasure isn't paid for with risk.

In some contrary way she was aroused by the muted undertow of hostility. They began to touch and kiss again, with a slow, inevitable uncoiling of excitement.

'You know what, Sadie,' he whispered. 'That last time was the best fuck ever.'

30

'Here, Daisy!'

She heard a shout from behind and turned her head, mildly exasperated at someone wanting to stop and talk in this summer downpour. Picardy Street was awash, the gutters overflowing with rapid water, puddles forming like lakes. Daisy had borrowed a large shawl of Mamma's. With her left hand she held the two sides of it together under her chin. She'd managed to drape a fringed tail of the material across the basket clutched in her right. It held a stale loaf the baker had let her have half-price. But if she stood and talked, the thin wool would be no protection at all.

'Wait, Daisy!'

It was Annie running up the road. She must be in a state to go bareheaded in a cloudburst like this. Her hair was black with the rain and plastered to her neck and forehead. Her skirt was heavy with water, her blouse had gone transparent, showing the flesh colour of her arms. Daisy cursed inwardly. She couldn't imagine anything Annie could have to say would be worth a soaking like this.

'I just seen Beth Coster!' Annie called from a few yards away. She was breathless, one hand laid dramatically across her chest.

Beth Coster was one of the scabs. She was notorious in the district, a big, ebullient woman who still clung to her job at Ballard's. Anyone who quit could be sure of a public tongue-lashing from the foul-mouthed virago. If it weren't for her, so Annie maintained, there'd be no one left at Ballard's by now. The two women detested one another cordially.

'What did she have to say?' Daisy pulled her shawl tighter over the basket on her arm.

'She's sick as a dog.' Annie's grin was cocky, radiant. Daisy could see rivulets streaming down her sharp cheekbones and off her chin. 'And she told me something.'

'What's that?' She wished Annie'd get on with it.

'That bastard Floyd's got the sack.'

When she got home Daisy found that the top two inches or so of her loaf were saturated. Not wanting to spend money on gas to dry it out, she sliced the bread lengthways, putting aside the top layer for the time being. She cut slices from the bottom section for the children and Mamma, waiting like hungry fledglings in the nest. Mouths to feed. The phrase played tinnily in her brain like a stale tune.

In one way she was relieved that the children no longer protested about the everlasting bread for every meal. But they looked shrunken, and so listless it hurt her. Perhaps they no longer had the energy to complain. Or maybe they'd forgotten that anything else existed.

Then she went into the other room to take off her drenched clothing. As she peeled the wet cloth from her skin, Daisy's mind was filled with the piece of news Annie had passed on. She wasn't sure what to make of it. It didn't have to mean the strike was won, as Annie claimed, with her big, triumphant smile. Daisy clung to her doubts because she dreaded disappointment. She towelled her hair on an old piece of sheeting they used to dry themselves. But it was too thin, neither use nor ornament.

Since the last time she'd seen Edward she felt low. Life was back to normal, worse than normal. There was nothing to look forward to. She missed the excitement of seeing him, the feeling of sharing in his world for a time. She missed the fillip of being admired by a man who was rich and charming, and could take his pick.

Sometimes Daisy imagined herself being kept by him, eating well, feeling full after meals, the children plump and rosy, her own looks set off by smart new clothes, far away from this bug-hole. But she made herself think of the other side of the coin. Having to please him, agree with him, sleep with him whether she felt like it or not. And any time she stepped out of line he could cut her off without a shilling and there wouldn't be a thing she could do.

All the same, times were harder than ever. The shop she used to sell her work to had turned nasty when she tried to go back to them. At the moment all of them were living on Andrew's wages, poor kid. She felt like a blood-sucker, and he was so good about it . . .

In fact he seemed full of beans recently, and he was hardly ever home. There must be some girl . . . Ever since he was eighteen or so Andrew had come and gone as he pleased. He always kept quiet about his courting – and she minded her own business – but there was generally someone in the background.

This time seemed different, though. Special. The other night in bed she'd had the wild idea that it might be Mercedes – Daisy hadn't seen so much of her in the last two or three weeks – but next morning she decided that her empty stomach was to blame, making her imagination run riot.

Daisy put on some dry clothes. An old cotton dress she wore for housework and her other set of underclothes, the bad ones, worn thin, and patched. But after her soaking they were welcome, soft and dry against her skin. Now if Edward was keeping her she'd probably have several sets – silk ones even. She'd look quite different in those. Thoughts like that stole up on her often now, but she pushed them away.

She bent and picked up her wet clothes from the bare floor of the bedroom. How on earth was she going to dry them without using gas? The air was still damp, they'd take days. Her saturated boots lay on the floor. She hated them. Broken down as they were, the rain would have done them a power of no good. She picked them up, stowing them neatly in the corner where the morning sun – if there was any – would dry them. She couldn't stop herself thinking of a pair of soft grey leather high-heeled shoes she'd seen in a shop on one of her jaunts to meet Edward.

She *did* wonder if he'd sacked Floyd because of what she'd said about him. Perhaps he was sending her a sort of message . . . The idea struck her as unlikely, then she thought about it again and it made a kind of sense. What if Annie was right and it did lead to the strike being over? No one'd ever know the part she'd had in it.

Outside it was still raining. Inside the weather made no difference. Come blizzard or heatwave, the church hall – loaned courtesy of Father Simpson with his piercing, disapproving brown eyes – was chill as a tomb.

Mercedes scanned the twin rows of women, ranged along the sides of the two decorators' trestles. Perversely, she was put in mind of a picture someone had showed her of The Last Supper – the heads poised at different angles, the mix of expressions and physical types. Remembering the very first time she'd come here. She had felt like a missionary from one of her childhood storybooks, encountering a mutinous tribe, quaking inside, but trying to project a convincing air of calm and authority. Since then things had changed. Mercedes had no illusions about belonging, but there was familiarity. She had a place. Her eye picked out details. Edie's grin, with the black spaces of her missing teeth, Annie's top-knot of stringy curls, Rose Gretton's cloth cap and the puffy sadness of her eyes below it. She knew them now. For nigh on two months she'd come here almost every day, and had been admitted to the shabby intimacy of their homes.

263

There was a bubbling feeling in the air today. It wasn't triumph – it was far too early for that – more a fresh welling of hope that they tried superstitiously to keep within bounds. Edward Ballard had requested a meeting with the strike committee for the following day. Friday. Of course, nothing might come of it. All of them kept repeating that, as if hostile, invisible spirits were hovering in the vast emptiness of the hall, above their heads and below the steepled rafters, ready to pounce on any signs of over-confidence. But they recognized the secret expectations in one another.

Mercedes had called a meeting, thinking it would be a good idea to remind themselves about exactly what they'd been fighting for, going hungry and doing without for. Dying for, Rose Gretton might have said.

'Annie gets reinstated. That's the first thing.' Mercedes disliked her voice when speaking publicly. To her own ears she sounded like some painfully earnest school prefect. Her eyes slid round the table, gauging the women's reaction. But if anyone objected, they weren't prepared to say so out loud. 'We're agreed on that then. I think there are some points we've got to hold out on. On others we can afford to give way a little.'

'No scabs to be kept on, neither,' Annie proclaimed with calm certainty. She raised her voice not at all, and yet immediately everyone turned towards her . . . Mercedes envied her instinctive self-assertion, her magnetism. Always Annie made her feel young and shrill. And yet, as her mind framed the familiar thought, Mercedes understood that it was less true than it had been once.

'No compromise,' Annie emphasized. 'All the scabs are out!' There was a buried heat behind her eyes. Murmurs of agreement came from all sides. Mercedes guessed that some of Annie's vehemence on this score came from a desire to punish Kate Reeves, partly for her defection but, more specially, for her spineless refusal to contribute to Bobby Gretton's funeral.

'Right. We're inflexible on those two points,' Mercedes continued. 'Now what about the question of a minimum wage? It's my feeling we should ask for fifteen shillings, but I don't honestly hold out much hope . . . I think we should be prepared to compromise . . .'

'All the same,' Daisy cut in, 'we should stick on one thing. If we go above our targets, it's *us* that gets the bonus, not the manager . . .'

'And written rules,' Edie said. 'So we know where we are . . .' Another thought occurred to her. '*And* we don't have to buy our own thread.'

As they worked out the standpoint to be taken the following day, Mercedes couldn't rid her mind of an image of Edward Ballard, red and sweating with exertion, trying to beat her down over some point in a tennis-match, using his maleness, his superior age and overbearing presence. She had a sudden vivid sense of this conflict, too, as a personal struggle. She'd forced him to back down on that occasion and – incredible as it seemed – it looked as though she might be able to do it again.

31

Edward's father used to have an ebony statuette, about a foot high, that some buccaneering uncle had brought him from Africa. It was long and slender – shaped rather like a large cigar – with the merest indentation to suggest a neck. The features were flat, the nose barely projecting beyond the surface of the face. The closed eyes were indicated by two faint semi-circles.

It stood on a mahogany and brass dumb-waiter in the dining-room. As a boy, when the room was deserted, Edward used to creep in and take hold of the figurine, trace its streamlined contours with his hand. It was miraculously smooth, like satin, yet black and hard.

Later, when he was sent away to school, and had to fight for survival, he used to picture the statuette whenever circumstances threatened to show him in any kind of foolish or shameful light – when he was laughed at for blushing like a girl or calling some older boy he knew by his childhood pet-name, or once when he fell off the wall-bars in the gym and let out a loud, inadvertent public fart. At times like this he used to think of the figurine, with its blank features and smooth, hard exterior. He used to try and become it, to cover up his mortification with a similar empty serenity.

It helped a great deal and he'd never lost the knack, though as he grew older he had less and less need to use it. As time went on he controlled his own universe, and everything in it was arranged to display him to his best advantage.

Today, though, he was faced with the situation of negoti-ating, from a position of weakness, with three semi-literate harpies and a woman – his social inferior – he'd offered

266

himself to and been refused. It was enough to tax all his powers of sublimation. But afterwards he thought he could say quite truthfully that he hadn't betrayed, not by the flicker of an eyelash, the slightest awareness of the ignominy of his position.

Edward's patience had already been sorely tried earlier in the week, when he'd attempted to rid himself of Leonard Floyd. Naïvely he'd expected the interview to be subdued, a bit embarrassing, perhaps, but quickly over and done with. He'd thought Floyd would go quietly. He approached the manager with a bluff man-to-man air, explaining that he intended to reorganize the factory along different lines and offering him a handsome pay-off.

Floyd had gone berserk. Edward realized later that he should have foreseen it. He'd expected the financial sweetener to silence all protest, but the man was a fanatic. Edward had read it in his eyes from way back.

The manager's flush was like a dramatic chemical change. Great beads of perspiration stood out on his forehead. He cursed vilely at the top of his voice, and all but threatened Edward with a drubbing from some plug-ugly friend of his.

In his own defence, Edward brought up the matter of the under-age skivvy. The blackmail only made matters worse. Floyd came and stood menacingly close to him, giving off a stench like fusty mutton-stew.

'Didn't you ever dip your wick where you shouldn't?' he bellowed. His breath smelled like a long-dead sewer-rat. His hot eyes narrowed in a way that seemed piercingly meaningful, and made Edward wonder what he knew. The row he made must have been heard by the roomful of substitute workers beyond the closed doors of the manager's office. It was a scene of pure farce.

Edward was profoundly rattled. He wasn't used to being threatened by his employees. It had never happened to him before. By a massive effort of will he managed to stay calm, reminding Floyd tersely that his relationship with the girl called Dot was a police matter, which he wouldn't hesitate to report if Floyd made it necessary.

A great deal of time seemed to pass before Floyd saw the sense of this, reluctantly cooled off to a lower level of trembling fury, grudgingly accepted the pay-off and left. Edward still lived in fear that he hadn't heard the last of the man.

Now he was faced by a deputation of four women workers, three of whom gave off a discreet but offensive aura of insolence – Edward thought hard of his father's statuette. Daisy, on the other hand, looked subdued and fragile. It gave him a jolt to see how thin she was, though it was only a matter of days since he'd seen her last. She seemed to be lurking behind the others. Far from flaunting a mocking awareness of the secret between them, Daisy seemed almost abashed.

As ever he was dazzled by her pale, peculiarly potent European beauty. After an interval of days it struck him with renewed force. But her lack of assertiveness gave him courage and heart. He addressed the women with scrupulous courtesy, but like a man whose time is valuable, with the tacit suggestion that they should be business-like and to-the-point with what they had to say, as he himself would be.

'I've sent for you ladies in the hope that we can finally sort out the nuts and bolts of the problems that still remain between us . . .' He spoke as if their differences were mere matters of detail. He found himself able to ignore Daisy completely, with the insulting implication that she was simply one of a rather trying bunch. Edward marvelled again at the way in which his public school conditioning had perfected his powers of hypocrisy.

Before anyone could reply Edward offered an ingratiating disclaimer. 'You'll have heard, I'm sure, that Mr Floyd has been dismissed. And confidentially I'd like to say that

I can in many ways sympathize with your dissatisfaction with him as a manager . . .' He trotted out the blinding insincerity without turning a hair.

Mrs Durrant stood behind him, mute and monumental, as she had at the previous interview, when the strike was in its early days. Today Edward had the impression that she exuded an unnerving sibylline quality. The heavy planes of her large face had a massive, omniscient repose. Her crossed fleshy arms, the straight folds of the brown dress were positively statuesque. He must be overwrought. Edward felt judged by her, and knew the verdict would remain locked in some unfathomable recess deep inside her.

He continued with his dogged pretence of poise and control. 'I haven't yet appointed a new manager. But I'm about to see a man who's been highly recommended. I'll keep you informed . . .'

Floyd's office, where they were gathered, was as bare, highly polished and geometrically neat as the manager had left it. The stuffy, sweet-rank smell of his perspiration still hung in the air, a legacy that would no doubt last for some time to come.

He eyed the women ranged in front of him as if they were enemies. The least imposing, but perhaps the most offensive, was the gingery, bovine creature, Edie Black. There was a youngish, dark, hard-faced woman, with tightly braided black hair, who hadn't been at the previous meeting. She would have been attractive, with a bit of flesh on her, but her spirit seemed dulled by hunger. Perhaps it was as well. Her eyes had a sceptical look that might have spelled trouble under more favourable circumstances.

But it was Annie Tyrell who stood out as the leader. She was smaller and more emaciated than he remembered her, but she'd have made her mark in any company. There was something compelling about her olive colouring and jaunty crest of curls, the cynical humour of her brown eyes. There was a stubborn dash in the way her worn clothes sat on her erect, underfed frame, the effect enhanced rather than destroyed by the stout men's boots that peeped out from beneath her skirt. He saw her as the kind of uncrushable proletarian the middle-class instinctively feared. For one fanciful moment he pictured her storming the Bastille, avid and vengeful, full of a heathenish joy. At that moment Edward hardly felt her equal.

It seemed to him that the women tolerated his charade, the mask he'd assumed of a busy man graciously allotting them some of his precious time, but they weren't impressed by it. No matter. He asked no more than that they keep up their end of the pretence, however half-heartedly, and save his face.

Annie Tyrell stepped forward. 'If you'd run your eyes over this, Mr Ballard . . .' Her voice lacked completely the wheedling note he'd been used to all his life from his inferiors.

She presented him with a typed sheet of discussion points, prepared no doubt by the meddling brat, the MacInnes girl. The document enraged him with its pretentiousness. But he bore with it in a similar spirit of enforced tolerance.

He scanned the paper. Their claims were pretty well the same as those they'd made almost two months ago. Salvaging as much dignity as he could, Edward ran through the points cursorily, agreeing briskly to the most obvious, as if they were matters of no importance. He balked at the fifteen shillings minimum wage, beating them down to thirteen and ninepence, to be reviewed after six months. As far as the written code of rules was concerned, the details would have to wait until the new manager was appointed, but he thought they'd find both the manager and himself quite reasonable. It was, after all, in everyone's interest – Edward looked at them reprovingly over the rims of his reading-glasses – that the factory should begin normal production as soon as possible.

He kept his manner deliberate and firm, as if he were fully in command of the situation, but he could see confusion on the women's faces at the ease with which their demands were being met.

'If we're all generally agreed I can see no reason why normal working arrangements shouldn't resume as from Monday . . .'

Dumbstruck, the women nodded their assent. Edward stood up. The interview, and the strike that had cost them so much grief, was at an end.

'I'll leave you to sort out the details of your return with Mrs Durrant, who knows far more about the day-to-day running of the factory than I do . . .'

From his standing position Edward surveyed the deputation. Their expressions showed more surprise than anything else. For a brief moment his eyes locked with Daisy's. Her normal composure seemed to have cracked. Inexplicably she appeared stressed and stricken. His heart went out to her, but he turned away with deliberate indifference.

'Good day to you, ladies.'

Edward strode towards the door. His gait was erect and assertive. Still, it felt like a retreat.

The Lanchester waiting outside in the yard was a refuge. The elegant lines of its bodywork, the high black gloss of its finish, the rich smell of the leather upholstery, all represented a little piece of his own world.

'Everything work out all right, sir?' Waters, his chauffeur, asked. Stocky and spruce in his grey uniform, he was solicitous, respectful, man-to-man, conveying the fact that he was on Edward's side.

'We've sorted something out,' Edward replied carelessly.

They exchanged a wry smile. Waters saw the strikers as rabble. He'd a niche in Edward's world and couldn't waste sympathy on those he'd left behind. What was more, they were women. There was a male free-masonry in the smile, a shared contempt, that was soothing to Edward's soul.

As the Lanchester glided through the factory gates, Edward noticed what a beautiful day it was. After forty-eight hours of heavy rain, the world seemed cleansed and refreshed. Even the repulsive back-streets of Bermondsey showed all their charm, with a ribbon of radiant blue winding between the blackened chimney-stacks and warm champagne-coloured tones glowing in the grey brickwork. His spirits rose. A walk in the park, followed by lunch at the club, would do him the world of good.

A female figure lingered outside the gates. Edward recognized her immediately. It was the MacInnes girl, waiting no doubt to join her cronies in rowdy celebration. Wearing a blue and white summer dress, she looked slight and child-like. Falsely innocent, like a poisoned ice-cream.

'Stop the car a second, Waters.'

A mood of savage bravado filled him, fuelled by the certainty of his chauffeur's approval.

Edward leant out of the window and called to the girl. 'Hasn't your father had the guts to spank your arse yet, you meddling little virgin?'

He experienced a fierce pleasure in breaking the taboo, using coarse language to the daughter of a social acquaintance. She'd mucked him about quite enough. The taunt pleased him. It was unanswerable and cut her down to size. It would demean and shock her, make her blush. He heard Waters chuckle appreciatively.

Mercedes hadn't seen him. She started and turned. He saw bewilderment in her eyes, like that of a child waking from sleep, then recognition. It was superseded by an unemphatic look of mute disdain. The look struck at him, chilled him, reversing his imagined scenario. For what seemed like an age, their eyes stayed locked.

His chauffeur restarted the car. Edward was thankful that the man hadn't waited for him to give an order. But he wished to God that Waters hadn't been there to witness the crass encounter.

They'd agreed to meet outside the factory gates at one o'clock, but by a quarter to most of the Ballard's women had already arrived, and stood waiting, chattering but apprehensive, looking drab and ill-nourished in the fresh brightness of the sunshine.

Mercedes had been there most of the morning. She'd travelled to Bermondsey early, bringing the typed sheet with the women's demands. After that she'd simply stayed put, knowing that no amount of purposeful activity could distract her mind from the suspense of waiting for the outcome of the meeting.

'Have you heard anything yet?' she was asked time and again, as new women arrived on the scene. All she could report was that Ballard had left twenty minutes or so ago. But she kept quiet about the strange encounter she'd had with him.

He'd certainly seemed rattled. Cautiously she interpreted that as a good omen. His outburst had amazed her. Not the insult itself – in his eyes she more than deserved it – but the unvarnished crudity of it. Mercedes would have expected some devastating, smilingly sophisticated, stiletto-like slur. She'd simply gazed at him, unable to think of any effective retort. But her very silence seemed to unnerve him. He looked quite sheepish as he drove away. Mercedes cherished the memory of his discomfiture.

'Good morning, Miss MacInnes.' It was Nathaniel Hardy, the photographer from the *Advertiser*, who'd suffered a dousing at the hands of Leonard Floyd. Through the weeks Mercedes had kept contact with him, and he was eager to be in at the kill, as he put it. She hoped his optimism would turn out to be justified.

His tubby, bowler-hatted figure put Mercedes in mind of a cheerily smiling poster for Webster's port cordial to be seen all over London recently. He began to set up his equipment. The photographer was popular with the women, they saw him as an ally. Some of them began to josh him, striking provocative picture-postcard attitudes.

'What about this, Mr Hardy!' A sparky, prune-like creature Mercedes knew as Belle, parodied the S-shaped pose of a music-hall siren, breasts and buttocks out-thrust.

'Luv-v-ly.' Hardy pretended to snap her. He was flushed and flustered with his reception.

'Here they come!' someone shouted.

The women crowded round the gateway. Annie and the others were leaving the factory by the back door. They began to walk towards their waiting colleagues, two and two. Annie and Edie in front, Queenie and Daisy behind them.

It was impossible to tell anything from their appearance. Approaching across the yard, they seemed demure and impassive, almost maddeningly so. Mercedes was faint and dizzy with the suspense, her whole being tensed, as though life and death hung in the balance. A deep and deathly silence had fallen.

Then, a few paces from the waiting women, Annie bounded forward. With the suddenness of a marionette, she spread both arms wide and threw back her head.

'We've done it!' she yelled. 'We've beaten them!'

For a split second there was hush. The echo of Annie's shout hung in the air, as its sense was assimilated.

'We've done it!' someone else called out, parrot-like, shrill, as if testing the truth of the words.

Then cheers erupted, a babble of triumphant shouts and cries of amazement. Mercedes found herself seized and embraced by Belle, Rose, Queenie, a succession of other women she knew, though she couldn't have named more than half. The next few minutes were a sunlit jumble of arms and smiling faces, disjointed snatches of conversation and tight, emotional weeping. Mercedes was hardly aware of what she was saying, doing. She was incredulous, enraptured. The reason why seemed almost lost in the welter of shared jubilation.

'Oi, Mercedes! Over here!' Confusedly she heard Annie calling.

Mercedes pushed her way through the throng in the direction of the voice. Annie was standing with the photographer, Hardy.

'You and me, girl,' Annie said.

In the thick of the turmoil they posed, smiling broadly – Mercedes through tears – their arms round one another's shoulders.

'That's the ticket!' Nathaniel Hardy disappeared beneath his black cloth. A second later the camera clicked. Afterwards he snapped them both separately, then the deputation of four, in every possible permutation. Mercedes thought Daisy looked dazed and out-of-sorts, but it was far too public here to question or comfort her.

But she was distracted from the reflection when the jubilant buzz of sound around her changed its tone, seeming suddenly to become sharper, expectant. Mercedes turned her head. A ragged jeering had broken out. She saw that the scabs were emerging from the factory for their forty-five-minute meal-time break. Her first reaction was one of surprise at how few of them there seemed to be. Everyone knew they'd been drifting away, but it dawned on her that their number must be depleted by half, or even more. Under the circumstances it was hardly surprising that Ballard had been so eager to come to an agreement.

They looked apprehensive as they crossed the yard. A good handful of them dodged back inside, but the others had children to see to at home, so they had no option but to run the gauntlet of the triumphant regulars who watched them coming with breezy malice.

Among the scabs Beth Coster stood out, a huge woman with a face like a slab of beef, her thin grey hair pulled back tightly into a sparse bun. She walked towards them with lumbering unconcern, the only one of the substitutes to appear unabashed by the reversal in her fortune.

'Where're you going to work next week, Beth?' Edie called, as the massive scab ploughed her way through the crowd outside the gate.

Beth grinned sardonically. 'Thought I might try the Leonard Floyd home for old soldiers,' she joked, raising a flurry of laughter among the regulars, disarming their hostility for a moment.

Kate Reeves skulked among the remaining workers. She'd tucked in behind Beth like a dinghy in the wake of a man o'war, her shoulders hunched as though she hoped to pass unnoticed. She looked scared. Mercedes pitied her.

But Annie caught her old co-worker by the sleeve. She was grinning, but her eyes were hard and vengeful. 'Your Jack's going to be upset, eh, Kate? No cash to count next week.' Annie shook her roughly by the arm. Kate's eyes opened wide in sudden panic. The older woman smiled at her fright. She stared at her for a moment, leisurely, like a snake exercising its sway over some small, helpless animal. Then she pushed Kate contemptuously away. 'Tell you what, love,' she called after her. 'Don't bother coming round my house trying to borrow a tanner!'

'Back to the sweatshop Monday,' Annie said, as she and Mercedes sauntered down Picardy Street an hour or so later, in the soft, bright sunshine. 'What'll *you* be doing then, Mercedes?'

'I've got no end of work to catch up on at the Association,' Mercedes replied equably. The thought of a few days of desk-work wasn't unwelcome, now everything had been brought to a successful conclusion down here.

She felt euphoric. Uppermost was a kind of drained, satisfied relief at the outcome of the strike, the sense of a job well done by everyone concerned. There was also a physical well-being, as the sun shone down on her face and body, baking her pleasurably through the cotton of her dress. And buried beneath both these feelings lay the secret anticipation of seeing Andrew tomorrow night. The knowledge was a delicious counterpoint to outward events, like a hidden chamber full of treasure that she could visit at any moment.

'Think of us,' Annie said, 'Heads down over the old machines again . . . First week's wages, I'm going to buy the biggest eel and meat pie from Bentley's and cook a whole bag-ful of potatoes. Then me and the kids and Will are going to eat till we bust . . . You know . . .' she glanced wryly at Mercedes, 'I got to be honest. I couldn't stick you when you first started coming down here. But . . .' She flashed a malicious-amiable grin. 'I suppose you can get used to anyone . . .'

Mercedes laughed comfortably. 'I suppose you can.'

The market that afternoon was busy and strangely festive. Perhaps it was her imagination, but with this sunshine after two days of solid rain, people seemed smiley and easy-going. Mercedes had come to know by sight a vinegary-looking woman called Nell who kept an old-clothes stall. She was notorious for peering distastefully down her nose at any wares people offered her, as if she were smelling bad fish. In today's heat Nell was still huddled in her shawl and mittens, but she was laughing, actually laughing, with Enoch who sold vegetables on the neighbouring stall. In mid-conversation he nodded a casual greeting to Mercedes, and she was warmed by yet another small sign that she was accepted here . . . taken increasingly for granted.

Twenty or so yards away, among the crowd of female shoppers, Mercedes saw a striking-looking woman approaching them. She had noticed her once or twice before in the market, and each time she'd been unsettled and impressed by the sheer sensuality of the stranger's appearance.

The woman had a slim, but rounded figure. She stood out, in the poverty of Picardy Street, for her look of health and vitality. Her complexion had a warm apricot tint and there was a smudge of a darker rose colour on each cheekbone. Mercedes couldn't tell whether it was natural or not. Her hair, black and kinky, with a bluish gloss, was pinned up, but loosely, so that tendrils escaped and curled round her face. As she made her way down Picardy Street, the woman smiled with careless bravado at friends and acquaintances, crinkling her brown eyes and showing soft dimples in her cheeks, yet, at the same time, it was as if she kept something back, some private, sensuous secret. She wore a plain white blouse and a blue skirt which emphasized the camber of her waist, the shapely bounce of her breasts. Her walk was slow and indolent, graceful as a dance: she seemed to lean backward a little, leading with her hips, flexing her shoulders now and then, as though in pleasure at the warmth of the sun.

Mercedes could imagine her mother's friends pursing their lips and summing the woman up as a dreadful, flashy creature. But, looking at her, Mercedes felt slight and sexless, clumsy, graceless. The woman was no longer in her first youth. Twenty-eight perhaps, or twenty-nine. But Mercedes couldn't imagine any man seeing her without being dazzled by the powerful earthiness of her presence.

Annie saw her looking. 'That's Bessie Carter.' Her tone was half-disapproving, half-admiring. 'Bit of a merry widow, that one.'

The woman drew level. 'All right, Bess?' Annie called.

'Not so bad, Annie, love.' Her voice was throaty and uncompromisingly cockney. The widow smiled, looking cat-like and pleased with herself.

When she'd passed, Annie indicated her with a jerk of the head back over her shoulder. 'You know Daisy's brother, Andrew? Well, he's been knocking about with Bessie Carter for months.'

quite shamelessly buy himself a young working-woman, and suffered no qualms about inflicting his paunch and wrinkles on her, all the staleness of his middle-aged self.

Even more galling was the knowledge that, just as long as Edward was discreet, none of their friends would think any the less of him. In fact, if anything, it would probably raise his stock. It wouldn't surprise her to know that half the husbands had secrets of their own. As far as they were concerned Edward was only doing what any man would, given the chance.

And as for the wives, far from supporting her, they were probably agreeing among themselves that it rather served her right. Mildred had always given herself airs, tried to be different, idled away her days with novels and painting, looked down on all things domestic . . . And now the chickens had come home to roost. She was no better off than they were, not different at all.

'Poor Millie's going to have to learn to grow old gracefully.' She could imagine Bridie's complacent, mock-concerned smile.

Mildred took deep breaths, trying to control the anguish, force it down. Since last Saturday neither she nor Edward had referred to that awful scene. That night she'd wept without shame or moderation. She'd howled, ignoring the unseen mockery of the servants on the floor above. She even thought of suicide.

But, with daylight, life had reasserted its claim and Mildred saw reason and sense. She'd no redress, no power. What could she do against Edward? Where could she go? With revulsion she had pictured herself stuck in some genteel hotel in Brighton or Bournemouth, all alone, living on a pittance. No friends, no status, belonging nowhere. She shivered again, now, at the very idea.

Satirically she struck an attitude in the mirror, one hand clenched against her breast, theatrically defiant. With a huge effort of will she forced her anger into retreat. She needed to be calm. Tonight was important. The news of Edward's peccadillo would have spread like wildfire. It was up to her to face their friends with serenity and charm. With a touch of insouciance, if she could muster it. Mildred reappraised her image in the glass, arranging her features into a gracious smile of welcome. Above all, she didn't want anyone pitying her. A tot of brandy might steel her resolve, and get her through the early stages. Furtively she turned towards her bedside cabinet.

At first Mildred found it easier than expected to ignore the newly-discovered spectre of her husband's mistress and carry on as normal. As she sipped a light, dry pre-dinner sherry with Edward, the Bertons and the Kirkpatricks – the French windows open on to a hazy blue summer evening – the whole scene was so pleasant and familiar that she slipped quite instinctively into her usual social role.

And perhaps that was the mature thing to do. She might be shaken, her feelings badly hurt, but life went on. They were still a couple, she and Edward, entertaining two other couples of similar age and background. Their collective friendship was long-standing and pleasurable. It was tolerant, adapting itself to the ups and downs of all involved. It had the solidity of an institution.

If you were feeling difficult – as Mildred frequently did – you could pick holes in everyone here. You could find fault with all the hypocrisies and compromises that shored up marriages, friendships. But the relationships remained, with a solid, sterling value greater than the sum of their parts.

To begin with, traditionally, everyone had exclaimed over Mildred's appearance.

'Ravishing, Millie,' Neville Kirkpatrick told her. The smile on his hawk-like features was as it always had been, amused, sardonic, amiably civilized. 'A dream of a dress. Very Jane Austen. A delicious anachronism.'

She replied with the flirtatious playfulness she'd shown towards him ever since they'd both been in their twenties. 'An anachronism, Neville, but also, let me point out, the very latest thing.'

'That new hairdresser of yours is a genius. I saw Fay Hogarth the other day – her hair was a mass of adorable little curls, like a Greek boy's . . . I've half a mind to poach him,' Bridie teased.

'Fellow looks like a professional tango-dancer,' Edward growled, playing up his antipathy for public consumption.

All six of them sat and gossiped the way they'd always done, without the slightest acknowledgement of Edward's fall from grace, the ordeal of Mildred's discovery. It all made her think of a mediocre comedy she'd seen staged a couple of weeks ago, about a hot-blooded Italian nobleman in love with a cool English beauty, the young wife of the visiting Duke of Melmothshire, or some such fabricated county.

'*Madonna*, you British!' the grandee had expostulated at some point during the play. 'If the Black Death were raging at your gates, you'd avert your eyes just a little and carry on talking about the weather!' The remark had raised a positive storm of self-congratulatory laughter among the audience.

'Hasn't today been too beautiful,' Bridie sighed, as if she'd read Mildred's thoughts. 'The rain really washed away all that stickiness . . .' She leaned blissfully back against an eau-de-nil satin cushion, took a sip of her pale gold drink and smoothed the silk of her dress, a tasteful riot of pink and white roses.

'You look like a summer's day yourself, Bridie,' Edward told her with easy gallantry. A cool bath and that dram of whisky appeared to have restored his good humour. Mildred had to admit he looked distinguished, framed

283

in the rectangle of the French windows, glass in hand, his sweep of yellow hair surmounting the crisp black and white of his dinner dress. In spite of herself she warmed to him, reassured by his sameness, his charm, the familiar smile that made him look like a secretive lion. A flash of cowardly, abject gratitude seized her for the status he conferred on her. Without him she'd be nothing. It would be madness on her part to rock the boat.

Over the whitebait at dinner, though, hairline cracks began to develop in Mildred's serenity and she drank rather a lot of chilled Pouilly Fumé to keep herself feeling light-hearted and vivacious.

The particular object of her irritation was Veronica Kirkpatrick. In fact, if the truth were known, Veronica always got her goat. Privately she thought Neville's wife a smug and rather humourless person. Veronica was grave and poised, with a creamy skin and hair prematurely white. The combination lent her an eighteenth-century air, as though she were a young woman in a powdered wig. She played up the look with a black velvet ribbon round her throat, and a grey and white striped dress with a scooped and ruffled neckline.

She offered her opinions in cool, measured tones. To Mildred's mind Veronica's views had no particular merit or originality. It was simply her manner that lent them authority and weight. But Hugh Berton and Edward were immoderately impressed, falling over themselves to defer to her, as though Veronica were some wise, all-seeing matron and they a pair of unworthy school-boys.

Tonight it seemed to Mildred that Neville's wife was paying particular attention to Edward, questioning him in her deep, smooth voice as to his thoughts on the Irish Home Rule question, encouraging him to expound. Edward's knowledge of the subject could be writ large on

284

the back of a postage stamp. Veronica would have done far better to approach Mildred on the matter.

But the point was that she didn't approach her, though Mildred put forward some rather telling and well-informed ideas. Veronica appeared to wave them away, listening instead with rapt intensity to Edward's halting, hastily-cobbled viewpoint. Mildred found herself quite hot with suppressed indignation.

After McKellen had supervised the serving of the sirloin and they'd all switched to Médoc, Edward continued to bask in Veronica's attention. She'd set a ball rolling. He became expansive and talkative, the focus of the table. Everything he said was greeted with gales of merriment.

'Teddy's certainly on form tonight,' Hugh Berton, Bridie's husband, murmured to her, as another of Edward's sallies set them all laughing. Mildred was fond of Hugh, a barrister, round and curly-headed as a cupid. But she couldn't help feeling out of sorts at his adulation of her errant husband.

She managed to smile thinly and nod in agreement. But Mildred could feel the old destructive anger rising again. She simply couldn't control it. Edward had behaved disgracefully towards her, and yet here he was fêted, admired, made much of. The wages of sin, so it seemed, were success.

'A little bird tells me your strike's over at long last,' Bridie ventured cautiously – they all knew Edward could be touchy on the subject. But she was encouraged by his obvious high spirits.

'That was a very well-informed little bird, Bridie,' he replied easily, in too high a humour to be cast down by the reminder. 'Yes, we're back in business come Monday.' Edward grimaced with appealing ruefulness. 'The harpies have relented, thank the Lord.'

'And what of the settlement, Teddy, the conditions? Did you have to make hundreds of horrid concessions?' Bridie looked self-conscious, a little amused with herself, like a child talking business with an adult.

Edward took his tone from her. 'Heavens no, Bridie. Just a few teeny ones on the money side.' He looked round the table, including the rest of them in the dialogue. 'In fact, I've agreed to a fixed minimum wage,' he reported casually, as if the decision had been partly his own. 'Not quite as high as they wanted, but fair, I think. One does what one can . . .'

In the right mood Mildred might have been quietly amused at the deft way her husband had marshalled the facts, presenting his galling personal defeat in the light of an exercise in practical philanthropy. But tonight his amiable bad faith annoyed her beyond reason. She managed to hold her peace, picking up her glass of Médoc and draining it in rebellious reflex.

The breezy atmosphere had spiralled into something more sanctimonious. Over the good roast beef and excellent wine everyone was inclined to agree that, within reason, the poor deserved a decent, basic standard of living. It was the bully-boy tactics they used to obtain it that were deplored. Neville Kirkpatrick shook his head. Socialism run riot.

'It's socialism that gives the working-classes a bad name,' Hugh Berton summed up chirpily, with his irresistible choirboy smile.

'What they *won't* admit is that *we* have to make a profit simply to employ them.' Soberly Edward went to the heart of the matter. 'We're not in it for love, either.'

'There's profit and profit,' Mildred put in sotto-voce. Edward glanced at her sharply, but was distracted by the ministrations of the servants.

The main course was cleared away and small lemon water-ices were served, palate-cleansers before the magnificent meringue and strawberry bombe which was to follow. Veronica and Bridie refused the dessert wine, a chilled, fruity German white. Mildred accepted, distancing herself from their lady-like moderation. She noticed Bridie cast a censorious glance in her direction.

In the slim glass engraved with languorous art-nouveau tulips, her pale wine caught the sparkle of the central chandelier, reflecting it with twinkling clarity. Mildred gazed with private absorption. The combination appeared to her extravagantly beautiful.

After the servants had faded once more into the background, Veronica took up the discussion again in her cool, omniscient tones. 'Of course, if I had my way, no mother of a child under ten or eleven would be permitted to go out to work. I'm convinced it leads to neglect, whatever arrangements are made . . .'

'Absolutely!'

'True, true . . .'

Murmurs of agreement hummed from all sides of the table.

'But we don't live in a perfect world, and these things go on – sometimes circumstances even make the situation unavoidable. And then, I think, a fair minimum wage is in everyone's interest.' To counteract the solemnity of her words, she turned to Edward with a dry, teasing smile, one eyebrow raised. 'Teddy, I think you've set a very good example . . .'

He smiled in return, with a graceful show of modesty. 'Thank you, Veronica.' A light, self-deprecating sincerity in his voice.

Mildred could stand the hypocrisy no longer. She yearned to debunk both Edward and Veronica.

'He didn't do it voluntarily!' she exclaimed in full-blooded tones. 'He'd much rather have gone on as before, leaving the manager to do his dirty work, screwing as much graft out of the poor devils as he could and bleeding them white with fines . . .' Her voice rang boisterously in her own ears. All faces had turned towards her, as though frozen in mid tennis-match.

She grinned at Edward and her guests and took a swig of the beautiful wine. It was like iced nectar.

Mildred felt the need to explain further. 'It's been a complete rout, the whole thing. He's had to give in on every score. Re-instate the old battle-axe that started it all, sack the manager, get rid of the women who shored up the firm between-times . . . He's upped the wages, rewritten the rules . . .'

The bewildered faces ranged round the table amused her immoderately. They seemed a long way off, small, distorted and yet terribly clear. She was the cynosure of all eyes. Silly phrase. Mildred giggled. She felt talkative and confidential.

'They were awfully well-organized, actually. Edward hasn't told you about the little MacInnes girl, has he? Do any of you know her? Father's a doctor. Harley Street wallah, in fact. She's just a slip of a thing . . . Horrible socialist, though, Hugh . . .' Mildred smiled at him saucily. 'She got the strike all sorted out. They'd never have lasted so long if it hadn't been for her . . . It's little Mercedes Edward's got to thank for his defeat,' Mildred stated blithely, though she knew precious little about the facts of the girl's involvement.

Bridie said in a shocked, hushed voice, 'You sound as if you're pleased, Millie . . .'

'I'm only telling the truth, Bridie.' Mildred attempted a challenging smile, but knew that it failed. She sipped her wine, anticipating the full, fruity flavour, but this time it tasted different, not so nice. It occurred to her that she felt peculiar, a little sick. The familiar, painful anger sparked inside her. Suddenly she saw herself as a cornered animal spitting defiance, but doomed.

With heavy sarcasm she asked Bridie, 'Why in the world should I be pleased that my dear husband's been

288

humil . . .' She couldn't get the word out and let it pass. 'Heaven forbid!' Mildred congratulated herself. She hadn't mentioned the mistress, yet no one could be in any doubt as to what was in her mind.

Distantly she heard a murmur from Hugh, 'Millie, are you quite well . . . ?'

It was overlaid by Edward's louder tone. 'Mildred, I think you should go and lie down . . .'

Their words barely registered. She was busy coping with the convulsions of her own body. She *did* feel sick. The strength of the nausea threatened to overwhelm her. She found herself on her feet, stumbling towards the door.

33

Mercedes dragged herself towards the basement room in Southwark that Andrew had borrowed from a friend for the evening. The journey involved a train and a deal of walking. She accomplished it with blind instinct, barely aware of what she was doing. Her head ached dully. The contours of her right eye-socket seemed etched in pain. Her skin was hot, her lips dry. Sounds and movement reverberated in her brain with unpleasant intensity, as if she had a fever. Vaguely she'd noticed her parents eyeing her anxiously, but there was scant communication between them recently.

'Is everything all right?' she could remember Florence asking, though she could no longer visualize when or where. She must have replied, but the question had seemed just a mild irritation like the far-off buzzing of a bluebottle. She'd left the house this evening without explanation.

'Does he bring Bessie Carter here?'

The question lay sour and heavy on her mind. With a hot, bright clarity, she saw Andrew arranging the loan of the room with his unknown friend, pictured their knowing smiles, the furtive exchange of coins. All that night she'd lain awake in the dark, thinking of Andrew and Bessie together, imagining her feline smile and soft, apricot flesh. She'd pictured him caressing her with a focused, lascivious urgency, whispering husky obscenities, thrusting himself deep into her body. She'd tortured herself with the images, deliberately, so that they couldn't steal up on her and catch her unawares with the dizzying pain they held.

Her own body felt like a scraggy appendage, a carcass

she was dragging to the rendezvous. She was famished, hadn't eaten for twenty-four hours and couldn't imagine ever wanting to again. Yesterday night and this morning she'd retched into a bowl, bringing up just thin, bitter bile. She longed to be at her destination, ached to see him. And yet she had no faith that seeing him would bring relief from the agony of betrayal.

When he opened the door, a part of her reacted as it always had done, confirming almost with surprise the sheer desirability of him in the flesh, the narrow-hipped mobility, the pronounced Slavic bones of his face. Her body tugged towards his solidity. She could so easily envisage melting against him when his arms reached for her. But the new doubt was stronger, making her stiff and unyielding in his embrace.

'Sadie.' He kissed her, cupping his hand tenderly in the nape of her neck, but Mercedes remained resistant. She shivered. Outside the air had held a residual baked warmth like the heat left in brick after the sun has gone, but in the bare basement room it was chill.

'What is it, Sadie?' The kindliness in his voice was at odds with the treacherous image she'd manufactured in her mind. She pulled away and stood looking into his eyes. The concern in them was genuine, with no shadow of guilt.

Mercedes plunged in without preamble. She had to know. 'Annie Tyrell says you're keeping company with Bessie Carter.'

His eyes changed. A wariness flickered through them, followed by a reluctant honesty. 'I *was*.'

She accused him harshly. 'You never told me!'

Andrew shrugged, his eyes remaining steady. 'It's over since I knew you.'

In her mind's eye she saw a ray of hope, saw it physically, a pale gleam on a black horizon. 'When did you see her last?'

'Last night.' The words rang with a sort of truthful defiance, as if he were entrenching himself in a battle position.

'Last night!'

Mercedes thought of the hours she'd spent in torment, feeding on her mental images of Andrew and Bessie, like some insect gorging off rotting meat. While he . . . 'Did you sleep with her?'

'No.' The reply came quick and conclusive. The way you'd expect, whether it were true or not.

He offered some words of explanation. 'Bessie and I've been close for a long time. She's fond of me. I can't just cut her off.'

His consideration for the creature damned him. She could have borne it if he'd belittled or insulted her.

'Did you tell her about me?'

He shook his head. 'You're secret, Sadie. We agreed on that. Tell Bessie and it'd soon get round.' What he said was true, and yet it seemed too pat an excuse.

A silence. The neat, bare room was a hostile environment, his environment. Behind him she could see the bed spread with a worn, floral quilt, its outer layer patchily eaten away by time, exposing the discoloured wadding inside. Mercedes had made love with him in the bed, and suddenly it seemed sinisterly invested with the ghosts of other lovers.

With a wild and pitiless clarity her overwrought senses conjured up the image of Bessie Carter, lying there naked, with her secret smile, vital black hair, her opulent flesh. Standing by, Mercedes felt herself wizened, a scarecrow. In reflex her hands flew to her eyes, as if in some confused way she meant to pluck the image from her head. She crumpled to the floor.

'I can't stand it. The thought of you and her.' The words erupted into the silence, convulsive, a kind of sob.

Andrew knelt beside her, trying vainly to gather her

spiky, resistant body to him, murmuring reassurance. 'It's over, Sadie. That was before you came along. It'd be lying to pretend I lived like a monk before . . . pointless. But it's over and done with . . .'

She braced herself against him, feeling like some sharp, spiny sea-creature. The thought came to her that she should have known. It was obvious he was no novice where sex was concerned. He'd always led her on, showed her the way. It seemed madness now that she'd never wondered how he came by the expertise . . . Or perhaps she'd simply, perversely, closed her eyes to the evidence.

'There've been others, too?'

'Yes, but . . .' He gave an unconscious shrug that signalled the irrelevance of the question.

'So I'm just one of a string.'

'You make it sound . . . I love you, Sadie.'

'That's easy to say.' She was scornful. 'You probably said it to Bessie too.'

'Yes, I did.' An edge to his voice, as if his patience had limits. 'But I didn't know you then.'

One sliver of her brain saw the logic in this. The rest was occupied with the ever more threatening mental picture of her rival. She recalled the flaunting, indolent walk, the throaty voice with its vulgar sensuality.

'You said you loved that slut!'

Once again there was a hush while the echo of her accusation hissed in the chill air. It seemed that Andrew deliberately said nothing, waited, giving her time to appreciate the implication of her own words.

When he spoke his voice was cold, and clear as the cracking of a whip. 'You despise her, don't you, because she's common?' He paused. 'Like me.'

'To think I . . .'

She was speaking to herself now, but his assertion hit home. Perhaps the cruellest element in her suffering was snobbery. A profound, ingrained snobbery she hadn't recognized until now. She held herself to be above Bessie Carter. Above Andrew, if the truth were told. He'd had them both, could compare them, might prefer Bessie . . . The idea was too humiliating to contemplate. The rivalry of a woman of her own class she might have been able to take . . .

Mercedes recalled imagining the reaction of her mother's friends to Bessie, picturing their exaggerated distaste, which now seemed to her to be based on fear. And she knew that deep down her own instincts were no different from those of the self-righteous matrons she so despised.

Andrew coaxed, 'Come on, Sadie. We have good times, don't we? Why dwell on what's past?'

Mercedes turned away. His gentleness didn't change anything. She began to weep in earnest, with passion, the sobbing torn from her, the reasons jumbled and confused – an agony of jealousy, a black self-loathing, the sickening conviction that she was demeaned and compromised.

In time her closed, obstinate grief made him resentful in his turn. 'I've done nothing bad towards you, Sadie. I even talked about us getting wed and you laughed it off. Don't you think that hurt me?'

In her destructive passion she saw a chance to wound him, as she'd been wounded. 'Can you see us, the two of us?' she asked him with harsh ridicule. 'What kind of a wedding would that be?'

She could see from his face that her mockery had cut him to the quick. His reaction was to withdraw, like a worsted enemy to his own camp, to recover his defences. Leaving her huddled on the floor, he got to his feet, and stood smiling down at her with a pitying malice.

'What d'you want then?' he taunted. 'To marry some stuffed shirt like your sisters?'

She looked up at him standing above her, hips thrust forward, hands hooked in his belt. On his face the look her friends and relatives dreaded above all from their inferiors.

The look they called dumb insolence, that challenged their fragile dignity, their view of the world and of themselves. At that moment his attraction for her had never been greater. But her anger at his arrogance was stronger, the suggestion that he was the one to rescue her from a stuffy bourgeois marriage. She hated him above all for the terrifying truth that lay behind his words.

He was exciting to her and alien. He'd too much power over her. Her desire for him was devastating. She'd laid herself bare to him, writhed and cried out in his arms, made crazy by lust. She'd thought their passion unique, and now she saw that it was commonplace.

The best thing, then, would be to put an end to his physical dominance and make a clean break. Regain control of her life and her soul. Mercedes could see the interlude suddenly as a form of madness. It had taken the annihilating jealousy to make her understand. Only she was determined to strike the first blow, and so punish him for all he'd made her suffer.

She stood up in her turn, collecting herself, light-headed and heavy-eyed. She looked at Andrew. 'I don't know what it is I want,' she told him, and shivered again in the chill air of the room. 'But it isn't you any more . . . There's no future for you and me together.'

'You love me,' he told her simply. Then, in a sudden snarl, 'You can't keep your hands off me!' In the instant of silence that followed she secretly acknowledged the truth of what he said. Andrew shook his head. 'But you'd let your bloody pride win out.'

Mercedes shrugged her shoulders. 'Anyway, I'm leaving you.' Keeping her face free of expression, though inside something was dying.

34

Mercedes lay between the smooth sheets of her bed. The light, filtered through red curtains, altered, shifted, or disappeared entirely, depending on the hour, but she had no sense of the continuity of night and day. People came and went on tiptoe, monitoring her comfort, adjusting the bedclothes and curtains, washing her gently with a soap that smelled faintly of cloves, bringing a regular change of clean, soft nightgowns.

There was always a jug of Florence's cool lemonade by the bed, with a little poured into a glass, so she could simply reach out – though that was an effort in itself – and take a sip to quench the parched feeling that was with her all the time.

Every so often a thermometer was pushed into her mouth for a minute or so and then removed. Above her head she would hear murmured consultations, George and Florence clucking over her, talking about what should be done.

'A hundred and three. I think she should be sponged down.'

'Lower tonight. A hundred and two.'

'Up again, I'm afraid.'

'Smooth that sheet, dear, it's all rucked . . .'

But none of it seemed to concern her. With a feeling of relief, Mercedes abandoned all forms of responsibility. Sometimes she had the impression she was on a boat, floating to somewhere far off. All she could do was lie back because it would take a very long time to get there.

Occasionally, though, she would start up with a sudden, urgent sense of anxiety and swing her legs over the side of the bed, convinced that she should be somewhere, doing something, sorting something out. Sometimes she'd even get to her feet and take a couple of unsteady steps before remembering that the obsessions and passions and concerns of the last two months were over and done with. And then she'd fall back again into bed, into the luxury of her semi-stupor.

But she had company at times, mainly in the hours of darkness when the solicitous visits of parents and servants were fewer. She didn't question whether they were inside her head, these hallucinations, or a literal, quivering presence in the faint candlelight of the room. The apparitions had a stronger-than-life vitality, with black, intense eyes and lips drawn back in wolfish grins over predatory teeth. They came and went with a will-o'-the-wisp unpredictability, posturing and seeming to mock her, taking on the personalities of her companions from Bermondsey – Andrew above all, Annie, Daisy, Queenie, Bessie Carter – but distorted like cartoons in newspapers, gaunt and elongated.

Mercedes watched them with the blank, wondering acceptance of a child. Sometimes they came in pairs, with an aura of hostile conspiracy. Andrew and Bessie, brazenly embracing, then eyeing her spitefully. Andrew, bone-white, strangely allied with Annie Tyrell. And, odder still, Daisy conniving quietly with a florid, bulbous Edward Ballard.

She lay there and endured passively the macabre images, twirling and coiling like smoke, as if they simply confirmed what she'd discovered. That the safe, simple world she'd been raised in was an illusion and that life held all manner of unsuspected contradictions, ambiguities and betrayals.

Once Mercedes cried out in panic and horror. She'd dreamt that she and Andrew were Siamese twins then, seeming to wake from the nightmare, found that the flesh down one side of her body was raw and bloody as if he'd been forcibly torn from her. That night she lay for a long time, clenched in fear, while her heart hammered against her ribs like a maddened captive animal hurling itself repeatedly against the bars of its cage.

'What day is it?'

Florence turned from the act of opening one red curtain. She wore the tartan blouse she'd brought home from Scotland and she had a smile on her face that seemed close to tears. Mercedes felt a welling of love for her, as if she'd come upon her mother unexpectedly, in a crowd of strangers.

'Are you feeling better, Sadie? We've been terribly worried about you. Daddy was even thinking of asking Donald Fielding to come and examine you. For a second opinion.' She mentioned a colleague of George's.

Mercedes stretched her arms into the air above her, then linked her fingers behind her head. She considered. 'Yes, I suppose I do feel better.' What she felt more than anything was a sense of calm, as if she'd returned safely from the perils of some epic journey. How strange, when she'd simply been lying between the four walls of her room for . . . how long was it?

'It's Tuesday. You've been in a sort of delirium for more than a week. There *is* an odd kind of fever going round, but Daddy says it's more than that. He says you're exhausted. Physically and mentally.'

Mercedes turned down the corners of her mouth in scepticism. 'How could I be?'

Her first conscious thought was that she'd missed the women's return to work. They'd have been back for more than a week now, taken home their first wages. Perhaps there was even a new manager in place. And, unthinkably, it had all happened without her.

This reflection was followed almost immediately by the realization that she had no place now down in

Bermondsey. She was redundant. Neither her services nor her encouragement were needed. Life at Ballard's would go on, as it had before the strike, without her. She framed the thought with an abrupt sense of loss, but also of relief.

'I wish you'd eat something, darling. Daddy says I'm not to force you, but it's days since you touched a morsel . . .'

'Milk. And a peach – are there any?' It wasn't hunger exactly. But suddenly she craved coolness, freshness.

'Menzel's have been selling some French ones. I'll send one of the maids out.'

For a few days Mercedes lived the life of a semi-invalid while Florence and George fussed round her, ordering her to rest a great deal and bringing a succession of small, bland meals to tempt her appetite.

'It's so wonderful to have you back, darling,' Florence confided one day. 'It's as if you've been somewhere else for ages, for much longer than just the days you've been ill.'

Mercedes was shocked by the extent of her physical weakness. Simply to walk upstairs left her exhausted. The idea of journeying to Bermondsey, or even to Victoria, to the Association's offices, seemed ambitious beyond measure. But she was ill-at-ease with her inactivity, the solicitude of servants and parents. She resisted the idea of sinking into the role of cherished daughter of the house. The freedom she'd seized had cost her too much friction and heartbreak. With constant hints Mercedes reminded George and Florence that the situation was temporary. As soon as feasible she intended to come and go again as she pleased. Her parents were non-committal. She suspected they were unwilling to cross her at present, in case she had a relapse. Mercedes guessed they were simply biding their time.

It had been on impulse that she'd broken with Andrew, a wilful, vengeful, stricken impulse. The thinking came later. After her illness she had all the time in the world for that.

As Mercedes sat in her study on the second floor, with her shelves full of books, her old rocking-horse in the corner, a white cotton blanket Florence seemed to think of as essential tucked across her knees, trying to read, his presence closed in on her, his face and voice filled her head, making her forget where she was, leaving her with a raw, regretful ache. If someone knocked on the door or entered the room, she would start, with a nervousness that surprised her.

'Gracious, Sadie. You must have a guilty secret,' George teased her one evening, as he came to drink his malt whisky night-cap in her company. At times Mercedes had the rueful impression that this was precisely how her parents liked her best, weakened and immobilized, forced to play the game of family life.

Shakily she laughed off her agitation. 'If only you knew . . .'

If he *did* know, she reflected, how quickly George's joviality would turn to dark, atavistic horror. For a gently-bred girl, hers was perhaps the ultimate in guilty secrets.

In bed at night her body still craved his. She dreamt about him constantly with a graphic vividness that was often accompanied by involuntary orgasmic cramps. Frequently the dreams featured scenes of jealousy and would wake her into darkness and hours of lone anguish as unendurable as the first time. In the morning she would fantasize that she could feel the warmth of his body all down one side of her, then find it was an illusion, and be seized by the fear of discovering her flesh as she'd imagined it before, torn and bleeding from the brutal severance.

'This is crazy.' She struggled to sit up in bed, damp with sweat, exhausted as if from some long drawn-out ordeal.

A little later one of the maids came to draw the curtains

and bring her breakfast tray. Hot chocolate and brioches Florence had ordered to be freshly baked for her each morning. Mercedes ate and drank, propped against a pile of pillows, enervated.

As an antidote to her night-time frustrations, she tried to picture a life they could realistically have shared if her relationship with Andrew had been taken to its logical conclusion. The scenario she pieced together depressed her with its bleakness.

She imagined a hasty, utilitarian wedding down in Bermondsey, with none of her own relatives present. A shabby furnished room – try as she might Mercedes couldn't picture it as inviting or cosy. Then the endless monotony of Andrew going off to work at the factory and coming home at night . . . And herself. Either days spent between four walls, washing clothes, cooking, dusting and cleaning her tiny world, or some job that paid a pittance and put her at someone's beck and call throughout the long day, a hireling, a dogsbody.

'I know I couldn't stand it . . .'

It was one thing to befriend the poor, assume an active, glorious role in bettering their lot, but quite another to become one of them. She could see the attraction – for a few weeks – in playing at being a working-man's wife like Marie Antoinette acting the role of a milk-maid. But the reality, the sheer, endless grind of it, was something else entirely.

So, her life would go on as it had before she met him . . . Her work with the Association fascinated and absorbed her. And her experience with the Ballard's strikers would, Mercedes anticipated, have raised her stock there immeasurably. She was ripe for further responsibility and avid for new campaigns.

All the same, the aching suspicion persisted that, in rejecting Andrew, she'd lost something she'd been looking for all her life – that everyone was looking for – something passionate, addictive and fundamental that her blood craved. She could renounce and belittle it, but in the despairing truthfulness of the night her subconscious self would continue to protest.

After a further week of submitting to an invalid's routine, the cosseting attention of the household, Mercedes had had enough.

'I'm discharging myself,' she told George and Florence.

Her parents argued fiercely. George brought all the heavy weight of his professional mystique to bear. But Mercedes put her foot down. She was conscious of having lost ground in her move towards self-determination. It was time to act before the loss became irreversible. She left the house and caught an omnibus to Victoria, still weak, but boosted by the flexing of her will.

She spent the day in the Association's office, catching up with neglected paperwork, making a list of all the things that wanted doing, taking pleasure in ticking off item after item, bringing order to chaos.

The functional shabbiness of the office, with its shelves of papers, spartan desks and chairs, acted like a tonic after the rugs and cushions and tempting little meals of the last fortnight. Women came and went during the day, busily passing through, intent on reports they had to write, meetings to attend. Their bustle was exhilarating.

In the afternoon Hannah dropped by, looking cool and elegant in pale green shantung. By about three o'clock she and Mercedes were left alone in the office. Hannah was in a chatty mood and seemed impressed with the outcome of the Ballard's dispute.

'You've shown great determination, Mercedes.' She perched with unaccustomed informality on the edge of Mercedes' desk. 'Verbal fireworks are all very well – emotional pyrotechnics – but they can burn out pretty quickly. Give me someone with staying power every time.

Someone who can keep going through all the deadlock and discouragement of the average dispute.'

Mercedes was warmed quite wonderfully by her praise and offered a token show of modesty. 'I've neglected them awfully since . . . I've not once been down to Bermondsey . . .'

'Quite right, too!' Hannah cut in fervently. 'You've done your job down there, Mercedes. It's over and done with!'

Mercedes was caught off-balance by the feeling in Hannah's voice, and couldn't think of anything to say.

'I used to get terribly involved,' Hannah explained. 'Much, much too involved. You're there to do a job, you know. It's a mistake to let it spill over into your personal life.' She'd picked up a coloured glass paperweight from the desk and fiddled with it absently as she spoke, not looking at Mercedes. Her words came in a rush, quite unlike her usual measured delivery. 'It took me an awful lot of time and a lot of heartbreak to learn that . . .'

Mercedes was astounded and intrigued by this glimpse of a more vulnerable Hannah. Was it possible that this poised creature had once been as full of self-doubt as herself? As confused? Feeling her way, with only a sort of dogged belief that things could and should be changed to guide her?

She would have loved to find out more, but Hannah hopped down from her perch and presented Mercedes with a sheaf of manuscript pages densely covered in her black, even handwriting.

'Could you possibly make a start on this today, Mercedes, dear? It's really quite urgent.'

35

In mid-July the MacInnes family and the Pimletts had, from time immemorial, rented two adjacent houses in the Lake District near Cockermouth. The habit persisted even now, when the children were all grown, and the party generally included a sprinkling of grandchildren.

'You *will* come this year, darling?' Florence cajoled. 'The fresh air will be marvellous for you . . . Walter's going to be there,' she added, as a further inducement.

The presence of Walter was less of an attraction than it once might have been. Recently Mercedes had discovered a little pocket of reserve in her feelings for him. She'd sensed a slight priggishness in his attitude towards her involvement in the strike, though there was nothing you could really put your finger on. She'd not seen him since the evening meal at Hannah's flat. All her free time and energy had been wrapped up in Andrew.

Mercedes dithered. Last year she'd refused to go. It had been an act of self-assertion more than anything, a kind of protest against the family's taking her presence for granted. But today she was beguiled by the prospect of lazy, undemanding days spent in gardens or on the beach, long walks across rounded green hills, picnics and laughter.

She nodded and smiled. 'I'd love to come.'

'Wonderful!' Florence's face lit up like a child's and Mercedes felt as if she'd given her some splendid present.

Sybil, one of her sisters, would be coming too, she learned, with Leon her husband and their two young children. The Pimlett party would consist of Tom and Winnie and all three of their children – Walter, his elder brother Peter, with Cassie, his very pregnant young wife, and Walter's sister Allie, with her two toddlers, but without her husband.

The two large, white cottages stood cheek by jowl in the green hollow of a hill. They belonged to a manufacturer who'd pretty well stopped coming there himself, but who let them out to regulars who'd had the good fortune to discover them via word of mouth.

They were spacious, but furnished in homely style, the rustic wooden cottage furniture made hospitable by carpets and cushions and easy chairs. The gardens had an air of being hewn from the wilderness. An area of lawn in front of the cottage gave way to meadow and trees, beyond which lay naked moorland.

The two houses had always been a home from home for the MacInnes and Pimlett children. A place of enchantment where the normal rules didn't apply, where they could run wild and get dirty, eat in the open air, ignoring the bedrocks of their everyday life, like bedtime, piano practice and regular meals.

The families took with them the bare minimum in the way of help. The MacInnes party included just Mrs Carter and a young kitchen maid. Two women from Cockermouth came in daily to do the heavy cleaning and a local farmer's son cut the cultivated area of grass each week.

Apart from that, they shifted for themselves, laughing about the simple life, going back to nature and roughing it. The joke had a hollow ring to Mercedes after the grim little hovels she'd encountered of late, and women on strike for the privilege of working a sixty-hour week for less than fourteen shillings, but she closed her mind to the anomaly. She'd come here to enjoy herself and was determined to keep the small, niggling voice of her conscience at bay.

And the magic of the place reasserted itself. She rediscovered her old bedroom with its whitewashed, sloping ceiling and patchwork quilt. From the window she drank in the view of rolling hills, studded here and there with small, white cottages, reminding herself how the shadows of the clouds scudded across the sunlit slopes.

Each night the families met up for an evening meal in one or other of the two houses – plain, wholesome stews, flans or baked meats, salads and summer fruits. They had to push tables together and carry chairs back and forth between the cottages in order to accommodate everyone. Then they'd sit up talking or playing games till around midnight. The children stayed up too, till they dozed off on someone's lap and were carried upstairs sound asleep.

The days were free and unstructured. As the spirit moved her, Mercedes would walk or read or join in some improvised game of tennis across a clothes-line on the lawn. Everyone did as they pleased. Food was cold and portable, to be eaten when and where desired.

Sometimes they'd all agree to go to the beach together, and then the servants would pack hampers. Leon and Peter had motor-cars, and they ferried food and bodies to St Bee's in relays.

Mercedes' pleasure in the sunny, informal days was clear and conscious, as if she'd emerged from a tangled forest into a bright meadow. Her dreams of Andrew still came disturbingly at night, but in the day-time she banished thoughts of everything except the present. The weather was scorching. Days on the beach were idyllic, with echoes of her childhood. She played sandcastles with the children, paddled or showed them rock-pools. She took part in huge, hilarious games of cricket, running barefoot on the wet sand, or rigged up a windbreak where she could sit in the sun and read books and newspapers.

None of the Pimletts ever referred to Mercedes' part in the dispute at their friend, Ballard's, factory, though by now something of the story must be known to them. She guessed that George must have had a private word, making much of his daughter's illness and physical exhaustion, presenting the episode as the indiscretion of a headstrong girl, asking their indulgence.

It became a habit for Mercedes and Walter to walk the mile and a half into Cockermouth each morning to collect the mail and the previous day's newspapers. In the bright blue dawning of the brilliant days the jaunts were pure pleasure. In this nostalgic setting it was hard to remember the small resentments she'd harboured against him. Walter became again simply her childhood playmate, almost a brother. They drew closer again in the shared privacy.

'This year I feel as if I appreciate everything about this place more than I ever have before,' she confided to him. 'All the ordinary family things seem to have a special magic to them . . . It's all so familiar, but at the same time it's as if I'd never really seen it before.' She was exhilarated and held up her arms to the high, cloudless sky. The turf under her feet felt rich and springy.

They walked in companionable silence for a while, then Walter said, 'There's such a sense of continuity about it all, what with the elders, then our generation, and the sprogs toddling about. And we all belong. When I'm here it makes me think about having my own kids and bringing them here one day . . .'

He flashed her a wry smile from beneath his moustache, suddenly conscious of how solemn he sounded. Mercedes felt fond of him and touched his hand. But as she did so that serious look came into his eyes, a vulnerability. The look she hadn't seen for some time now, that used to disturb her, its insistence ruffling the carefree surface of their friendship. It made her thoughtful for a while.

'I feel as huge as an airship.' Cassie Pimlett sat fanning herself under a large, striped parasol her husband, Peter, had rigged up for her on the beach. Her swollen belly ballooned in front of her looking to Mercedes like some monstrous appendage, attached to her body, yet not a part of it.

'You're the very picture of glorious fecundity,' Leon, Mercedes' brother-in-law, remarked daringly. Beneath the ruffled, boyish brown hair there was a slight flush to his cheek. Mercedes wondered absently whether he didn't have a little bit of a fetish for expectant women. She remembered him during her sister Sybil's two pregnancies, sitting on the floor at his wife's feet, gazing up at her as if she were some majestic goddess of fertility.

'Glorious elephantinity!' Cassie retorted. She lowered her voice, with a conspiratorial smile. 'Look at my medical advisers.'

Watched by their wives, Thomas Pimlett and George, barefoot and wearing straw hats, their trousers rolled to mid-calf, tunnelled vigorously in the sand, to the squeaking delight of their respective grandchildren.

Through lids half closed against the brightness of the sun, Mercedes gazed at Cassie as she sat, serenely inactive, beneath the umbrella. A sea-breeze blew wisps of her child-like ash-blonde hair across her peachy face, and she wore an unconscious smile. Cassie seemed to feel herself blessed, to bask in her pregnancy, laughing lazily at her own clumsiness.

There was something about the holiday atmosphere and Cassie's wry humour that liberated the two families. Her condition was mentioned shamelessly, even joked about. Only a short time ago, when her two sisters were carrying, their pregnancies had been hedged about with a sense of embarrassment and hardly mentioned in mixed company. There was something in the air, Mercedes thought, some imperceptible change, quietly dispatching the stuffiness of Victorian days, gradually making people more free and easy.

'Can I get you some lemonade, Cass?' she called, with

an enquiring glance towards the two wicker hampers containing the families' provender.

'Just half a glass, Sadie.' Cassie turned her dazed, contented eyes towards Mercedes. 'But only if you're getting some for yourself.'

Throughout the holiday Mercedes had been fascinated by Cassie. Her interest stemmed from the incredulous suspicion germinating inside her that she herself might be in the same condition. The obsessive speculation formed a secret counterpart to the glorious summer days, in some strange way intensifying rather than spoiling her enjoyment.

Mercedes looked dreamily about her, at the golden spread of the sand beneath the chalky cliff-face, at the blissful blue of the sky, the glittering sea melting into a far-off haze on the horizon and, halfway down the beach, the figures of her parents and the children clustered eagerly round their expanding earthworks. At times like this it was impossible to credit the thought that a child might be growing inside her. It was too unreal. She was only just over a fortnight late. There could be all manner of reasons . . .

But sometimes, when she walked alone across the moorland behind the house, or lay with her eyes open in the dark underneath the patchwork quilt she used to love so as a child, then the possibility took on shape and substance, and she experienced a pang of terror, but also a perverse excitement.

'What if you turned out to have a bun in the oven?' She could still hear the very tone and timbre of Andrew's voice when he'd said that. Then and now her reactions were confused. Above all there was the deep-seated fear of scandal, but at the same time a reckless curiosity as to what would happen and a strange attraction to the idea of surrendering to fate.

Mercedes emerged from her dreaming to find herself

pouring Cassie the offered glass of lemonade. It was gloriously cold. The ice in it had not yet completely melted.

'Thanks, Sadie . . . Anything in the papers?' Cassie asked idly, as if world events were a form of entertainment unrolling for her benefit, but not concerning her.

'Plenty.'

'Anything about that divorce case?' Cassie put in quickly, before Mercedes could bore her with anything political.

'Yes . . . Here, look for yourself.' Mercedes pointed out the relevant column.

With time on her hands, Mercedes had begun to read the newspapers avidly, the way she used to before the strike and Andrew began to claim all of her time and attention.

That summer English eyes were turned towards Ireland, where the situation bristled like dry grass just waiting for a match to set it alight. Civil war threatened and private armies drilled quite openly. Leon, Peter and Walter talked about the Home Rule question *ad nauseam*, over meals and pre-dinner sherry, while motoring, and on the beach. Leon had been run out during a family game of cricket last week, engrossed as he was in discussing developments in Ireland with George, who was keeping wicket.

In the end Mercedes was satiated with all the talk. There was nothing new anyone could say. In reaction she began to follow events in Europe. At the end of June a little Serbian anarchist had shot the heir to the Austro-Hungarian empire. Absorbed in her own personal drama, Mercedes had been unaware of the happening at the time, and she had only the foggiest idea as to the whereabouts of Serbia. But as July passed the assassination seemed to be producing repercussions all over Europe – in Russia, Germany and Romania, as well as Austria. Mercedes began to get involved in the daily developments of the situation, and to regale the rest of them with readings from the foreign news. They were less than enthusiastic.

'I'm sure it's fascinating, Sadie,' Sybil remarked languidly as she and Mercedes, Walter and Leon flopped on the grass one day recovering from the exertions of a tennis match, glasses of Mrs Carter's home-made ginger-beer at hand. 'All the same, it's got nothing in the world to do with us.'

'Long live insularity!' The jibes between Mercedes and her sister tended to have a mild edge of hostility.

'Put a sock in it, Sadie.' Walter was an instinctive peacemaker. '. . . Sadie's obsession,' he observed quirkily, supplying a humorous whistle on all the sibilants.

It became a catch-phrase that they all trotted out whenever she tried to interest them in the matter. But towards the end of the month Austria declared war on Serbia in earnest, and willy-nilly they all became more interested in the affair.

Events began to snowball. Each day brought international ultimata that were ignored, and threats of mobilization. France was involved. The whole thing was moving a little close to home. The newspapers invoked the *entente cordiale* – French interests were tantamount to British. 'Sadie's obsession' became the preoccupation of them all.

As they basked in the hot sunshine, the figurative storm-clouds seemed unreal. But Mercedes remembered that two months back Hannah's husband, James, had been gloomily prophesying war in Europe.

'You were there, Walter, that evening,' she recalled. He nodded and they shared a brief, reflective silence before Mercedes added, 'How terrifying if he turns out to be right!'

Mercedes' birthday fell on 3 August. For as long as she could remember, whatever the weather, the two families had celebrated with a communal picnic. Whatever else was on the menu, there had to be chocolate cake. It was traditional. Mercedes used to have a passion for it as a child. Champagne was the other essential ingredient. At first she was allowed just a sip of George's, but at fifteen she graduated to a glass of her own. For the rest of her life, the taste of it recalled those special birthday picnics.

When she was a small girl Mercedes used to pray for rain. There was something so deliciously incongruous in the sight of the grown-ups crouching beneath umbrellas in the garden, with the glasses and their plates of cake, while the relentless summer rain fell all round.

She had a mental picture of a younger, thinner Florence, pink-cheeked below the black spider-web shape of her umbrella, holding up a long, fluted glass and proclaiming, 'The show must go on!'

The laughing, indomitable determination of the two families to celebrate in the face of wind and weather used to make her feel enormously important and loved.

This year the idea of such discomfort seemed a world away. It was Bank Holiday Monday and the sun shone gloriously, as it had for weeks. They all agreed that the beach was the place – for the last two weeks they'd commandeered a spot just a little way along from St Bee's. It was empty and sheltered, with a good stretch of smooth, even sand. There could be no better venue.

The two families planned to curtail their holiday due to the volatility of the international situation. Germany was threatening to invade Belgium, violating her neutrality, and it seemed unlikely that the British Government would simply stand by . . . The servants were already packing, in preparation for an early departure the next day.

As Walter set up deck-chairs for the parents and Sybil and Mercedes spread rugs on the loose, warm sand, they were infected by a giddy, nervous gaiety. You could almost see a black question-mark hanging in the air. Today things were the way they'd always been. But tomorrow?

For Mercedes the sense of uncertainty was heightened still further by the pregnancy anxiety she could share with no one. The picnic would be a kind of last supper. It seemed to her that the clear, tender light of the summer morning was illuminating each separate second, revealing it as fragile and precious.

A folding table was erected. Walter had a flamboyant way with champagne. To the children's delight he made the corks pop and filled the waiting glasses with a showy twist of the wrist.

Thomas Pimlett, a slight figure in blue blazer and light trousers, took on himself the role of toast-master. He was in an emotional frame of mind and made a small speech.

'Sadie's birthday has always been a day we've spent together. Even last year, when she couldn't be here, we went ahead and celebrated in the same old way.' Momentarily a ray of sun angled off the glass he held in front of him, sparking a dazzling dart of light. 'It's got to the stage when I see August the third as a kind of communal birthday.' He stressed the phrase as if it pleased him.

'The MacInneses and the Pimletts have grown up together.' Thomas gestured expansively, slopping a little of his wine on to the sand. His silver hair was whipped by an on-shore breeze. 'And each year Sadie's picnic reaffirms the friendship between our two families.'

'Hear, hear.' The rumble of George's voice filled a slight pause.

Given the circumstances, Thomas obviously felt some topical reference was called for, and he continued doggedly. 'As a nation we're facing a tricky situation . . . which could develop in any number of ways . . . But whatever happens we know we can rely . . . The close ties between our two families will endure . . .' He was beginning to struggle a little, but recovered himself to propose the triumphant toast. 'To Sadie. And friendship!'

'Sadie and friendship . . .' The words were repeated in a buzz of different tones and pitches.

'Down the hatch!' To amuse the children, Walter drained his glass in one long gulp. Charlie, Sybil's five-year-old, followed suit with his lemonade.

Two large tears trickled slowly down Winnie Pimlett's amiable horse-face. Her daughter, Allie, put an arm round her shoulder and passed her a small, lacy handkerchief. Florence smiled broadly, but her eyes were suspiciously bright.

'Thank you, Thomas . . . I'm touched.' Mercedes took a sip of the chilled champagne. There was a lump in her throat. She felt sentimental and knew it. But sentimentality had its own truth.

She looked round at the circle of familiar faces. Beyond them the blue surface of the sea danced with bright, fragmented reflections of the sun. And, just for a moment, by some obscure association, her mind caught an echo of the hopes and passions of that summer in Bermondsey, a momentary drifting, like a lace curtain stirring in a current of air. Mercedes had a sudden sharp sense of how spacious life was, how diverse and mysterious.

'I wish I could keep this moment,' she exclaimed impulsively.

It was too much for Winnie, who crumpled into fullblooded weeping.

'Grandma's crying,' came the hushed, wondering voice of Allie's three-year-old, Louise, making them laugh and providing an honourable British exit from the embarrassment of unbridled emotion.

Late afternoon, when the picnic was over, Mercedes and Walter found themselves left alone on the beach, guarding the hampers and other effects while Peter and Leon drove the rest home. The two of them would be picked up on a second journey.

They took off their shoes and walked for a while on the shingle, letting the cool waves lap over their feet. The heat of the day was heavy and torpid now. Thoughts of the impending crisis mixed elegiacally, and not unpleasantly, with sun and sand, and with her memories of the afternoon.

'It's an awfully shallow thing to admit,' Mercedes said. 'But all the menace in the air seemed to make this year's picnic more . . . memorable, and more enjoyable even.'

'Like dancing on the edge of an abyss.' Eyes narrowed, Walter skimmed a stone. It hopped on the calm surface of the sea four times, before plopping out of sight beneath the waves.

'I'm going to do a better one than that.' She cast her eyes around for a good, flat pebble.

'If it *is* war, I'm joining up,' Walter said.

Mercedes looked up from her search. 'I can understand that. I really can.' She paused and shrugged her shoulders. 'But it's a pity it's not a more inspiring cause. Like Sybil said the other day, it hasn't got a thing to do with us.'

'Not stopping a small nation from being bullied?'

'That's just a little part of it. The whole thing shouldn't be happening. It concerns about . . . point nought nought nought nought one of the population. And people will die . . .'

He didn't reply. Mercedes had the feeling there was something quite different he wanted to say. She found a stone and skimmed it.

'Five!' she said, smiling triumphantly at him.

'You're the birthday girl. I let you win.'

She gave him a push. 'But you went first.'

They began to walk up the beach again, towards the rugs and hampers.

'You know, I felt quite sentimental today,' Walter said. Mercedes was struck by the fact that in her mind she'd used the same word.

'Mmm. It's terribly easy to take families for granted and

315

see all the faults in them. Then suddenly you realize how much they mean . . .'

He turned to her eagerly. 'You felt that, too?'

'I've been feeling it all holiday.'

They reached the baggage and sat down to wait on an old tartan rug.

Walter leant on one elbow, gazing absently out to sea. 'Watching the young 'uns – Allie's and Sybil's – and being with Cassie, I've been imagining being here with my own children. Feeling broody and dynastic.'

For the umpteenth time that day Mercedes pictured the tiny life forming inside her, becoming less of a possibility, more and more probable. To cover her preoccupation, she teased him. 'You can't do it on your own. You must have set your heart on someone.' Before she'd finished the sentence, the thought came that she was fishing . . . that he wanted her to fish.

'Sadie.' He turned to her with a tentative, strained smile. 'It's you. I've set my heart on you.'

'Oh.' The idea wasn't new to her. For months Mercedes had caught that look in his eye. And yet somehow she'd never thought it would go any further. A sort of panic gripped her. She dreaded hurting his feelings.

'I'm surprised.' Mercedes looked gravely into his eyes. Openness seemed to be the best approach. Taking him seriously.

'Are you? I feel as if I give myself away all the time.' He reached out and took her hand, then gave a rueful smile, seeming ill-at-ease with the solemnity. 'It's devilish hard to say I love you to someone who's been your friend for . . . twenty-four years.'

'Walter!' Her tone was a mixture of affection, regret, confusion. In a brief flash she visualized marrying him, saw herself standing outside a church, her veil blowing round her, being photographed next to him. There was a proud, proper smile on his boyish face. She saw the genuine delight of their parents. For the first time she understood her sisters' marriages, saw the temptation in doing the right thing.

At the same time the charming image filled her soul with iron. It was so . . . dynastic was the word he'd used. After the sentimental lull of the holiday she re-awoke to the danger of being strangled by chains of love and habit.

'If it's war, I'm joining up.' He repeated the resolution. 'And I couldn't face going without asking you . . .' His voice had a dying fall, as if her lack of response had chilled him.

Her heart went out to him, painfully, as if he were a cherished younger brother. If only he'd left things as they were. She hated to wound him.

At the same time she had the reckless urge to tell him she was carrying another man's child, to smash the wholesome, homogeneous image he had of her. He thought she fitted into his cosy mental jigsaw of home, hearth and children. And she didn't.

'Walter, listen. You're my dearest friend. I can say quite truthfully that I love you . . . But not in a marrying way.' A spark of pain lit up in his eyes. 'I'm so sorry, Walter.'

How difficult she was, what a misfit. She'd turned her back on passion, in Andrew. And now she was refusing conventional happiness. Mercedes felt suddenly alone and lost. But what else could she do?

36

The repetitive rhythm of the train had a soothing, hypnotic effect on Edward Ballard. Outside the window a domestic late-summer landscape baked beneath the steady heat of the sun. The countryside became flatter and more predictable as they approached London, and so peaceful you could imagine that all the febrile war chatter back at the hotel, the wild speculation, had been a dream.

Only the train was full of young and not-so-young reservists travelling to join their units. To Edward's displeasure, a couple of them had been billeted on their first-class compartment for the final leg of the journey. But they'd turned out to be pleasant, respectful lads who, anyway, preferred to stand and smoke outside in the corridor.

From his pocket Edward slipped a small, silver-capped hip-flask that used to belong to his father, and took a swift nip of whisky.

Mildred, opposite, looked up from her book, pale and a little bleary – it had been a wearing journey from Gleneagles where they'd been holidaying, and there had been delays and cancellations.

She gave a gently ironic smile. 'Touch of war-panic? Steadying the old nerves?' But her teasing had a tentative quality. Since the dinner party when she'd overplayed her hand so publicly and so disastrously, Mildred had been gratifyingly biddable.

'No, old thing. Just staving off the boredom.'

Their relationship had settled into a pattern which suited Edward very well. He could afford to be affable, paternal even, restraining the whip-hand which he so manifestly

318

held, unless Mildred showed signs of straying from the narrow paths of compliance that were her territory from now on. The more so since he'd succeeded in convincing her that she'd wronged him, and that – worse luck – there had never been anything between himself and the young working-woman he'd been seen with.

'Only another hour or so.' The old Mildred would never have bothered with such an insipid, factual remark. But nowadays she made efforts to be meek and pleasant.

He nodded. 'Not long now.'

It would be good to get home. Edward was fatalistic about the fact of war – all the self-appointed experts had been predicting it for years. What he couldn't stomach was all the bombastic, jingoistic nonsense everyone had suddenly started spouting. He'd had a bellyful at the hotel in Gleneagles. An old fart with a face the colour of raw liver had all but challenged him to a duel for suggesting that the Germans might be better prepared than God's chosen nation. Between his own four walls he could escape from all that hog-wash.

Edward's seventeen-year-old son, Toby, seated next to his mother, closed the Forster novel he'd been immersed in and looked up with glazed, faraway eyes.

'Back to earth then, old chap,' his father remarked heartily.

Toby gave him a vague smile. 'Yes.'

Edward constantly felt at a loss with his eldest son. He ached to make contact, but was aware in advance of the banality of his approach. Toby wasn't like the two younger boys who were roaming the train's corridor, exhilarated by the aura of masculine swagger and purpose that surrounded the soldiers

'Good book?' Edward pursued his sterile efforts.

Toby nodded carelessly. 'Excellent.' He made no effort to elaborate.

Silence. Edward looked across at his son with a mixture

of exasperation and love. The boy had a seraphic beauty. Edward's golden hair combined with the clear-cut features Mildred had in her youth. The purity of his looks was accentuated by a pair of gold-rimmed spectacles. Toby played the piano with a passionate facility and painted with a skill that astonished his father.

Though Edward wasn't artistic, he saw in his son a quality he'd once possessed. A gentleness. The lack of a self-protective shell. These vulnerabilities had been stamped and shamed out of Edward by a mixture of fatherly contempt and school conditioning. But he'd never had the heart to try to change Toby. He loved him too much as he was. Thank God he was too young yet for soldiering. Edward prayed that the know-it-alls who claimed this whole thing would be over by Christmas would turn out to be right.

The train was approaching a level-crossing. Outside, vivid against a field of bleached wheat-stubble, a young woman in pink, with a dark fringe and side-curls, stood with two bemused young children, smiling and waving ecstatically to the soldiers as they passed.

'Eh there, nippers!'

The two reservists who'd shared their carriage leant their heads and arms out of the window, waving enthusiastically to the children.

'Ma's all right, too,' one of them called more softly.

Edward watched with blank, misanthropic eyes. For the life of him he couldn't see why the fact of war should throw everyone into this state of communal euphoria.

The night before last he'd sat up late in the hotel with a couple of holiday companions, sharing a bottle of brandy and waiting for the telephone to ring. Neville Kirkpatrick had promised to let him know the moment the ultimatum was rejected.

As it happened, the two men were both manufacturers, like himself, and in their snug, panelled retreat they mused on their prospects in the light of this new twist of fate.

Oliver Browning was about Edward's age and, like him, had inherited wealth. Harold Bull was younger and frankly self-made. Sneakingly Edward admired the man's shrewdness and self-confidence.

Bull had made him think. Already he'd devised a strategy in case of war. And he wasn't one of those who thought it would all be over in a matter of weeks.

'There's fortunes to be made if you move at the right time. I'm closing down for a while. Save on costs. And give the workers a scare.' His light eyes glinted with a flash of chill amusement. 'Stops the buggers getting above themselves . . . Everything'll be all to hell for a bit. Shipping disrupted, all that. I'll be watching the lie of the land.' He'd reached forward to splash a little more brandy into his glass. 'Spot the gaps – and fill 'em. No use crying about what can't be helped.'

His attitude had impressed Edward. Bull was right. Chances were raw materials were going to become pretty well unobtainable. Everything was going to be haywire. Best to cut your losses and close down till the situation had stabilized. Then diversify.

But it wasn't just prudence that attracted him to the idea of a shut-down. He pictured Harold Bull's hard smile. 'Stops the buggers from getting above themselves.' It'd certainly be one in the eye for those harpies who'd played merry hell with him all summer. Briefly, and with the old ache of useless regret, he pictured Daisy's fair skin, the opaque pools of her eyes. Edward felt for his hip-flask and took another swallow. Then he leaned his head luxuriously back against the lace-edged linen antimacassar and anticipated his revenge.

Arriving home at Devonshire Place, Florence embarked on an orgy of housekeeping and stocking-up. She seemed driven by some kind of self-fuelling inner logic, incomprehensible to anyone else.

'It's as if you were getting ready for a party.' Mercedes was bemused by an energy that appeared to her pointless and misplaced. 'The Germans aren't coming to tea.'

George chose to play the heavy father, taking Mercedes aside and emphasizing that she owed it to Florence to stay home and play her part. 'It's a trying, uncertain time. None of us knows what to expect. Your mother's doing what she can and she *needs* your support,' he whispered with dramatic confidentiality. An insistent look in his eye told Mercedes that this wasn't the time to assert her own rights.

Resignedly she stayed to help Florence supervise the efforts of the servants in scouring the house from top to bottom and reorganizing the pantry.

Food was a problem. Due to panic-buying the shops were well-nigh empty and, where stocks lasted, the prices had more than doubled.

'What *are* we supposed to do?' Florence fretted. Soberly Mercedes pointed out that they'd a pantryful of dried pulses and fruits, sugar, pickles, tinned stuff – they were hardly likely to starve.

Florence was shocked. 'They're reserves! They mustn't be touched.'

Mercedes put her foot down about joining her mother on shopping expeditions to the poorer parts of London in search of goods she couldn't find closer to home.

'It's immoral,' she insisted. 'And totally selfish. Just because you can afford to pay inflated prices . . .'

But Florence was as predatory as a jungle creature foraging for her young, and as single-minded.

'If I don't do it,' she declared, 'someone else will!' But she took Mrs Carter with her on her trips.

Mercedes felt stifled in the house and slipped out a couple of times a day to stretch her legs and widen her horizons a little, trying to work off a deeply personal impatience that was growing inside her, almost an aversion, to the drama of the war as it was played out around her.

People seemed to be acting the roles they thought they should – a breezy patriotism or a calm and smiling self-sacrifice, while at the same time all their worst instincts were running riot.

She passed two well-dressed, well-coiffured women of about Florence's age, friends, exchanging a dignified fare-well kiss. To Mercedes' critical eyes their every movement appeared conscious, as if they were two gracious actresses on public display.

'Our prayers will go with Miles,' she heard one of them coo. 'Dora, darling, you must be so-o proud of him.'

The other lifted her head, arranging her features into a brave, tremulous, womanly smile. 'I am,' she said simply.

It happened that they were standing outside Menzel's, the shop where Mrs Carter had bought their fruit and vegetables ever since Mercedes could remember. Two days ago it had been ransacked, because of its German name, by a crowd of drunken patriots. The windows had been broken and frail, wispy-haired Mr Menzel insulted and manhandled. The shop stood boarded-up now and desolate. Neither woman appeared to notice.

When she was feeling alienated from the people and happenings around her, Mercedes' thoughts turned inward, to the unformed, unknown being in her belly. It was becoming more and more real to her and, increasingly, wonderingly, she welcomed its presence.

Not that the prospect of breaking the news to her parents had grown any easier. Florence's tizzy over her war-preparations seemed an ominous harbinger. Over the last few days Mercedes had quite decided that she was going to move away from home into a room of her own at the earliest opportunity. At long range, so it seemed to her, all of them might find the situation a mite easier to bear.

As she walked down Upper Regent Street – hot and dusty and more deserted than usual due to the present disruptions – Mercedes tried to imagine her future. She wasn't without funds. Her bank-balance was relatively healthy – she never managed to spend the whole of her quarterly allowance and it had mounted up. As soon as she'd found a room, Mercedes decided, she would invest in a typewriter. She pictured it foursquare and reliable, insuring her against starvation. Mercedes quickened her pace, feeling resolute and equal to the situation. With a flicker of self-awareness she recognized how the *fait accompli* of a child was altering her outlook, mentally transforming the kind of drudgery she'd always dreaded into a daring new challenge.

'Landings! Troops in France!'

Mercedes bought a *Daily Mail* from the gaunt, one-armed vendor at Oxford Circus. Hard facts about the British landings in Europe were cushioned on a billowing swell of patriotic rhetoric. Mercedes' eyes moved down the page and were caught by a smaller headline. WIDE-SPREAD FACTORY CLOSURES.

Her attention sharpened. A multiplicity of factors, the paper stated, accounted for the shutting down of a large number of factories in all Britain's major cities. It went on to cite credit restrictions, bank closures, the disruption of transport and the general uncertainty of the outlook.

Mercedes lowered the newspaper. As if no time-lapse had intervened she was transported back to the early summer, to her intimate, day-to-day preoccupation with the progress of the Ballard's strike, and a black certainty filled her. That the women's triumphs had been dashed, wiped out at a stroke, leaving them unemployed again, worse off even than they had been before.

For just an instant Hannah's advice flashed through her

mind. Your job's over. It's a mistake to get involved. But she brushed it aside as she would a fly on a sunny day. The impulse to go straight down to Bermondsey and check on the situation for herself was irresistible. Mercedes began to walk at a fast pace down Oxford Street. She wasn't sure what buses or trains were running, but she'd get there somehow.

Daisy was at home in her rooms in Aquitaine Street. It was Saturday afternoon and Mercedes had hesitated in case Andrew was there. But she decided to call anyway. Some unreasonable corner of her mind ached for a glimpse of him. At the same time she was frightened – that she wouldn't cope, that her self-possession would crumble . . . Protectively one hand strayed to her stomach. Whatever happened she wouldn't tell him about that.

She need not have worried because he wasn't in. Daisy opened the door and seemed pleased to see her, but also abstracted, as though her mind was elsewhere. She confirmed that Ballard's workers had been paid off the previous afternoon and the factory was closed for the foreseeable future.

'After all you went through!' The irony was too cruel. 'It's a tragedy.' Mercedes was sick to her heart.

Daisy shrugged. 'We *were* pretty cut up.' Perversely she seemed to be taking the news far more calmly.

Immediately Mercedes was eager for action. 'First thing Monday morning I'll get on to the Association . . .'

'They'll have a job on,' Daisy remarked soberly. 'There's hundreds out of work round here.' Faced with her phlegmatic realism Mercedes felt hysterical and over-dramatic.

They sat and talked for a while in the living-room. It was cool in there – the sullen stickiness of the afternoon was filtered through the freshness of the plants on the window-sill and the shifting blue curtains. The conversation was an effort. To Mercedes it was like trying to connect with someone she'd known a long time back. She could hear the children playing in the next room, and their grandmother murmuring from time to time, but the door remained shut and Daisy made no attempt to call them in.

A couple of times she apologized for her own preoccupation and smiled wanly. 'Too much on my mind.'

'Of course.' Mercedes disliked the drawing-room politeness of her own reassurance.

Quite late on a thought occurred to Daisy. 'Did you know? Andrew got married a couple of weeks back. To that Bessie Carter. Did you ever come across her?'

'I think I've seen . . .' Mercedes felt the colour drain from her face. She gritted her teeth and braced her body against any show of emotion. Hold on, she told herself inwardly, hold on. Till later. You can think about it then.

'He's been moody lately,' Daisy told her, then, 'He's enlisting. The silly little fool.'

Through her turmoil it occurred to Mercedes that Daisy probably now had no means of support. She seized on the thought to distract her from her own disarray.

'What on earth are you going to do without Andrew's money?'

'He'll send a bit for Mamma . . . I haven't decided – something'll turn up.' A hastiness in Daisy's manner made Mercedes feel that she was being evasive. 'I'll have to think,' Daisy added unnecessarily, reinforcing the impression.

In a little while their conversation lost all momentum. Mercedes stood up to go, feeling disappointed at the strangeness between them, but telling herself it was hardly surprising considering Daisy's anxieties. At the same time she felt jolted and shaken at the news about Andrew and longed for privacy to think about it.

'I really will try to sort out some kind of subsidy to tide everyone over,' she said as they stood awkwardly in the doorway.

'Thank you.' Daisy's eyes were distant and her words sounded automatic.

Annie took the two loaves out of her basket and set them disdainfully on the table. Back to bloody short commons. They'd cost almost double, and she'd only got them because the baker's wife had put some away for regulars. Paid off only yesterday, Annie had been prepared to buy meat for a big final blow-out. But it had all gone for the army, or else the big dealers had got there first. She wasn't giving good money for the wizened little sausages Dick had offered her, and she'd told him as much.

He'd just shrugged indifferently. 'There's others that will.'

A knock came at the door. She guessed it'd be Edie or Queenie come to have a moan. They were all running around at the moment like chickens without their heads, and no wonder. This whole business was a pig's ear from beginning to end and it was the workers who suffered as usual. Queenie's Harry was a reservist. He'd been called up at half a day's notice and left her with five bob for herself and the kids. And God knows how long it'd be before his first pay came through.

'Thank the Lord *I'm* in work,' she'd said to Annie last Wednesday, then lo and behold come Friday they'd all been laid off. She pictured Ballard making his closing-down speech, all thin-lipped and patriotic. If he'd been honest he'd have been dancing up and down, grinning like a clown, and thumbing his nose at the lot of them.

Annie went through to the hall and opened the door. 'Good Gawd.'

On the doorstep stood Mercedes like a ghost from the past. She looked drawn and anxious but Annie was struck by the tan on her face and arms. Affronted almost. While they'd been slaving over their machines – and thankful to

327

be so – their comrade-in-arms had been sunning herself on some beach by the look of it.

'I read in the paper about the closures,' Mercedes said. 'And I had to come down. Annie, I can't tell you how sorry . . .'

'Way it goes, isn't it?' Mercedes was sincere, she meant well. But Annie couldn't face the outpourings of regret and cut her off. 'One moment you've sorted yourself out. Next thing you're back where you started . . . I won't ask you in, love. Will's sleeping in the other room. He gets tired nowadays.'

'I can't stop anyway, but . . .' Their eyes met and Annie thought what a kid she was, her face so open and earnest. ' . . . I wanted to say that you can count on the Association's help. We'll be doing what we can . . . At the very least we'll be raising cash for the worst cases of hardship . . . I'll keep in contact.'

Annie looked at Mercedes with grudging affection, but also with weariness. The girl cared, no doubt about it. But when it came down to it the people here were a sort of hobby for her. *She* was in no danger of going hungry. 'That's good, Mercedes. We can use any cash you get hold of. But it's like trying to block off the ocean with a cork . . . It's the whole system needs changing, top to bottom.'

'Yes.' Mercedes nodded, her eyes honest and somehow shamed.

For a moment they said nothing. Then Mercedes asked, 'Are your boys enlisting, Annie?'

Annie gave a contemptuous laugh. 'Over my dead body. Not till they have to.'

Mercedes flashed a quick, approving smile. Then she seemed to hesitate and want to say something, but shrugged her shoulders. 'I'll be seeing you, Annie.'

As she turned to go Annie had an impulse to stop her, to explain. 'All I want is to live steady, you know, Mercedes.

No shocks. No charity. Just a regular wage. All the ups and downs make you tired in the end.'

She saw the stirring of a surprised sympathy in Mercedes' eyes – pity – and instantly regretted the momentary lapse into weakness. In reflex Annie pasted a tough, well-worn grin across her face. It felt to her like the cheap plaster Will used to hide the cracks with when he was decorating.

'Oh, sod it, girl. We'll pull through. We always have.'

37

Setting out, Mercedes had felt fit and full of beans. Now, on the way home, she was bothered by a nagging, dragging pain in the pit of her stomach and permeated by a muffled sense of disappointment that her meetings with Daisy and Annie hadn't been more momentous.

The expectation had been childish, she knew, and it reflected the difference between her life and theirs. For her that summer had had a romanticism to it. The Ballard's strike and all that surrounded it had given her the most significant months of her life. For Annie and Daisy the goal was quite simply survival. Floundering, trying to keep their heads above water, they had no energy left for reunions or reminiscences.

The fact remained that there was work to do. 'I'll phone Hannah tonight,' Mercedes resolved. With this war the Association would have to tackle a whole new set of problems.

As she crossed London Bridge the evening seemed to resonate with the suppressed heaviness of a thunderstorm that never quite materialized. The purple-grey sky hung above the river like a threat. Her head began to ache and, in the sultry, airless heat, her dress stuck to her neck and armpits. At the back of her mind the news of Andrew's marriage lay coiled and avoided like a snake. She couldn't think about it now. A dull sense of loss ached inside her. She'd address it later when she had peace and silence.

The debilitating pain in her stomach was getting worse. A rare bus loomed suddenly on her right. It was going to Oxford Circus and had slowed at a junction. She was able to hop aboard.

'Naughty!' the conductor admonished. 'I'd put you off if there wasn't a war on . . .'

Mercedes sank down thankfully on to a seat. What blessed relief to be rid of the effort of walking.

'You all right, duck?' The conductor had a round, red face that seemed designed for cheeriness and joking, but his brown eyes, half-buried in flesh, were serious. 'You're white as a sheet.'

'I'm fine. Honestly.' She experienced the British desire to keep her suffering to herself.

Later, as she retraced her steps towards Harley Street, Mercedes was aware of a sudden gush of blood between her legs. She hastened her step. The blood oozed again, hateful, thick and sticky, seeming yet another element in the stifling oppressiveness of the evening. She closed her mind to the significance of the bleeding, praying that her underclothes would be sufficient to soak it up, re-living an adolescent nightmare. The terror that her dress would be stained with the dark, shameful, tell-tale evidence. For the time being that was her chiefest concern.

Why did she feel like a nun lying here in her bed? Was it the peace, the emptiness? Or because she had nothing – nothing left to show for the last eventful months of her life. The triumphant strike negated and wiped out, Andrew definitively lost to her, the child she'd begun to plan for flushed from her body. She lay back, tracing with her eyes the sinuous moulded curves of the cornice snaking round her ceiling.

She was left drained, with no emotion, no reaction. Nothing. For two days Mercedes watched the shadows cross her room, marking the passage of time.

The calm was ruffled for a while on the second day by a thunderstorm and Mrs Carter bursting in to close her window.

'Phew,' she sighed. 'About time, too.' Pulling her dress

and apron away from her chest and shaking the material, so that a cool current of air played on her skin.

Twice a day George came to see his daughter. He'd helped put her to bed when she arrived home in a state of near-collapse. And he knew.

'Take it easy,' he told her. 'Get plenty of rest.'

She could see in his eyes that he knew about the miscarriage, but he said nothing, either to her or to Florence. It was a can of worms too dreadful to broach.

Florence was oblivious, bustling in and out, bringing drinks and coaxing her to eat, revelling in her usefulness. Mercedes let her fuss. She lay doing nothing, her mind a blank.

'Mrs Spalding's called.' Florence was bending over her bed. 'She's downstairs. She says if you're too weak to see her she'll . . .'

'No!' Mercedes sat up with a jerk. 'Send her up. I *want* to see her.'

Florence hesitated. There was a lingering, dubious look in her eyes. She would obviously have preferred to send Hannah away.

'Please, Mother.'

A minute or so later Hannah knocked and entered. Mercedes' spirits lifted at the sight of her unashamedly fashionable figure in a slim dress of dark brown gaberdine with a face-framing hat. There were times when she found Hannah pretentious, abrasive and resistible, but for better or worse they had aims and attitudes in common. They were fellow-campaigners.

'Mercedes, there's so much I need to talk to you about . . .' Her tone was eager and intense. With a swift movement she sat herself down on the rush-seated chair by Mercedes' bed and removed her hat, revealing her sculptured mass of chestnut hair. She made a token gesture towards Mercedes' weakened condition. 'You *must* stop me if I'm tiring you . . .' But the briskness of her manner dismissed the unlikely eventuality.

'I imagine you agree with me that this war is pointless, pernicious and wrong,' Hannah began with crisp certainty.

'Absolutely!' Eagerly Mercedes sat forward, ruffling the bed-clothes, sending a book she'd tried to interest herself in rattling to the floor. She was enchanted with Hannah's heretical statement, so baldly and shamelessly expressed. Isolated in the heart of her family with only the newspapers for information, she had begun to feel herself a freak, the only person who saw nothing glorious in the departure of young men to fight for no principle that could be honestly stated. 'And there's this great smoke-screen of humbug surrounding the whole thing. You feel like a . . . spy, if you're not jumping up and down waving a flag!'

Her mind flashed back to what she'd seen in Bermondsey three days ago. 'There's all this patriotic fol-de-rol and yet complete callousness about the circumstances of the families left behind. They can starve for all anyone cares . . .' The blanket of inertia that had wrapped her disappeared at a stroke, burned away by a hot indignation. Symbolically Mercedes pushed the constricting bed-clothes off her and turned to sit sideways on the edge of the bed.

'Mrs Spalding, I wonder if you'd like some tea . . .' Florence put her head round the door. At the sight of Mercedes' upright posture she stiffened. 'Sadie, dear, you know what Daddy said . . .' Without altering her expression she managed to convey her disapproval of the disrupting presence of Hannah, who was old enough to exert a calming influence.

'No, thank you, Mrs MacInnes. You're very kind.' Hannah's brisk lack of ingratiation obviously alienated Florence still further. She shot Mercedes a meaningful glance, with eyes as lugubrious as a bloodhound's, before disappearing again.

Hannah turned away as if Florence's interruption had been a slight, unimportant distraction. Mercedes sympathized with her mother, but was quietly amused. Hannah's lack of understanding for the susceptibilities of humbler souls was both her weakness and her strength.

'Listen, Mercedes.' Hannah lowered her voice impressively and Mercedes guessed that she was about to get down to the main purpose of her visit. 'I've come to put a proposition to you . . .' She held up her hand as if Mercedes might be about to butt in with a barrage of questions. '. . . But I want you to think very hard before committing yourself.'

Mercedes was baffled and hugely intrigued. She couldn't imagine what Hannah was going to say.

'The suggestion comes from Lady Flowers. We both agreed that, if anything, this war – and there's no knowing how long it will last – this war is going to throw up more and greater problems than we've had to deal with before . . .' Hannah's quiet vehemence lent a warmth to the matt ivory of her skin, animating the classic haughtiness of her looks. Like her or loathe her, Mercedes thought, she was an imposing woman.

'Lady Flowers feels – and I agree with her – that under present circumstances volunteer participation, however dedicated, just isn't enough. We need a core of people we can really count on. She's proposing to create three salaried posts – one secretarial and two itinerant, practical workers. Both of us immediately thought of you in connection with the latter.'

'I see . . .' Hannah's proposition was a bolt from the blue, yet immediately Mercedes' brain raced, imagining herself in the new circumstances, creating instantaneously a whole new way of life for herself. Here on offer was paid work which, far from being the drudgery she'd always envisaged, would absorb and interest her passionately. Planning for a future with her child, Mercedes

334

had imagined a place of her own. The idea had grown on her, and now it would be within her reach . . . child or no child.

'You're not to answer.' Hannah rose to go. Crossing to the dressing-table, she adjusted the set of her hat. 'In fact I absolutely forbid you to. I want you to think hard about the whole thing for a day or two.'

38

'I think I liked you better in the rose-coloured one . . . I don't know, though. Perhaps we should take both.'

In a side-room of the shop in Bond Street called Étienne Vergé Daisy stood centre-stage, surrounded by an expanse of soft jade-green carpet. A multiplicity of full-length mirrors – each bordered with a pair of engraved long-legged herons – reflected her own image back at her from all angles. The blue-grey cashmere dress she was wearing draped across her breasts and upper arms in the most artful and flattering fashion. On her feet were grey kid pumps with Louis heels. She'd never in her life looked so elegant or felt so humiliated.

Edward Ballard stared appraisingly at her from a green and pewter-coloured *fauteuil*, seeming totally at ease and supremely unaware of the sly amusement of the rouged and red-haired woman, Madame Enid – so-called – who was assisting them with their choice.

Her hands traced wafting arabesques in the air. 'The drapery, it's exquisite, sir.' Addressing all her remarks to Edward, as though Daisy was simply a doll to be dressed.

She insisted on accompanying Daisy into the adjoining dressing-room and helping her on and off with her clothes, while her expressionless fish-eyes lingered insultingly on Daisy's worn camisole and drawers. Several salty comments crossed Daisy's mind, but the affluence of the surroundings and the ambiguity of her relationship with Ballard left her powerless.

'Which do *you* prefer, Daisy?'

'I like this one.' Her reply was neutral, factual. She

couldn't afford to appear ungracious, but wouldn't stoop to simpering gratitude.

'Choice is more limited than usual, sir, due to the hostilities,' Madame Enid confided pretentiously.

'Plenty to be going on with.' Edward's manner was affable and bluff. 'We'll need an evening-type gown as well.'

'Of course, sir.' The woman hurried off to the showroom trying to subdue a rapacious smile.

'You look delightful, Daisy.' Ballard uncoiled his long body from the chair and crossed the empty stretch of carpet to where she was standing. With finger and thumb he tipped up her chin. 'Ever since I've known you I've imagined buying you clothes that would do you justice.'

She had a view, very close, of the tiny wrinkles and roughnesses of his skin before he bent to kiss her, bringing his body disconcertingly close. Cautiously she breathed in. He smelt not unpleasantly. Tobacco and cologne predominated, with only the faintest hint of the more pungent odour of flesh.

He gave a kind of growl of appreciation, gathering her closer to him, cradling her head in one of his hands, sliding his tongue between her lips. She wasn't ready, found it difficult to breathe, but didn't like to pull away. Daisy thought the kiss presumptuous, but she no longer had the right to object. She felt chilled and unresponsive, and prayed she wouldn't ruin everything later on, when they went to bed.

Hearing the soft, brisk patter of Madame Enid's returning footsteps, they sprang apart. She re-entered the room, followed by a pale child who seemed almost enveloped by the rich garments she was carrying.

'Perhaps something here will be suitable for madame, sir.' A discreet complicity in the saleswoman's smile signalled that she knew what they'd been up to.

Gritting her teeth, Daisy paraded self-consciously in

front of Ballard's lordly, speculative gaze, wearing a succession of grand frocks. She'd chosen this – it was simply a means to an end.

Finally, Edward picked out a cream and black square-necked dress, the sleeves and bodice embroidered with hundreds of tiny jet beads. While he and Madame Enid rhapsodized, Daisy wondered about the woman who'd sewn them, and what rate she got for the job.

A little later, while the saleswoman fussed and bustled, pointing out to the wraith-like child which dresses she could take away, Edward ordered Daisy sotto-voce, 'Put the rose-coloured dress on to leave in. Tell them to wrap up that old coat and skirt of yours . . . And get that Enid woman to help you choose some pretty underpinnings . . .'

Daisy's face flamed. She spent an excruciating ten minutes with the subtly prurient Madame Enid, looking at the kind of embroidered drawers and petticoats she'd made herself until a few days ago. It seemed to Daisy that the rouged saleswoman held up the garments with an unnecessary, flaunting lewdness, but she was overwrought by now and probably imagining it.

Daisy stood by while Edward signed, with a genial flourish, a cheque for what must have amounted to several years' wages, and Madame Enid fawned on him in the most sickening fashion. Then she and her erstwhile employer left the shop arm-in-arm.

'D'you know what I'd like to do, Daisy?' Edward said, with an amused droop of the lip. 'Drop that disgraceful old coat and skirt of yours into the first bin we come to.'

Edward had booked them into a suite for the night at the Kilbracken Hotel in the Strand. It was a huge place, full of honey-coloured wood-panelling, mirrors, carpets and amber-pink lamps shaped like tulips or lilies. All the people in the foyer and corridors seemed to Daisy to exude a confident air of belonging. Even in her new clothes, she herself felt wretchedly out of place. And surely, in a hotel like this, Edward could well run into someone he knew. But he seemed oblivious to the danger, addressing the staff in the same loud, affable tones as he'd used with Madame Enid, supremely conspicuous with his high colour and abundant yellow hair.

They were shown to a huge room on the second floor with long windows overlooking the Strand, framed by wine-coloured, floor-length velvet curtains. The porter opened a side-door to reveal a dressing-room and a bathroom, with a WC, a shell-shaped hand-basin and a large shiny white bath-tub on curved mahogany legs carved with acorns and oak-leaves.

Edward pressed a coin into the man's hand and they were left alone. Daisy was unnerved by the dominating, predatory presence of an enormous dark red ruched and valanced double bed. For a moment her head spun and she had the vivid, disconnected impression that she was trapped in someone else's dream.

'Well, Daisy, do you like it?' Edward asked. The tone of his voice and the look on his face made her think of a benevolent adult demonstrating some splendid new toy to a child.

'Yes,' she smiled. His manner didn't allow for any other reply.

He confessed, then, that he had to leave her alone for a couple of hours. He'd made an arrangement – days ago – to meet his banker for a heart-to-heart.

'I couldn't be more sorry, Daisy.' His features arranged themselves into what seemed to her a well-practised expression of regret – perhaps he used it on his wife. 'But I really can't cancel, my dear. All manner of things to discuss what with the present complicated situation . . .' Edward promised to be back by half past eight to take her to dinner. He seemed apprehensive, as if she might turn petulant and feel slighted by his absence.

In fact Daisy was relieved to have a couple of hours on her own to compose and mentally prepare herself for the night ahead. It was difficult to keep a fresh sense of purpose while at the same time frittering away her energy in constantly trying to be what Edward wanted her to be.

Before leaving he pulled her to him again and gave her a series of short, soft kisses and murmured her name, permitting one hand to cover and squeeze her breast. Like a housewife testing fruit, Daisy thought, but she tried hard to banish the mental picture. She allowed herself to melt against him and sigh a little, which seemed to please him. She felt woefully out of touch with the practice of flirtation and seduction.

When he'd gone she ran herself a bath, scenting it with some violet-coloured crystals from an array of fancy glass bottles on a shelf in the bathroom. While the tub was filling she wandered round the bedroom, familiarizing herself with this new luxury, feeling the softness of the curtains, sitting on the matching velvet chaise-longue, helping herself from a basketful of grapes on the table. The fruits were blackish-purple, with a blue hazy bloom to them, perfectly firm and spherical, so flawless that at first she thought they might be artificial.

Afterwards it was sheer delight to lie and let the hot, perfumed water lap round her body. The best she'd managed in her life up to now was a tin tub in front of the fire on a Saturday night. Here there were scented soaps and big, soft towels. She abandoned herself to the wonder of it.

But as she began to dress herself for dinner in the clothes that Edward had bought her, the semi-revulsion she'd experienced in the shop in Bond Street washed over her again unawares. In the chic little dressing-room her reflection gazed back at her wherever she looked, dressed in a suggestively cut ivory silk camisole and drawers. She was making an offering of herself, wrapping herself up like a present for Edward Ballard. Daisy felt sick.

'Oh, for God's sake, what does it matter?'

Impatiently she dismissed her qualms. She needed Ballard. She was using him as he was using her. Both of them were adults, both understood the situation. She took the cream and black beaded dress down from its hanger, stepped into it and slipped her arms into the sleeves, then reached behind to fasten the buttons. Her image in the mirror did the same. Even with her hair unruly and curling from the steam of the bath, Daisy began to perceive that she looked more beautiful, more . . . special, than any of the rich, confident women she'd seen downstairs. The thought helped to stiffen her resolve.

She crossed to the dressing-table and sat down to do her hair. In the mirror her eyes were still wide and apprehensive. All this luxury was nice – no point in denying that – but she didn't think she could look her fellow-workers or Mercedes in the face if she met them now. It had been hard enough to talk to Mercedes the other day, knowing all the time what she, Daisy, was planning to do.

She began to brush her hair with punishing vigour. Forget them. Forget all of them. Daisy focused her mind on the imagined bright, pleasant rooms she'd be living in as Edward's mistress. Pictured Janie's dark curls and Alex's blond head bobbing among the flowers and shrubs in the garden and Mamma sitting out in her chair, safe and secure, looked after. That was what all this was for.

The food shortages that were affecting everyone else didn't seem to have penetrated the kitchens of the Kilbracken Hotel. There was a succulent Scottish roast beef on offer, and a featherlight meringue and blackberry dessert. It was all delicious and Daisy sipped steadily at the wines that went with them. The alcohol made her feel braver and more flirtatious, able to cope with whatever lay ahead.

In this situation Daisy felt a great deal less ill-at-ease than she had when they first arrived. Their smart fellow-diners were anchored to their own tables, their attention focused inward to their own little groups. Though she couldn't help noticing that a number of heads turned sharply to watch her progress through the restaurant. The new dress lent her a protective colouring. She felt pleasantly anonymous, mysterious even.

Daisy had the impression that Edward Ballard relished the sensation of being seen with a handsome younger woman. Tonight his figure seemed to her to loom across the silver and crystal of the dining-table, occupying all her attention, larger and clearer than life, like a hallucination. From a distance Ballard looked a distinguished figure, with his worldly air and expensive clothes. Close to, she thought, there was a coarseness to his red face. Her memory still smarted at the remark he'd made about her coat and skirt. Next to the costly dress she was wearing it was heavy and ugly of course. But she'd been proud of the skilful way she'd salvaged it from a man's suit, and she resented his belittling of her possessions – and by extension her life – however poor.

She warmed to him a little, though, when they began to discuss the flat where she might live.

'A ground floor, Daisy, don't you think? Some leafy suburb. With a garden and French windows if possible . . . Space enough for your mother and children to be comfortable. With a couple of rooms where you and I can be private . . .'

His heavy face glowed with anticipation and she understood abruptly that what he wanted was a homely relationship with her, sex in a domestic setting. Tonight's luxury was for seduction purposes. His tastes were simpler. Somehow she liked him a bit better for that.

'You know, Daisy, I'd quite given up hope,' he confided over coffee and sugared almonds. He seemed a little drunk. His eyes, innocent of any self-protective veil, were hard to meet. 'I was overwhelmed when you came to me . . .' Edward's hand reached across the table for hers. He seemed overcome with emotion. Daisy was impressed. She observed him wonderingly and thought secretly that, barring accidents, she was home and dry.

Upstairs, in her overwrought imagination, the enormous crimson bed seemed to pulsate subtly in expectation. Someone had been in and turned down the top coverlet, exposing snowy starched pillow-slips and sheets. One corner of the top sheet had been folded invitingly back, and a red rose laid on the white triangle it formed. Edward took up the flower and presented it to her with a gallant flourish. The gesture struck her as awkward and she wasn't sure how to respond.

'So, Daisy,' he said heavily, as if some point of no return had been reached, and he gazed at her searchingly. She looked back, her smile non-committal and slightly puzzled. But her blood was still heated by the wine and she felt capable of doing whatever she had to.

'Take off your dress,' he said quietly. Daisy was caught off-guard by the cool directness of the order after his show of emotion downstairs. But in a sense she was relieved that a move had been made.

She hung her dress in the adjoining room. When she returned Ballard was naked, in the act of climbing into the big bed. For a brief second she caught a glimpse of a slightly sagging belly, bone-white legs. Daisy found it bizarre to see him thus reduced to basic status. To her he'd seemed all of a piece with his protective Savile Row carapace.

Still wearing the silk camisole and drawers, she climbed beside him between the cold, stiff, slippery sheets. As she did so a sudden sharp awareness came on her, that she was alone in the world, responsible for people who were helpless without her. Lying down beside her former employer, Daisy had the illusion that she was going into battle.

'Daisy,' Edward murmured throatily. He began to kiss and caress her, slowly at first, but with a mounting passion. She closed her eyes and moved with him, moaning softly. A corner of her mind conjured up a brief, aching vision of Frankie's young body, the warmth of it, the familiarity. Edward's caresses became more frenzied, but she sensed that something was wrong. Reaching out her hand, she found him still limp and flaccid.

'Sod it!' He sounded ill-tempered. It chilled her, but she mustn't let it show.

Daisy became aware that he was pushing her down, exerting pressure on her shoulders, pushing her head down below the coverlet. She was affronted, realizing what he expected her to do. The act wasn't new to her, but with Frankie it had never been taken for granted, her compliance assumed.

There was no choice. She took his soft penis in her mouth. After a while, to her relief, she felt it respond and bloom. As she laboured beneath the bedclothes, Daisy kept in her head the picture of two children in a sunlit garden.

39

.On the floor of Mercedes' bedroom a brass-nailed trunk lay open. Clothes and books were strewn all round as she tried to make choices. It was impossible to take everything. She'd been absorbed in the problem for some hours, hadn't even taken the time to do her hair. It hung round her intent face and streamed on to the shoulders of her blue-green autumn dress.

Mercedes felt calm, but she never lost touch with a heavy sense of the momentousness of the day. She was leaving home. Beyond the red-curtained window of her bedroom a drift of clouds showed, dull and whitish-grey, casting a dampened, subdued air over everything that lay beneath. Mercedes wondered idly whether her mood would have been different if the sky were blue, and the bed and floor of her room striped with two sharp, sunny rectangles.

It still amazed her that she had permission to go. All their lives George and Florence had looked askance at the idea of well brought-up girls earning their own living or lodging apart from their families. In their own circle they knew only one such – a hefty, strong-willed woman called Margery Cannon, who had a frank, hiccuping, unfeminine laugh and taught history in a progressive girls' school.

'Poor dear, she never had much luck with the men,' Florence had clucked many times. Margery was a bit of a joke to her and she found it inconceivable that she could have any other motive for pursuing her career than disappointment in love and making the best of a bad job.

But George's attitude to his daughter's bid for independence had changed ever since the evening she'd staggered into the hallway, legs plastered in her own blood. The incident was never acknowledged, never referred to. It was as if the truth of that day had been buried somewhere deep inside him and denied. But the switch in his standpoint was total.

'If that's what you want, my dear,' he'd replied evenly when Mercedes had approached him, ready for confrontation, with the news of a paid job and her decision to move out.

He must have persuaded Florence, too. There had been three days when her mother wandered round the house like Lady Macbeth, face set, her eyes tragic and swollen. But she made no protest and today she'd gone to visit a female friend to spare herself the reality of her daughter's departure.

Mercedes looked about her, mildly dazed. How on earth had she collected together so many useless objects of sentimental value? She picked up a statuette of a cross-eyed, smiling drunkard holding up a lamp-post that Walter had brought back from Edinburgh once as a joke. Its grotesque, leering ugliness never failed to cheer her up.

'It'll remind me of you,' she told him, laughing, when he presented it to her at a family dinner. Since the holiday Mercedes hadn't seen Walter. He was training now at a camp in Gloucestershire and it wouldn't be long before he found himself in France . . . The twenty-year-old son of one of George's patients had already been killed at a place called Mons. She'd met him a few months ago when walking with her parents down Shaftesbury Avenue. He'd seemed so young, a blushing, callow boy. Mercedes shivered and packed Walter's statuette, giving in to a mixture of fondness and foreboding.

The room she had found was on the second floor of a tall house in Tachbrook Street, Westminster, a brisk fifteen minutes' walk from the office in Victoria.

'It's nothing fancy, but it's got everything you need,' the no-nonsense landlady had told her with a hint of aggression in her tone. 'There's no rules here. Long as you're quiet, you can come and go as you please.' Then she'd given a long, appraising look Mercedes found a bit unnerving.

But the room did have all the basics, an iron bedstead, a wardrobe, a table, a cupboard, chairs – plain, heavy items of furniture without style or distinction. There was a gas-ring, and a bathroom, shared with the other tenants. Most people would have said it was all functional and unremarkable, but Mercedes' imagination was fired by the large windows with sills broad enough to sit on comfortably, a curved alcove with shelves, the warm russet-coloured chenille of the curtains. She thought the room could be made individual and welcoming, and already scenes from the independent new life ahead of her were flickering in her head.

Mercedes examined the clothes she'd pulled out of her wardrobe and laid pell-mell on the floor, chair and bed, so she could see them all at a glance. September was here. She'd need the thicker things. Best to take those and leave her summer dresses behind. With a burst of energy she began to pick up skirts and blouses and underclothes, fold them smartly and lay them in the trunk. Better get this finished. A day off for moving house was a luxury the Association could ill afford. There was so much to do.

Last week they'd been contacted by the fiery trade-unionist Mary MacArthur of the National Federation of Women Workers. Her interest was an accolade, reflecting the growing reputation of the Association's work. The Federation was planning to set up a series of workshops for the women left in need by the outbreak of the war, and the Association was invited to cooperate. The case was urgent. Makeshift solutions were needed to plug the glaring gaps revealed in the military bureaucracy, which had left thousands without means of support. Soldiers' wages were trickling through to their dependants as slowly as sand through an egg-timer, and separation payments were scandalously overdue. Tomorrow, with Hannah and Lady Flowers, Mercedes was going to a meeting to thrash out the whole question.

Mercedes scooped up an armful of the garments she was leaving behind and hung them hastily back in the wardrobe. A saucepan and a kettle stood on the dressing-table, lent her by a sceptical Mrs Carter who clearly thought she was mad to leave her home comforts and shift for herself. She placed them on top of the clothes in the trunk. Room still for a few books. Mercedes turned her attention to a pile left on the floor.

'Miss Mercedes!' The childish voice of Lily, a new young maid Florence had engaged, floated up the stairs.

'What is it?' She went on to the landing and leant over the banister.

'Someone to see you, Miss . . . A soldier.' A note of doubt on the final word.

Walter? She hadn't known he was in town. Mercedes was pleased, she'd had the feeling of coolness between them.

'He's waiting in the green room,' Lily whispered, as Mercedes reached the hall. Her thin face wore an odd expression, curious and somehow speculative.

Eagerly Mercedes pushed the door. The soldier was standing by the window and turned when she came into the room. For a moment she was disorientated. His features weren't those she expected to see. He was paler, fairer, taller . . . Andrew.

'Hallo, Sadie.' She recalled the huskiness of his voice as if from a dream.

'Hallo.' The word came out almost as a whisper. She shook her head. 'What a surprise.'

They stood facing one another, wary, like two confronting children. The stiff new uniform made him look not quite himself, lent him a public quality, when her memories of him were so private.

'How are you?' he asked.

She smiled. 'Fine, I suppose. I'm packing – moving out to a place of my own. I've got a paying job.'

The news, so significant to her, seemed not to touch him. All the unmarried women of his acquaintance had work.

'I saw Daisy a little while ago,' Mercedes said. 'She told me you'd got married.'

A flicker of emotion showed in his eyes. 'Yes, I married Bessie . . . Before I go, like.'

'And when do you go?'

'Four o'clock this afternoon.' A pause. 'I said goodbye to Bessie three hours ago. I've been walking round, wondering whether to come. I wanted to see you. Say goodbye. Just see you.'

She smiled again with a look of tentative friendship. 'I'm glad you did.'

Another silence, then, 'Look at you.' The old shy, teasing grin crossed his features. 'What a state. You 'aven't even done your hair.'

Impulsively Mercedes suggested, 'Shall we go for a walk? Regent's Park or somewhere?'

He looked relieved at the prospect of escaping the constraint of her handsome household.

'Wait a minute – I'll fetch a coat.'

Up in her room she tied her hair back hastily with a black ribbon, put a black jacket on over her dress, and a blue and green tam o'shanter she used to like when she was younger and had rediscovered in the upheaval of packing.

As she and Andrew left the house together Mercedes had a brief glimpse of Lily's fresh face, alert and nosey. She'd be down in the basement like a shot to report to Mrs Carter and the others. Mercedes revelled in a conscious, buoyant sense of indifference. She was leaving home and the servants' gossiping was a matter of heady unconcern. By the same token, she and Andrew never used to go to Regent's Park together. It was far too close to home. Now she strolled side by side with him, not caring which of her neighbours stood twitching the lace curtains. As a working woman living alone, she would soon, in any case, become an object of scandal and surmise.

As he walked alongside her she marvelled anew that the taut body, the unique, arresting, uncliché'd features had been lent to her to have and hold. The thought was abstract and Mercedes took care to keep it so. She had no wish for dormant feelings to be re-awakened.

'What's this job then?' he asked.

'The same. For the Association. Only it's salaried now. Partly because the work's become more urgent than ever – it's just vicious, the lack of provision for families . . .'

Andrew nodded sagely. 'There's people down our way just don't know where to turn . . .' He added pointedly, 'I left Bessie with five pounds – Annakin's gave the enlisted men a damn good send-off. Should tide her over till my wages come through.'

'It won't last, I'm sure, this chaos. It stands to reason, with the men gone, women workers are going to be needed more than ever before.' It was a conviction she was beginning increasingly to hold. Mercedes shrugged her shoulders. 'If we can just get through the early days . . .'

Diffuse, sluggish, slate-coloured clouds hung in the sky over Regent's Park so that the grass took on an intense, fevered shade of green. The park had a brooding doomsday look that pleased her.

'How's Daisy coping?'

Andrew smiled. He had good news. 'Stroke of luck. She's found herself a live-in housekeeping job. For a widower she says. Big house in Ealing. Room for the kiddies and Mamma, and no bones about them living with her.'

'Good for Daisy. You must be relieved, too.'

The lake lay in front of them, shining metallically grey-white beneath the bleak sky. A little flock of ducks glided past as if propelled by some smooth underwater mechanism. They sat down on a bench that overlooked the water.

'Why did you enlist?' Mercedes asked him suddenly.

Andrew looked straight ahead, out across the water. He seemed to consider as if he hadn't given the question much thought. 'It wasn't a mad burst of patriotism, if that's what you mean. Only I could've lived and died in Bermondsey and never, ever . . . Curiosity, Sadie, that was about it.'

As they sat there a young girl, about fourteen years of age, walked past, pulled by an eager, rough-haired terrier on a leash. She was a bonny creature, with a wild-rose complexion, and bouncing brown curls beneath a pancake hat, cosily dressed in a brown velvet coat. A heartening contrast to the bleakness of the day. She smiled and scolded the dog. Mercedes thought what a picture of health and well-being the girl presented, straightforward, all of a piece. But appearances were deceptive. Already the child was probably as complex a mixture of strength and weakness, joy and sadness, light and shadow as anyone else.

All at once Andrew blurted, 'I've wanted to tell you, Sadie. You were right to leave me. You and me were too different.'

'You're better off with Bessie?'

'We're the same. We're comfortable together. We take the world as it is . . . Not like you, always wanting to change things.' He shrugged and searched for the words to explain himself. 'Don't mistake me. I like it in you. I respect it. But me and Bessie just want to live our lives . . .'

They were silent. Then Andrew grinned at her with amiable malice. 'I can just see you, Sadie, ending up living in sin with some bomb-throwing anarchist.'

She laughed doubtfully at his view of her.

'Only I never was as . . . shaken up by a girl as you. And, just now, when you walked into the room, with your hair all hanging, I could just have . . .' He let the sentence peter out as if he might already have said too much.

For a minute or two Mercedes debated with herself before confiding, 'I didn't want you to know, but I got pregnant. And I got so I really wanted to have the child, come what may. But I miscarried.'

'Sadie!' He gazed at her with awed disbelief. 'If I'd known . . .'

'No!' Defensively Mercedes wrapped her arms about her body. 'It would have complicated things. Oh . . .' She smiled at him with a wry look. 'I had such a passion for you, but – you said it – we're too different.'

'Did you feel bad?'

'It wasn't just one simple emotion. I was half-relieved and half . . . I'd pictured it so clearly, it was like a private happiness, and then . . . Afterwards the offer came of a job and it gave me something . . .' Mercedes gave a small grimace, 'to spend my energy on.'

She felt his hand close over hers. He was warm where she was cold and stiff. He held it tightly as if to communicate – compassion? Solidarity?

'I dream about it. The baby. And about you.' Mercedes didn't look at him. The feeling that lay between them was sober and elegiac. She knew how easily it could be fanned back into the wildness that had invaded her that summer.

'I ought to get back,' she said. 'There's so much I've got to do.'

Outside the house he stooped and touched his lips to hers. The kiss held a subdued awareness of what they'd shared. She recalled the soft, dry touch of his mouth.

'Take care,' she said.

'You, too.'

He smiled and turned to go. She watched as he walked away from her down the road. At the corner he turned and waved, looking slight and earthbound compared to the potent figure who still inhabited her dreams.